"THIS WOMAN I CLAIM AS MY OWN—AND MINE ALONE! I WILL SLAY THE MAN WHO DARES TO LAY A HAND ON HER!"

Without warning, Wulfgar reached out, taking Rhowenna unaware as he grabbed her and possessively jerked her to him. A slow, deliberately wolfish smile curved Wulfgar's lips as he stared down at her, his eyes dark, unfathomable. Before she realized what he intended, he roughly yanked her head back, and abruptly crushed his mouth down on hers—hard, hungrily.

Never in her wildest imaginings had she dreamed that a man would, or could, kiss her as Wulfgar did, as though he were draining the very life and soul from her body and then pouring it back in again. She felt as though the deck had suddenly canted beneath her, making her knees buckle, so she would have fallen had he not clasped her tightly, inexorably molding her body against his own, making her intensely aware of him as a man who wanted her . . .

Also by Rebecca Brandewyne

Across a Starlit Sea
And Gold Was Ours
Desire in Disguise
Desperado
Forever My Love
Heartland
Love, Cherish Me
No Gentle Love
The Outlaw Hearts
Rainbow's End
Rose of Rapture
Upon a Moon-Dark Moor

Published by
WARNER BOOKS

REBECCA BRANDEWYNE

SWAN ROAD

WARNER BOOKS

A Time Warner Company

WARNER BOOKS EDITION

Copyright © 1994 by Rebecca Brandewyne
All rights reserved.

Cover design by Diane Luger
Cover line art illustration by Artery Graphic
Cover illustration by Elaine Duillo
Hand lettering by Carl Dellacroce

Warner Books, Inc.
1271 Avenue of the Americas
New York, NY 10020

 A Time Warner Company

Printed in the United States of America

First Printing: January, 1994

10 9 8 7 6 5 4 3 2 1

For Loyal and Ilse Gould,
Basil C. Raffety,
and in memory of Thomas H. Thompson,
all the best and wisest of mentors and friends.
With much love and appreciation.

The Players

IN WALAS:

Pendragon, king of Usk,
Igraine, queen of Usk, wife to King Pendragon

Their daughter:

Rhowenna, princess of Usk

Gwydion, kinsman to the House of Pendragon
Morgen, a serving woman
Father Cadwyr, a priest
Owain, a bard

IN NORTHUMBRIA AND MERCIA:

Aella, king of Northumbria
Cerdic, a prince of Mercia
Mathilde, a princess of Mercia, sister to Prince Cerdic

IN THE NORTHLAND:

Ragnar Lodbrók, a Viking *konungr*

His sons:

Ivar the Boneless
Ubbi
Halfdan

The Viking *jarlar*:

Björn Ironside
Flóki the Raven
Hasting
Olaf the Sea Bull
Wulfgar Bloodaxe

Yelkei, a slave and spaewife

Contents

9th Century Europe & Scandinavia

Atlantic
Ocean

The
Northland
Kingdoms

Baltic
Sea

North
Sea

Caledonia

Jutland

The
Slavic
Kingdoms

The British
Kingdoms

Erin

Wales

Frisia

The
Germanic
Kingdoms

Severn
Sea

The
Frankish
Kingdoms

Swan Road

The old gods touch her sleeping thoughts
With a dream that soars on night's soft breath
'Neath outstretched wings of long-necked swans
And mighty dragons breathing fire and death
From a-crest foam-flowered waves
Swelling o'er seafarers' graves
Of shifting bones that seaweed shrouds
enwind.
By fair winds caressed and deeply kissed,
Hoist'd on high and billowing wide
Against the sun-washed blue of summer skies,
Sails spill like blood, a crimson tide
That flows unchecked to distant strands,
And in its wake, on violated sands,
In silent voices speak the corpses left
behind.

Yesterday's princess is tomorrow's slave,
Quick as the moment between beats of a heart
That pounds with terror, blind and cruel,
And weeps for lovers torn e'er apart
As warriors, each riding serpent's spine,
Dismount and plunge into frothy brine
That seethes and swirls like a storm
before

Violent surge the sweeping combers in
Upon what was, just past, the tranquil beach
O'er which the misted mountains rose
And palisade kept watch from falcons' reach.
Now shouts a wild, barbaric cry—
And from dying lips, the last, low sigh
Of those who'll fight the battles brave
no more.

With baubles and bangles of amber and silver
And a treasure far more precious than gold
Loaded onto their longships of mammoth oaks felled,
Set sail, homeward bound, those marauders so bold.
Swift up the Swan Road do they flee,
North, toward the white Frozen Sea,
At whose edge lie the lands of the mid-
night sun,
Where swords light the heav'ns when on snowy steeds
Odinn's Valkyries come to fetch the home the slain,
And in the great mead halls, by low-burning fires,
The skálds sing a tale of Wulfgar the Dane
And of fey Rhowenna the Fair;
Sweeter than siren's snare,
Is love when two hearts twine fore'er
as one.

Prologue

The Old Gods

The Dream

==

The Southern Coast of Usk, Walas, A.D. 865

Rhowenna awoke with a start.

Panicked, she gasped and cried out, sitting bolt upright in bed and clutching her fur blankets tight against her trembling body. Wildly, she gazed about her shadowy sleeping chamber, fearing to be set upon at any moment, seized by the strong, barbarous hands of which she had dreamed so vividly that even now, she could still feel them upon her, sweeping her up, crushing her against a broad, hard-muscled chest that belonged to no Usk man, or even to a man of Walas, but to a stranger, a savage worse than those who inhabited the lands to the east and, across the sea, the isle of Erin to the west. But as always, she found no one in her chamber save her waiting woman, Enid, who slept on a pallet at the foot of the bed, her slumber undisturbed by the low wail of terror that had issued from Rhowenna's lips. Although she was now fully awake, Rhowenna's fright did not diminish. Rather, it increased. This was not the first time she had had the nightmare. Each time it recurred, she grew more frightened, worried lest she had been beset by some madness. Part of her even hoped that it was so, for if it were not, she must accept the fact that she possessed the Sight and confess as much to Father Cadwyr. He would surely think her accursed; perhaps he would even accuse her of being a witch. And perhaps he would be right.

Even now in her ears, the primitive drums still pounded, the arcane chanting still echoed, and the piercing screams still rang—although her father's royal manor was as silent as a grave and, outside, only the raw night wind stirred. As though she had run a long way, her heart beat as loud and fast in her breast as the drums in her mind; and despite the winter cold, she was so drenched with sweat that her fine white wool nightgown clung to her skin. The fire in the brazier had burned low, and as the wind snaked through her father's royal manor, slithering over her clammy body, she shivered violently.

Pushing back her tangle of long, heavy black hair, Rhowenna slowly rose, dragging one of the fur blankets about her for warmth. Quietly, so as not to waken Enid, she moved to pour herself a cup of dark, rich, spicy mead from a clay jug set nearby. Then, grasping the goblet, she knelt beside the brazier to feed sticks of wood to the blaze. Soon, the tongues of flame licked high, and they and the mead, of which she drank deep, pervaded her body with their welcome heat.

It was still night, when not only the wild animals, but also the old gods roamed the earth. This, despite her Christian upbringing, Rhowenna deep in her bones believed; for on the wings of the night wind, had not the ancient ones come to her again, bringing the dream? It was a premonition, a warning, she knew. She had spoken of it to no one—not even to Gwydion, her beloved kinsman—for she longed with all her heart to deny that it was a true vision. If she remained silent, she felt she might somehow prevent it from breathing life, from becoming real. Still, it so terrified her that tonight, she was sorely tempted to rouse the household, to speak of what she had seen. Only the thought of Father Cadwyr's penetrating eyes and thunderous wrath as he denounced her as unholy, the devil's handmaiden, dissuaded her. Still, compelled by her inner turmoil, Rhowenna rose abruptly. Despite the inclement weather and the certainty that she would be punished if she were caught sneaking from her father's royal manor into the night, she knew she must go down to the Great Sea, whence came what haunted her.

She gathered up her warm fur cloak, wrapped its folds about her, and tugged on soft leather boots. Then, willing its creaking iron hinges to silence, she carefully eased open the door to her sleeping chamber and peeked out. By the light of the low-burning fire in the central hearth of the great hall beyond, she saw to her relief that the housecarls—her father's warriors—and the servants slumbered on, undisturbed by her furtive gambit. Her feet whispering across the rushes that strewed the stone floor, she swiftly ventured past them and into the darkness.

Because Rhowenna's father, Pendragon, was king of Usk, his royal manor not only occupied the central position in the village, but was also the grandest dwelling of all, the only one constructed of stone. Situated on a knoll overlooking its domain, it contained a great hall, a kitchen, and private chambers for the royal family. It was surrounded by the chapel, various outbuildings, and an earthwork girded with a wide ditch and topped by a stout wooden palisade. Beyond the palisade were the huts and workshops of the *ceorls*, the serfs, each structure built of wattle and daub, roofed with thatch, and located on a hide, a single measure of land. The village itself sprawled along the shores of the river Usk, which poured into the Severn Sea and thence into the Great Sea to the west, with the gentle green hills and the rugged, mist-enshrouded mountains of Walas rising behind.

Her father's small kingdom of Usk was bordered by the larger ones of Glamorgan to the west, Gwent to the north, and, beyond the immense ditch and earthwork erected by the Bretwalda Offa and known as Offa's Dyke, vast Mercia to the east. In these uncertain times, when war was all too common and alliances shifted as suddenly as the wind, all three larger kingdoms posed a threat to Usk—but Mercia threatened most of all. To the south, across the Severn Sea, loomed the isles of what had once been the Summer Country, the largest and holiest of these the Tor that rose above Glastonbury or *Ynis-witrin*, the Isle of Glass, as it was sometimes called. Woad, used to make blue dye, grew there, and apple trees; and there, too, the High King Arthwr and his second queen, Gwenhwyfar, were buried. In Arthwr's time, the Tor and Glastonbury had been places of the old gods; now, like much else, they belonged to the Christ and to the priests who served Him. Once, long ago, beyond the craggy black cliffs of West Walas in the distance, had stretched the land of Lyonesse, where fortresses had towered more magnificent even, it was claimed, than those of the Romans. On a cloudless day, some said, one could see the strongholds shimmering beneath the Great Sea; for Lyonesse was lost now, drowned by the treacherous, unending, whitecapped waves that rushed in to batter the coast relentlessly, crumbling and eroding the land, leaving long, gnarled fingers of black rock behind, which would someday also disappear. What lay beyond the isle of Erin to the west, beyond the Great Sea itself, no one knew. On the few maps Rhowenna had seen, dragons were pictured as inhabitants. Bards sang also of another drowned land, called Ys, to the south, which had once lain beyond Brittany, and of a mighty kingdom, Atlantis, even farther away, which had once risen from the waves, and of its towering, magic crystal mountain, so powerful that it had even harnessed the sun. But in the end, the forces the mountain had sought to command had proved too potent for it, and it had exploded, wreaking havoc upon the kingdom and causing it, like Lyonesse and Ys, to sink into the Great Sea. Although she had never been beyond the boundaries of Usk, Rhowenna had acquired this information through the years by listening intently to those who came to her father's royal manor to seek his favor.

By the priests, she had been tutored about the Christ who was the one true God. From the bards, she had learned of the old gods and of those who had, with blood sacrifices, worshiped them: her ancestors, the Picti—the Old People of the Hollow Hills—and the Tribes, who had tattooed themselves with blue woad and who had understood, or so she had been told, even the mysteries of the standing stones and all the lore that had been lost through the ages, since the advent of the Christ. There had been wise and learned men and women in the old days—the priests and priestesses of the Druids and of the Houses of Maidens. But when the High King Arthwr had fallen in battle at Camlann, a great and terrible darkness had come upon the land—the twilight of the gods, some called it; and as the Great Sea had drowned Lyonesse, Ys, and the mighty kingdom of Atlantis, so the Christ had vanquished the old gods. The merchants who traveled far and wide—from the east by horses across the mountains, and from the west by ships upon the Great Sea, up the rivers Usk and Severn—told their own tales of foreign and forgotten lands; and from these, as well, had Rhowenna gleaned further erudition.

As a squirrel stores nuts for the long winter, so did she hoard in her eager mind every scrap of information that came her way. Knowledge was power, her mother, Queen Igraine, often said to her, a weapon more formidable even than a broadsword or a battle-ax—and one that a woman who was wise would learn to wield skillfully, both to defend and to advance herself in a man's world. Yet there was a force even more powerful than knowledge, Rhowenna thought, troubled: fate, destiny. It was this she believed she had seen in her dream, written in the stars, immutable; and despite all her learning, she felt herself helpless against it.

A silver moon ringed with pearly mist shone in the black-velvet night sky, illuminating her way as she slipped through the postern gate of the palisade to traverse the stony, narrow, serpentine track that led down from her father's royal manor to the shore below. From past experience, she knew she would spy nothing there. Still, she could not banish the frisson of fear that this time she would see in reality what she had hitherto seen only in her mind; and she was driven to reach the strand, to make certain all was as it should be. If she did not, she would not sleep again this night.

The winter wind, while not strong, was nevertheless bitter, permeated with drifting mist, drizzle, and salty spindrift from the Severn Sea. Against the chill, Rhowenna drew her cloak even more closely about her as she hurried along. So often had she made this short journey of late that her feet seldom faltered upon the rough, frost-encrusted path, although it was occluded by mist and darkness. Regardless of its possible dangers, she loved the night. It was magical, mystical; it belonged to the old gods who called to her, came to her, as though to entice her from the Christ, whose realm was of the light. Beneath her cloak, her hand sought the Celtic crucifix that hung from a slender gold chain about her neck. On such a cross had the one true God died, the priests said. But the old gods lived, as elemental as wind and fire, as the earth and the Great Sea. Over all things celestial, terrestrial, and infernal, they yet ruled. Rhowenna did not doubt this, despite all she had been taught by the priests. The ancient ones spoke with the voice of the wind—a sigh, a moan, a warning that prickled the fine hairs on her nape; and in answer, the cry of some night creature echoed through the mountains that hove up behind her, dwarfing her. What was she compared to the mountains, to the old gods? The minutest grain of sand upon a beach, cast hither and yon by the mighty sea whose name was fate, destiny. Had she not seen in her dream that this was so?

She had gained the shore; and now as she stood looking out at the cold, dark, frothing water that sluiced in upon the strand, her hair and cloak billowing about her in the wind, Rhowenna was struck anew by her own insignificance in the vast scheme of things.

Yet the old gods spoke to her now.

She did not want to listen—but she heard them all the same. The surf pounded like the drums in her mind; the wind chanted its lyrical refrain; the unknown beast in the mountains screamed. All about her, the sinuous mist twisted and twined like the ghosts of the blue-woaded pagans who had danced amid the standing stones aeons ago. The Great Sea stretched before her—boundless, empty. Yet in her mind's eye, the images unfolding in slow motion, Rhowenna saw upon the far horizon a tide of phantom riders as crimson as blood, mounted upon the spiny backs of monstrous sea dragons that rose and plunged upon the foamy waves, drawing ever nearer to the coast, come to ravage and to rape, to maim and to murder. Down from the north, along the Swan Road that was no road at all but the course the migrating swans followed when they winged their way across the Great Sea, the longships with their bloodred sails came. As swift as the wind, as silent as the earth. But in Rhowenna's ears rang the pounding of the drums, the chanting of the pagans, and the screams of dread at the sight of those savage riders of the seas.

Caught up in the throes of her vision, she saw the vessels spill forth their army of marauders. Shouting their war cries, their broadswords and battle-axes held high, the giants leaped into the sea, a gold-headed god at their vanguard. Against their massive thighs, the breakers crashed and churned; but still, the giants surged forward, as though they and the sea were one. And now, the screams of the wounded and of the dying began as her father's housecarls and *ceorls* were set upon and slaughtered, as the women were flung down violently wherever they were seized, skirts ripped away, thighs spread wide for the giants who defiled them. All around Rhowenna, terror reigned. The acrid smoke that rose from the burning village stung her eyes and filled her nostrils. Coughing and choking, she stumbled on amid the cacophony and confusion, frantically seeking escape, slipping on the blood that ran red upon the ground, seeping into the dark, dank earth. Before her stricken, disbelieving gaze, a broadsword flashed in the sunlight, then reddened as the blade bit deep into Gwydion's neck, severing his head from his torso.

Gwydion! Gwydion!

Rhowenna was not even aware of the terrible, animalistic cries that erupted from her throat as he slowly crumpled before her, of the powerful arms that, even before her beloved kinsman's body hit the ground, grabbed her up, enfolding her tight against a brawny chest. Her head fell back against her captor's shoulder. Shocked and dazed, she stared up into eyes as deep blue as a summer sky, a face framed by a halo of tawny hair gilded by the sun. The old gods had come for her, she thought. Soon, she would be reunited with Gwydion in heaven. Desperately, she clung fast to that hope as a merciful blackness swirled up to engulf her.

It was at this moment in her nightmare that Rhowenna always awakened, driven by fear to search out the strand, to make certain a clutch of dragons had not come fleet and fierce from the north, down the Swan Road of the Great Sea, a gold-headed god at their fore.

In her lifetime, they had not come to Usk.

Only from the tales of the warriors and the songs of the bards had she knowledge of how the marauders were wont to swoop down from their Northland to attack, to plunder, and to lay waste to the kingdoms of the Shetlands, Orkneys, Caledonia, Britain, Erin, Frisia, Brittany, Normandy, and the Frankish and Germanic lands of what had once been the vast Carolingian Empire ruled by Charlemagne. Yet in her mind, she beheld the red-sailed longships as clear and sharp in detail as though she had seen them a hundred times before.

Fate. Destiny.

Trembling, Rhowenna knelt upon the sand beneath the pale, misty stars that gleamed like the eyes of a thousand distant dragons in the night sky. Bowing her head and clasping her crucifix tight, she began earnestly, fervently, to pray— not to the old gods, but to the Christ, who was merciful, or so the priests said. Her lips moved as she whispered the litany over and over, as though it were a spell to protect her:

"A furore Normannorum, Domine, libera nos. A furore Normannorum, Domine, libera nos."

It was the only Latin that Rhowenna knew—but like all in Walas, young or old, she knew it by heart: From the fury of the Northmen, O Lord, deliver us.

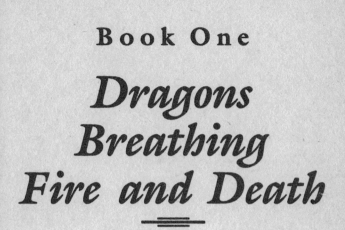

Book One

Dragons
Breathing
Fire and Death

Chapter One

Check to
the King

The Southern Coast of Usk, Walas, A.D. 865

The morning was half gone when Rhowenna finally awoke, although she was hardly rested, even so. When she had returned from the shore, she had been so troubled and torn by her dream that she had not closed her eyes again until the gloomy grey dawn had broken on the horizon, shrouded with mist, bleak with drizzle. She had shivered and been glad to burrow deeper beneath her fur blankets; and presently, sleep had claimed her at last. But the rest of the household had been stirred to wakefulness by the slowly lightening sky; and now from beyond her sleeping chamber, Rhowenna could hear the familiar noises of both her father's royal manor and the village beyond the palisade: the chatter of the servants as they cleared the morning meal from the long trestle tables in the great hall, the clank of pots and pans in the kitchen, the shouts and laughter of the housecarls outside, the blowing

and stamping of horses shivering in the wet bailey, the barking
of dogs, the cackling of geese and chickens, the snorting of
pigs, and the bleat of goats and sheep from the hides of the
ceorls.

Loath to leave her bed's warm confines, Rhowenna mar-
veled that all should sound so normal, that life at her father's
royal manor should go on as though a cloud of doom did not
hang over it. But then, why should it not? She alone was
privy to her dream. Not for the first time did she shudder at
the thought that perhaps with her very silence, she ensured
the truth of her vision. If she gave no warning and the Northmen did come to commit their carnage, would she not be as
guilty as they for the slaughter of her people? Surely, that
must count as a sin greater than the Sight, more evil than the
witchery against which Father Cadwyr would assuredly rail
should she speak of what she had foreseen.

In the old days, before the advent of the priests, her dream
would have been revered as a gift from the old gods and she
herself regarded as a seeress. Rhowenna yearned for that time
when her people had understood the mysteries of things that
now appeared beyond their ken, that were called evil by the
priests, the work of the devil. The priests claimed to bring
enlightenment to the world; yet their words were as dark as
their robes, and for all their talk of mercy, their God was a
jealous and vengeful God, Rhowenna thought. Sometimes,
her faith in Him faltered; she did not comprehend why so
much that seemed natural and right to her should be considered sinful by Him. Sometimes, she thought that the priests
themselves did not understand what they preached, or even
that they twisted God's will and words to suit themselves; for
who was to know or to say any different? But these were
blasphemous thoughts; she should confess them, she knew.
Still, she did not. She did not want to tell her innermost
thoughts to the priests, especially to Father Cadwyr.

Thus, although Rhowenna longed for guidance, she did not

know whom to ask for it. Although he was a fierce warrior, renowned for his prowess in battle, her father, Pendragon, feared the priests, with their talk of eternal damnation and hellfire and brimstone for the souls of those who did not follow the way of the Christ. Her father would be frightened by her dream, by the thought that Father Cadwyr might believe him to be rearing a godless daughter or, worse, one dedicated to the old religion, to the old gods, who were false idols. Her mother, Igraine, more inclined to put her faith in her own good judgment than in the counsel of the priests, was a likelier prospect for advice. But upon such a serious matter, perhaps she would feel duty-bound to consult her husband. Nor could Rhowenna bear to tell Gwydion she had envisioned his death at the hands of the Northmen; and Enid, her waiting woman, would only be stricken with panic at the notion of the Northmen's descending upon the kingdom of Usk. There was no one to whom Rhowenna could turn.

Sighing heavily, she rose, deeply distressed and knowing, as well, that for her tardiness this day, she would be rebuked by her mother. After washing her face and hands in the icy water of her bronze basin, she stripped off her nightgown to don a workaday dress of plain, undyed wool. She had just finished dressing when Enid appeared in the doorway, with a cup of milk, a bowl of thick porridge, and a cake of laverbread that had been fried in pork fat and spread generously with honey, all of which she had kindly saved for her mistress from the morning meal. As Rhowenna sat down upon a low stool to eat, Enid took up a comb of fine, carved horn and began to work the snarls from Rhowenna's long hair and to plait it into a single braid tied with a simple thong. Mistress and maid had been together since childhood, so it was a familiar morning ritual they shared, most often with companionable talk and laughter. Today, however, Rhowenna, lost in her disheartening reverie, was inclined toward silence; and Enid, sensing this, said little, although, once, she did remark that Rhowenna looked tired, even ill, and then quietly fussed over her more than was usual.

As she gazed at her reflection in her polished bronze mirror, Rhowenna agreed with Enid's assessment of her appearance. Her face was drawn and wan, and beneath her eyes, crescent smudges of mauve shone dark against her milk-white skin. She resembled the witch Father Cadwyr would surely name her if he learned of her dream, she thought dully; for her heavy mass of knee-length hair was as black and shimmering as a raven's rain-soaked wing, and her eyes were startling, a strange, crystalline violet in color, like amethysts, and slanted and heavily fringed with sooty lashes. No one in Usk had eyes like hers, and because of that, there were many who believed her fey, a changeling, and made the ancient sign against evil when she passed by. Should he be given a reason to condemn her, Rhowenna knew that Father Cadwyr would have no difficulty in finding supporters for his cause.

She had never liked the priest. His black eyes burned like hot coals when he looked at her, and she saw in his fervid glance a licking flame of covetous desire that did not belong in the eyes of a celibate, a man devoted to the work of the Christ. In the village, she had heard rumors that Father Cadwyr lay with women, for which he despised and condemned them bitterly, and flagellated himself mercilessly afterward. But if such were true, he was careful to conceal his sins and always showed an appropriately pious face to her father. Still, Rhowenna mistrusted him.

Yet there were those, too, who thought her beautiful and who loved her well. Her kinsman Gwydion was one of these. She trembled whenever she thought of him—and she thought of him often these days; for if there were other men who looked with favor upon her, Rhowenna did not see them. She saw only Gwydion—tall, as dark as bronze, as lithe as a sapling, his young body as graceful and swift and hard as an arrow on the fly, his hair as black as her own, his eyes as grey as the mist, as the Great Sea. In Gwydion as in Rhowenna herself, the blood of the Picti and of the Tribes was strong and marked. Perhaps that was why she was so drawn to him. She had known him all her life; yet it was not until they each had stepped over the threshold of adulthood that she had come to regard him with more than just sisterly affection.

At age ten, Gwydion had been fostered to one of her father's earls, and Rhowenna had seen him only rarely until the day when, his training completed, he had returned home. A boy when he had gone away, he had come back a man—no longer merely her kinsman, her childhood playmate and friend, but a stranger, in ways that had excited and intrigued her. The touch of his hand upon hers had scalded her. Even now at the memory, heat rose within her, making her cheeks flame.

Glimpsing herself again in her mirror, Rhowenna turned away quickly, biting her lower lip, her lashes sweeping down as though to veil her thoughts from her own image. Flustered, she took up from her dressing table the gold circlet, engraved and nielloed, that she wore as princess of Usk and clasped it about her head. It was a reminder, however unpleasant, of her rank, of the fact that no matter how much she hoped otherwise, her father was unlikely to choose as a husband for his only daughter a mere kinsman, when she might command a prince—or even a king. Rhowenna shrank from the idea of being sent away to some foreign land, of being wedded and bedded by a man who, however royal his blood, would be a total stranger to her. Still, even that would be better than being a captive of the Northmen who rampaged through her nightmare.

Glancing once more into her mirror, she pinched her pallid cheeks hard to put some color in them. Then, overhearing her mother asking Enid about her, Rhowenna stepped from her sleeping chamber into the great hall, hoping fervently that

Father Cadwyr would not be there, as he often was, looking, with his dark, flowing robes and his black, glowing eyes, like some fierce bird of prey waiting to swoop down upon her and tear at her young flesh. To her relief, the priest was absent, as was her father, who had gone hunting with several of the housecarls. Only a few of the elderly warriors had remained behind. Two of them contested over a chessboard; the rest sat around the fire in the central hearth, repairing and cleaning armor, reminiscing about the hunts of their youth and, with cups of mead and mulled wine, warming their old bones, glad to be inside on this dismal winter's day. Here, too, Rhowenna discovered her mother, assisted by a few of the serving maids, at the large loom that stood in one corner.

"The morn is well advanced. You slept late this day, daughter," Igraine observed in greeting as she looked up from where she sat, her fine black eyebrows arching with gentle reproof when she spoke. But there was concern, too, upon the Queen's beautiful face. "That is the third time this week. Are you ill, Rhowenna?"

"Nay, just not sleeping well, Mother."

Which was the truth, Rhowenna thought, casting her eyes down to hide the fact that there was more to it than that and hoping that her mother would be satisfied by the response. The Queen was very good at discerning a lie; beneath her steady, dark blue-eyed gaze, many a housecarl, servant, and *ceorl* grew uncomfortable and faltered during the telling of some false story and finally confessed the true tale. Even Pendragon's earls were wary of Igraine's sharp scrutiny; much of the King's power and many of his decisions had their roots in the Queen's shrewd, uncanny perception.

Now, as though sensing there was indeed more to the matter than Rhowenna had admitted, Igraine frowned. For a moment, it seemed she would press the issue. Then, glancing about the great hall at the housecarls and serving women, she appeared abruptly to change her mind. In these troubled times, only an innocent was trusting, a fool, careless—and the Queen was neither. Words heedlessly spoken before warriors and servants often—for a handful of coins or baubles, or to avenge a grievance, whether real or imagined—found their way to the ears of one's enemies, to be used against one by the ambitious and unscrupulous. Strategically located Usk was neither a large nor a powerful kingdom. That it was yet whole and independent owed more to its natural boundaries and to the cleverness and diplomacy of its rulers than to the might of its army; for its warriors, although fierce, were few compared to those of its neighbors. As a result, Usk wisely minded its own business and did not attract attention to itself by dabbling in the struggles and intrigues of others. Its great hall was not ostentatious; it did not display the riches garnered from the land and from the Great Sea or from the traders. Although Usk's coffers were full, Pendragon was frequently heard to lament a bad harvest, the poor hunting and fishing, and an empty purse, so Usk—when thought of at all by those who would conquer and carve up what was not theirs by birthright—was often discounted by the foolish as a petty kingdom of no great wealth or importance.

"I will prepare you a sleeping draught this evening, daughter, if you like," Igraine offered after a moment, casually.

Rhowenna had inherited her mother's intelligence and insight, and she was not deceived by the Queen's tone. It held a note she recognized as a harbinger of a private conversation later. Her heart sank at the sound, for although she yearned to unburden herself to her mother, the unknown consequences of that act discouraged her. Still, she nodded.

"Aye, perhaps 'twould help," she said.

And perhaps that, too, was the truth, she thought as she dragged a low stool over to the circle of women and, taking up her reel and spindle, began her own work for the day. Being neither vain nor lazy, the Queen turned her hand as quickly and easily to a bone needle as she did to a bone

chessman; and through the years, she had trained Rhowenna
to do the same, instilling in her the belief that idleness and
ignorance led to no good, and teaching her not only the
knowledge required to manage a royal manor, but also the
lore of the Picti and of the Tribes, which had been handed
down through the ages from female to female. There was no
task of either chatelaine or serving woman that Rhowenna
could not perform. She should have thought of a sleeping
potion herself, she realized belatedly. The various properties
of flowers and roots, herbs and spices, how to make medicinal
tinctures and decoctions, were as well known to her as to her
mother. Perhaps with a sleeping draught, the dream would
vanish. That, instead, it might well be enhanced by a potion
was a thought that, shivering a little, Rhowenna did not dwell
on as her nimble fingers twirled the reel and spindle, turning
carded wool into a fine, even yarn she would later weave
upon her own small loom. If she dyed the fabric Tyrian
purple, it would make a handsome cloak for her father, she
mused as she spun, and perhaps she could speak to one of
the metalworkers about fashioning a brooch to pin the cloak,
a gold circlet with a winged, serpentine dragon at its heart.
That would please her father, for the dragon was his emblem.

Focusing on such matters as these, Rhowenna forced herself to occupy her mind as she occupied her hands with her
work. She would ponder her dream no more, she told herself
sternly, but put it from her head. If the priests spoke truly,
the vision was false and wicked, sent to her by the devil to
tempt her to damnation if he could. She would not imperil
her immortal soul. Even the old gods had warned of the
consequences upon those who would commune with demons.

Rhowenna listened with only half an ear to the shallow
chatter of the serving women as they bickered about the
simple, mundane matters that were their own lot and that did
not interest her. There was little to be gleaned from workers
who grew more quarrelsome during the long grey winter

months, when there was little to do except to sit beside the fire in the shadowy great hall and to sew, to spin, or to weave. Sometimes Owain, the bard, entertained the women with his songs and storytelling, but he was nowhere to be seen this day. Like as not, he had joined the hunt, eager to escape from the dreary confines of the royal manor. Rhowenna did not blame him. She, too, would have been glad to venture outside for a while, despite the inclement weather. She felt torpid and thick-headed from lack of sun and sleep. She wished she were a fat bear, who could just hibernate all winter and have no worries beyond being safe and snug in some cave, slumbering, dreamless, until spring instead of sitting and spinning and fretting.

But there was no surcease from any of this as the seemingly interminable day wore on, the noon meal but a brief respite for Rhowenna from the turning of her reel and spindle. She returned dully to her work, feeling like Clotho, one of the Greeks' three Fates, who had spun endlessly, drawing out and twisting the fibers of men into the threads of life. Was there no more to be had from life than this? she wondered. Was there no more in store for her? Then, determinedly, she compelled herself once more to shake off her melancholy thoughts. They were born of the winter months and being cooped up for so long inside the royal manor, she reassured herself. She had grown as fractious as the serving women, who had begun yet another spat among themselves.

"A dull needle and ragged stitches do not a fine gown make, Cerys," dour, shrewish Winifred chided. Always, her cold, censuring eyes watched the rest of the women avidly, alert for the slightest mistake. With her sharp, spiteful tongue, she made it her business to chastise them for any perceived fault or mistake. "That seam will never hold—and you've sewn the sleeve in crooked, besides, stupid wench!"

As she gazed down at her botched handiwork, tears trembled on the lashes of silly young Cerys, who was gentle and harmless and meant well but who, in truth, could not be trusted with any save the simplest of tasks. She was frequently to blame for broken crockery in the kitchen and cross words in the great hall.

"I—I do not know how I—how I came to do such a thing," Cerys whispered, contrite and cringing in the face of Winifred's admonishment.

"Like as not because your mind is on Rhodri—instead of your work!" dark, sly, malicious Morgen gibed. She was fair-faced and ripe-bodied, the siren and mischief-maker of the lot, as eager to tumble into a man's bed as she was to shirk a hard task or to start trouble. She had had her eye on the warrior Rhodri for some time and, resenting the fact that it was Cerys he preferred, was quick to side with Winifred.

"Aye, well, that is the way of it when a maid is in love," plump, jolly Jestina observed affably, as though there were no argument brewing. With her capable, willing hands and kind, generous heart, she was forever smoothing over the upsets and the quarrels of the others. Taking the gown from Cerys, she began patiently to undo the ragged stitches of the crooked sleeve. "'Tis not so bad, after all. A turn here and a tuck there, and 'twill soon be put aright. Fetch a sharper needle from the sewing chest, child," she directed to Cerys, "for Winifred spoke truly when she said that your own needle is dull. That is why you had to push it so hard through the fabric and so twisted the sleeve."

"I did that once—twisted my knee. 'Twas so painful, I remember. . . . You will need to put a compress on it and to bind it well," frail old Gladys chimed in querulously from where she half dozed by the fire, her embroidery sliding from her lap. Deaf and senile and so invariably muddled, she was often inadvertently humorous and so a favorite target of the housecarls' good-natured baiting and jesting.

Glancing up from her spinning as she joined in the laughter that greeted poor old Gladys's contribution to the conversation, Rhowenna had banished from her mind her fears of impending doom. In that instant of laughter, she thought only, with pride, that her mother, the Queen, was like a swan amid ducks where she sat among the circle of serving women. Lovely and serene, graceful of form and movement, keen of mind and wit, Igraine alone took no part in the mirth at Gladys's expense. Instead, her head was cocked a trifle, as though she were lost in reverie or, more likely, listening for the sound of Pendragon's return. But then Rhowenna saw her mother's face go suddenly still and heard, too, the loud squawking and violent fluttering of panicked hens in the bailey, the thudding hooves of horses ridden hard and furious, the discordant jangle of bridles yanked up short and spurs upon booted feet, and the urgent, frightened shouting of men outside; and she knew then, even as her mother did, that something was wrong, terribly wrong.

The Queen rose abruptly, accidentally knocking over her chair, a clumsy action so unlike her that Rhowenna felt a sudden fist of fear clutch her heart. Igraine's face was now drained of color; one fragile hand trembled at her throat for an instant before, recovering, she glided swiftly toward the doors of the great hall, through which the housecarls were even then bursting in a biting gust of rain and wind that brought with it a whorl of brittle leaves and old straw blown up from the bailey, and that set the rushlights in the great hall wildly aflicker.

For a moment, as the massive oak portals swung inward, Rhowenna could see naught but the men's faces, grim and angry and afraid beneath their helmets dripping with rain, for the broad shoulders of those who came foremost blocked her view. So at first, she felt only a deep sense of relief that the faces were familiar, that the royal manor was not under attack by some enemy force. But then she saw that between them, the warriors bore the bloodstained body of her father, the King, and she was struck dumb with anguish and disbelief.

Time seemed to slow then, and Rhowenna viewed her surroundings through a shadowy vignette, blurred at the edges, unreal. An afflicted cry rose to echo amid the heavy timber rafters of the great hall. She was only dimly aware that the wail came from her own throat as she, like the rest, pressed forward to reach the King. Metal clanged against metal and upon stone as one of the housecarls swept the cups of mead and wine from the long trestle table by the fire to clear a place to lay Pendragon; and as the other men carefully maneuvered the King's body onto the table, the dark, rich liquor from the scattered cups flowed and puddled like blood upon the rushes that strewed the stone floor. The mead, made from honey, would be sticky and difficult to clean up, Rhowenna thought stupidly, then was stricken and ashamed that she should think of such when her father lay so silent and unmoving upon the table.

"Is he alive?" The Queen's voice was low and sharp with fear; for it seemed to them all as she bent over Pendragon that he did not breathe and that the pallor of death had already crept upon his flesh.

"Aye, my lady," Pendragon's head warrior, Brynmawr, replied soberly, "but badly hurt, and I fear that the wound may prove mortal."

"Jestina, fetch my medicine chest and clean linens for bandages! Winifred, set a pot of water to boiling! Morgen, I will need mud and cobwebs to staunch the bleeding! Cerys, send for the healer! Rhowenna, you will assist me! Brynmawr, your knife!" Like stones cast rapidly from a sling, Igraine's orders flew as, taking the speedily proffered blade, she began carefully to cut the King's blood-stiffened leather garments from his body so that she might see what damage had been done.

As sharply as Brynmawr's dagger sliced through Pendragon's clothing, so her mother's words pierced Rhowenna's shock. Gathering her wits, she moved to stand at the Queen's side, her insides knotted with terror as she stared down at her father's handsome, bearded visage, as ashen as though all his life's blood had poured from it. There was a smear of mud upon his cheek and bits of twigs and leaves in his dark beard. He had been struck down in the forest, then, and had fallen to the earth, she surmised. The hounds of the hunting party must have flushed a wild boar, she thought. Savage and dangerous, a wild boar could gore a grown man to death, even a man so large and powerful as her father. One of his housecarls had died that way once, long ago, when she was just a child, she vaguely recalled. But now as her mother probed the injury, Rhowenna spied the cruel iron barb and the small, broken piece of wood embedded in her father's flesh, just above his heart; and she knew then, horrified, that he had been brought low by an arrow. A hunting accident? Or had someone attempted to murder the King?

"Brynmawr, how did this happen?" Igraine asked, her voice harsh and throbbing with emotion, her midnight-blue eyes dark and huge in her pale, fine-boned countenance.

"An ambush, my lady. We were set upon in the woods— by whom, I know not, except that they were men of Walas and not the Saxon wolves from east of Offa's Dyke; for they were wise in the ways of our hills and forests, my lady, and of our style of fighting. Most like, they were warriors of Glamorgan or Gwent. If so, my lady, it may be that they will believe the King dead and will lay siege upon us!"

Rhowenna shivered at Brynmawr's words, for until now, except for her dream, she had never really thought of Usk as being vulnerable to assault, and certainly not from other kingdoms of Walas. She had not suspected treachery from one of Walas's own.

"Go, then, and make the necessary preparations to ward off such an attack," the Queen ordered to Brynmawr, looking suddenly, Rhowenna thought, as though the blood flowing from Pendragon's wound somehow sapped her own strength, as well.

Why, she is no longer young, Rhowenna recognized, startled, *and I never realized it until today; and without Father, she is vulnerable, as I am.* . . .

What might befall them if her father died? This time in which they lived was not like the old days, when a queen could rule in her own right. If Pendragon were to die, one of his kinsmen would claim the throne, and she and her mother might have little say about what became of them. Worse, Usk might be conquered by enemies and she and her mother taken prisoner, raped, or even killed. For the first time in her life, Rhowenna longed to be a man, so she might wield a sword and a shield to defend herself. Of its own volition, her hand dropped to the small dinner dagger she carried in the mesh girdle around her waist. If the worst should happen, she would not be seized without a struggle, she vowed silently, fiercely. She would fight to the death if need be to protect herself and her mother.

Bowing to the Queen, Brynmawr strode to the doors of the great hall, taking several of the housecarls with him to set about fortifying the royal manor and the palisade that bulwarked it, while Igraine and Rhowenna strove to save the King's life, Igraine calling for more rushlights to be brought and placed upon the table to drive away the shadows where Pendragon lay. Her hand trembling as she took Brynmawr's knife from her mother, Rhowenna passed the blade through the flames of the fire in the central hearth, as she had been taught by her mother to do when using any kind of instrument to perform surgery upon an open wound. When the knife glowed hot, she poured a small amount of wine upon it to cool it. Then she handed the blade back to her mother, watching anxiously as, setting her teeth against the pain she must cause her husband, Igraine grimly pressed the knife point into the congealed blood and torn flesh around the broken shaft of the arrow that protruded from just below Pendragon's collarbone.

How long they labored over the King's body, Rhowenna did not know, although it seemed like forever. Daylight faded to dusk and then dusk to darkness as, back and legs aching from standing motionless for so long, she bent over her father, wiping the perspiration from his feverish brow and, with a cloth dipped in a bowl of warm barley water, moistening his dry lips, hoping and praying that he would gain a little nourishment to sustain him through his ordeal. Now and then, at her mother's direction, she felt his heart, which beat faintly and unsteadily beneath her palm, and her eyes were huge and scared when they met her mother's. More than once, as the King groaned and stirred restlessly at the Queen's ministrations, his breath rasping and rattling in his throat, Rhowenna was forced to press him down to hold him still. But to her relief, he did not regain consciousness as, little by little, her mother dug from the wound the iron barb that had caused it. Then, at last, grasping the broken shaft, Igraine pulled the arrowhead free. Blood gushed from the gaping hole; Rhowenna gasped as her father made a terrible choking sound. But the Queen did not falter, mopping away the blood, while with boiling water, and a fresh cloth lathered with soap from a medicinal plant, she cleaned the wound. After that, Rhowenna poured wine into the injury to ensure that putrefaction did not set in. Then, sweat beading her own brow, she pulled the jagged edges of her father's skin together, while her mother carefully sewed the laceration shut with a needle and thread. Despite the stitches that had closed it, the wound still bled, but this Igraine stanched with a poultice of the mud and cobwebs she had earlier sent Morgen to fetch. Then, folding one of the linens into a pad and tearing the others into strips, the Queen bound the injury tightly. During the whole, the

King roused only briefly, then lapsed once more into an increasingly delirious unconsciousness—not a good sign, Rhowenna knew.

At her mother's direction, the warriors who had remained behind in the great hall following Brynmawr's departure lifted the King's body and carried him into his sleeping chamber, where they laid him upon his bed. After that, there was nothing to do but to wait, to hope, and to pray. Her face grave with sorrow and fear, Rhowenna sank upon a low stool by her mother at Pendragon's side, knowing that the vigil would be long and its outcome uncertain. Somber-faced, talking softly, earnestly, among themselves, the housecarls moved slowly to leave the two women alone with the King. Feeling a quick, gentle touch, in passing, upon her shoulder, Rhowenna glanced up to see Gwydion gazing back at her reassuringly as he left the sleeping chamber, quietly closing the door behind him. She had not realized until now that he had been one of those who had stayed behind when Brynmawr had gone to gird the royal manor against a possible assault. A wealth of love and unspoken words had been in Gwydion's steady grey eyes; and now, the cold knot of fear in Rhowenna's belly warmed and loosened a little at the understanding that no matter what, her beloved kinsman would be at her side to support and to defend her. She yearned to go and seek him out, to lay her head upon his shoulder and to feel his arms hold her close against his hard young body, loving and protecting her. But the memory of his hand upon her shoulder must be enough to comfort her until she could slip away from her father's bedside.

The healer came at last, bled Pendragon copiously, then retired to the great hall, declaring that the Queen's treatment had been exemplary and that there was nothing more to be done. Hard on the healer's heels followed Father Cadwyr, with his burning eyes and dark robes, to proclaim that whatever came to pass, God's will would be done and that the two women must trust in Him—to which Igraine retorted, rather sharply, that God helped those who helped themselves. Still, she did consent to kneeling beside the priest while he lamented the attack upon the King and prayed for Pendragon's swift recovery. But as Rhowenna, too, knelt and bowed her head, she could not repress a shiver at the thought that for all his pious pronouncements and prayers, Father Cadwyr resembled nothing so much as a huge carrion crow hovering over her father, waiting to pick the flesh from his bones.

Chapter Two

Loki's Wolf

The Shores of the Skagerrak, the Northland, A.D. 865

Wulfgar Lodbróksson was caught between two worlds. Neither *jarl* nor *thrœll*, he was the bastard son of the great Ragnar Lodbrók, a powerful *konungr*, a king, of the Northland, and a captive Saxon woman, Goscelin, whom Ragnar had brought home to the Northland one year from a raid down the coasts of Caledonia, Britain, Frisia, Normandy, and beyond. Ragnar had taken Wulfgar's mother as his concubine, but, in truth, she had been nothing more than a slave, for he had never deigned to marry her, since he already had more than one wife; and when, presently, he had tired of her and cast her off, she had been reduced to serving as a scullion in his kitchen and—as a result of her subsequent lowly place in his household—as a whore for his *jarlar* and *thegns*. Indeed, there were many who doubted that Ragnar had actually fathered Wulfgar. The first and foremost of those who cast aspersions upon Wulfgar's paternity were Ragnar's three legitimate sons: Ivar, called the Boneless—not for his shapelessness, but, rather, for his fluidity of movement—and Ubbi and Halfdan. Yet because no one, least of all Ragnar and his sons, could ever really be certain Ragnar was not, in fact, Wulfgar's father, Wulfgar was never compelled to wear a thrall's collar. Instead, from the time he was born, he was a *bóndi*, a freedman. This alone was his salvation, the one thing to which he clung ferociously against all odds; for in reality, his lot in life was little better than his poor mother's had been.

As a child, Wulfgar had been given to his half brothers and made to understand that his livelihood, indeed his very existence, depended solely upon how well he served them. Although once he had attained his manhood, he could, as a freedman, have left them at any time, he had no means to do so, and he had, besides, come to understand that out of sheer perversity and spite, his half brothers would not have tolerated his breaking away. Being the true sons of their father, they would have found some foul manner of forcing Wulfgar's acceptance of their claims upon him—or, worse, have seen him dead in his grave. Even Yelkei, the sly old spaewife who had been his wet nurse, who had reared him when his mother had died, and who in the past had fought like a she-wolf to protect him, could not have stayed their hands against him then, Wulfgar thought. Whether he be driven to subjugation or to death mattered not to his half brothers; but he must continue to serve and to obey them because he dared to call himself their father's son—and so held a claim, however tenuous and remote, to Ragnar's kingdom and throne.

Of his father and half brothers, it was Ivar whom Wulfgar most hated; for being the oldest of Ragnar's three legitimate sons, Ivar was heir to Ragnar's vast holdings, a prince of the Northland, and the handsomest of men, besides, while Wulfgar was naught but a bastard and believed himself nothing uncommon to look upon. But these things alone, although cause for jealousy, would not have earned Ivar Wulfgar's enmity; there was one thing more: Ivar was also the cruelest of Wulfgar's half brothers. Many times over the years had Wulfgar felt the stabbing sting of Ivar's needle-sharp wit and scorn, an injury piercing Wulfgar's pride and manhood more deeply than the smart cuff to his ear or the swift boot to his backside, which he often received from Ubbi or Halfdan. Although those two were mighty warriors, as bold and blood-thirsty in battle, as ambitious and hungry for power as their older brother, they were rougher, simpler men, lacking the complexities and subtleties that made Ivar clever and cruel. Unlike Ubbi and Halfdan, who cared not what any man thought—and even less for a woman's feelings—Ivar made it his business to know the hopes and dreams of all who served him; and Wulfgar, in his youth, had been foolish enough, once, to blurt out his own aspirations during a heated quarrel, when his ingrained wariness, forbearance, and plain common sense had fallen prey to the fierce prick of Ivar's needling. Wulfgar had regretted ever since that evil day when his own pride and temper had placed such a weapon in Ivar's ruthless hands.

Ivar would not, Wulfgar thought, have much grudged him the small farm that would have been his by birthright had his father been a freedman and not Ragnar Lodbrók, a king. Wulfgar would have been of little consequence then, merely one of the many entitled to speak at the *Thing*—the assembly of all freemen: *bóndi, thegns*, and *jarlar* alike—who, under the law that, a hundred years later, would come to be part of the great Frostathing Law, would have been permitted to acquire three thralls of his own, provided he had also pos-sessed no less than twelve cows and two horses. But being no one's heir and so having little enough to his name, Wulfgar called no square of land his. Nor would Ivar, knowing that it was Wulfgar's one burning desire in life, agree to his half brother's joining the ranks of the *thegns*, the warriors, and going a-*víking* in one of the square-sailed longships that had made the Northmen the scourge of the seas for over two centuries.

It was for this prohibition most of all that Wulfgar hated Ivar.

So it was that Wulfgar was little more than his half brothers' lackey, as was proved this winter's day by his driving of their sledge, piled high with equipment and supplies for the hunt upon which they had embarked earlier that morn. It had snowed the night before, and the wind was raw, the air frigid. Shivering a little, Wulfgar might have wished for the heat of the fire in Ragnar's *skáli*, a great mead hall, or at least for a heavier fur cloak; but he was accustomed to the cold, having known naught else all his life. There was a stout, iron-ringed barrel of mead on the sledge, and one, too, of *bjórr*, a highly fermented fruit wine. Doubtless when the hunting party paused to rest, he would be given a cup of one or the other to warm him, its never before having been his half brothers' whim that he should freeze to death. Meanwhile, to take his mind off the day's chilliness, he dwelled on the strange warning that Yelkei had given him earlier that morn. Since the two sturdy, yoked oxen harnessed to the sledge were prone to plod placidly after the horses being ridden and so had scant need of any real guidance, a low command, a gentle tug on the reins now and then were all that were required to maintain the pace and direction of the sledge, which left Wulfgar's mind free to wander where it willed as he hunched on the seat, his bare blond head bent, his blue eyes downcast to avoid notice, as was his habit. He had long ago learned that like a slave, a freedman, if he were poor and wise, did not attract to himself the attention of the *jarlar* and *konungrs* of the Northland—especially of those who had reasons of their own for singling him out and wishing him ill.

Like the thick snow clouds massed in the pale, sullen sky,

the breath of the dogs, oxen, and horses billowed and swirled, mingling with the fine clouds of powdery snow churned up by paws and hooves alike, and with the white wisps of clammy mist that curled and drifted across the low-lying land, clinging to its wet hollows. Ahead, beyond the wide stretch of wild, snowy plain and the icy edges of the still, weed-grown mere, where swans and ducks could be flushed aplenty in the shorter summer months and brought down by the great gyrfalcons of the *jarlar*, rose the dark-forested hills that were the destination of the hunting party, cutting a jagged oblique against the horizon. At the fore of the hunting party, the dogs danced, yapping and straining at leashes held by the hunters; and beside his father, Ivar rode, mounted upon a strong, spirited steed as white as the new-fallen snow.

There were in the Northland two kinds of men: those who were short and dark, and those who were tall and fair. Ivar was one of these last. His long, flowing mane of red-gold hair gleamed like flame-kissed wheat in the grey light of day, reflecting the frosted rays of the dull sun in such a way that it seemed a halo shone about his proud, handsome head. But he was no angel such as Wulfgar had heard populated the heaven of those whose god was the Christ. In truth, Wulfgar thought Ivar a demon, the personification of the giant Loki, who had insinuated himself into Asgard, the realm of the gods, and who was the contriver of all wickedness. Except when alight with malice or cruel mirth, Ivar's blue eyes were as hard and cold as ice—even stern Ragnar's had more warmth—and as watchful as those of a predator alert for prey. His face was lean, the bones finely molded, and in combination with his aquiline nose gave him a fierce, hawkish appearance. As was customary, the ends of his long mustache were neatly braided and his beard was short-cropped, both forming an elegant frame for his sensual lips, habitually curved in a faint, arrogant sneer.

Although tall, broad of shoulder, long of limb, and powerfully muscled, there was nothing slow or ponderous about Ivar. He moved with such suppleness and grace that he had on his first raid earned his sobriquet, the Boneless, when, blessed with the ability to contort his body in ways that were uncanny, he had effortlessly evaded enemy weapons and dealt his foes many a death blow. Now he was in his prime, and his lithe figure and superior skill with a broadsword were such that his very name struck terror into the hearts of men. But Wulfgar's own heart held jealousy and hatred for Ivar, as well as a grudging respect and admiration for his prowess as a warrior. Only now and again, when Ivar turned those pitiless blue eyes on him, did Wulfgar scent a mortal danger. Someday, Ivar would slay him, he thought, or he would be forced to kill Ivar. This, Yelkei had told Wulfgar once, long ago, insisting that his destiny and Ivar's were forever intertwined, like the interlaced branches of the pine and spruce trees that stood close and thick in the woods. But young and frightened by Yelkei's eerie prophesying, Wulfgar had flung away from her angrily, crying out that she was an old fool and a fraud and a spiteful-tongued witch. Since then, hurt and offended by his rejection, she had held her peace and had not spoken to him again of what she saw in the fires and mists, and in her castings of the rune stones.

Still, Yelkei had done a strange thing this dawn as Wulfgar was tightly strapping the last of his father's and half brothers' gear and provisions onto the sledge: She had glided up beside him, as dark as a raven of ill omen in her old, worn fur cloak, and laying one yellow, bony, clawlike hand upon his arm, she had muttered:

"Have a care, Wulfgar. This day, you will decide your destiny."

To Wulfgar's deep frustration, there had been no time to ask what she meant by her cryptic words; for just then, talking and laughing boisterously, Ragnar and his sons had exited the great mead hall of Ragnar's *hof*, a large longhouse, and

Yelkei had slipped away as silently as she had come, leaving Wulfgar standing there, staring after her, a chill in his bones that had had naught to do with the biting wind. Now, as he thought once more of her low, enigmatic pronouncement, he was unable to repress a shudder. Although Wulfgar professed scorn for Yelkei's unworldly power, this was because he did not understand it, and so it frightened him—as all things not understood by men are frightening. Much of her knowledge, he judged, came from nothing more than an innate shrewdness about human nature, and from her keeping her eyes and ears open in such places as Ragnar's great mead hall and the marketsquare. Yet there were times, Wulfgar was forced to admit, when Yelkei's slanted black eyes took on a blank, farseeing gaze in her wrinkled moon face, and she spoke in a voice that did not seem to come from her own throat, foretelling what could have been known to no man, unless he were told it by the gods. Even mighty Ragnar feared her at those times, and although she was naught but a yellow slave from the vast grassy steppes of the Eastlands, did not dare to lift a hand against her. Only Ivar was brave enough to deride her; but his laughter too died away uneasily when she stared at him steadily, her small, stooped figure suddenly looming large and forbidding in the face of his mockery. Because of this, Wulfgar deep down inside thought that Yelkei was a true spaewife, and he could not deny that her words earlier this morn haunted and troubled him. With all his heart, he wished he knew what her warning had meant.

He was so lost in contemplation of this that he did not hear Ragnar's terse command to halt, and only Ivar's drawled taunt, inquiring whether Wulfgar were bent on going a-*víking* in a heavily laden sledge, and the laughter of the rest of the hunting party in response to the gibe, brought him to his senses. At that, flushing a dull red with anger and embarrassment, Wulfgar drew the oxen up sharply. Then, springing lightly from the seat, he moved to untie the thongs that secured the provisions and to unwrap the hides that contained generous quantities of salted bear meat, smoked fish, dried fruit, and hard bread; for the gelid air and riding both quickened a man's hunger, especially during the long, dark winter months, the *mørketiden*, the murky time. The stout barrels of mead and *bjórr* were opened and cups filled. When all had been served, the hunters, Wulfgar, and the other freedmen and slaves who accompanied the hunting party were permitted to take their own shares. Hunkered down beside the sledge to block the worst of the wind, Wulfgar tore off with his fingers chunks of the tough meat and coarse bread, chewing slowly to savor each bite and washing the food down with long swallows of mead. Gradually, his belly grew replete, his body warmed from the strong drink. For a moment, he closed his eyes, longing to curl up by a fire somewhere and to sleep until the summer sun woke the earth from its winter slumber. But too quickly the small meal was finished; the short break was ended; and at Ragnar's order, the hunting party was already mounting up.

Yelkei was just a fool, a spiteful old fool, Wulfgar told himself again darkly as he repacked the sledge, clambered back onto the seat, and once more took up the reins. She had spoken so to him merely to frighten him, to put him on his guard against perfidy this day; for she feared that Ragnar and his sons would slay him, given the chance to do the deed without fear of blame or reprisal—and more than one man had failed to return from a hunt. The bears, wolves, lynx, badgers, wolverines, and elk that stalked the long-shadowed forests were dangerous creatures, not so easy to kill as the foxes, reindeer, roe deer, lemmings, beaver, martens, and hares that also abided there. Accidents happened, just as they did upon the seas, whether the prey was whales or sea lions— or the towns of the kingdoms of the Eastlands and the Southlands. Still, Wulfgar did not think it likely that Ragnar and his sons would seek to be rid of him when there were others to bear witness against them, *jarlar* like Björn Ironside and Hasting, who bore Wulfgar no grudge and, indeed, found no small amusement and satisfaction in his being a thorn in his father's and half brothers' sides. There were those who had as great a desire as Wulfgar to see Ragnar and his sons laid low, and who, if the opportunity arose, would be quick and glad to speak against them before the *Thing*. Although he had carved out his own kingdom in the Northland, Ragnar was still subject to the Jutish king across the Skagerrak, and he was no fool, besides. Yelkei was the fool, Wulfgar thought again, with her fires and mists and rune stones, meddling in what was the business of the gods, not of men. Like as not, she would cause the wrath of the gods to fall upon *him*, and he would wind up accursed, doomed to wander Náströnd, the Shore of Corpses, along Hel's river Gyoll until Ragnarök, the twilight of the gods.

Then, as he remembered how Yelkei loved him and had cared for him after his mother's death, Wulfgar's heart softened and he felt ashamed of his uncharitable thoughts. She only sought to protect him, as she always had. It was not her fault if her powers disturbed and unnerved him—and if he, being too proud and stubborn to admit that fact, grew angry in order to hide his fear. That was the way of a man; as a woman, Yelkei should understand that—and perhaps she did, for she never reproached him for his harsh words, but quieted like a small, nesting bird and bent her head and hands to her tasks. Later, she would see to it that he had a second bowl of broth or stew to ease his hunger, or an extra cup of mead or *bjórr* to warm him against the winter wind that crept through the chinks and cracks of the tiny, wattle-and-daub hut he had, as a freedman, been allotted within Ragnar's palisade. The hut had only one room, heated solely by a small stone hearth set in the center of the hard earth floor; but resting there was better than sleeping in the crowded slave pens or bedding down outside in the snow. Yelkei slept curled up in a corner by the door of the hut, and saw to Wulfgar's needs in her spare time, cooking or preserving whatever small game he killed or fish he caught in his own free moments, and cleaning, washing, and sewing for him late into the night, by the dim glow of the fire and the rushlights.

As he thought now of these things, Wulfgar knew in his heart that whatever Yelkei had meant by her words, she wished only to protect him from harm. It would be wise to be wary of treachery in the dark forest, he thought, unconsciously laying one hand upon the scramasax he carried in a leather sheath at his belted waist. He had forged the single-edged knife himself, of iron, setting the blade into a fine, well-polished handle he had fashioned from the strong bone of an elk.

Except for Ivar, Wulfgar feared no mortal man, only the elves who stalked the woods, and the dwarves, giants, and trolls who lurked in the caves of the hills and the mountains alike. He had never forsaken his dream of becoming a warrior, and every chance he found, he practiced in secret with the weapons he had made from materials foraged or filched here and there: a case-hardened spear, its smooth shaft of ash, its sharp head of iron; a longbow, and arrows tipped with iron barbs and fletched with feathers stolen from the gyrfalcons in Ragnar's mews; a round, leather-covered, lime-wood shield with an iron boss and rimmed with strips of gilt-bronze; and his most prized possession, a battle-ax formed of a keenly honed blade he had engraved with battle scenes and Odinn's runes, and mounted to a stout, thong-wrapped ash haft long and heavy enough that wielding it required two hands. He called the weapon Blood-Drinker.

He had no broadsword, for without formal training in its use, he could not have hoped realistically to prevail over those experienced in its maneuvers. But although wielding the battle-ax, too, required a certain amount of skill, its effectiveness relied more upon its user's strength, of which Wulfgar had no mean measure. More than one bush, branch, or young tree had met its demise at the hands of Wulfgar and the blade of his battle-ax; and although it was not meant for hunting, he had, some years back, blooded the weapon on the throat of a great red stag. He had first wounded the animal with his spear, bringing the mighty beast to its knees before setting its soul free, inhaling its last, dying breath, and, afterward, marking his face with its warm, thick blood in his own initiation rite as a man, a hunter, and a warrior. He and Yelkei had eaten well for many long weeks after that.

As most *thegns* did, Wulfgar carried his favored weapon at his back, in a wide leather scabbard; and the feel of it beneath his fur cloak reassured him, just as his scramasax did, that if trouble came this winter's day, he would be prepared for it. If he must die and spend nine days and nights wandering Náströnd, the Shore of Corpses, to the barred gates of Hel (for being no true warrior, Wulfgar had no thought of being claimed by a golden Valkyrie and borne as a hero over the rainbow bridge, Bifröst, unto Valhöll, Odinn's great mead Hall of the Slain, in Asgard), he would not go without taking his enemies with him.

Yet, curiously, Yelkei had not warned of his death, only of his destiny. At the thought, Wulfgar sighed heavily. There was no point in his dwelling further on her words; he could not fathom their meaning, and he was not an old dog to worry a bone long after its meat had been picked clean and its marrow sucked dry. He would trust to the gods and to his battle-ax to protect him. A man could do no more than that.

The hunting party had reached the edge of the forest now. There, Wulfgar drew the sledge to a halt and jumped down from the seat, for from here, he must go on afoot; the oxen and sledge were unable to keep pace with the horses on the narrow, winding trails in the woods. As did the other freedmen, he filled flasks with mead and *bjórr* for his masters and wrapped some of the food, as well, into a pack he hefted onto his back. Then he strapped on his snowshoes and, gathering up the spears of his father and half brothers, set out at an easy trot behind the hunters and mounted men, leaving only the slaves behind to guard the oxen and the sledge.

Upon the heath, the winter's day had been twilight-dim, and the forest was duskier yet, long with shadows and deep with silence, so it seemed a place not of man and beast, but of the gods and mythical creatures, and the hunting party intruders, daring to trespass where it was not meet or safe to tread. He was not alone in this feeling, Wulfgar thought. Even the *jarlar* and the *thegns* talked more softly as they entered the woods—although it might have been because sounds carried in the forest hush and would alert the herds of elk and deer to the presence of men—and there was awe and not a little fear upon the faces of the freedmen, who came seldom to the woods, which was a place not only of elves, but also of other beings not human and of fantastic beasts, as well. It was said that not only dwarves, giants, and trolls, but also dragons lived in the caves of the forested hills and breathed a fire as deadly as the thunderbolts that flew from Thor's great hammer, Mjöllnir, during a thunderstorm. Wulfgar himself had never seen an elf, a dwarf, a giant, a troll, or a dragon; but as the *skálds*, the bards, sang of them, they must exist, he thought, and he was glad the hunting party moved so quietly, almost furtively through the woods.

Like stalactites, icicles hung from tree and bush alike, and snow weighed down the boughs and lay thick upon the ground; in places, the wind had blown drifts several feet deep against thickets, brambles, and tree trunks. Scattered upon the snow's whiteness were green needles and brown cones from the evergreen trees, and brittle, dead leaves from the deciduous trees. The naked branches of these last, entangled and heavily encrusted with ice, resembled an enormous cobweb spun by some unearthly, gargantuan spider, Wulfgar thought, and they swayed and creaked in the wind, singing a ghostly song that sent a grue up his spine. Sometimes, the burden of the snow and ice was so heavy that without warning, a dead limb would snap from its trunk to crash to the ground below. He had seen a man struck and killed that way once, long ago, and so he kept a wary eye out for rotten boughs.

But there was beauty as well as danger to be found in the forest. The tall, feathery pine and spruce trees were haunts from which the winter birds chirped their plaintive songs above an earthen floor thickly carpeted with aromatic heather, lichens, and moss underneath the snow. From the summits of the hills, clear-running rills with sweet melodies all their own twisted and tumbled down through deep, narrow, rocky crevasses and shallower, wider gullies they had carved out over the years; they spilled in waterfalls over stony outcrops into small, secluded pools, half frozen now in the dead of winter and whose gentle rippling was a harmonious whisper on the wind. The crisp air was clean, untainted by the smells of smoke from cooking fires and burning fat from rushlights and whale-oil lamps, and fragrant with the scents of pine and spruce and the wintry decay of the rich, dark earth. Inhaling deeply of the forest perfume, Wulfgar trailed along in the wake of his father and half brothers, his shuttered gaze enviously regarding Ivar, who rode upon the showy, snow-white steed. It was not fair, Wulfgar thought bitterly, that one so wicked should be so blessed by the gods. But then, Yelkei had told him often enough that life was seldom fair, and from the time he was old enough to grasp such things himself, Wulfgar had seen that this was indeed so. Some men were born to the great mead halls of the *jarlar*, others, to the slaves' iron pens, and most, like him, to that place in between, where a man must struggle to survive, having neither riches of his own nor a master bound by law to ensure his welfare.

Beneath the dark canopy formed by the overhanging branches of the trees, along rough paths dimly dappled with grey sunlight, the hunting party wound its way steadily upward through the wooded hills until at last, along a stream that elk, reindeer, roe deer, and other animals were known to frequent, the hounds caught the fresh scent where tree bark had been scraped away by the antlers of stags, and great patches of snow had earlier that day been trampled and pawed by herds feeding on the moss and lichen beneath. The rocks that strewed the stream banks and protruded from the icy water were slimed with moss; the earth all about was slick and muddy. The stream itself, half frozen, flowed sluggishly, and so was easy enough to ford when the dogs, barking and impatiently straining at their leashes, were freed by the hunters to plunge into the water and to wade across, their tails waving like gay banners behind them. After shaking themselves off vigorously on the far bank, the hounds again put their noses to the ground, then eagerly set to running and baying as they once more picked up the scent, their voices echoing through the woods, above the high-pitched wail of the chief hunter's horn.

At the sound, Ragnar and the other *jarlar* and *thegns* spurred their horses forward, splashing through the frigid water, with the hunters and freedmen racing swiftly behind. Once on the other side of the stream, Wulfgar fairly flew over the snowy earth, using the spears of his father and half brothers both to keep his balance and to pull himself along in the wake of the horses. After a time, despite his wet leather breeches and sealskin boots, he no longer felt the cold, but was as warm as though he sat before a too-hot fire. Beneath his fur cloak and leather garments, he could feel sweat trickling down his body, and his breath came fast and harsh, forming clouds in the air. Still, he, like the hunters and the other freedmen, was accustomed to running with the horses and so did not lag behind as the hunt wore on, but pressed on determinedly, keeping to the tracks that snaked through the forest until reaching higher ground, where the trees thinned and there was more room to maneuver as he drove the spears hard into the snow, sliding and swishing forward on his snowshoes, exhilarated by the chase.

The hounds, who had scrabbled over fallen logs and through snarls of brush, where the horses and men could not follow, had long been lost to sight. But an occasional blast on the chief hunter's horn brought distant, answering barks in response, drawing the hunting party on in the right direction; and sometime past noon, the men swung eastward, up a slope to a crest where the pine and spruce trees were sparse, and there, across the way, in the distance, they spied a herd of fleet roe deer, twenty to thirty head strong, Wulfgar estimated, bounding through the woods. At the sighting of their quarry, the chief hunter once more blew his horn, and the dogs, who had been silent for the better part of an hour, hard on the trail as they sniffed out the scent, now renewed their baying with vigor. Breaking from the trees to the north, they spotted their fleeing prey and scrambled down the acclivity to strike out across the wide, misty valley below and then up the opposite hillside, streaking after the roe deer.

"Björn Ironside! Hasting! Take half the men and circle around behind the herd!" Ragnar directed as he drew his snorting steed up short, lifting one hand to bring the hunting party to a halt behind him. "The rest of us will ride south and head them off before they reach the pass."

With exuberant shouts, the men were off and away, setting spurs to mounts to thunder in a cloud of churning snow from the crest, down the incline to the floor of the valley, where the trees were few and on the forest fringe, although boulders and smaller rocks swept down from the hills through the years by avalanches hove up from the ground, and the scrub was more prolific, the earth choked with the sodden tangle of brush and dead weeds that spread across the marshy ground. At the heart of the valley, where the mist hung low, a shallow mere stretched, and this slowed Wulfgar and the other men afoot, so that by the time they had slogged across the icy water, the men ahorse to the south had succeeded in turning back the herd of roe deer and driving them toward the hounds and the rest of the mounted men led by Björn Ironside and Hasting to the north. For a moment, it seemed the panicked herd would fly deep into the forest to the east, heedless that the going would be difficult at such a pace, with low-hanging boughs to hinder the lead stag's antlered head. But in the end, the dogs prevented this, snarling and snapping and streaming out in a wide half circle to cut off the herd's course of escape; and the magnificent lead stag swung hard about to the west, toward the only perceived route to freedom, which lay across the mere and the valley, on the hillside whence the hunting party had come.

Realizing this, Wulfgar and the other men afoot stealthily advanced, making little sound upon the snowy earth, using the stones and thickets and brambles for cover, their furs and hide garments providing additional camouflage from their prey. Silent and alert, they watched from their places of concealment, waiting to show themselves as the herd came, leaping agilely over rocks and scrub alike, afraid, upwind, into the snare laid by the men. From where he crouched behind a stout bush to avoid being trampled, Wulfgar could now see through its skein of bare branches the blur of laboring greyish sides and white underbellies as the roe deer pelted toward him, the whites of their terrified eyes and the frantic flaring of their black-velvet nostrils as the hounds came hard on the herd's heels and the *jarlar* and *thegns* closed in from the north and the south, yanking mounts up short and readying bows and arrows. At Ragnar's signal, the chief hunter sounded his horn long and loud; and at that, the hunters and freedmen rose up from their hiding places, clambering onto boulders and outcrops for safety, yelling fiercely and waving their arms wildly at the oncoming roe deer, throwing them into further panic and disarray. The violence that erupted was fatal to man as well as beast as, in the confusion, Wulfgar saw a hunter knocked down and crushed beneath stampeding hooves, and a freedman gored by lowered antlers in passing. But most of the startled herd instinctively shied away from the shouting men, crashing into other roe deer as bows were drawn tight and notched arrows loosed amid the chaos.

One of the roe deer stumbled and went down then, an arrow protruding from its heaving side, and then another roe deer and yet another fell as, too late, the lead stag realized the trap and raced on out of sheer instinct to survive, sailing over a hummock and then bounding into the mere, striving to gain the trees at the foot of the western hills, the majority of the herd coming hard and fast behind, nearly trampling one another in their haste to escape as some of their number ran crazily in the opposite direction, impeding the flow, and stragglers struggled to catch up. But the slender, fletched shafts of the *jarlar* and *thegns* drove true; like stinging bees, sharp iron barbs bit deep, bloodying greyish winter coats that would never again turn red-brown with the summer, and a second barrage of arrows followed the first as at least half a dozen more wounded roe deer, bleating with pain and fear, staggered and rolled in a tangle of thrashing limbs to be viciously fallen upon by the frenzied dogs.

Then the hunters were there, shouting, cursing, and jerking the hounds back by the collar and leashing them, while, with wild whoops of triumph and bloodlust, the men ahorse dismounted to surge forward, as well. Now, like the rest of the freedmen, Wulfgar rushed to catch the reins carelessly tossed to him by his father and half brothers, and to give them their spears, with which they brought low the few injured roe deer still endeavoring to lurch on. Then, scramasaxes in hand, the *jarlar* and *thegns* waded into the melee to deliver the death blows to those roe deer downed but still alive.

It was then that in the cacophony, a streak of grey fur burst with a ferocious snarl from a misty hollow beneath a rocky outcrop amid the scrub, where, wounded in a fierce fray with a much younger foe and driven from its pack, it had sought refuge. Across the wet, low-lying ground, the creature leaped, its brain clouded from its injuries, its belly sharp with pain and hunger. For a moment, caught up in the slaughter of the roe deer, the men were only dimly aware of the flash of grey fur that bolted into their midst. Then Ivar cried out hoarsely, a terrible sound, so the eyes of all who heard it were drawn to him; and coming to their senses, the men realized that the beast that had sprung from the hollow was a lone wolf, maddened with rage and fever and the smell of blood. It had knocked Ivar down where he had knelt over one of the fallen deer, and was now at his throat.

In that instant, it seemed that time stopped and that all in the hunting party were paralyzed, frozen with horror and disbelief. Never had Wulfgar seen a wolf so huge; and it came to him in that seemingly eternal moment that it was no ordinary wolf at all, but a were-wolf, Fenrir, progeny of the wicked Loki and brother to Jormungand, the monstrous Midgard serpent that girded the earth, and also to Hela, who was Death. The gods had created the strongest of fetters to chain Fenrir, but he had broken the bonds as though they were made of cobwebs. Angry and alarmed at seeing this, the gods had then dispatched a messenger to the mountain spirits, and they had forged for the gods a chain known as Gleipnir, fashioned of these six things: the sound made by a cat's footfall, the beards of women, the roots of stones, the breath of fish, the nerves of bears, and the spittle of birds. When complete, the fetter was as slender and soft and delicate as a silken riband. But the were-wolf, suspecting that it was enchanted, had refused to be bound by it unless he could hold in his mouth the hand of one of the gods as hostage for their good faith. Knowing how they planned to trick Fenrir, only Týr, the god of battles, had proved brave enough to place his hand inside the were-wolf's massive jaws with their sharp, carnivorous teeth; and when Fenrir had discovered he could not escape from the chain called Gleipnir, he had bitten Týr's hand off at the wrist as punishment for deceiving and imprisoning him.

But now, Wulfgar thought, the were-wolf had at last somehow broken free of his magical bonds and descended to Midgard, the earth. Wulfgar shuddered with fear at the notion, for if that were indeed so, it could mean only one thing: that Ragnarök, the twilight of the gods, was at hand. Now, too, would Garm, the hound of Hel, howl; Jormungand, the terrible Midgard serpent, rise from the seas to spew venom upon the earth; the giant Hrym sail forth Naglfar, the Ship of the Dead; and the watchman, Heimdall, blow his horn, a call to battle. Wicked Loki would join the enemies of the gods—the followers of Hela, who was Death, and the Frost giants; and the sons of Muspell, with their leader, Surt, at their vanguard, would ride over the rainbow bridge, Bifröst, breaking it beneath their weight, on their way to the last battlefield, Vigrid. There, all the gods and their foes would be slain; then the universe would burn up and be no more—or so the *skálds* sang in the great mead halls of the *jarlar*, and so all his life, Wulfgar had believed. Nor was he the only one of the hunting party to think that their doom was come upon them. Stricken, the rest of the freedman had fallen to their knees as though awaiting retribution, and even the *jarlar* and *thegns* were stunned and uneasy, uncertain what to do.

Ivar was still locked in mortal combat with the giant wolf, twisting and turning to avoid its great, snapping jaws and terrible, bared fangs. Another man would have been dead by now, Wulfgar thought. But Ivar had the strength of two men and was gifted, besides, with the uncanny ability to contort his body in that unnatural fashion—as though he had no bones. He had his hands firmly about the wolf's throat to hold the creature at bay, and he and the wolf thrashed and tumbled across the ground as they grappled desperately for supremacy, a blur of grey fur and brown leather, stained with blood—although whether this was from wounds of their own or from the roe deer killed earlier, Wulfgar could not tell. The snow was red with the blood that had poured from the injuries and the opened throats of the roe deer, and the battle of Ivar and the wolf had brought them near to one of the slain does that lay silent and still upon the earth, large, liquid brown eyes glassed over now, limbs already stiffening in the cold.

It seemed forever before at last gathering their wits, Ubbi and Halfdan raised their bows and notched their arrows to take aim at the wolf, only to have their weapons abruptly and savagely struck from their hands by their father, who swore at them wrathfully.

"By the God of the Runes and Valhöll!" Ragnar roared as he cuffed his sons again roughly, nearly knocking them down; and Wulfgar thought he had never seen his father so angry—or so afraid. "You fools! 'Tis plain you did not drink from Ymir's well of wisdom and wit at Jötunheim ere you were birthed, else you'd have more of both, you stupid whelps of a mongrel bitch! Why, you cannot tell man from beast in that fracas! Do you want to slay Ivar by mistake?"

"Nay, but neither are we of a mind to stand idly by while a crazed wolf mauls him to death, Father!" Halfdan, younger and bolder than Ubbi, shot back, his breath coming harsh with ire at Ragnar for shaming him before the hunting party, and with fear for Ivar.

"So you say!" Ragnar growled, his clear blue eyes blazing like sunlight reflecting off ice. "But 'tis more like you cared not if your arrow pierced him, Halfdan, for then would his death set Ubbi on my throne—and you be one step closer to it, by Odinn!"

"Nay, Father!" Halfdan protested. "That was not the way of it—"

But Ragnar, in his upset, did not want to hear Halfdan's indignant words; and with his fist, he backhanded Halfdan across the mouth before roughly shoving him aside; then, breathing hard, he strode toward Ivar and the wolf, spear in hand, poised to strike. Now, of all Ragnar's sons, Ivar was not only his heir, but also his best beloved, and this must have been foremost in his mind, Wulfgar thought; for Ragnar's hand trembled ever so slightly as he watched for his chance to intervene in the deadly struggle, and when he finally did thrust his spear downward, he missed the wolf's side and instead drove it so savagely into the creature's haunch that the shaft broke in two. Still, the wound did not prove fatal. If anything, it only incited the wolf to further violence; for after making a spine-chilling sound that was neither snarl nor squeal, the creature appeared, incredibly, to gain strength and redoubled its assault with a vigor, its jaws suddenly clamping viciously about Ivar's sword hand and wrist. There was an audible snapping and grinding of bone, and a fearsome cry issued from Ivar's white lips as he tried but failed to wrench free. The hunting party gave a collective gasp, for a man so maimed he could not wield a weapon was better off dead, and it seemed to them all that the wolf would tear Ivar's hand clean off his wrist.

That was when Wulfgar decided his destiny, as Yelkei had warned he would that day; for surely, he thought afterward, it was not ill chance alone, but fate, the gods' decree that Ivar's battle with the wolf should have brought the two of them so close to him, and at a time when the creature was on top, so that for a moment, he had an unobstructed swing at it. If he had remembered Yelkei's words in time, Wulfgar might have hesitated and the opportunity been lost. But he did not think of Yelkei's warning; he had no clear thought in his mind at all, really, except that of saving Ivar's life. Shouting a mighty cry as he yanked his battle-ax from its leather scabbard at his back, Wulfgar whirled the weapon about his head, then brought it down hard and true. The song Blood-Drinker sang was a song of death as it bit deep into the wolf's neck, spraying blood, and killing the creature almost instantly. As though in anger and protest and certainly pain at its demise, the wolf growled low and fierce in its throat, an anguished snarl; its back spasmed grotesquely. Then, finally, as Wulfgar jerked his blade free, the creature toppled to one side and lay still, its jaws still locked about Ivar's wrist.

Only the hard rasp of Ivar's breath broke the silence then; even the dogs were quiet, as though sensing the import of the moment. All eyes were locked on Wulfgar and the battle-ax he held in his hands, its blade slowly dripping blood onto the soaked earth; and of a sudden, regaining his senses, he realized with dismay that in the space of his weapon's descent, he had brought upon himself what he had all his life sought to avoid: the attention of the *jarlar* and of Ragnar, their king.

"By the Norns!" Björn Ironside crowed in the hush. A powerful *jarl*, his fame and exploits rivaled those of Ragnar himself, so there was a certain wariness and enmity between the two men, with neither being loath to stick an oar into the other's water. "That was a brave blow for one who is no warrior—and a true strike against what was surely no ordinary wolf, but a mighty were-wolf, Loki's get, loosed from the very gates of Hel! Well done, Wulfgar Bloodaxe!"

At the bestowing of this title, the rest of the *jarlar* and *thegns* roared their approval. But although Wulfgar's heart soared with pride and joy at the sound, his eyes were watchful; for neither Ragnar nor his sons joined in the cry, and Wulfgar knew that his deed had not won him their love, that they would rather have seen Ivar dead in his grave than alive and beholden to an upstart bastard with a claim, however slight and distant, to Ragnar's kingdom and throne.

"How came you by that battle-ax, Wulfgar?" Ragnar asked softly when the shouting had died down. The words were spoken pleasantly enough, but Wulfgar was not deceived by their tone. A flame of fury burned deep in Ragnar's eyes, and there was a flicker, too, of what, in another man, Wulfgar would have called fear. "'Tis the weapon of a *thegn* and not that of a lowly *bóndi*. Yet you had it near to hand and were skilled in its use. 'Twould seem your free moments have been spent aping your betters rather than in studying how best to serve your masters."

"With all due respect, lord, my free moments are my own." Wulfgar's reply, while courteous, was not humble, for he had naught to lose now by any boldness, he thought. If they had not been before, his father and half brothers had this day become his bitterest foes, and caviling would not lessen their hate or soften their hearts toward him; indeed, it would earn only their amusement and contempt for his weakness. "The battle-ax I made with my own two hands, lord, and taught myself to wield. I named it Blood-Drinker, although it has tasted only that of animals and not that of the Northland's enemies, for which it thirsts."

"Spoken like a true *Víkingr*!" Hasting observed stoutly before Ragnar could answer. As close as brothers were Björn Ironside and Hasting, each quick to support and to defend the other. "Why, a *jarl* could do a lot worse than to call you his man, Wulfgar Bloodaxe, I am thinking. At the midspring *blót*, when we make offering to the goddess of spring, Eostre, you must count yourself among those who set their right hands to the sword hilt of a *jarl*, thus pledging him loyalty."

"Wulfgar is a *bóndi*—not a *thegn*," Ragnar ground out tersely.

"Is the life of your heir worth so little to you, then, that you would not raise up the man who spared it?" The words of Björn Ironside had a scornful sting, which goaded, as he intended. "Or can it be that you wear so much gold jewelry not as proof of your prowess as a *Víkingr*, but to blind us, so we cannot see how small the great Ragnar Lodbrók is, in truth!"

There was a huge clamor of laughter at this, for the North-men were not so afraid of their kings as the men of the Southlands were of theirs, and the Northmen loved a good jest, besides—no matter if it were at the expense of a slave or a king. Gold was rare and, so, highly prized; and indeed, Ragnar wore more than his fair share of it. But Wulfgar did not join in the mirth, for he saw that Björn Ironside's gibe had angered Ragnar, whose face had reddened and grown dark with a scowl. Wulfgar knew that Ragnar would not forgive him the men's glee, but would add it to the growing list of grievances against him.

"The chance to swear oath at the festival, in exchange for my life"—Ivar spoke for the first time as, gritting his teeth against the pain, he slowly pried the wolf's jaws from his wrist. Then, grimacing, he staggered with some difficulty to his feet, cradling his injured wrist and hand. But while a whole man might be made the butt of a joke, a wounded *thegn* was an object of neither ridicule nor pity, it being the lot of a warrior to suffer without complaint whatever the Norns, the Fates, bestowed. So no one was foolish enough to offer Ivar assistance. "It sounds like a fair bargain to me," he said, and then he smiled a strange caricature of a smile, and his blue eyes leaped with a queer light.

With those coolly voiced words was Wulfgar's lifelong dream made possible; yet the taste of it was as ashes in his mouth, and a grue chased up his spine. What had he done? Had Goscelin, his Saxon mother, not named him for his brother spirit, the wolf, who would this day have slain Ivar? Too late, Wulfgar recalled Yelkei's warning—and at last understood it; for had he not, with a single stroke of his battle-ax, killed the wolf who would have disentangled his destiny from Ivar's and, by doing so, thereby decided his own? Fool was he, Wulfgar thought, the fool of all fools! He should have let Ivar die. Why had he not? He did not know. He knew only that, like Ragnar, Ivar would neither forget nor forgive this day—and yet was perversely glad Wulfgar was to become a *thegn*, a *Víkingr*.

Long did Wulfgar ponder this curious fact as the hunting party lifted the corpses of the two slain men, and bound the dead roe deer to spear shafts, which the freedmen, in twos, hoisted onto their shoulders for carrying back to the sledge. The wolf, Björn Ironside declared, was Wulfgar's own prize; and when, out of long habit, Wulfgar glanced instinctively to Ivar for confirmation of this, Ivar slowly nodded his agreement, earning a glare from Ragnar, who muttered a curse and then spat on the ground before turning away to mount up and gallop off, leaving the rest of the hunting party scrambling to catch up. Wulfgar tied a rope about the body of the wolf to haul it home behind him. It was an extraordinary beast, its hide worthy of a mighty warrior; and that, he would strive to become, Wulfgar vowed, to honor his dead brother spirit.

Chapter Three

The Betrothal

The Southern Coast of Usk, Walas, A.D. 865

To Rhowenna's great relief, her father did not die. But he never quite recovered from the treacherous attack upon his life, either, being plagued thereafter with a sudden weakness that would come upon him when he had taxed his strength, and a shortness of breath he had never suffered before. Although the royal manor had not come under assault, as had been feared, the King worried about the security of his kingdom, nevertheless, afraid that because of the attempt upon his life, Glamorgan or Gwent had come to view Usk as a tasty morsel and was intent on devouring it. For this reason, when he learned that Cerdic, a prince of Mercia, was in search of a wife, Pendragon sent messengers to Cerdic's court, proposing an alliance between Usk and Mercia, and offering Rhowenna as Cerdic's bride to seal the bargain. Rhowenna herself knew nothing of this, however, until the day when her father called her before him to tell her what he had done, and that Cerdic had agreed to the proposal and to take her to wife. She was as stunned by her father's words as though she had been stricken a dreadful blow, for although she had known she was destined someday to wed a prince or even a king, she had not thought to find herself betrothed to one of the Saxon wolves east of Offa's Dyke, who, since the time of the High King Arthwr four hundred years ago, had been Walas's bitterest enemies. Unable to restrain herself, she cried out softly in protest at the news; and at that, so she knew he was not without sympathy for her plight, her father said gently:

"I know that this arrangement is not what you had hoped for, daughter, or even what I would have wished for you. But I am not . . . as strong as I once was." The admission came slowly, so she knew how difficult it had been for her father to make. "I must ensure that Usk is secure from those who would swallow us whole or piecemeal, and Mercia is a kingdom far more powerful than Glamorgan or Gwent, whence this attack upon me must have come."

"I—I understand, Father," Rhowenna choked out, fighting to recover her composure and to hold at bay the tears that started as she thought of Gwydion and all her hopes and dreams, now dust in the wind. "And I will honor my duty to Usk—if not with a glad heart, then at least with an obedient one."

"Prince Cerdic is a rich and handsome man, the emissaries assure me, whole of body, sound of limb, and in his prime, well able to provide for you and to defend you. So you need not be afraid on that score, daughter." Pendragon handed her a small wooden casket he held on his lap. "He has sent you this as a token of his regard."

Opening the casket, Rhowenna could not suppress a gasp of surprise and astonishment as she spied lying upon a bed of purple silk a magnificent gold necklace set with amethysts that matched the violet of her eyes. Despite being princess of Usk, she owned no piece of jewelry to compare to this, and some of her hurt and disappointment was assuaged at this evidence of the unknown Prince Cerdic's esteem. The necklace was not only resplendent, but also suited her coloring, bespeaking not only a desire to honor her, but also a thoughtfulness of character that was a mark in his favor, she thought. Perhaps he would not be so hard and cruel as she had at first feared when she had learned he was one of the Saxon wolves east of Offa's Dyke.

"'Tis beautiful, Father. Please have the emissaries convey my thanks and appreciation to Prince Cerdic, informing him that I am honored and that I shall treasure his gift always."

Her father was pleased by her response, Rhowenna could tell, and for that, she was grateful, for she did not want him to worry over her unhappiness; he had enough problems to fret him as it was. Nodding his approval of her, Pendragon spoke no more; and realizing the interview was at an end, Rhowenna left him quietly, taking the small casket away with her to lock it away inside her own larger, heavier jewel chest in her sleeping chamber, where it would be safe. Then, after she had closed and secured the lid of her jewel chest and returned her chatelaine to the fine, gold-mesh girdle about her waist, she tossed her light wool cloak about her shoulders, and made her way down the winding path that led to the beach where the Severn Sea merged with the Great Sea beyond.

Spring had come to Walas at last, the snow melting from all but the highest peaks of the land, leaving the gentle hills and the rugged mountains behind her as green as raw, uncut emeralds scattered against the lapis-lazuli backdrop of the endless sky, where the sun shone as golden as the necklace Prince Cerdic had given her and, wings spread wide, the gulls soared and cried their forlorn song. The wind was a melodious sigh that stirred the flowers and the grass, setting them a-ripple like the waves of a vast, strange, and wonderful sea that somehow soothed her aching heart a little. She had hoped to be alone to reflect on her father's devastating news and what it meant to her, but now as she drew near to the strand, Rhowenna saw Gwydion there below, his coracle drawn up onto the sand. Glancing up at her, he smiled and waved, causing her heart to turn over in her breast as he motioned for her to join him.

"I'm going fishing," he called gaily. "Do you want to come along?"

"Aye. Aye, I'll come!" Torn between sudden gladness and despair at seeing him, she gathered up her skirts to hurry on down to the beach. She was a trifle breathless when she reached him, her cheeks flushed becomingly, a strand of hair tumbled loose from her single long braid and billowing in the wind as she gazed up at him from beneath sooty lashes half closed against the bright sun. "It seems ages since I've been fishing."

"My own thought precisely. Here, help me shove off, then, and we'll get under way."

Together with an ease born of skill and long practice, they pushed the coracle into the water, then climbed into the light, round craft and settled themselves in its bottom. As Gwydion rowed them forward across the waves, Rhowenna fell silent, not knowing how to speak to him of her betrothal. She inhaled the cool, briny wind and watched the sunlight play upon the water, and it occurred to her now, for the first time, that although Gwydion had in the past told her that he loved her, he had never done more than kiss her cheek and, once, tenderly, her mouth. Yet, surely, she had not misread the expression in his eyes whenever he looked at her. Surely, he would be as dismayed by the arrangement her father had made with Prince Cerdic as she had been when she had learned of it.

At last, when they reached a spot where Gwydion thought that the fish would be plentiful, he drew in the paddle and laid it aside, letting the coracle gently drift as it would, while he and Rhowenna between them cast a small net.

"You are uncommonly quiet this day, Rhowenna," Gwydion observed finally after they had worked for some time in companionable silence, although with only a modest catch yet to show for their efforts, "and pensive. Something troubles you. What has upset you?"

For a moment, Rhowenna's hands stilled on the net she and Gwydion had emptied into the bottom of the craft. The fish they had caught thus far shimmered silvery in the sunlight, gasping and twisting and flopping. The fish were helpless out of their natural milieu—just as she would be in Mercia, Rhowenna thought, far away from home, a stranger amid strangers in a foreign land.

"Only a short while ago," she responded at last to Gwydion's question, turning away from the dying fish, "I discovered that my father . . . my father has arranged a . . . betrothal for me, Gwydion—with Prince Cerdic of Mercia."

"I see," he said softly, after a time, very still. "My felicitations. Prince Cerdic is very wealthy . . . and handsome, I have heard."

"Oh, Gwydion!" The cry was low and anguished. "Have you nothing more to say to me than that?"

"What more *is* there to say than that, Rhowenna?" he asked, a muscle flexing in his set jaw, his voice rough with feeling. Then, glimpsing the expression upon her countenance, his own face and his tone gentled. "I'm sorry. Did you dare to dream for us, then? I didn't know. You never said—" Gwydion broke off abruptly, striving visibly to master his emotions. Then, after a moment, he continued quietly. "I was not so brave, you see. I never dared to hope that there could ever be anything more between us than what we already share. You are princess of Usk, Rhowenna . . . and not for the likes of me, with no kingdom to call my own. Did you truly think that 'twould prove otherwise?"

"I—I don't know. Oh, I suppose that deep down inside, I knew better. But . . . oh, Gwydion! You are right! I *did* dare to dream! And now . . . now, all is changed, and will never be the same again. When you went away for your fostering, you knew you would return, but I won't be coming back, Gwydion. I will have to spend the rest of my life among the Saxon wolves east of Offa's Dyke, with a husband who is a stranger to me. . . ." Her voice, sad and bitter, trailed away as she uttered the painful thought aloud, making it seem, finally, real and not just some dreadful misunderstanding or an event so far distant as to appear unlikely.

"'Tis small comfort, I know, but strategically, from Usk's point of view, an alliance with Mercia is the wisest course of action, Rhowenna, considering the nature of the attack upon your father this past winter. We can no longer trust Glamorgan or Gwent to keep to its own boundaries. To launch an assault against Usk, Mercia would have to send its armies across Offa's Dyke and the river Severn both, so we would have ample warning of their approach and time to prepare to hold out against them. That means they would be the lesser threat and a more desirable ally."

"I know, I know. My own mind tells me the truth of your words, Gwydion. 'Tis my heart that rebels and calls them lies and wishes I were only a plain serving maid instead of princess of Usk, to be bartered away as the price of a treaty!"

"And I wish I were a prince worthy of your hand, Rhowenna. But I am not, nor likely to become one; and so I have loved you as a brother loves his sister, and spoken of no more than that, because it was not meet or possible and because I did not want to cause you pain. That I have done so anyway grieves me sorely."

"Nay, Gwydion." Rhowenna shook her head, blinking back tears and attempting to smile, although the result was pitiable. "If there has been fault between us, 'twas mine—

and mine alone. I heard what I wanted to hear in your words. I longed for the moon when I knew in my heart that it was beyond my reach. 'Twas you who were wise and I who was foolish. You are not to blame for that.''

But even as she spoke the words and although she recognized their truth, the fact that Gwydion had deliberately built a wall around his heart against her wounded her; she felt he could not have done that unless his love for her had been a shallow thing, unworthy of what she had felt for him in return. Had he loved her deeply, he would have taken her in his arms, kissed her feverishly, and begged her to run away with him, Rhowenna thought, to set sail in the coracle and to cast their fate to the wind, believing that wherever they were bound, whatever they must endure, it was enough that they were together, of one heart and one mind. Some part of her had hoped desperately for that, she realized now. But perhaps that, too, was a notion as foolish as all the rest of her romantic dreams had proved. Still, she could not put it from her head; and her disappointment in Gwydion was as painful to her as her father's news of her betrothal had been.

If Gwydion sensed this, however, he did not show it, but turned their conversation to light, inconsequential matters, seeming not to notice that Rhowenna made only monosyllabic replies and bowed her head and busied her hands at their tasks more than was necessary to avoid meeting his eyes. She would see naught save pity there, she thought; and she could not bear that, not from Gwydion. She would have thrown away kingdom and crown for him had he but stretched out his hand to her and asked her to go away with him. But he had not, and so her only refuge now was her quiet dignity and this pretense that there was nothing more between them than devotion and kinship.

When he remarked that it was growing late and that they had best be getting back to shore, she raised her head finally from the shining, dead and dying fish. The westerly sun reflected off the sea into her eyes, and it seemed that for a moment on the far horizon, a clutch of dragons rode the waves, crimson sails unfurled wide against the sun to catch the wind. She could not suppress a wail of terror.

"Rhowenna! What is it?" Gwydion's voice was sharp with anxiety as he stared at her eyes, huge and scared in her pale face, and filled with a stark blankness, as though she were tranced and saw something he did not. "What is it? What do you see?"

The sound of his voice penetrated Rhowenna's senses at last, and blinking her eyes, she realized with some confusion that the horizon was empty save for the fiery sun sinking into the sea, that what she had seen had been nothing more than a trick of the light, after all. Yet the vision had seemed so real that she could have sworn that it was . . .

"I thought . . . I thought—Gwydion, for many long nights now, I have had a dream, a hideous dream of the Northmen's coming to ravage Usk"—without warning, her terrible secret came spilling out—"and for a moment, I thought I spied their longships there in the distance, on the horizon. 'Twas only the sun in my eyes; I see that now. But I was so frightened—"

"The Northmen! Rhowenna! Have you told anyone else of this?"

"Nay." She shook her head, biting her lower lip contritely, suddenly ashamed that she had permitted her fear to silence her when so many lives were at stake.

"But . . . why not?"

"I was afraid," she confessed, her voice low and remorseful, "afraid that Father Cadwyr would denounce me, would call me accursed, a witch. He has no tolerance for the old ways, for the old gods whence my dream comes to me, I know, Gwydion. He would not think it a true vision, but a wickedness visited upon me by the devil—and I've no wish to be burned at the stake because of a priest's blindness and stupidity!''

''Of course not. Still, Rhowenna, the Northmen! Do you not remember the tales of the slaughter and ruin they wreaked upon Anglesey some years ago?''

''Aye, I do. I do. That is why I have been so troubled and torn, not knowing whether to speak or to remain silent. . . .'' She paused for a moment, contemplating her dilemma. Then, finally, slowly, she continued. ''There is still more, Gwydion, the worst of all, the reason why I did not tell even you about all this before. In my dream . . . in my dream, I saw the Northmen . . . strike you down and—and slay you, Gwydion!''

He went very still at this last announcement. Despite all the priests' exhorting, Gwydion was reluctant to accept that the old ways, the old gods, were false. He believed in her vision, too.

''Your dream is a strong and serious portent,'' he said after a long minute of consideration. ''But 'tis also only the shape and shadow of what *may* happen, Rhowenna, not necessarily what *will* be. Now that we have been blessed with warning of it, we can change the future. If the Northmen do come, I need not perish as you feared. I will be on my guard, and I will survive—as will Usk. Together, we can surely think of some pretext that will alert the King and the Queen to the possibility of danger from the Northland—perhaps we can claim that some passing fisherman warned us that there have been several recent attacks along the coast—without mentioning your dream or exposing you to denunciation by Father Cadwyr.''

''Aye, 'tis worth trying.'' Rhowenna brightened at the thought, feeling that perhaps something good, after all, had come of this day.

"I *do* care for you, you know." Gwydion spoke softly as his grey eyes met her violet ones steadily. "Come what may, I will always be your kinsman and your friend, Rhowenna."

"Aye." She nodded, swallowing hard to choke back her tears and turning away to gaze once more at the far horizon, which was barren and bleak—and bloodred.

Chapter Four

The Festival
of Eostre

The Shores of the Skagerrak, the Northland, A.D. 865

For some unknown reason, Ivar had told Wulfgar he could, until the midspring festival, remain in the hut he shared with Yelkei inside Ragnar's palisade. But this apparently magnanimous offer, Yelkei had strenuously urged Wulfgar to reject, reminding him that Ivar did nothing without an ulterior motive and that whatever it was in this case, it surely boded no good for Wulfgar. Remembering Yelkei's warning to him the dawn of the hunt and what had come to pass, Wulfgar had reluctantly agreed; and gathering his few belongings, he had left the relative protection of the palisade for a hut he built for himself at the edge of the forest, near the weed-grown mere, beyond the boundaries of Ragnar's markland.

Until Wulfgar completed the hut, he slept out in the open on the ground, beneath a hastily constructed shelter of pine boughs. But for the first few nights, he hardly closed his eyes, missing the security of the palisade, the familiarity of the hut he had called his own there and Yelkei's comforting presence. He was not accustomed to being alone and regretted that Yelkei had not been able to come with him. But she was Ragnar's slave, and Wulfgar had lacked the means to purchase her freedom; nor had either Ragnar or Ivar offered to let her go, although they feared her and considered her of little use. Until he was on his own, Wulfgar had not realized how much he had depended on her. In the beginning, the sounds at night of the woods and of the heath unnerved him; he started at the hoot of an owl or the howl of a wolf, and he longed for her to chase away the shadows as she had done when he was small. More practically, he missed her skill at cooking and sewing when his first attempts at those chores produced poor results.

But gradually, as the murky winter turned into spring, the anemones making their appearance and the thunder of *islossning*—the great cracking and breaking of frozen rivers, which warned of impending floods—sounding, he grew used to the calls of the night creatures, and he learned to cook and to sew in a rudimentary way. Only his loneliness was constant, although it gradually faded to a dull ache. He began to savor his freedom once he was past his feeling of being lost without his half brothers to structure his days, and he established, by trial and error, his own routine. He took pride in the hut he erected, and his talent as a hunter burgeoned now that he was able to devote so much of his time to the task. His proficiency with the weapons he had made also mounted with his ceaseless practice; and Yelkei, whenever she managed to slip away to visit him, cackled with delight when she saw him.

"Confess, Wulfgar Bloodaxe!" she crowed in her raucous, rasping voice. "Despite all the scraps I stole for you over the years, you never ate so well at Ragnar's hearth as you do at your own. Look at you! You've become a fine figure of a man now that you've a full belly when it suits you. You were always tall, but now . . . now, by the gods, you've the weight for it, Wulfgar. Broad of shoulder and chest, long and strong of limb. Aye, if there were those before who doubted that you're Ragnar's own get, they'll question it no more when they see you again. Why, you're enough like Ivar the Boneless to pass for his twin even with the sun at its zenith in a summer sky!''

Wulfgar scowled darkly at her words.

"If you thought to find favor with me with such flattery as that, why, then, you've failed badly, old woman!'' he growled, angry and offended. "What have I done that such an insult should trip from your spiteful, worthless tongue?''

"Spiteful? Mayhap, when it suits my purpose, Wulfgar; for malice often proves a useful weapon when keenly honed and properly wielded—as your nemesis, Ivar the Boneless, could tell you, for he makes good use of it himself. But worthless? Nay, I'll not abide that—for a Mongol king of the Eastlands once offered a sackful of gold coins for this tongue of mine.''

"Aye. Aye, that I can well believe—were it cut clean from your head and delivered up on a silver plate to him!''

"Why, that might have been the way of it, in truth!'' Yelkei admitted, and barked with laughter. "But . . . do you observe that no man is the richer for my tongue—save you, Wulfgar, to whom it has ever spoken the truth. If you doubt me, why, you've only to take a look at your reflection in yonder pond . . . or are you afraid of what you might see?'' The taunt stung, as was intended.

"Nay, I fear naught but the gods and those creatures not human.''

With that boast, Wulfgar strode to the edge of the mere and, kneeling, parted the slender yellow reeds that grew tall there, and gazed into the still water shining silver in the sunlight. To his utter shock, it was indeed the handsome bronze visage of his half brother Ivar who stared back at him, long mane of gilded hair falling about finely molded bones set with deep, sky-blue eyes, an aquiline nose, full, carnal lips framed by a silky mustache and beard, and a strong jaw with an arrogant thrust. For a long moment, Wulfgar yearned violently to claw at his face until it was unrecognizable. Then, he had another thought. Leaping to his feet, he stalked to the hut he had built and went inside, banging the door wrathfully behind him—although even that did not silence the sound of Yelkei's mirth.

After a time, she followed him inside, and screeched with fright to see him standing there, naked to the waist, his face covered with lather, and a sharp knife in his hand.

"Are you mad?" she cried, sidling away a little and peering at him intently in the semidarkness.

"Nay, I had a mad desire, at first, to cut my throat," Wulfgar said curtly, indicating the blade and giving a snort of laughter at her alarm, glad to have got a bit of his own back against her. "But I've thought better of it, having no wish to wander the Shore of Corpses to the barred gates of Hel any sooner than I must."

From the cauldron on the hearth, he had ladled steaming-hot water into a bowl, which he had set upon the hard-packed dirt floor. Now, using the water as a mirror, he hunkered down over the bowl and began carefully with the whetted edge of the knife to shave off his mustache and beard.

"What are you doing?" Yelkei's normally inscrutable moon face, shocked and appalled, peered down at him.

"Ridding myself of some of my unfortunate resemblance to Ivar."

"But a mustache and beard are the mark of a man!"

"Aye. Even so, a man may still be a man without them— and if any man is so foolish as to mistake me for less, why, then, I shall have the advantage of him and soon teach him the error of his ways."

"Well, do as you wish and suffer the consequences," Yelkei said. Taking up a blade of her own and hitching up her leather tunic a little, she squatted on the earthen floor and deftly set to skinning and butchering a brace of fine, fat hares Wulfgar had snared earlier that morning. "Still, you will miss all that hair on your face, come next winter, I am thinking."

"Perhaps," Wulfgar conceded as he scraped at his beard, then rinsed his soapy knife off in the bowl of hot water. "And then again, perhaps by then, I shall have gone a-*víking* in a mighty longship down the Swan Road, to plunder the kingdoms of the Southlands, and have carried away a lusty young Christian maid as my slave, to keep me warm beneath my blankets of a cold winter's eve—instead of a shrewish old woman who would sooner geld a man than bed him and who snores like a drunken grey-beard in a corner, disturbing my slumber!"

"Why, it gladdens my heart to learn how you have missed me, Wulfgar." Yelkei chuckled as she tossed chunks of the hare meat into a pot and began to chop fresh greens and roots she had brought in a basket. "Still, if 'tis a flame for a Christian wench that burns between your legs, you'd have done well to spare your mustache and beard until after the midspring *blót*. 'Tis no *jarl* worth his salt who will be wanting to risk the wrath of Ragnar and his sons to take oath from a maiden-faced *bóndi*!"

"By the four harts who bite the buds of Yggdrasill!" Wulfgar swore as he flung away the cloth he had used to wipe the lather from his now-smooth face. He jumped to his feet and began angrily to pace the hut. "So that's the way of it, is it? Well, I expected that my father and half brothers would seek to prevent my pledging oath as a *thegn*. But are you sure that *no jarl* is brave enough to accept me, Yelkei?"

"Although he is subject to the Jutish king across the Skagerrak, Ragnar is a power to be reckoned with in the Northland, Wulfgar, and even Björn Ironside and Hasting, bold and formidable men in their own right, dare defy him only so far and then no further. But there is one who has the judgment of a fool and who drinks deep of his cups, who could be persuaded to take you as his man."

"And who is that?"

"Olaf the Sea Bull."

"That foul, mead-swilling old—"

"Aye, he is all that you say, and more, Wulfgar. But listen to me, and heed my counsel"—Yelkei's voice was stern and sharp now—"remembering that to you alone, my tongue has always spoken truly. Did I not warn you the morn of the hunt that that day, you would decide your destiny? And did you not that day do so by slaying your brother spirit, the wolf, who sought to protect you by killing Ivar the Boneless?" Rising from the fire where she had put the stew to cook, she gestured to Wulfgar to stand with her on the great wolfskin spread upon the floor. Then she laid one yellow hand upon his arm, her bony fingers digging like talons into his bare flesh. "Listen to me, Wulfgar," she exhorted again. "Olaf the Sea Bull is no great *jarl*, 'tis true. But his beard has been grey for many long, dark winters now, and during the murky time just past, I heard Hela's death rattle in his bones. His *thegns* are brutes, grown as soft and slovenly and slack as their lord. But with a strong leader at the rudder of Olaf's *Dragon's Fire*, they could be turned to account once more. The Sea Bull's sons have all been carried home on their shields, slain in battle; his wife is long dead; and the husbands of his daughters have the spines of jellyfish. There is no one to follow in Olaf's footsteps, Wulfgar; and so when the old Sea Bull dies, a man who is quick and daring and clever enough may seize Olaf's markland for himself and claim the right of *jarl* over it all!"

"Aye." Wulfgar nodded slowly, as though carefully considering the matter, although his heart leaped with excitement at Yelkei's words. "It could be that you are right. I will think hard on what you have said."

Until Yelkei had spoken to him of Olaf the Sea Bull, Wulfgar had had in his mind some vague notion of building a longship of his own, although he had known how impossible that would be when he had neither the men nor the oxen, the sledges, the cattle, nor the sheep required for such a massive undertaking. Preparing for the day when he would have those essentials, he went out into the forest with men who did. He watched them seek out the tallest and the strongest of the oak trees to chop down with stout iron axes. He observed how they cut off the tops and boughs of the felled oaks and stripped off the bark, then strapped the great trunks to sledges pulled by several teams of oxen to be hauled to the shores of the Skagerrak. There, upon the fjord-riddled sands, log rollers were already in place for the building of the longships that had made the *Víkingrs* the scourge of the seas for over two centuries.

Large enough to rival a whale, measuring approximately one hundred feet in length, twenty feet wide at the beam, and over six feet deep from the upper edge of each side to the bottom of the keel, the longships were built from the outside in. Each massive, true keel, which formed the longship's backbone and gave it its vast superiority over enemy vessels, was fashioned from the trunk of a single oak and deliberately bowed amidships, so that in battle, the longship could be spun about practically on her own axis, providing incredible maneuverability. The stempost and the sternpost were also made from a single piece of timber, often intricately carved into a dragon's head and tail on war boats, a snake or swan on ceremonial vessels, of the kind used at the midspring festival. From a metal rod attached to the prow would hang a gilt-bronzed wind vane.

The shell, thickest at the bottom and gradually thinning toward the water line, was composed of overlapping planks bent by hand and affixed to the stempost and the sternpost, working from the keel up. Once in place, the strakes were caulked with moss or tarred rope or animal hair and fastened together with iron rivets; then ribs of naturally bowed oak limbs were set into the shell, and the strakes were lashed with spruce-root withies to the ribs, all of which resulted in a hull capable of flexing in rough seas and still maintaining a watertight seal. A leather covering, made from the hides of tens of head of cattle, could be stretched from side to side and secured for protection when the longship encountered stormy seas or rode at anchor.

Crossbeams, attached with wooden knees to the sides, bridged the hull above each rib to provide lateral reinforcement, and upon these, the deck planks were laid in such a way as to rise at the stern, forming a slight poop for the steersman to stand upon and which boasted a small roof against bad weather. At the heart of the hull, beneath the deck planks, was the "old woman" or keelson, a huge oak-block base into which the mammoth spruce take-down mast was set, and atop this block, upon the deck planks, was yet another block, shaped like a fish and so called the mast fish, which supported the mast. Three Y-shaped trestles or crutches standing upright from bow to stern held the yard, spars, or sail when the longship was being rowed. At the starboard stern was the rudder, also cut from a single plank of oak and attached by a spruce root to the wart. A thick rope of osiers running through a cramp in the rudder's paddle allowed it to be immediately hoisted in shallow or rocky waters.

Along the elaborately painted sides of the longship were the oar holes, which could be plugged when the longship was under sail, and over each of which could be hung two shields, each shield overlapping the next to form a continuous, decorative line from bow to stern when the longship was in harbor or was to be used for the burial of its *jarl*. The oars themselves were of pine, twenty pairs strong, and made in successive lengths so they would all strike the water in unison, the freeboard's being slightly higher at bow and stern than that amidships. To demonstrate his bravery and agility, a daring *jarl* would sometimes hoist himself over the side of the longship and leap from oar to oar while they were moving. There being no thwarts, each oarsman sat upon his own sea chest when rowing; and along with the sounder, a drummer stood in the bow and beat the rhythm upon a hide-covered drum. A spruce-wood gangway provided the men access to and from the longship when the vessel was moored to a wharf.

The square sail that caught the breath of the wind was woven of coarse wool two layers thick, and usually dyed red. Occasionally, a pattern of alternating red-and-blue or red-and-white stripes, squares, or diamonds was chosen by a *jarl* who wished his longship to be instantly recognized by friends and foes alike. When wet, the sail was heavy and, especially during capricious winds or storms, so difficult to manage that even a strong warrior could be knocked overboard by a swinging yard—his own or that of another longship sailing close alongside. Still, with her magnificent square sail, a longship could sail not only across the wind, but also well into it, giving her an additional advantage against her enemies and making her hard to catch. The sail's rigging was fashioned of tough whale, walrus, or seal hide, measured in ells and so strong that it could not be pulled apart by a tug-of-war among more than fifty men.

Like the beat of a longship's drummer upon his drum, Wulfgar's heart pounded with exhilaration as he watched the longships take shape and counted the days to the midspring *blót*, when the longships would be named. During that time, he practiced with his weapons for even longer hours to ready himself for the games that would be held at the festival; and he made it his business, as well, to learn everything he could about Olaf the Sea Bull—although it was hard to find much to that *jarl*'s credit. Olaf's situation was indeed as Yelkei had said; and although the Sea Bull looked healthy enough for a grey-bearded drunkard, Wulfgar could not help but recall Yelkei's insistence that she had that past winter heard Hela's death rattle in Olaf's bones, and he shivered at the thought that the spaewife could foretell a man's doom, which was only for the gods to know.

Then, at long last, the morning of the vernal equinox (and so also of the midspring *blót*, the wild, promiscuous rite of spring) dawned, the sun's tongues of flame setting the sky ablaze, burning away the last of the night's mist that had swept in from the sea to linger over the land; and in the harbor that gleamed as blue as an aquamarine in the sunlight, a herd of sea dragons rode the combers, breathing crimson fire until square sails were furled and heavy iron anchors cast overboard to chain the dragons where they lay. From far and wide, the *Víkingrs* had come to Ragnar's vast domain to celebrate the goddess of spring, Eostre—old grey-beards who had ravaged the Eastlands and the Southlands for nearly half a century, and callow youths with faces as silk-smooth as Wulfgar's own and who, like him, had yet to stand upon the deck of a longship and to feel the sea swell and ebb beneath their sealskin-booted feet. With them came their wives and sweethearts and daughters, gay ribands woven through their long braids and wearing long, flowing woolen gowns, brightly dyed in a multitude of colors and fastened with ornate round brooches above each breast. Much to Wulfgar's surprise and pleasure, he observed that despite his lack of mustache and beard—or perhaps because of it—the eyes of more than one female strayed toward him and many an inviting smile was cast in his direction. The maidens he flirted with gladly, knowing that later that night, after the day's wassailing, there would be even more drunken reveling, wild dancing to the savage, rhythmic strains of flutes and drums, and frenetic coupling in the Sacred Grove, beneath the moon; Wulfgar was as eager as the next man for the feel of a lusty wench moaning and writhing beneath him. But the married women he assiduously avoided; for the crime of adultery, an unfaithful wife and her paramour were punished by being sold into slavery, severely flogged, or beheaded. Wulfgar had no wish to suffer any of those penalties for a fleeting night's dalliance, no matter how beautiful and desirable the woman.

To the nine-day festival, the *bóndi* from all the surrounding farms brought *nabid*, a strong beer, horses, and other offerings to the goddess of spring. The animals were ritually slain, after which the walls of the *templum*, the temple, that stood in the *lundr*, the Sacred Grove, on Ragnar's markland, were smeared outside and inside with the fresh, warm blood, and the meat itself cooked slowly in earth-covered pits lined with hot stones, in preparation for the feasting later in Ragnar's *hof*, his large longhouse, which looked especially splendid. Inside, the timber walls, packed with clay, showed evidence of having been freshly scrubbed, although even this had not removed the dark stains left by the ubiquitous smoke from the hearth and the whale-oil lamps; and all along the *langpallar*, the raised side aisles of the *skáli*, the great mead hall, long benches spread with plump cushions had been placed before long, narrow tables. Such furniture was rare in the Northland, belonging solely to *konungrs* and to the richest of *jarlar*, and used only for festivals and other special occasions. The shutters of the tiny, high-set windows covered with pigs' bladders admitted only the dimmest of sunlight. But the numerous whale-oils lamps hanging from the smoke-blackened, free-standing posts that supported the thatched roof burned brightly, illuminating the walls adorned by bleached-linen tapestries elaborately worked in colored wool. Although several feet wide, the striplike tapestries were also very narrow, no more than a foot high, and placed at a man's eye-level, so that they could be seen in the dim, smoky atmosphere of the great mead hall. Near the hearth, the *skálds*, accompanied by flutes and lyres, sang their epic poems, and jugglers and acrobats performed to entertain the *jarlar*.

Wulfgar had not stepped foot inside the *hof* since leaving the hut he had previously inhabited within the palisade, and he had no wish to linger now as he made his obeisance before Ragnar, regally ensconced upon the high seat on the central dais flanked by two mammoth, intricately carved pillars at the far end of the great mead hall. Upon Ragnar's head was his ornate, gilt-bronzed, horned helmet, never worn into battle, but only upon ceremonial occasions and for the initiation of young men as warriors; and his blue eyes, behind the helmet's masklike eyeholes, were hard and cold as he stared down at Wulfgar. After paying his respects to Ragnar, Wulfgar quickly made good his escape, eager to be gone and to take part in the games outside.

The Northmen were fond of all sort of games, particularly board games such as chess, draughts, and fox-and-geese; and several of the women, as well as the grey-bearded men too old for physical sport, had laid their boards on the tops of stout, iron-ringed barrels and, seated on low stools, were deeply engrossed in their next moves. But the games Wulfgar joined were strenuous contests such as running, swimming, and rowing, designed to challenge a man's physical strength and agility so the *jarlar* might judge his worth before accepting his oath as a *thegn*. His age and prowess were such that he easily stood out from the crowd of mostly untried youths against whom he competed. But it was as Yelkei had warned him: Even bold Björn Ironside and Hasting, for all that they had brought about his chance to become a *Víkingr*, gave no sign of being disposed toward accepting him as their man; nor, to Wulfgar's discouragement, had Olaf the Sea Bull shown a flicker of interest—and Ivar's arrogant, mocking half-smile was a barb that stung and made Wulfgar burn with anger and shame.

"Be patient," Yelkei counseled, her black eyes narrowed to cunning slits, her voice low, "like the lone wolf who lurks in the reeds at the edge of the misted mere, waiting for the ducks to grow greedy and careless as they fatten on the fish."

Eight times the sun rose and set, and the maiden chosen to play the roll of Eostre, the goddess of spring, was driven about in her elaborately carved, ox-drawn cart to be feted by all present; and afterward, a solitary slave was beheaded each day and seven animals slain, all of which were hanged from the trees in the Sacred Grove as Eostre's sacrifice, so that at the end of the festival, seventy-two corpses, a magic number, would have been offered to the goddess.

And still, Wulfgar had not pledged himself as a *thegn*.

"The ducks waddle from the fullness of their bellies, and bask in the sun while preening their feathers. Now does the wise wolf draw near—but slowly, stealthily, Wulfgar," Yelkei cautioned, "so the whisper of his coming is but the wind among the reeds."

On the ninth day, the longships were named and consecrated with blood, pushed over the log rollers on the sand and then, just before being shoved into the sea, the bodies of slaves were crushed to death beneath the massive hulls to assure the blessing of Aegir, the sea god, and his wife, Ran. The waves of the sea were the nine daughters of Aegir and called by such sinister names as Grasper and Howler. No man wished to lie in their watery arms; and a prudent warrior always carried a single piece of gold with him on board a longship, to pay their mother, Ran, should he drown, so he could be certain of gaining entrance into Valhöll. Even if it meant distributing coins or jewelry from his own hoard, it was the duty of every good *jarl* who captained a longship to ensure that each of his *Víkingr* could afford this offering. But despite Yelkei's words of wisdom, Wulfgar despaired of the chance to know that in his purse, he bore a *Víkingr*'s piece of gold for Ran. But then Yelkei said:

"There is a fat old duck who has foolishly strayed from the rest at the mere and fallen into a little crevice, easy pluckings now for a hungry wolf. Go you down to the foot of that small hill yonder and see if I do not speak the truth."

And indeed, she did; for that was how he found Olaf the Sea Bull—lying facedown in a rill that gurgled through a shallow clove at the foot of the small hill—so that afterward, he was never certain whether Olaf had toppled in a drunken stupor from the knoll, or whether Yelkei had given him a shove. Wulfgar always suspected the latter. Hastily, he dragged Olaf's heavy bulk from the stream, relieved that as he pressed down hard upon Olaf's back, the grey-beard began to cough and to sputter, a trickle of water running from his mouth. After a moment, the Sea Bull lurched to his hands and knees, retching, and Wulfgar smelled the stench of sour wine and ale and the remnants of the midday's horsemeat stew. Then, at last, his stomach purged of its contents, Olaf managed to sit up and, bleary-eyed, peered at Wulfgar beside him.

"That'd not be something stronger than water in that flask of yours, would it?" he asked Wulfgar, indicating the leather flask slung over the younger man's shoulder. "Ale, perhaps, to wash this foul taste from my mouth."

"*Nabid*," Wulfgar returned shortly, unstoppering the flask and handing it to him, "but you are more than welcome to it, lord."

Taking a generous swig, Olaf swished the beer around vigorously in his mouth for a moment, then spat it out on the ground before gulping another long draught, which he swallowed. After recapping the flask and passing it back to Wulfgar, Olaf rose and staggered to the rill. There, hunkering down and cupping his hands, he splashed his pasty face several times with cold water, shaking his head to sling his wet hair from his eyes and, with one hand, wiping his scraggly, dripping mustache and beard.

"How I came to roll down that hill, I do not remember," he said finally, grimacing as he gingerly probed his brow, which he had struck on a rock in the stream. "There must have been more of a bite to old Brunhilde's ale than I thought, or else, more like, she tried to poison me—which I'd not put past her, the vile-tempered shrew. Ah, well. 'Tis no matter. I reckon 'tis thanks to you, lad, that I'll not be going to my burial mound this day."

"Aye, well, 'twas no more and no less than any other man would have done had he spied you lying there, lord." Wulfgar carefully kept his eyes lowered, his tone respectful, knowing how another in his place would have roared with laughter at Olaf's tumble and made him the butt of many a jest far and wide. "You'd have pulled your own self out of the water had I not happened along—for surely, 'tis Odinn's fondest desire that a *jarl* such as Olaf the Sea Bull die in battle, to be borne by the Valkyries to Valhöll."

"You know me, then, do you?" Olaf inquired, obviously flattered and pleased.

"Why, who does not, lord? 'Tis said from shore to shore of the Northland that a man may count himself lucky to serve as *thegn* to Olaf the Sea Bull—and so I would count myself, lord, if you would have my pledge."

"What, lad? You've not yet sworn oath? Why, what ails you?"

"Naught, lord, save that I came late to the festivities," Wulfgar lied boldly, realizing suddenly that Olaf was not only still slightly drunk and dazed, but also short of sight and so had not recognized him. With his mustache and beard shaved off, Wulfgar thought that Olaf, in his stupor, had probably mistaken him for one of the younger, untried men who had come to the midspring *blót* in search of a *jarl*. "And no matter a man's worth, there is only so much space on a longship— and much of that has already been claimed by those who arrived sooner than I."

"Well, by the gods, my *Dragon's Fire* has room for one more, if you're of a mind to bend knee before me!" Drawing the broadsword at his back, Olaf plunged it, point down, into the soft earth along the stream, so the blade stood upright, quivering a little before him. "So, kneel you, then, lad, and set your right hand to her hilt and swear your fealty."

This, Wulfgar did, and when he rose, he was at long last a *Víkingr*.

Chapter Five

The Taking of the Bride

What Olaf the Sea Bull thought when he sobered up and discovered the trick Wulfgar had played him, Wulfgar never knew. Olaf said naught of the matter to him—or indeed to anyone Wulfgar knew—doubtless because the older man would have been made to look worse than a fool in light of Ragnar's open enmity toward Wulfgar. Although Olaf was drunk more often than not, he had both vanity and pride; and so in the end, he put on a brave face and declared that he would not be told how to stoke his own hearth fire, not even by his king, and that it would be a sorry day in the Northland when the *jarlar* could not count themselves masters of their own marklands. So unexpectedly shrewd and potentially incendiary were these words that afterward, doubtless fearing the hue and cry that would be set up against him by every freeman entitled to speak at the *Thing*, Ragnar prudently offered no challenge to Olaf, but chose instead to bide his time, pretending as though the entire business of Wulfgar's oath-swearing were beneath notice.

Wulfgar strove mightily to ensure that Olaf should have no other cause, save that of Ragnar's animosity, to regret accepting his fealty. Wulfgar rose earlier and worked harder than half a dozen of Olaf's other men, which was not difficult, considering how shiftless and lazy they had grown, serving a lord who seldom made his authority felt.

Olaf's longship, the *Dragon Fire*, was beached on the shores of the Skagerrak, where she had ridden out the winter; and now, the first thing his *thegns* did after the midspring *blót* was to clean and to repair the vessel to make certain she would be ready to sail, come summer. That was the time when the *Víkingrs* rode the seas. They set sail for home when the first of the trees began to change color, so as not to be caught without winter quarters, or upon the seas when they turned rough and stormy with winter winds so cold that sometimes, to the west, the Baltic Sea froze and the Kattegat became a solid mass of ice between Smaland, Sjælland, and Jutland.

The *thegns* carefully scraped the *Dragon Fire*'s sides free of the now-dead marine life and debris, recaulked her strakes, and retouched her paint where necessary. Then they shoved her over log rollers into the harbor and moored her to the wharf, where they scrubbed her deck and polished it with holystones until it shone as smooth as new, mended her square red sail, and replaced oars too battered by heavy seas to be of further use. She was not so grand a longship as some; still, Wulfgar's heart burst with pride when he gazed at her bobbing on the waves. Almost, he could imagine that she were his; and he dwelled on Yelkei's description of a man bold enough to seize Olaf's markland at his death. Wulfgar rebelled at the thought of the *Dragon's Fire*'s being dragged inland and covered by the earth that would serve as Olaf's burial mound. Would that she could be Wulfgar's own longship instead!

Olaf had originally planned to go a-*víking* that summer down the river Elbe, into Frisia and the Germanic kingdoms of the Southlands, where good wines, fine weapons, jewelry, and cloth could be found, and pottery and glass that could be traded in the marketplaces at Sliesthorp, Ribe, Kaupang, and Birka. But that was before Yelkei slipped away one night from Ragnar's *hof* to Olaf's own, where Wulfgar lived now that he was Olaf's *thegn*. All along the *langpallar* of Olaf's great mead hall stones were set to divide the raised side aisles into sleeping quarters for his men. Wulfgar had been allotted one of these alcoves, which afforded him and Yelkei a modicum of privacy as she bent near to him, her black eyes glittering with such excitement that he knew, even before she said as much, that she had news of great import. Still, she restrained herself long enough to inquire about Wulfgar's welfare before saying, very low, so as not to be overheard:

"Now, then, do you listen sharp to me, Wulfgar, for here is a tale that could win a bold man riches beyond counting! It happened that this day, a *skáld*, Sigurd Silkbeard by name, came to Ragnar's great mead hall, from Jutland, where he traveled the Hærvej, the Army Road, up from Sliesthorp to Schleswig, Jelling, Vor-Basse, and thence to Viborg, with a small detour, on the way, to the marketplace at Ribe. 'Twas there that this *skáld*, Sigurd Silkbeard, heard from a trader newly arrived from the kingdoms of Britain that Cerdic, a prince of Mercia, is to wed at summer's end. Prince Cerdic's bride is the only daughter of Pendragon, king of Usk—which lies in the land of Walas, west of that dike built by the sea wolf Offa, who was the Saxons' Bretwalda."

"Aye, I am not so ignorant that I have not heard of this great earthwork, like the Danevirke the mighty King Godfred of Jutland built to hold back the advance of Charlemagne's Frankish hordes from the Southlands. But what has all this to do with me, old woman?" Wulfgar asked, beginning to grow impatient.

"Hold your tongue till I'm done with my story, and you shall learn," Yelkei chided crossly, frowning at him. "And use the head on your shoulders for more than turning a comely wench's eye! Think you that the only princess of Usk goes empty-handed to her husband? Nay, she will carry a dowry of chests full of silver and gold and jewels—and that alone worthy plunder! But the maiden herself—if unharmed and yet a virgin—would be a hostage for whom either her father or her betrothed would pay a large ransom. Do you doubt it?"

"Nay, I do not. But if the *skáld* Sigurd Silkbeard has told this tale in Ragnar's great mead hall, why, then Ragnar himself will set out to capture both dowry and maiden; for he's no fool and not slow to seek a prize that will prove to his advantage."

"Ordinarily, nay. But he has burned his fingers more than once, stealing from the kingdoms of Britain, and there's a rich reward to be gained by the man who delivers Ragnar's head on a silver plate to King Aella of Northumbria. If Ragnar seeks to conquer all of Britain, he needs more treasure and *thegns* than even he has at his command; and he dare not trust Björn Ironside or Hasting not to sell him down the river Humber, to Aella, in York. So, instead, Ragnar sails up the river Seine to sack Paris again; twenty years ago, from King Charles the Bald, he got seven thousand pounds of silver there to take his plunder and to go in peace, and it may be he thinks to get twice as much now, with which to support an army. 'Tis your nemesis, Ivar the Boneless, whom Ragnar sends after the princess of Usk—may the gods have mercy on her if she's as fair as Sigurd claimed; for Ivar lusts for any pretty wench and won't scruple to play the cheat by taking her maidenhead and then saying he did not."

"Aye, well, that is no doubt the truth, and in that case, I am sorry for her," Wulfgar said as he thought of the many young women his oldest half brother had raped on raids and brought home as his slaves. "For if her father or her betrothed learn that Ivar's plowed her field, they may not think her worth ransoming, and then she'll surely wind up a slave and a whore of the *thegns*—as my poor mother did when Ragnar had tired of her. Still, none of this has aught to do with me, old woman; so why do you tell me this tale?"

"Because nine times this day, I cast the rune stones—for nine is a magic number—and nine times, they spoke to me the same: *You* must go after this princess of Usk, Wulfgar! Ivar does not sail for several days yet. If you can persuade Olaf the Sea Bull that this venture is worth his while, you can be gone from the Northland before Ivar leaves—and capture the prize yourself ere he discovers that you seek it!"

"Art mad, Yelkei?" Wulfgar stared at her, aghast. "What would that profit me? Save to give Ragnar and Ivar a good excuse to declare a feud against Olaf and to march on his markland. Moreover, whether seized by Ivar or Olaf, neither the maiden nor her dowry would be mine. 'Tis mad you be— or else you grow witless in your old age."

"Haaa!" Yelkei snorted, a harsh sound like the call of the ravens that haunted the woods along the strands. "You did not think so when I told you to seek Olaf the Sea Bull as your *jarl*. But, so be it. There is no use wasting good reindeer milk on a babe who refuses to suckle. I must return to Ragnar's *hof*. Thorkell has concluded his business and is leaving. 'Twas he who brought me here in his ox-cart, and if I do not ride back, I must walk."

Rising slowly from where she squatted upon the pelts that served as Wulfgar's blankets and pallet, Yelkei drew on her cloak and slipped away as silently as she had come, leaving Wulfgar gazing after her, scowling darkly with anger at the guilt and shame he always felt whenever he rejected the counsel born of her powers. She had not told him everything, he sensed, and that, too, troubled him; for he could not guess what she might have held back and what it might portend for him. He should not have been so impatient and irritated with her. If he had been wise, he would have held his tongue and listened to Yelkei more closely, as she had advised, Wulfgar thought, cursing himself for his foolishness. Truly, he must learn to restrain his temper and to overcome his fear and suspicion of Yelkei's prophesying; for he had seen for himself the truth of her words far too often to doubt them.

Muttering under his breath, he lay down upon his pelts, but his emotions were in such a turmoil that sleep would not come easily. His last thought as he finally drifted into slumber was a nebulous notion that perhaps it would do no harm, after all, to speak to Olaf the Sea Bull about the princess of Usk and her dowry. Then the matter would be out of his hands, Wulfgar told himself; its disposition would then be Olaf's decision to make. If Olaf chose to risk the ire of Ragnar Lodbrók by racing Ivar the Boneless to Walas for possession of the maiden and her dowry, then he, Wulfgar, surely could not be held to blame for whatever repercussions might follow. The responsibility for those would fall on Olaf's head. Yet even as Wulfgar comforted himself with that idea, he could not rid himself of the gnawing disquiet that somewhere in Asgard, the gods heard his thoughts—and laughed.

Rhowenna ferch Pendragon was happier than she had been in many a long week. Since she had told Gwydion about her dream, it had not come to her again; and now that summer had arrived and still nothing untoward had occurred, she had begun to think that the dream had not been a true vision, but nothing more than a nightmare, after all. Still, it was a relief to know that the false story she and Gwydion had spun of a fisherman's warning them of recent attacks along the coast, by Northmen, had resulted in the King's posting watchers along the shore. Rhowenna had observed that the Queen's dark-blue eyes had been thoughtful when she had heard the tale and that she had glanced at Father Cadwyr's avid face, then back at Rhowenna's own pale countenance, but had chosen not to probe too deeply into the origin of the lie. Rhowenna felt as though a great burden had been lifted from her shoulders; and grateful for that, she had tried very hard to prepare herself for her coming nuptials if not gladly, at least diligently. Prince Cerdic had sent envoys to Pendragon's court; and she had lessons daily with them to learn the Saxon customs and the language of her betrothed so she would not disgrace either herself or Prince Cerdic before his courtiers. Although the emissaries had on the surface been polite, she had nevertheless indignantly discerned from their attitude toward her that they—whom she had always thought of as ignorant savages and sea wolves—believed her to be both uneducated and a backward barbarian, lacking more than a few words of Latin, the tongue of the learned, and Pendragon's great hall judged poor and crude by their scornful eyes. Because of this, she was proud that she had proved a quick learner and was gradually earning the envoys' respect.

But today on this warm summer afternoon, Rhowenna had forgone her lessons to search for cockles and mussels along the seashore. With knife, rake, and basket in hand, she had set out earlier with several others of the young housecarls and serving maids from the royal manor; and now, her skirts pulled up and tucked into her mesh girdle, she waded, bare-legged and bare-footed, in the salty, sun-dappled water, using her blade to dig the cockles from the sand and her rake to probe the deeper waters favored by the mussels. Her basket was nearly full; the sun and water felt good against her skin, and her spirits were higher than they had been in weeks. Only an occasional glimpse of Gwydion in the distance marred her happiness. No matter how hard she tried, Rhowenna could not forget how everything was changed between them, how easily he had relinquished her to Prince Cerdic of Mercia.

Each time she thought of it, her heart ached in a way she had not known was possible. Because it hurt her so to see Gwydion, she avoided him as much as she could; and he, doubtless understanding her feelings, did not press himself upon her—although, despite herself, she sometimes wished fervently that he would come to her and tell her what a fool he had been, that he would take her away with him before it was too late. Rhowenna knew that this was foolish, wishful thinking, but she could not seem to stop herself from imagining how wonderful it would be to marry him.

All her life, she had witnessed the deep love between her parents; and she yearned for such a love for herself but thought it unlikely she would find it with Prince Cerdic, who, for all that he was to be her husband, was still a Saxon. Old prejudices died hard; and despite all her lessons, Rhowenna was uncertain whether she could ever grow to embrace life willingly in Mercia, much less Prince Cerdic himself. It was a disheartening thought; determinedly, she shoved it from her mind, knowing that it would do no good to dwell upon it, that she could not change her future and so must learn to make the best of it.

She hunkered down, and with the sharp point of her knife, she dug again into the wet sand, taking pleasure in the feel of the sodden grains that squished between her toes as she pried another cockle from its hiding place, then tossed it into her basket. Those at the royal manor would eat well this night, she thought, smiling with satisfaction as she gazed at her booty.

"'Tis indeed a fine haul, my lady," Morgen, who worked beside her, observed, plainly glad to take a break from their laborious task. Getting to her feet, Morgen stretched lazily, like a sinuous cat, her hands at her back, which, like Rhowenna's own, ached from stooping. Then, pulling her tucked-up skirts from her girdle, Morgen slowly wrung out the most sodden portions of the fabric. "We'll not be able to lift the basket between us if we fill it much fuller."

"One of the men can carry it, then," Rhowenna said carelessly, sitting back and driving her blade into the sand beside her. She untied the thong that bound her long, damp braid, then loosened the plait and shook her hair free, running her fingers through the tangled mass. The wind caught the strands, whipping them about her gently as, after a moment, she closed her eyes drowsily and lifted her face to the sun, basking in its heat. "Fetch Hueil or Daffyd or one of the others."

"Aye, my lady." Morgen nodded, pushing her own heavy black mane of unbound hair back from her face as she turned away. Then, suddenly, her attention caught by an unfamiliar shimmering on the far horizon, she paused, her hand held to her brow to shade her eyes against the glare of the sunlight reflecting off the waves of the Severn Sea. "Good Lord in heaven, what is that? Some kind of—of horrible sea monster, it looks like. Two of them! No, three! Look, my lady!"

For a moment when Rhowenna opened her eyes, the sun blinded her, and she could see nothing. But then, at last, as she stared off into the distance to where Morgen pointed, she spied the clutch of sea dragons that rose and plunged upon the waves, widespread crimson sails spilling like blood across the deep-blue summer sky. Her breath caught in her throat; her heart leaped with terror at the sight—for this time, she knew that it was no dream, no vision, but the terrible reality she had foreseen and feared. Grabbing her knife from the sand, she lurched to her feet, glancing about wildly for the housecarls. But while the men were within shouting distance, they still well down the coast. Rhowenna had not realized until now how far she and Morgen had strayed from the rest and from the royal manor, too.

"Those are not sea monsters!" she blurted, her voice ris-

ing. "They're ships . . . longships! Dear God! 'Tis the Northmen! They're coming! They're coming to Usk! Run, Morgen!
Run!"

Morgen's eyes widened. Her face blanched with fright as
she suddenly understood the danger. Abandoning their rakes
and basket, the two women gathered up their skirts and
pounded desperately down the shore, crying out as they ran,
their bare feet skimming the edges of the combers and sending
water and sand flying. Rhowenna's heart lodged in her throat
as she glanced back over her shoulder and saw how rapidly
the longships were gaining on them, drawing ominously
nearer and nearer to the coast, square red sails billowing in
the wind. She had never seen vessels sail so swiftly, as though
they flew over the sea; and she realized in terror that Morgen
and she would not reach the palisade in time. Her breath came
in hard rasps, and she had a painful stitch in her side that,
without warning, doubled her over.

"My lady!" Morgen whirled about, racing back to Rhowenna. "Are you all right?"

"Aye. I just . . . need to . . . catch my breath. . . ."

"There is not time! We must hurry! Come on!"

Clutching her aching side, Rhowenna forced herself to
stagger on, sobbing, hearing now the urgent, warning wail
of the horns blown by the watchers stationed along the coast,
the shouts of the housecarls and the screams of the serving
women who had been among those digging for cockles and
mussels earlier and who now, like Morgen and Rhowenna,
fled in fear for their lives toward the haven of the palisade.
But already, flight was futile, Rhowenna recognized with a
sinking heart. The sea dragons were swooping with impossible speed toward the beach, furling their wings, long necks
outstretched, bellies heaving and shuddering as their fierce
riders, yelling mighty battle cries, dismounted and waded
thigh-high into the frothy waves to drag the longships halfway
up onto the sand. After that, everything happened so fast that

for ever after, it was only a terrible blur in Rhowenna's mind, a nightmare that became reality.

She had never seen such savages as the *Víkingrs*; even the Saxon wolves east of Offa's Dyke were not so barbaric, she thought as, stricken, petrified where she stood, she watched the marauders surge forward from the sea, at their vanguard the gold-headed god she had seen in her dream. Aye, it *was* he! She was so stunned by the realization that only Morgen's screams of dread and frantic jerking on her hand urged her to movement when the tawny-haired giant of a Northman suddenly disappeared from her view, swallowed by a fearsome wave of horrifying warriors who howled and leaped forth like madmen, stark naked save for the bearskins flung about their massive shoulders. Rhowenna had heard macabre tales of such Northmen, who were said before battle to acquire the bears' ferocious strength and power by drinking the beasts' blood and by wearing their hides. From these *bearsarks*, bear shirts, had such warriors received their name— Berserks—a name that struck terror into the heart of all who heard it; for the Berserks were said to be not just fearless, but actually mindless in battle, bolstered by strong alcohol and so vicious and pathological that when battle fever and bloodlust were upon them, they could bite through an ironclad shield or walk through fire, without suffering any pain. Invariably, they led the foremost ranks of the Northland's warriors; and it was said that even the other Northmen were afraid of them—proof indeed of their fiendishness.

Like a pack of starving wolves, the Berserks fell upon the housecarls and *ceorls* who, alerted by the bellow of the watchers' horns, had charged forth from the palisade, the village, and the fields of Usk alike, shouting their own calls to arms, weapons in hand, to fend off the brutal attack of the Northmen. Everywhere Rhowenna turned, cacophony and confusion reigned as the first of the sickening blows were struck and the bloody battle was joined, the men becoming in moments a blur of flying pelts, bloodstained leather garments, and hacking and slashing weapons as each vanguard bravely met the other's assault. The harsh, metallic clanging and clashing of the warriors' broadswords and battle-axes and iron-bossed, gilt-bronzed shields filled the air, accompanied by the stout, ferocious *thwack* of the *ceorls'* wooden clubs, staffs, hoes, and rakes, the deadly *whoosh* of scythes and spears and knives that flashed in the sun as the reivers drove forward, the Berserks leading the way, swarming up from the shore to higher ground, an army of huge, crazed men against whom the warriors and *ceorls* of Usk could not stand fast. They buckled and broke ranks, scattering and falling back toward the knoll from which the palisade rose—so near and yet so far.

As the Northmen pressed on relentlessly, the high, piercing shrieks of fleeing women and children echoed above the clamor of the battle, mingling with the screams of animals that, in their panic, broke loose from tethers and pens to run about chaotically, adding to the pandemonium. Blood spattered and gushed, seeping into the rich, moist earth; and black clouds of acrid smoke billowed on the wind as torches were scooped up from their sconces, ignited by the marauders, and then tossed onto the thatched roofs of the *ceorls'* huts and byres, setting the village ablaze. There was no way to reach the safety of the palisade, no place to hide, Rhowenna numbly understood with utter despair as she stumbled on blindly through the cruel conflict, Morgen half dragging her forward as they slipped and slid upon the bloody ground, striving desperately to escape from the terrifying melee that had enveloped them. But there was no route to freedom, no refuge to be found from the fighting and dying. The battle was thick all around them, the Berserks cutting a wide swath in the ranks of Pendragon's housecarls and *ceorls*, and the rest of the Northmen coming hard and fast behind. In their wake, corpses littered the ground, people Rhowenna had known and cared for all her life, although there was no time to mourn for them. It seemed a miracle to her that she and Morgen were still alive and somehow as yet unharmed. But surely, they would not remain so much longer, Rhowenna realized as, now, from the circular timber wall of the palisade, arrows began to rain down, the iron barbs with which they were tipped finding their marks. One of the Berserks staggered back, an arrow protruding from his eye; another of the reivers was shot through the throat, his frenzied gnashing of teeth and howling abruptly muted to a blood-bubbling gurgle, his back arching spasmodically before he toppled facedown into the dirt.

Reins trailing, a riderless horse galloped by, white-eyed and snorting, nearly knocking the two women down, and as, with all her strength, Rhowenna pulled Morgen from its furious path, they tripped over a body, sprawling headlong upon the earth. The stench of fresh-spilled blood filled Rhowenna's nostrils, and she could feel it, warm and slick and sticky, upon her flesh. Crying and gasping for breath, she lay there beside the corpse, shaking and thinking dully that surely in moments, she would be dead herself. All around her, men were at one another's throats, fighting to the death. To her utter horror, a *ceorl* was decapitated right before her eyes, his head flying away, a fountain of blood spewing from his neck. Another man had his belly ripped open, his insides spilling out as he slowly crumpled forward and collapsed. Gorge rose uncontrollably in Rhowenna's throat at these unspeakable sights, and she retched violently onto the ground before struggling mindlessly to crawl on toward the royal manor.

Dimly, she realized she had lost Morgen in the fray, her last link with all she had ever known that was safe, secure, and sane in this world so suddenly and horribly gone mad. This could not be happening, she thought hysterically, tears streaming down her cheeks. This could not be real. But the arms that, without warning, caught hold of her, swinging her up and crushing her against a broad, muscular chest, were strong and warm and all too tangible. Shocked and dazed, her head rolling back against her captor's shoulder, Rhowenna stared up into eyes as blue as the summer sky, a face framed by a halo of hair gilded by the sun. It was he, the Northman she had seen in her dream.

"I knew that you would come for me—" she whispered, her voice catching on a ragged sob. "The old gods warned me that you would."

Then, as in her dream, a merciful blackness swirled up to engulf her, and she knew nothing more.

Book Two

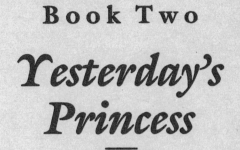

Yesterday's Princess

Chapter Six

The Shore
of Corpses

The Southern Coast of Usk, Walas, A.D. 865

Wulfgar had never before been in battle, so when the battle
fever and bloodlust came upon him, he did not at first know
them for what they were. He knew only that he burned with
a raging madness that was consuming his entire body. Time
and time again, his battle-ax, Blood-Drinker, soared and
plunged and sang a *Víkingr*'s song to Odinn, the god of war;
and to Wulfgar's pride and satisfaction, many a Christian man
of Usk fell beneath its whetted blade. Its engraved scenes of
battle, the like of which Wulfgar had only imagined before,
he now experienced firsthand. Only once, when he had first
stood upon the deck of Olaf the Sea Bull's *Dragon's Fire*,
with the endless blue sea shimmering and swelling all about
him, had Wulfgar felt as exhilarated as he had when he had
raced pell-mell behind the howling Berserks up from the shore.

of the Severn Sea, to the village of the Usk men and into the heart of the slaughter.

Presently, he was to learn there was a third cause for such a fire to blaze within a man. He felt its licking tongues of flame flicker deep inside him when, toward the end of the brief but devastating battle, he first beheld Rhowenna, princess of Usk, she whom the Northmen would in time come to call fey Rhowenna the Fair, because of the dreams sent to her by the old gods and because of her beauty. By Rhowenna's long, silky hair—as black as the ravens that nested in the woods along the strands of the Northland—and by the fine gold, engraved, nielloed circlet about her head did Wulfgar know her. Although he had not thought to find her outside the palisade that perched like a falcon's aerie upon the top of the hill, green and rocky, which towered over the burning village, he knew she could be none other. His breath caught in his throat at the sight of her; and his heart leaped with excitement in his chest and, if he were honest in the telling, with coveting, too—for bedraggled as she was, her beauty shone forth.

She was half crawling, half dragging herself through the melee, trying desperately to reach the palisade; although she was weeping and obviously terrified, there was, too, upon her countenance a grim expression of bravery and determination that touched something deep inside him. Without thinking, Wulfgar hacked his way toward her through the fighting and caught her up, crushing her weakly struggling body close against him, as though to protect her from the mayhem and killing taking place all about them. She was not so tall and robust as a maiden of the Northland, but as light as a veil of mist in his arms, her garments torn and so covered with blood that for a moment, he feared she had suffered some wound during the battle, although he could discern no injury but a pale bruise upon her ashen cheek. When his eyes met hers, he saw that her own were a startling shade, as violet as the amethysts the Greeks had craved as protection against drunkenness—although Wulfgar himself had never known such a stone to keep a man sober. Her lashes were as black as soot and so heavy that they seemed to pull her sloe eyes down at the corners and cast crescent shadows upon her cheeks in the sunlight. When she spoke, her voice was like the gentle caress of the wind; and although Wulfgar could not understand her unfamiliar Christian tongue, he felt, eerily, that the gods had deliberately delivered her into his arms. It had happened just as Yelkei had known it would when she had told him of casting the rune stones nine times, with nine times the answer the same: He, Wulfgar, must go after the princess of Usk.

The battle was dying down now, although the palisade upon the hill still stood strong and unravaged because the Usk warriors had hailed arrows and poured hot oil upon the Northmen who had attempted to breach the circular timber wall and forced them to retreat. As this was only a raid, the *Víkingrs* had not come prepared to conduct a lengthy battle or siege. They had thought to storm the palisade, set it afire, and take its inhabitants by surprise; they had not expected to find the Usk men on guard and ready for battle. Because of this, the princess's dowry was no doubt forfeit. Still, she herself would surely be worth her weight in gold, Wulfgar reflected as he gazed down at her in his arms. After speaking to him, she had swooned, overcome by fright and smoke, he surmised, and now lay with her head resting against his shoulder, her black lashes like fragile butterfly wings against her cheeks. So she would look when sleeping, wrapped in a man's embrace, he thought. Never had he seen a woman so fair, as lovely and graceful as the rare black swans he sometimes saw at the lakes and meres of the Northland, her bones delicate and finely molded. Suddenly, the idea of her belonging to Olaf the Sea Bull or, worse, Ragnar Lodbrók and Ivar the Boneless, angered and appalled him; for he could not believe that upon seeing her, any man could help but desire her. That she should be brutally dishonored and defiled sickened and shamed him. He had not thought of her as a woman before, with feelings, but only as the princess of Usk, a prize to be won and exchanged for riches. He should have left her in peace instead of listening to Yelkei's cryptic prophesying.

Almost, as these thoughts filled his mind, was Wulfgar tempted to leave Rhowenna behind. But the notion of laying her down amid the bodies that strewed the bloody ground as though it were Náströnd, the Shore of Corpses, filled him with revulsion and misgiving. Already, several of the other *Víkingrs* had the captive Usk women spread-eagled upon the earth, their skirts rucked up about their thighs, and were ruthlessly and raucously raping them before snatching them up and carrying them toward the longships. Such might prove Rhowenna's fate, Wulfgar thought, if he relinquished his hold on her; for in their frenzy, the Berserks, especially, might not notice the gold circlet about her head, which marked her as the princess of Usk, the one woman not to be harmed. So reasoning, he at last turned and made his way down the narrow, serpentine track that led to the strand below, where he bore Rhowenna on board the *Dragon's Fire* and set her down gently in the stern.

Her lashes fluttered slowly open then. Her tearful eyes were wild and dark with fear and hatred as she stared up at him, mute and trembling and offering no resistance. But when he tentatively stretched out one hand toward her, she abruptly jerked free the knife at her waist and attempted savagely to stab him. Reflectively, Wulfgar seized the wrist of her upraised hand in a cruel grip that made her cry out softly and that he knew to his regret would leave bruises on her tender flesh tomorrow. He had not wanted to hurt her. But despite his powerful hold on her, she continued to struggle like a wild thing against him, the fingers of her free hand curled like talons to strike viciously at his face before he managed to restrain her, compelling her to drop the knife and then pinioning her arms behind her back. At that, her chin setting mutinously, her violet eyes blazing with reckless anger, Rhowenna hissed some heated words at him in her strange Christian tongue that he could not understand, then spat contemptuously in his face.

"Be still!" he growled, infuriated, as he wiped the humiliating spittle from his face, then gave her a rough shake. "Be still! I am not going to hurt you!"

Rhowenna was startled and disbelieving as, to her confusion, she half grasped the meaning of his foreign words. Then, her voice low and trembling with emotion, she spoke to him again, this time, to his surprise, in the Saxon language of her betrothed, Prince Cerdic.

"Lying dog! Let me go—or I swear the first chance I get, I'll cut your heathen throat!"

"An evil deed for a Christian maiden," Wulfgar rejoined slowly, the Saxon language he had learned as a child at his mother's knee rusty from years of disuse. "For do not your priests claim that murder is a mortal sin, for which a Christian soul will be condemned to everlasting Hel?"

"Aye, but I would sooner burn in Hel than submit to you!" Rhowenna shot back, quivering at her own temerity before this Northman who now held her very life in his hands.

"Would you? Nay, I think not; for Hel is no fiery place such as you have been taught by your priests, lady, but a world of nine lands, cold and dark, and the worst of these is Náströnd, the Shore of Corpses, where there stands a bleak black fortress filled with hideous monsters to torture you and to devour your flesh from your bones forever, since in Hel, you are already dead and so there is no release for you—a cruel fate for one of your spirit . . . and beauty."

Deliberately, Wulfgar brushed the tangled mass of long, heavy black hair back from her face, then set his hand beneath her chin, tilting her face up to his, feeling his heart swell strangely with triumph and pleasure and desire at the way in which her eyes fell before his. A crimson blush stained her cheeks, and her breath came quickly and shallowly, making her breasts rise and fall enticingly beneath her bodice.

"Do not touch me so, brute!" All too aware of his overwhelming strength and nearness, the way he held her, his hand locking her arms behind her back, pressing her against his broad chest and preventing her from struggling to escape, Rhowenna tried to wrench free of him, to no avail. She was caught as fast as though by an iron band. "Let me go!"

"Look about you, lady, at the carnage and violation done to your people, and be glad that 'tis I and none other who holds you captive—and that I knew you for the princess of Usk, besides—else you would even now be laid upon the ground, your skirts thrown up over your head, your maidenhead forfeit to a moment's brutal lust, and you yourself carried away afterward to the Northland to become a slave and a whore of men far crueler than I. Do you doubt it?" When she did not respond save for the widening of her eyes, the paling of her face, the erratic beating of the pulse at the small hollow of her throat, Wulfgar continued more gently. "I do not wish to harm you, lady. But 'tis my duty to bind your hands and feet lest you make some foolish attempt at escape before we are under way; and much as I dislike the idea, if you persist in fighting me, I shall be forced to some unpleasantness you will regret, I promise you. So do not try my patience further."

At that, slowly loosing his steely grasp on her and drawing the scramasax from the leather belt at his waist, he swiftly sliced off an ell of spare rigging that lay coiled nearby on the deck. Then, being careful not to wrap the single strip of walrus hide so tightly that he cut off her circulation, he deftly tied Rhowenna's wrists behind her back and her feet together at the ankles, so her lissome body was bent like a supple bow and she could not even stand, much less make any attempt, however futile, to run away. She could only sit where she was, heartsore and sick and afraid, longing for death and knowing with a terrible certainty that even that escape was to be denied her. She was a prisoner of the barbaric *Víkingrs* who had descended so suddenly and swiftly upon Usk, and they did not intend that her release should come easily—if at all. This morn, she had been a princess—and a virgin. Now she was a slave—and perhaps was soon to become a whore, as well; for had not that threat been implicit in the Northman's words to her? With difficulty, Rhowenna fought down the hysteria that threatened to overcome her at the thought, realizing that she would need to keep her wits about her if she was to survive.

Some primal instinct made her cling to that thought, and when Wulfgar again squatted beside her, an unstoppered flask in his hands, she did not refuse the *bjórr* he pressed upon her. The wine had an unfamiliar, fruity flavor and was far more potent than that to which she was accustomed. But she was glad of the sudden warmth that spread from her belly to the rest of her body. She had not recognized until now how strangely cold she was, despite the summer sun that shone brightly overhead. At Rhowenna's greedy gulps, Wulfgar swore softly, angrily, causing her to cringe as, fearing she intended to drain it dry, he abruptly snatched away the flask he had held to her lips.

"You must drink slowly, lady," he cautioned sternly, "small sips, or you will grow drunk and violently ill, besides, once we've put out to sea. I have seen it happen before— even to men with stout heads and strong stomachs."

Rhowenna nodded weakly to show she understood. Even so, Wulfgar offered her no more of the *bjórr*. The last of the *Víkingrs* were now approaching the beached longships, laden with the corpses of their slain companions, with screaming, weeping, and struggling women, and with booty plundered from the dead bodies of the Usk men and from the burning village of the *ceorls*. Many a flask was uncorked and tilted high, spilling wine and ale down throats hoarse from the shouts of victory and all over the triumphant *Víkingrs* themselves as they tossed their captives and spoils into the longships, then dragged the vessels from the sand into the sea. Rhowenna's heart ached with horror and pity as she saw the hysterical women carelessly cast onto the decks of the longships, battered and bruised, half naked, their clothes ripped and begrimed, and blood staining the thighs of those who had been maidens earlier that day. Highly valued armor and weapons callously stripped from the dead Usk men, jewelry and cloth, tools and utensils, and other goods stolen from the blazing huts and byres of the *ceorls* were tossed, as well, into piles soon heaped high upon the decks. Alongside, the corpses of the reivers were ceremoniously laid out with their arms folded across their chests and their shields placed upon them.

Rhowenna gasped and then cried out softly as Morgen, moaning with pain and bound hand and foot, was roughly thrown down beside her in the stern of the longship. Like the rest of the women, Morgen had obviously been beaten and raped, perhaps even by more than one man. Her face was bruised, her lower lip cut and bleeding; her bare shoulders and half-exposed breasts showed the marks of brutish mauling, and her soiled bodice and skirts were nearly torn away. For a long moment, the wind knocked from her by the violent force with which she had struck the deck, she lay sprawled upon its planks, unmoving.

"Morgen—" Rhowenna whispered urgently, her voice catching on a broken sob, for she half feared that the serving maid was dead. "Oh, dear God, please let her be all right! Morgen! Can you hear me? Are you all right?"

"Aye, as well as . . . can be . . . expected, my lady," came the low response at last as Morgen slowly raised her head and began weakly to inch her way across the deck to where Rhowenna sat braced against one side of the longship. "At least, I'm . . . alive," she continued as she struggled with difficulty into a sitting position. "Did they . . . did they . . . hurt you, my lady?"

"Nay, not yet, anyway. One of them . . . one of them recognized the circlet I wear as princess of Usk, and so I was spared—Oh, Morgen! I am sorry, so very sorry for what has happened to you and the others—"

"'Tis not your fault. You are not to blame for it, my lady—and I, at least, was no virgin." Morgen confessed this last wryly. "How I thank God for that! Some of the rest were not so lucky; and worse lies ahead for us all, I fear, slavery and whoredom, if the tales of the Northmen are to be believed—and after today, who among us could doubt them? Not I."

"Nor I," Rhowenna replied, tears stinging her eyes and a hard, painful lump rising in her throat as she looked at all the women ravished and taken captive, and then back at the corpses that littered the burning village and the ravaged shores of Usk. It was very like the Shore of Corpses the Northman had described to her.

She realized suddenly—stricken—that she did not even know if Gwydion was among the dead. She had not seen him fall in battle, as she had envisioned in her dream; and as the *Víkingrs* shoved their longships into the sea, she clung fast to the slender thread of hope that perhaps Gwydion was still alive, that he had somehow survived the terrible battle, despite the fact that so much of what she had foreseen had indeed come to pass when the tall, gilt-haired Northman had swept her up and carried her to the vessel. Even now, she could feel his intense blue eyes upon her, and she shivered uncontrollably, her own gaze involuntarily drawn to him. He seemed different from all the others. Perhaps he would not use her too cruelly, Rhowenna thought; for she had witnessed his desire for her earlier, and she felt that despite his assurances to the contrary, it was only a matter of time before he forced himself upon her. Why should she alone escape rape, or worse, at the hands of these savage Northmen?

"Where is Olaf the Sea Bull?" Wulfgar inquired as he and the rest of the *Víkingrs* leaped from the lapping waves into the vessels. The oarsmen were taking their places on their sea chests and the drummers beginning to beat the rhythm to which the oars now rose and fell in unison to send the vessels shooting forward over the waves of the Severn Sea.

"Chosen this day by the Valkyries to drink forever with Odinn, in Valhöll!" One of the men pointed to Olaf's bloody body, stretched out on the deck of the *Dragon's Fire*. "May we all prove so fortunate as to die so gloriously in battle, to become one of the Einheriar of Odinn!"

"Aye!" the other men crowed loudly, laughing, drunk on wine and ale, on battle fever and bloodlust, and on the sweet, heady taste of their victory this day. "Aye!"

Only Wulfgar was silent, an icy grue creeping up his spine as he stared at Olaf's mortally wounded corpse, its sightless blue eyes gazing up unblinkingly at the sun, its scraggly grey beard fluttering a little in the wind. Was this the answer Yelkei had received in her casting of the rune stones? Wulfgar wondered uneasily, half afraid that for his heeding, however reluctantly, the counsel born of her sorcerous meddling in what was their business only, the gods would smite him down where he stood. Was this the knowledge she had withheld from him: that Olaf would not survive the raid upon Usk? Yelkei had claimed she had heard Hela's death rattle in Olaf's bones. But perhaps that had been only a lie, Wulfgar thought; perhaps *he* was responsible for his *jarl*'s death—for surely if he had not suggested this venture, Olaf might still be alive.

Yet, despite these fearful and guilty thoughts, Wulfgar

could not still the sudden, irrepressible thrill of excitement that coursed through his veins at the realization that Olaf the Sea Bull was dead. Unbidden, Yelkei's vision of a man bold enough at Olaf's death to seize his markland crept into Wulfgar's mind; and it came to him then that he had already taken the first step in that direction: He had without even realizing it assumed Olaf's vacant place in the stern, at the tiller—and surprisingly, no man aboard the *Dragon's Fire* had challenged his authority to do so. Right now, they were probably all too drunk and buoyed up by their triumph to notice or to care who captained the longship, Wulfgar told himself. But surely when they sobered, one or more of the *thegns* would cry foul at his usurpation and would attempt to take his place. He would not let that happen, Wulfgar resolved. He *could* not—for whoever held the tiller of the *Dragon's Fire* could also surely claim Olaf's markland, as well as the princess of Usk; and as he gazed down at Rhowenna at his feet, Wulfgar was suddenly determined that no matter the cost, that man would be he.

"Lady"—he spoke quietly to her so as not to be overheard, for he did not know which, if any, of Olaf's *thegns* might understand the Saxon language—"my lord, Olaf the Sea Bull, lies dead there on the deck, slain in the battle with your people. He was an old grey-beard, grown slack and slovenly with age, and more often than not, he was deep in his cups. But in his own way, he was a good lord to me, and it could be that I would have had some small influence with him where you are concerned. Now, we are both of us without his protection, and although you will doubtless not believe it, I am afraid for you.

"There will be those besides myself who will covet Olaf's markland—and even more who will covet the ransom you are sure to bring from your betrothed, Prince Cerdic of Mercia, or your father, King Pendragon of Usk. There were others besides my lord Olaf who knew of your betrothal and dowry, and who intended to take you hostage, lady. They will be enraged that Olaf the Sea Bull beat them to the prize. Foremost among them are Ragnar Lodbrók, who is a powerful king of the Northland, and his son and heir, Ivar the Boneless. They are my bitterest foes, and so you may be certain that upon our arrival in the Northland, they will demand that I deliver you up to them, and that if I do not, they will march upon me and Olaf's markland to take you by force.

"Are you listening to me, lady?"

"Aye—for all the good it may do me." Rhowenna, too, kept her voice low. "I am powerless to defend myself even against you, much less your enemies, so what do you hope to gain by telling me this tale—unless 'tis to terrify me into submitting to you?"

"I would rather have you knowing naught but a maiden's fear of her first time with a man, and willing in my arms." The answer was blunt and made Rhowenna flush scarlet with shame at the image he evoked in her mind. "But neither Ragnar Lodbrók nor Ivar the Boneless is so particular; and although I doubt that Prince Cerdic will pay ransom for a sullied bride, your father might for a dishonored daughter."

"Nay, he will not! Be sure of that, Northman!"

"I cannot—nor can you be, I am thinking. Even so, I wish only to help you, lady. By the gods, I swear it! It has come to me that the wench beside you is a virgin no longer and, while not so beautiful as you, is much like you physically and comely enough to pass as the princess of Usk if she were of a mind to, with none but ourselves the wiser. We would need to keep our wits about us, for 'twould be a dangerous game we would play. Still, in this manner could I best keep you safe from harm, lady, for then you would be naught more than my slave and, as such, not likely to attract the interest even of Ragnar Lodbrók and Ivar the Boneless. But the switch must be made now, and quickly, while the *Víkingrs* aboard the *Dragon's Fire* are still drunk with wine and ale and victory, and so not likely to remember which ebon-haired woman was first wearing that gold circlet about your head.''

"Why—why should you care what happens to me?" Rhowenna asked, bewildered by Wulfgar's wholly unexpected offer of protection and assistance.

"Because I have never before seen a woman such as you. You are rare and beautiful, like a black swan, and I would not see you cruelly ravaged.''

"That is no answer. You are as barbarous as the rest of your kind. 'Twas *you* who kidnapped me and brought me on board this vessel!''

"Would you rather I had left you amid the battle and the corpses, where I found you, perhaps to be raped or even killed by the Berserks or the other warriors? Nay, I thought not. What answer will you believe, then, lady? I have no other save what I have already told you.''

"You are a liar!''

"May the gods strike me dead if I am.''

His blue eyes held her own violet ones steadily, and try as she might, Rhowenna could discern nothing but earnestness in his gaze. She did not understand it, but it represented hope and a chance for her that she was reluctant to reject.

"I—I do not know why you should wish to—to help me, but I will—I will ask Morgen if she will agree to the exchange,'' she said slowly at last, still puzzled by his behavior toward her and half suspecting some trickery. Still, he had sworn by his gods, and perhaps that did mean something to him, although he was no Christian, to whom such an oath was holy. Turning to Morgen, she explained what Wulfgar had told her.

"Do you believe what he has said, my lady?" Morgen queried thoughtfully.

"I—I don't know.''

"Still, you are yet a virgin, and afraid. But this I tell you, my lady: If your rank will not spare you from rape before you are ransomed, your shame will be more easily borne if it comes at the hands of one man rather than many. Although he is a savage and a heathen, the Northman is handsome and, if he speaks truly, perhaps not so cruel as the others.'' Morgen's dark eyes studied him covertly as she considered this. ''Mayhap he is indeed sorry for you, as I am, and does, in truth, want only to help you—or perhaps he is not so kind, and not only lusts for you, but also is greedy and thinking to win your ransom solely for himself. Even so, I do not see what other choice you have at the moment in this matter, my lady, but to trust him; and I am not so hard and unfeeling that I would condemn you to endure my own fate this day. Tell the Northman that we will go along with his plan for now— but add that if he is bent on some treachery, we will presently discover it, and he will regret it. Say that if such a day should come, we will reveal the deception and denounce him to any and all who will listen as a traitor to his king and his homeland. Say further that on that day, we will seek refuge with those who oppose him and will beg of them his head for his perfidy.''

''In the great mead hall of my enemies, you would soon learn that you had left the lair of a lone wolf for that of a vicious pack,'' Wulfgar declared soberly when Rhowenna had related Morgen's words and warning to him, ''as I have good cause to know. Still, 'tis a fair enough bargain when you've no reason to trust me save for my word, and I will hold to my end of it.'' So saying and after glancing about covertly to make certain he was unobserved, he swiftly bent and, removing the gold circlet from Rhowenna's head, placed it upon Morgen's own. '''Tis little enough protection I offer you, lady. Even so, you shall be glad of it, I am thinking, before this game is done.''

Miserably contemplating the price he might demand she pay in return for that protection, Rhowenna did not answer, but swallowed hard and turned away. Morgen's words rang in her mind: Better one man than many. Surely, that was true.

As the square red sail of the longship was hoisted and caught by the wind to send the vessel skimming swiftly over the waves, Rhowenna watched the rugged green mountains of her homeland, Walas, grow smaller and smaller in the distance, perhaps never to be seen by her again—and it suddenly occurred to her that she did not even know her captor's name.

Chapter Seven

Where the Wild Swans Soar

The abomination of the journey by longship to the Northland was surpassed, in Rhowenna's mind, only by her memory of that brief, brutal battle at Usk. Except for the small roof above the stern, there was little shade and, so, little relief to be found from the hot summer sun that beat down unmercifully upon her and the rest of the women, burning and blistering the delicate skin of Rhowenna, Morgen, and the other few serving maids, who, unlike the female *ceorls*, were not accustomed to working long hours in fields exposed to the sun. Fresh water, for drinking, was strictly rationed, and there was none at all for bathing, only the harsh, salty seawater for washing away the grime, blood, and defiling seed that soiled the women and their tattered garments. Nor was there any privacy whatsoever, any escape from the men's prying eyes, their plainly lewd if unintelligible jests in their foreign tongue, their raucous laughter, their slaking of their lust whenever they desired. Worst of all was the fact that the corpses of the slain *Víkingrs* still lay upon the deck. The *jarl* Olaf the Sea Bull and his *thegns* were to be taken to the Northland for interment; only the bodies of freedmen and slaves were pitched overboard at death. This was the custom unless it was a vessel's maiden voyage, in which case it was considered bad luck to bring home a corpse.

Rhowenna did not understand this at first, not until, once they were well out to sea, the oars were drawn in, and the sail was raised, the marauders pulled up several of the loose planks that formed the deck of the longship to reveal a shallow cargo space beneath, into which the bloody, stiffening bodies were carefully lowered, along with the plunder from Usk. Only then did she grasp the fact that the corpses would not be buried at sea, as she had initially assumed. Never had she imagined even the savage *Víkingrs* capable of such a barbaric practice as this; for as the afternoon wore on, it soon became clear what the gruesome result of storing bodies in the stuffy, humid hold would be. The smell alone was vile, nauseating, making Rhowenna and the rest of the women, some of whom were already seasick, retch violently over the side of the longship. But then, from nowhere, it seemed, the flies came in swarms, until Rhowenna thought that there must be millions of them aboard the vessel, so loud was the sickening drone of their buzzing in the hold. Drawn by the blood on her clothes and that of the other women, the flies came up through the planks to settle on the living as well as the dead, their bites making her skin sting; for with her hands bound, Rhowenna had no means of swatting the flies away. Only by tossing her head and writhing could she shoo them off; and she loathed the *Víkingrs* more than ever for their ribald gibes and howling laughter at her suffering and that of the other women.

Only her captor, Wulfgar Bloodaxe, did not take part in the malicious merriment, but stood protectively close at hand at the tiller, his face impassive, so she could not guess what he was thinking. Like the rest of the men, he had stripped off his bloodstained leather tunic and was now naked to the waist, clad only in his leather belt and breeches and sealskin boots. Despite herself, Rhowenna found her eyes surreptitiously straying more than once to his tall, powerful figure. His long tawny hair gleamed like burnished gold in the light of the sun creeping slowly toward the western horizon; his eyes shone as blue as the infinite summer sky. Like the body of some strong, sleek predator, his massive bronze arms, back, and chest rippled sinuously with hard muscle, disturbing her in a way she could not understand. There was something almost larger than life about him, she thought, as though he were indeed one of the old gods—for so had she imagined them.

Under his guidance, the longship sped forward, like a swan, Rhowenna reflected, long neck outstretched, wings spread wide upon the cool sea wind that was the only relief from the heat, the stench of the corpses, and the sting of the flies. She was glad of the small roof above the stern; at least she had a modicum of shade. Still, sweat beaded her body, making her thin, fine summer gown cling to her sticky flesh in a way that Wulfgar was only too aware of. Linen was rare and costly in the Northland, brought back from raids upon the Southlands and worn only by the wives and daughters of *konungrs* and the richest *jarlar*. It would mark Rhowenna as such, he realized suddenly, frowning, for he had not thought of this before. She and Morgen would have to exchange garments, as well as identities. This, he explained softly to them when, at sundown, he was, to his wary surprise, spelled at the tiller by a stout, bleary-eyed Knut Strongarm, reeking of blood, sweat, alcohol, and rutting, but lately Olaf's second-in-command aboard the *Dragon's Fire* and so the relief steersman.

"I am sorry for your discomfort and lack of privacy, lady," Wulfgar told Rhowenna as he knelt to untie her bonds and those of Morgen, also. "I know that you are gently bred and not used to such hardships as you have suffered this day. I will do what I can to ease your unhappy lot. But know you this: I have with no man's consent seized command of the *Dragon's Fire*, and it may be that at any moment, Knut Strongarm or one of the others will grow bold or sober enough to challenge my authority. Should that happen, I will be fighting not only for the captaincy of this vessel, but also for my very life.'' He did not add that until today, he had never fought a real battle, but only mock training duels within Olaf the Sea Bull's palisade. ''If I am killed, you must reveal your true identity at once, else you will not be safe from the rest of the *Víkingrs*. They are hard men, lady, and ruthless. Trust them not.''

''No more than I trust you—which is not at all!''

To Rhowenna's surprise, for she had expected Wulfgar to be angered by her words, he cupped her face gently in his strong hands, his fingers weaving through the tresses at her temples as he gazed down at her, his blue eyes glittering with approval in the fiery light of the sun sinking slowly into the sea.

''Good,'' he said shortly. ''You will be safer that way. I have brought a bucket of seawater for you and Morgen to wash yourselves and your clothes; you can trade gowns while you do that. Then will I bring you food and drink.'' Briefly, his hands tightened in her hair before he loosed her and, getting to his feet, turned away.

Chafing her wrists, Rhowenna herself rose slowly, unsteadily, her back and legs cramped and aching from the unaccustomed position in which she had been forced to sit for the last hours. But finally, she got her sea legs and managed to stand upright, glad she had lived all her life on the sea and had never suffered from seasickness. It was the foul odor wafting from the shallow hold that was making her feel so queasy. There was at least more privacy in the stern than elsewhere on the longship, and Wulfgar's tall, watchful figure as he stood between them and everyone else provided something of a screen. Even so, Rhowenna and Morgen did not linger as they stripped to their shifts and laved themselves and their garments as best they could in the wooden pail and without any soap. Despite its salty abrasiveness, the seawater was cool and welcome; Rhowenna longed to immerse herself in it, to scrub and to scrub until she was certain every part of her was washed clean, untainted by the blood of the dead and the dying. It even occurred to her, suddenly, wildly, simply to leap overboard into the sea itself, where she would surely drown; and she chided herself as a coward because something deep inside her strove to survive, no matter what might become of her.

Furtively, she and Morgen exchanged clothes, she donning Morgen's coarser gown, in worse shape than her own; and as she remembered the reason why, Rhowenna felt a sudden, deep sense of guilt and shame that she alone among all the women taken captive should yet be chaste. She had never been particularly close to Morgen; there had been some days when she had actually disliked her. But now, as she thought of the other serving maids and her own dear waiting woman, Enid—most of them still safe in Usk, behind the palisade of Pendragon's royal manor—Rhowenna knew she had rather have Morgen at her side now than any other: dark, bold Morgen, stronger in her own way than the rest, and not so hard and unfeeling as Rhowenna had once supposed.

"I won't forget what you've done for me, Morgen, I swear it! When my father ransoms me, I shall insist he pay whatever price is demanded for your own freedom, as well."

"I am counting on that, my lady, for no more than you do I wish to spend the rest of my life as a slave and a whore of these barbaric Northmen!" Morgen declared, the glint in her dark, narrowed eyes bespeaking a fierce sense of self-preservation—so Rhowenna realized that this, perhaps even more than pity, had driven Morgen to aid her.

When they had finished dressing in their wet raiment, Wulfgar brought the two women a cup of fresh water and one of ale, a single bowl of dried meat and fruit, and a thick slice of hard bread for them to share. As she and Morgen sat down to eat, Rhowenna observed to her relief that the other women had also been untied, permitted to wash, and were now being fed. At least their captors did not intend to starve them, she recognized, although none of the women, including herself, was especially hungry and some were plainly having difficulty keeping the food down. The *Víkingrs,* however, ate with gusto, seemingly unperturbed by the flies or by the stench of the corpses in the cargo space, and consumed large quantities of wine and ale, besides, talking and laughing all the while— although Rhowenna, who understood snatches of the conversation because of the similarity of the Northmen's language to that of the Saxons, felt that despite their apparent congeniality, there was among the men a certain wariness and tension that had not been present earlier, when their battle fever and bloodlust had still been upon them.

Now that the sun had set and twilight was seeping into darkness, the whale-oil lamps on board the *Dragon's Fire* had been lighted; by their soft glow, she could see Wulfgar's face, his guarded eyes, the muscle that throbbed in his set jaw. When he spoke, his voice was low but strong and sharp; and although he did not glance in her direction, the other men did, their eyes hard, sly, speculative, openly appraising, their voices heated, so she knew that they and Wulfgar were discussing her—or, more likely, Morgen, whom they must believe was the princess of Usk, if Wulfgar had kept his word. Remembering his warning earlier that he might be forced to fight for command of the longship, Rhowenna shivered, apprehensive that such a duel might be imminent. But at long last, it seemed that some sort of agreement was reached; for despite a few muttered curses, no weapons were drawn, no blows were exchanged. The *Víkingrs* finished their supper;

then all of them, including Wulfgar, drew lots for the women, all of whom, save for Rhowenna and Morgen, were then dragged away to the men's sleeping pelts now unrolled upon the deck. Rhowenna's heart leaped to her throat as she watched Wulfgar spread a huge wolfskin in the stern, then motion her and Morgen toward it; for she did not know what he intended, and from its dregs, her mind conjured shadowy images of rape and even worse perversions about which she had overheard whispered tales. But after binding their hands and feet again, Wulfgar said only:

"The gods are often capricious; but tonight, thanks be to Odinn, they decided to be generous, so I did not have to fight for you, lady. My straw was the shortest—and so my choice was the first. I chose you, lady, so you have naught now to fear. I will not force myself upon you. Lie down and go to sleep. 'Tis not confrontation, but rutting the men have upon their minds this night, so I do not think that any attempt to challenge me will occur before morning."

Then he did no more than to settle himself like a guard dog beside them, so they were between him and the sternpost. Still, he unsheathed his battle-ax and placed it close at hand; and Rhowenna knew from the tautness of his body next to hers that he was not so untroubled about the possibility of a nighttime attack as he would have her believe.

Although she was numb and cold in her sodden clothes, and exhausted, sleep did not come easily to her. She lay awake for hours, it seemed, unable to shut her ears to the dreadful, unnerving sounds of the *Víkingrs* forcing themselves upon the pitifully moaning and weeping women, or to the agitating drone of the flies belowdeck, a constant, hideous reminder of the hold's contents, although the offensive smell had dulled, carried away by the wind, or else her nostrils, unable to evade it, had grown used to the odor. Even the soothing lap of the waves against the longship was a painful reminder of how far from home she was. As she thought of her father and mother, hot tears scalded her cheeks. Did her parents miss her? she wondered. Did they cry for her tonight? Surely, they did, for she was certain of their love. And what of Gwydion? Had he escaped the carnage at Usk? Did he even now lie in the darkness thinking of her and wishing he had begged her to run away with him when he had learned of her betrothal?

Until this moment, she had never in her life slept beside a man, and this, too, kept slumber at bay. Although her initial, wild fear that Wulfgar intended to rape her and Morgen both had dissipated, Rhowenna nevertheless remained all too aware of his big body beside her own smaller one, of the subtle scents of sun and sweat and sandalwood that emanated from his flesh. She lay very still, trying hard not to touch him. But their quarters were cramped, and Morgen, on the other side of her, slept restlessly, so that now and then, Rhowenna was compelled to brush against him. He was warm, much warmer than she, as though a fire burned within him; and at last, gradually, that warmth seeped into her bones, and it and the gentle rocking of the longship lulled her into slumber. Her breathing grew soft and rhythmic; and at the sound, Wulfgar felt some of the tension drain finally from his body.

He had not realized that lying next to Rhowenna would affect him so strongly. He had had his fair share of women over the years. But he had spoken truly when he had told her that he had never before known one like her, with hair as black as a midnight sky, and eyes the color of violets. Her skin was softer and whiter than mist; her dusky cheeks were like rose petals; her mouth was as scarlet and moist as a sail kissed by spindrift. From her silken tresses and pearlescent flesh wafted the sweet fragrance of the heather that bloomed upon the sweeping hillsides of the Northland and that apparently grew also in Walas. There would be that, then, in his homeland to remind her of her own, so perhaps she would not feel so miserable and lost there as she obviously felt now upon the *Dragon's Fire*. No wonder Prince Cerdic of Mercia had wanted her. What man would not? Her beauty was the tale of bard song. Lucky would be the man who claimed her purity and heart, and who, in return, wakened her to passion and love. But neither Ragnar Lodbrók nor Ivar the Boneless would show her such caring and tenderness, Wulfgar knew, and his heart went cold and sick with dread at the thought. They would not have her, he vowed silently, fiercely. They would not despoil her and then make of her a slave and a whore if, afterward, her betrothed and her father refused to pay the ransom demanded for her return.

Yelkei, Wulfgar thought, *you were wiser than I knew when you bid me beat Ivar to the prize. Surely, Rhowenna, princess of Usk, is a maiden fashioned by the gods or from a man's dreams—and when has Ivar ever had a care for either? Sooner will I wander the Shore of Corpses to the barred gates of Hel than will I see her lie in his brutal arms, I swear it!*

Toward dawn, he slept at last, lightly, one hand on his battle-ax, the other wrapped tentatively in Rhowenna's long, unbound hair.

Rhowenna awoke bewildered, not knowing at first where she was, only that she could not move for the bodies pressed close against her and for her own hands and feet, bound fast. Then, in a rush, yesterday came flooding back to her, and she remembered she was aboard the *Dragon's Fire*, lying upon Wulfgar's wolfskin between him and Morgen. Morgen was turned with her back to Rhowenna, but Wulfgar was facing her, his battle-ax between them, one hand tangled in her hair, the other around her slender waist, his face so close to her own that she could see the rough blond stubble of his beard, she could feel his warm breath upon her skin. Somehow, he looked younger asleep and, in the pale dawn light, not so hard and fierce as he had seemed before, when she had first beheld him on the shores of Usk, at the vanguard of the *Víkingrs*.

There was an intimacy, however unconscious, in the way he touched her, held her, which unsettled her; and her breath quickened, her heart beat fast when his eyes slowly opened and he did not at once release her, but lay there staring at her, in his gaze a hunger that he did not trouble to disguise and that, despite herself, sent a strange, disturbing shiver through her body. Rhowenna had never before slept beside a man, nor had she ever awakened beside a man—and, moreover, known that he desired her at that moment. It was, to her confusion, not a wholly unpleasant experience; she did not understand why she should feel so in the arms of her enemy. She wished he would let her go. But when he did, slowly and reluctantly, it seemed, a peculiar pang shot through her, as though, somehow, there should have been something more; and she found she could no longer go on meeting his eyes. He had been kind to her when he might have been cruel, she told herself; that was all. She must not forget that he was her foe.

"Good morning, lady," Wulfgar said as he untied her, his voice low, his hands seeming to linger over the task. "I hope that you are rested, although your bed was no doubt not what you are used to. If you will look after your serving woman, I will fetch you something to eat and water for washing."

"I . . . thank you for your consideration," Rhowenna replied gravely, still not sure she could trust him, still marveling at his behavior toward her, when she had thought him a barbarian and a heathen, and still half expected rape or some other brutality at his hands. "I slept as . . . well as might be expected under the circumstances."

She loosed Morgen's bonds, then got slowly to her feet, her muscles aching even worse this morning, after the night spent upon the hard deck, than they had yesterday. In her life, Rhowenna had known pain and sadness and loss; but until now, she had never truly known hardship, she realized. She had been loved, sheltered, and pampered—princess of Usk. Now her world had been suddenly and savagely turned upside down, and she had become a captive and a slave. Was it any wonder, then, she asked herself, that she should be drawn, however unwillingly, to the one man who had treated her courteously, as befitted her breeding and rank, and who had offered her protection and assistance? Her mother would have counseled her to use Wulfgar's kindness and desire for her to her advantage, to gain from him as much information as she could about the Northland, its people, and its customs—because knowledge was power. The more she knew about her enemies, the more likely it was that she would survive her ordeal among them, would perhaps even manage to escape. The *Dragon's Fire* was not going to remain at sea forever; and while she could not hope to sail such a large vessel alone, she and Morgen together could handle a small boat the size of a coracle, if need be. She should have thought of all this before, Rhowenna told herself, angry at her dulled wits and resolving to do better. She was princess of Usk; she ought to have been acting as such, seeing to the welfare of the other women, giving them hope and reassurance instead of cowering in the stern, worrying about her own uncertain fate.

Wulfgar returned with a single bowl containing more of the dried meat and fruit and a slice of the hard bread; he gave the two women a cup of ale and one of fresh water to share as well. He also brought them a pail of seawater with which to perform their limited toilette. Clearly, his own ablutions were finished, for he had once again stripped off his leather tunic, and his hair and bare arms and chest were dripping water. But he carried a bowl of food for himself, and he hunkered down beside Rhowenna to eat, talking to her quietly during the meal.

"Lady, I will try to take the tiller again this morning. But I do not think that Knut Strongarm will easily relinquish it;

for he was Olaf the Sea Bull's second-in-command aboard this vessel and so no doubt believes that its captaincy by right belongs to him now. If that is the case, I shall be forced to fight him. If I am killed, do not forget what I told you about making your true identity known at once. It may serve to protect you from Knut and the rest of these men—although not from Ragnar Lodbrók and Ivar the Boneless. So if 'tis the will of the gods that I perish this day and the time should come when you must choose between father and son, be wise and heed my advice: Cast your lot with the old wolf instead of the cub, for Ivar is cleverer and crueler than Ragnar and more like to hurt you in ways of which I shall not speak, as you are a maiden and a lady. Do you understand?''

"Aye," Rhowenna whispered, trembling, all her earlier bravery and resolve seeping from her bones at his words, leaving her weak and cold despite the warmth of the sun that had crept up over the eastern horizon, dyeing the grey fabric of the morning sky in rich shades of rose and gold and aquamarine.

In the distance, a flock of swans soared, northward bound, their long necks outstretched, their white wings spread wide, their strange, wild, forlorn cries echoing on the wind, a song as plaintive as what she now heard in her mind plucked on the strings of her heart. When, at last, Wulfgar laid aside his bowl and slowly stood, of its own volition, her hand reached out to draw him back, then instead fell back lamely at her side. His impassive bronze visage was set, determined. She knew instinctively that it would prove futile to plead with him not to embark upon a course of action that might result in his death. She was nothing to him, nor he to her. Still, somehow, Rhowenna could not refrain from saying, very low:

"Have a care, Wulfgar Bloodaxe."

Have a care, Wulfgar. The words rang eerily in his mind, sending a chill up his spine. He could hear Yelkei saying them a lifetime ago, it seemed, that morning of the roe-deer hunt, when he had slain his brother spirit, the wolf, to save Ivar's life and, in so doing, had won the chance to fulfill his own lifelong dream of becoming a *Víkingr*. That Rhowenna should speak those same words to him now seemed an omen, but whether good or ill, Wulfgar did not know. He stretched out one hand to her, the brush of his fingers against her skin like the kiss of the wind as he touched her cheek gently, then turned away.

"I will take the tiller now, Knut," he said, calmly enough, although his every muscle felt drawn as tight as a thong inside him, his every nerve raw; for he sensed that here and now, he would either win the chance to seize Olaf's markland for himself or lose his life—and while he was not afraid for himself, Rhowenna's pale face haunted him.

"Oh, you will, will you?" Knut snarled, in a voice both challenging and overloud, so a sudden silence fell upon the longship, and the air became thick with tension and avid anticipation. "By whose authority? *I* was Olaf's second-in-command, while you were naught but an oarsman, Wulfgar Bloodaxe!"

"Strange that you did not remark upon that yesterday, when I stood in the stern as steersman, because Olaf was dead—and you were too drunk on wine and ale and bloodlust to remember your duty to the *Dragon's Fire* and to her captain and crew!"

"A valid point, Wulfgar Bloodaxe," spoke another man, Flóki the Raven, Wulfgar observed from the corners of his eyes, a warrior bolder and more honorable than most of Olaf's *thegns*. "How do you answer it, Knut Strongarm?"

"With the point of my blade in this upstart bastard's throat—and that of any other man foolish enough to think he can best me!"

"So be it, then," Wulfgar growled, drawing his battle-ax from its leather scabbard at his back and taking up his shield, "for I'll not sail under a fat-bellied old tosspot who cannot keep his wits about him and his shaft in his breeches when the battle's done and the sail's in need of hoisting!''

Knut Strongarm was so named for the strength of his sword arm, with which he had slain many a foe; and although he had twenty years on Wulfgar, he had not lived so long by being unable to defeat a younger opponent. He was not so tall as Wulfgar, but heavier, thick-necked, and resembling a walrus—slow and ponderous, but dangerous when attacked. His left eye was drawn down by a disfiguring scar from the slash of an adversary's scramasax during some raid years ago, and scars left by other wounds from other battles were revealed when he tugged off his leather tunic. After deliberately flexing his powerful muscles to demonstrate his strength, he pulled his broadsword from its sheath and picked up his own shield. Rhowenna thought she had never seen anyone so fearsome-looking; surely, Wulfgar could not hope to prevail against such a man. Her heart went cold and sick with fear at the thought.

The other *Víkingrs* were scrambling about the longship, furling the sail, clearing a space on the deck for the duel and tossing the heavy iron anchor overboard from the bow to hold the vessel in place until the matter of its captaincy was decided. Shouts flew back and forth across the sea to the other two longships, and those vessels, too, lowered sail and, drawing alongside the *Dragon's Fire*, dropped anchor, their crews lining up to watch the combat. When all was in readiness, Wulfgar and Knut began to circle each other warily, testing nerves, evaluating skill. Then, with a sudden, jolting clash of weapons that made Rhowenna flinch and gasp, the fierce battle was joined.

It was not, for Wulfgar, a fight of thrust and parry, for the battle-ax he wielded precluded that; but as a result, it also spoiled much of Knut's swordsman's technique, as well, compelling him to engage in a like hacking and slashing attack, during which his lumbering gait left him more vulnera-

ble than he would have been against an opponent armed with
a broadsword. Still, his strength coupled with his weight was
such that he drove Wulfgar back short moments after the duel
had begun. Wulfgar recognized immediately that brute force
alone would not win for him, that his best strategy would lie
in wearing Knut down by prolonging the battle. Wulfgar
concentrated on defending himself and on conserving his own
strength, relying on his greater quickness and agility to elude
whatever blows he could, his shield to hold firm against those
he could not. Still, each mighty *thwack* Knut landed with his
blade sent a bone-jarring tremor up Wulfgar's shield arm,
making him grit his teeth to keep from crying out and bringing
a malevolent grin to Knut's ugly face as he pressed his assault.

There was much to be learned about a man from a duel;
and as Rhowenna watched, she discerned Wulfgar's cunning
and proficiency against an opponent who, while stronger, was
less clever and adept, having for so long triumphed through
his brawn that he had grown smug and secure in thinking he
needed nothing more. But as the sun crept higher into the
sky, the conflict wore on, and as time and time again he failed
to penetrate Wulfgar's guard, Knut's smile gradually faded
to be replaced with a dark scowl of murderous rage, and his
onslaught grew increasingly violent and reckless. His fury
reminded Rhowenna of an afternoon in the bailey of her
father's palisade, when she had watched Brynmawr training
several young men who had been sent to Pendragon's court
for fostering. One of them, finding victory elusive, had lost
his temper in just such a manner, so Brynmawr had disarmed
him and struck him hard with the flat of a blade, knocking
him on his back before pressing the honed point to the young
man's throat.

"Never let anger get the best of you in a fight, lad!"
Brynmawr had chided sharply. "'Twill cause you to grow
rash—and that is a mistake that will cost you your life!"

Anger now seemed to possess Knut Strongarm, Rhowenna

observed, and perhaps, as a result, he might indeed make some fatal error. Wulfgar's eyes, although narrowed, did not blaze with wrath, but with calculation and exhilaration. He moved like a magnificent mountain cat, she thought, his tawny mane of hair streaming from his face in the wind, his hard, supple body crouching and whirling, his sealskin-booted feet dancing and springing lithely across the deck, the muscles in his naked, sweat-sheened arms, chest, and back quivering and rippling, filling her, as she watched him, with some peculiar sensation she had never felt before, a roaring of her blood in her ears, a fierce pounding of her heart.

Both combatants were covered with blood from minor wounds inflicted; the broadsword and battle-ax that earlier had gleamed in the rising sun now were dulled with red; the wooden shields were cracked and broken from forceful blows and now impatiently tossed aside as hindrances. Rhowenna feared greatly for Wulfgar then, for surely Knut's broadsword was the superior weapon, quicker, more flexible, less unwieldy. But then, she had never before seen a battle-ax wielded as, now, since casting away his shield, Wulfgar suddenly began to employ his as though it were not only a battle-ax, but also a staff. Deftly he twirled it through his fingers, holding its long haft raised and lengthwise to block Knut's increasingly slower, wilder downward swings; abruptly, Wulfgar reversed it and jammed the end of its leather-wrapped grip into Knut's stomach, doubling him over.

Knut's breath came in hard rasps now—through his mouth. Elation rose within Wulfgar at the sight, for a man who breathed so was not getting enough air into his lungs and was exhausted, too, ripe for defeat. Now Wulfgar began to press his own attack furiously, permitting Knut to become aware that he had only been toyed with before as a deliberate ploy to tire him. At the realization, Knut became even more infuriated, his blows more brazen, those of a man desperate, sensing he was but minutes from death. Eyes glowing with bloodlust, the *Víkingrs* were on their feet, cheering and yelling grisly, bloodthirsty exhortations. The women cringed on the deck, forgotten for the moment by their captors. Only Rhowenna stood upright, her eyes wide and dark, her face pale, her hands clenched so tightly at her sides that her knuckles shone white, her nails dug into her palms. In moments, not only Wulfgar's fate, but perhaps also her own would be determined. She would not meet her destiny cowering, but as bravely as Wulfgar had dared to seek it out, knowing what it might mean to them both.

Broadsword and battle-ax sang, a song of death, savage and discordant, punctuated by sharp rings and whacks as iron-hooped barrels and the Y-shaped trestles that rose from the deck and, once, even the mast were struck by the blades, sending wooden shards sailing. The planks were slick and scarlet with the blood that had trickled from the combatants' wounds. Now Knut lunged forward, sliding in the blood, his broadsword thrusting to stab viciously into Wulfgar's belly, only to be knocked aside at the last instant, struck hard by the blade of Wulfgar's battle-ax. Metal scraped upon metal, colliding in such a way that the hilt of Knut's broadsword was caught and jerked from his grasp, his weapon sent flying upward in a silvery arc that flashed in the sun against the blue of the sky before the blade swooped like a falcon to plunge into the sea. Wulfgar sidestepped and pivoted with a macabre gracefulness, the haft of his battle-ax hitting Knut in the back, driving him to his knees. Then Wulfgar caught the leather-wrapped grip, and the blade swung high, up and around, glittering, poised in the air for a moment before descending to bury itself in Knut's nape, decapitating him. Rhowenna cried out, horrified, as, seeming to move in slow motion, Knut's head flew from his torso to bounce upon and then to roll across the deck, and blood spurted and spewed from his neck, spraying Wulfgar's handsome face and broad chest. For an eternity, it seemed, Knut's body remained kneeling on the planks before gradually crumpling to sprawl upon the deck.

Breathing hard, Wulfgar stood there in the sudden silence, battle-ax in his blood-covered hands, and looking, Rhowenna thought, involuntarily shrinking from him, like some wild, savage predator as his eyes, burning with triumph, found hers. As he watched her cringe from him, his gaze hardened, growing distant and wintry, and a muscle pulsed in his set jaw, so that she knew she had angered him by recoiling from him instead of exulting in his victory. For all his previous kindness and gentleness toward her, she now knew he could be as brutal and deadly as the rest of the *Víkingrs*, a dangerous man to cross; and she shuddered and cast down her eyes, afraid that in his rage, he would strike her, or, worse, would suddenly seize her and rape her as was a man's wont toward a woman when he was filled with bloodlust. Perhaps he would even withdraw his protection of her.

But instead, he turned, and his voice rang out harshly, authoritatively, in the stillness.

"Is there another man among you who would seek to challenge my captaincy of this vessel? If so, let him come forward now and make his claim—or else hold his peace until this voyage is done!"

There was an interminable moment of tension and silence broken only by the soughing of the wind, the lapping of the waves against the hulls of the longships, the faraway cries of the flock of swans winging their way northward. Then, at last, when no one stepped forward to continue the battle Knut Strongarm had begun, the strained atmosphere slowly eased, and Wulfgar felt some of the tautness drain from his muscles.

"Then, henceforth, let no man aboard the *Dragon's Fire* defy my commands," he said, "and the first of those is this: There is the princess of Usk"—he pointed to Morgen—"she for whom we sailed from the Northland to Walas and for whom our lord, Olaf the Sea Bull, lies dead, slain in the battle with the Usk men. She is the only daughter of a king and betrothed to a prince, and while her dowry is lost to us, she herself is still a valuable hostage, worth her weight in gold— but only if she is unharmed and a virgin. Last night, there were among you those who would have cost us that ransom by slaking your lust upon her had not cooler heads prevailed. Now, I tell you that no man is to touch her, that he who is foolish enough to disobey this order will die, and that his corpse will not journey to the Northland for burial, but will be cast overboard to feed the fish.'' Wulfgar paused, allowing this warning to penetrate. Then he continued.

"This woman, the princess's waiting woman"—without warning, he reached out, taking Rhowenna unaware as he grabbed her by the wrist and possessively jerked her to him— "I claim as my own—and mine alone! Likewise will I slay the man who dares to lay a hand on her!''

At that, the silence of the *Víkingrs* was finally ended as first one and then another and yet another called out slyly— coarse jests and gibes that roused a great howl of laughter from the rest of the men and that, after a moment, caused a slow, deliberately wolfish smile to curve Wulfgar's carnal lips as he stared down at Rhowenna, his eyes dark, unfathomable. Before she realized what he intended, he ensnared one hand in her tresses and roughly yanked her head back. Startled, filled with sudden apprehension, she cried out softly, a small sound he smothered with savage triumph as, with a low snarl, he abruptly crushed his mouth down on hers—hard, hungrily, shattering her senses and taking her breath away.

No man had ever in her life dared to make so free with her, to kiss her so; and so Rhowenna had not known, had never in her wildest imaginings dreamed that a man would or could kiss her as Wulfgar did, as though he were draining the very life and soul from her body and then pouring it back in. She was totally unprepared for the shock and invasion of his kiss, for the hitherto unknown sensations he expertly wakened within her, frightening her and yet somehow perversely exciting her, as well, making her feel as though she would faint as his insistent tongue brazenly forced her resisting lips to yield and boldly insinuated itself inside, exultantly plundering the moist sweetness within, leaving no part unexplored, unravaged. Sparks of light, like the bursting of a falling star, exploded behind her eyelids, and her blood rushed to roar in her ears as a wild, unexpected thrill shot through her at his remorseless assault, dizzying her so, that years afterward, she was never to remember clearly that moment aboard the *Dragon's Fire* when Wulfgar claimed and kissed her as his. Instead, she was to see it only as though through a glass darkly, like the *mørketiden*, the murky time of the Northland she was to come to know. She had dreamed of this man; and now, he held her in his arms—no longer a dream, but vividly real, devouring her with his mouth. She felt as though the deck had suddenly canted beneath her, making her knees buckle, so she would have fallen had he not clasped her so tightly, bending her back, inexorably molding her body against his own, making her intensely aware of him as a man—and one who wanted her.

Scared, dazed by the magnitude of his desire, by his determined onslaught upon her senses, Rhowenna began belatedly to struggle against him, pummeling his naked, bloody chest, trying desperately to free herself from his imprisoning embrace, to no avail. Wulfgar was far stronger than she; if she had not known that before, she knew it now. She was frail, helpless against him, like a reed before the wind. He could do whatever he liked with her, *to* her, and she would be powerless to prevent him.

"Stop fighting me, vixen!" he muttered hotly against her lips, his hand tightening painfully in her hair to compel her to comply with his demand. "You will cause all I have gained to be lost, making me vulnerable, a laughingstock! Do you want these *Víkingrs* to think that while I can slay a man in battle, I cannot defeat a mere slip of a wench?''

In some dim corner of her mind, Rhowenna glimpsed an inkling of his purpose then. But before she could respond, his mouth closed over hers again, swallowing her breath until her hands ceased slowly to beat against his chest, creeping up of their own accord to twine about his neck, and a low, unwitting moan of understanding and acquiescence issued from her throat. A ribald bellow of approval rose from the men; and at that, at last, Wulfgar released her.

For a timeless moment, he stared down at her, taking in the dishevelment of the long black tresses that tumbled, witchlike and beguiling, about her piquant face; her wide, startled, sloe eyes, drugged with passion, fear, and confusion; the dark, crescent smudges her thick, sooty lashes cast against her pale cheeks when she closed her eyes against his piercing scrutiny; her finely chiseled nose, its nostrils flaring slightly, like those of an alarmed animal poised for flight; her tremulously parted lips, as lush and crimson as a full-blown rose, bruised and swollen from his unbridled kiss; the small pulse that beat jerkily at the hollow of her throat; the swell of her ripe, melon breasts beneath her bodice, rising and falling quickly, shallowly, straining enticingly against the coarse material.

She was his for the taking.

Wulfgar's loins quickened sharply at the knowledge. But then he saw how Rhowenna's hand shook as she suddenly scrubbed fiercely at her mouth, how she flushed scarlet with outrage and embarrassment at the taunts and laughter of the men; and he felt an abrupt sense of shame and anger. He was no better than any other *Víkingr*, he thought, disgusted, no better than Ragnar, no better than Ivar. Still, if he had not responded as he had to the jesting of the men, they might have wondered at his manhood; they might have doubted his ability to captain the *Dragon's Fire*; they could so easily turn on him at any time. And for her own safety and well-being, Rhowenna must learn to behave like a slave, a woman who belonged to him—and not a proud princess.

"Haul up the anchor! Hoist the sail!" Wulfgar barked abruptly, slinging over his shoulder the looped thong of his battle-ax's grip, so the weapon hung at his side. "We are wasting time here. Flóki the Raven, take the tiller, while I tend these wounds of mine. You will be my second-in-command. Some of the rest of you men get Knut Strongarm's body stowed in the hold." Then, turning back to Rhowenna but still speaking his own Northland tongue, he demanded imperiously, "Wench, fetch that bucket of seawater over here!" using gestures to punctuate his words so she would understand what he said.

For a moment, Rhowenna stood there stupidly, not quite certain he was speaking to her, such was the disrespect in his tone and the way in which he addressed her. But then, thinking of how he had killed Knut Strongarm before her very eyes and, afterward, had kissed her so savagely, she grew frightened by the fury that flared in his eyes when she did not respond, and she moved hurriedly to do as he had bidden, picking up the heavy wooden pail of seawater she and Morgen had used earlier for washing and, with difficulty, lugging it over to where Wulfgar stood impatiently.

"The next time I tell you to do something, wench, you had best not keep me waiting!" he snapped, still speaking in his own language and in a voice overloud, to be certain he was heard by the *Víkingrs*. "You are my slave, and if you are not quick to obey my orders, I will beat you. Do you understand?" At Rhowenna's mute, scared nod—for if she had not fully comprehended his words, she had caught their gist—he bent without warning and roughly tore away a strip of material from her tattered skirts. "You will cleanse my wounds," he said, handing her the cloth and then settling himself upon a stout, iron-ringed barrel, from where he eyed her expectantly.

"Have you—have you soap?" she inquired hesitantly, in the Saxon tongue, as she nervously dipped the cloth into the seawater, then wrung it out.

"Nay." Wulfgar spoke quietly now and in the same language. "But the salt will serve to stave off putrefaction, if that is your concern."

"Why should it be?" she dared to ask, her voice low and tremulous with emotion. "When you have this day proved you are no better than the rest of the brutes aboard this godforsaken vessel! I care not if you live or die!"

"If I should die, the day will come when you *will* care, lady!" Wulfgar rejoined heatedly to hide how she had hurt him with her words. "You will care very much, I am thinking, when you find yourself at the mercy of Ragnar Lodbrók and Ivar the Boneless—who will take more than a kiss from your lovely lips, and take it brutally, without care for your pain or shame—" He broke off abruptly, gasping, as, without warning, Rhowenna pressed the wet cloth to his chest and began to rub the seawater deeply into his injuries, so the salt stung and burned him unmercifully. His hand shot out, closing like an iron band about her wrist. "Lady, you did that apurpose!"

"You *did* order me to cleanse your wounds, did you not . . . my lord"—a falsely brave note of sarcasm crept into her tone as she addressed him thus—"and declared that as your slave, I must be quick to obey, else you would beat me?"

"Words spoken for the benefit of the *Víkingrs*"—Wulfgar scowled at her darkly—"as I thought that you would prove wise enough to understand, your having so far given me no cause to believe that you lack wits. Well do I know that you are not accustomed to such rough treatment as I have this day dealt you, lady. But if I am to protect you, 'twas necessary that I claim you as mine before the men; and for your own sake, they must believe you to be my slave, in truth—lest they learn that you are the true princess of Usk and reveal that knowledge to Ragnar Lodbrók or Ivar the Boneless. Do you understand, lady? I have this morn slain Knut Strongarm and so won the captaincy of this vessel, aye. Still, I would be a fool to think that what I have gained is by any means secure when 'tis not. 'Twould take only the suspicion that I have lied to them and deceived them to turn these men once more against me—and against you, as well. That is why the kiss I forced upon you was also necessary—although, in all honesty, I do not regret taking it, even so.''

Wulfgar's eyes burned again as they had before he had kissed her, like twin flames, blue heat that scalded Rhowenna as his kiss had scalded her. She did not understand why he should make her feel as she did: confused, conflicted, and as breathless as though she had run a long way. Her cheeks blushed crimson with indignation, humiliation, and some other emotion she could not name as she remembered the feel of his mouth upon hers, his tongue invading her, in a way she had not known that a man would dare. Her hands faltered over the washing of his wounds, trembled against his chest.

"You are not chivalrous, but crude—a beast!—to say such a thing to me," she whispered, her eyes downcast, unable to meet his own.

"Lady, I would be even more dishonorable and brutish if I lied to you—and that, I will not do. I am a man, aye, with a man's wants and needs, and you are a beautiful and desirable woman. Still, 'tis as I have told you: I will not harm you, so you need have no fear of me. I will have you willing in my arms, or not at all. The gods, in their wisdom, did not fashion you for less than that."

"How do I know that you speak the truth, that you do not seek to deceive me in some terrible manner?"

"I swear it, by the gods."

"You are a heathen, and so your oath means nothing. Your gods are false idols, so the priests say. There is only the Christ, who is the one true God." She touched the gold Celtic crucifix that she always wore about her neck and that had not yet been taken from her by the *Víkingrs*. "Will you—will you swear by Him?"

"Nay, I am no Christian, lady, but a *Víkingr* and so Odinn's warrior. When I die in battle, as every *Víkingr* longs to die, 'tis one of the Einheriar that I will become, and so be borne by the Valkyries to Valhöll, Odinn's great mead Hall of the Slain, in Asgard. If I am chosen as worthy of that honor. I will not be taken up unto your Heaven, by your God, about whom I know nothing, save that He was no mighty warrior and so cannot know the souls of such men."

"The priests say that He does, that He is all-knowing and all-powerful."

"Mayhap. Still, I do not fear the Christian God as some Northmen do, but only the gods of Asgard, and the giant Loki, who is wickedness. They are ancient—older than your Christ, lady, older than this earth, elemental and eternal, like the wind and the sea that carry us up the Swan Road to the Northland. Do you not sense the gods, lady? Do you not feel them—those guardians of fate, of destiny?"

A chill shivered up Rhowenna's spine at Wulfgar's words, making the fine hairs on her nape rise; for, in her dream, had not the old gods warned her of her fate, her destiny? Had she not sensed them, felt them all her life, and known that they existed, no matter what the priests said? Such beliefs were heresy, sinful; she knew she should confess them. But there would be no Christian priest in the heathen Northland; there would be nothing there of the life she had known in Usk, of the world she had left behind when this bold *Víkingr* had swept her up in his arms and carried her aboard the longship that now sailed so swiftly northward toward the cold, wintry lands of the midnight sun.

"Nay, I do not," she replied at last to Wulfgar's question. "The old gods are dead."

"I do not believe that, lady—nor, in your heart, do you, I am thinking."

Rhowenna did not answer him, but concentrated instead on the cleansing of his wounds, rubbing more lightly than before, so the salt of the seawater would not hurt him so badly, although she knew that it must give him pain, even so. Still, after that initial outburst, he bore her ministrations stoically; and in the silence, she became aware of the feel of his flesh beneath her palms, of the massive muscles that corded his arms and layered his chest and belly. She had never before known a man so big and so tall; she felt small and fragile in comparison, and she was not sure she liked the feeling. All her life, as princess of Usk, Rhowenna had wielded power. Now she did not. More than just physically, this man was more powerful than she—and the only thing standing between her and the rest of the *Víkingrs*. When, finally, she was done washing away the blood that encrusted his skin, she dropped the cloth into the bucket of seawater and spoke.

"Have you a healing salve for these injuries?"

"Aye." He pointed to his sea chest, which, having been moved by some of the men, now sat in the stern. "In there."

Rhowenna turned and, kneeling, slowly lifted the lid of his sea chest, feeling a sudden awkwardness as she did so, an unwelcome sense of prying and yet also of intimacy as she fumbled through his belongings, searching for the healing salve. His sea chest was nearly empty, containing little more than a change of clothes and a purse that, by the look and feel of it, held no more than a few coins at most. Wulfgar was not a rich man, she judged, only a bold one, a warrior bent on seizing what he could so that he might rise in rank and power—as he had seized her and the *Dragon's Fire*, and would no doubt take the markland of his lord, Olaf the Sea

Bull. Perhaps Morgen was right, and Wulfgar had offered her, Rhowenna, his protection and assistance because he sought her ransom for himself alone. She could not deny the possibility. Still, she must admit that so far he had kept her safe, as he had promised; so what did it matter if he was motivated to do so by greed instead of kindness?

Taking up the small clay jar of healing salve, she uncorked it and sniffed it tentatively, recognizing the scents of various herbs with medicinal properties. Satisfied that the jar contained nothing harmful—with which she might be accused of poisoning Wulfgar—Rhowenna dipped her fingers into the healing salve and began to spread it on his injuries.

"The wounds are not serious and will not require bandaging," she observed when she was finished. Replacing the cork in the jar, she returned the healing salve to his sea chest and closed the lid. "They need only to be kept clean to avoid infection."

"You are wise as well as beautiful. I thank you, lady."

"Then . . . grant me a small boon as a token of your gratitude, Wulfgar Bloodaxe," Rhowenna dared to entreat; for although he had claimed her as his slave, she knew that she could never accept that role willingly, that she must not permit herself to forget that she was the princess of Usk.

"What is it?" he asked, his eyes narrowed, so that she understood that he was not so bewitched by her beauty that he would allow her to make a fool of him. She was glad then that she had not demeaned herself by trying.

"Only this: that I and the other women no longer be kept bound hand and foot. Your men are many, and my women are few in comparison, and this vessel, this . . . *Dragon's Fire*, is many leagues out to sea, besides. There is no hope of our overpowering or escaping from you. Surely, then, we may be permitted some freedom of movement so we can more properly bathe and tend our own wounds?" Wisely, she asked for no more than this, knowing that to demand that the women be returned to Usk, or at least left alone at night, would prove fruitless.

"It sounds like a reasonable enough request," Wulfgar agreed at last, after a long moment of consideration. "Very well. I will allow you and the rest of the women to remain unbound. But mark my words, lady: The first time that there is trouble or that one of your women decides to throw herself overboard, there will be an end to it. You will—all of you— be restrained again. Do you understand?"

"Aye."

"Make sure the other women do, as well."

"I will. Th-thank you . . . my lord." Because Rhowenna was proud, two spots of color stained her high cheekbones as she forced herself not only to voice her appreciation, but also to call him by the title with which she had addressed him so scornfully before, knowing that he was but a warrior and not deserving of the honorific, save from a wife—or a slave.

"In time, you will grow accustomed to naming me so, lady, I swear it," Wulfgar said softly, an enigmatic half-smile curving his lips—although it did not lighten his eyes, which shone dark with a determination and desire that made her breath catch in her throat and her heart beat too fast in her breast.

"Nay, I will not!" she insisted fiercely.

"You are very sure of that, lady—now, at this moment. But this, I tell you: The day will come when you are not so certain; for the gods are mercurial, as those who tempt them inevitably learn, and no mere mortal can change what is written in the stars. We are, all of us, powerless against our fate, our destiny—even princesses, lady . . . even you."

Rhowenna did not answer, but thought of her dream—and knew in her heart the truth of Wulfgar's words.

Chapter Eight

Sliesthorp

In his time, Wulfgar had held the tiller of many a small boat, but never before this voyage that of a mighty longship; and he knew a joy such as he had rarely experienced in his life as, in response to the movement of his hands, he felt the *Dragon's Fire* rise and plunge on the glimmering waves of the sea, her graceful, towering dragon's neck outstretched like that of a swan, her crimson sail spread wide like wings to catch the wind. The sea was calm, the winds were favorable, and the three vessels sailed swiftly northward along the coast of Normandy, past the thriving marketplace of Quentowic, which lay directly across from the Straits of Dover, and thence along the coast toward Frisia and Jutland. Before last year, the *Víkingrs* would have put in at the largest marketplace in all of northern Europe, the Frisian town of Dorestad, located at the junction of the river Lek and an arm of the river Rhine, there to trade some of the captive women and the goods stolen from Usk. But over the years, despite its being protected by water, stout palisades, and gates, and being a Carolingian stronghold, Dorestad—once home to the great Charlemagne's silver mint—had been repeatedly sacked by the Northmen. Then, last year, massive tidal waves had overrun the sand dunes that were the sea's boundaries, sweeping in to flood several low-lying regions of the Frankish and Germanic kingdoms, drowning masses of people and animals, and diverting the course of the river Rhine toward Utrecht instead of Dorestad, effectively destroying the latter's trade and so the town itself, as well. For this reason, Wulfgar made toward the Jutish town and marketplace of Sliesthorp instead.

Although the longships covered the leagues swiftly, they still took several days to reach Jutland, days that Wulfgar put to good use by slowly furthering the ascendancy he had gained over Olaf the Sea Bull's *thegns*, accustoming them to his authority, so that when the time came, they would think it only natural that he assume ownership of Olaf's markland, too, and would not oppose him. With subtle comments dropped here and there, Wulfgar cleverly reminded the men that, although illegitimate, he was the son of the great Ragnar Lodbrók, their king, and of royal blood, regardless of the fact that Ragnar had never formally acknowledged him or his claim to Ragnar's kingdom and throne. Still, no man aboard the *Dragon's Fire* disputed Wulfgar's assertion that Ragnar was his sire, for even without his mustache and beard, Wulfgar's resemblance to Ivar the Boneless was still so marked that none could honestly doubt that the two of them were brothers.

Further, now that he saw the chance of an honest day's hard work's being justly rewarded, Flóki the Raven showed himself more than willing to deliver it, proving an able second-in-command, a staunch supporter of Wulfgar, helping him to whip the crew into shape. There were, of course, those *Víkingrs*—most of them grey-beards who had served Olaf the Sea Bull for years—who grumbled churlishly about the changes Wulfgar instituted. But there were also many more—younger, stronger, more daring men, like Flóki the Raven—who welcomed the fact that Wulfgar was a stern but capable and fair taskmaster, a bold, powerful leader who commanded and earned respect. Here was a man to whom a warrior could be proud to swear allegiance, to go a-*víking* with, and to follow into battle; a man who bore the blood of the mighty Ragnar Lodbrók and so might someday even become a king of the Northland, a man who, should he ever sit upon a throne, would want his own *thegns* as his *jarlar*. Under Wulfgar's captaincy, the *Dragon's Fire* vibrated with a level of activity and excitement she had not known for many a year. Even the other two longships, captained by minor *jarlar* who had sailed with Olaf the Sea Bull, seemed to catch the fervor aboard the *Dragon's Fire*; and as the days passed, no man again sought to challenge Wulfgar.

For that, Rhowenna was grateful; for astutely, she recognized that the stronger Wulfgar's position among the *Víkingrs*, the more secure her own. No man accosted her but, heeding Wulfgar's orders, kept away from her and Morgen both. Only Flóki the Raven spoke to them when necessary, having learned that Rhowenna could understand him, after a fashion. On his huge wolfskin, Wulfgar continued to bed down protectively beside them in the stern at night, with Flóki at the tiller, not only steering the longship, but also standing guard, so Wulfgar slept more deeply—although always with half an ear cocked, even so. In all his life, he had trusted only his mother and Yelkei, the better to ensure his survival and well-being. It was a hard habit to break; and so it was only slowly that he permitted himself to rely on Flóki, a reliance tempered with wry amusement as Wulfgar came gradually to realize that the support of his second-in-command was due in part to the fact that Flóki was enchanted by Morgen. In his spare moments, Flóki was doing his best to teach the "princess" of Usk to speak the language of the Northland,

and it was he who, from his sea chest, produced a chessboard so Morgen and Rhowenna could entertain themselves to help relieve the boredom of their days. Other than their meals and brief wash each morning and evening, there was little for them to do except to sit in the stern and to keep out of the way. To Rhowenna and the rest of the women, who were accustomed to busying themselves with their daily tasks, the tedium was difficult to bear.

Still, she would not be honest with herself, Rhowenna knew, if she did not admit that despite all she must endure, she experienced a certain sense of adventure and excitement during the voyage; for she had never in her life been farther than the boundaries of Usk. Her eyes grew wide at the sight of Quentowic in the distance. Even from afar, she could tell how large a town and marketplace it was. In her father's kingdom, there was no place like it; and for the first time, it dawned on her how small Usk was in the vast scheme of the world. Until now, Usk was the *only* world she had ever known, and she realized what a sheltered, limited world it had been. Wulfgar, observing how she gaped at the Frankish town, smiled secretly to himself. There were some things, it seemed, that could astonish even a princess, he thought, and he took pride in the knowledge that despite his low rank, he was more worldly than she. At least over the years, he had been to the towns and marketplaces of the Northland, most often to Kaupang, the summer marketplace on the western shore of the Oslofjorden, near the Vestfold. Soapstone-crafters, weavers, and metalworkers plied their trades there, and from there, too, eiderdown was shipped to the kingdoms of the Eastlands and the Southlands. But Kaupang was quite small compared to Sliesthorp, which was the largest town and marketplace in the Northland, boasting even a mint. Slaves and imported wares brought good prices there, so the plunder from Usk was bound to fetch coins aplenty for him and the rest of the *Víkingrs* to share between them.

Wulfgar's only real worry as he stood upon the deck of the *Dragon's Fire* was that he would at any moment spy Ivar's mighty longship bearing down upon him—for surely by now, Ivar had set sail from the Northland, heading toward Walas. Wulfgar did not want to be forced into a confrontation with Ivar at sea. He could only hope that from the Northland, Ivar had sailed west to follow the coast of Britain south and west to Walas; for if Ivar had chosen instead to strike south along the shores of Jutland, Frisia, and Normandy, he would shortly be upon them. But to Wulfgar's relief, his luck held; and presently, the *Dragon's Fire* lay at anchor in the river harbor of Hollingstedt, without his having set eyes on Ivar's distinctive red-and-blue-striped sail.

Sliesthorp itself lay on the east coast of Jutland, at the head of the Schlei, a narrow but navigable fjord at the western tip of the Baltic Sea. To reach the town and marketplace from the west, it was necessary, from the North Sea, to sail up the rivers Eider and Trene to put in to the tiny port of Hollingstedt, and thence to travel ten miles by ox-cart to Sliesthorp. For this overland journey, Rhowenna and the other women not only had their hands bound tightly behind their backs once more, but also, to her anger and shame, suffered the additional indignity of having ropes tied around their necks, so they could be led about like animals. In this fashion were they taken to be herded like cattle or sheep into the waiting ox-carts; and as Rhowenna felt the curious and appraising stares of passersby upon her, her cheeks flamed with humiliation, and she unwittingly stumbled against Wulfgar, who held the end of her tether.

"I am sorry. I go too fast for you, lady." He realized suddenly the difficulty she was having, keeping pace with his long stride.

"'Tis not just that, but the fact that you would leash me like a dog! No man has ever dared to treat me so! Nor am I accustomed to being stared at so rudely, so—so—" She broke off abruptly, biting her lower lip hard to hold back the heated words, the ragged sob that threatened to erupt from her throat.

"Although you are my captive and my slave, lady," Wulfgar began, frowning now, "I have shown you far more courtesy and consideration than is wont for a man of my ilk, a warrior and a *Víkingr*. Yet, like a high-spirited filly you still chafe against the bit and your master. You are princess of Usk no longer, lady, and you must learn your place—lest you be the death of us both! Would you have me endanger us both by favoring you to the point where 'tis said of me that I am besotted by you, so other men will think me weak, easy prey, to be ruled by a woman, and Ragnar Lodbrók and Ivar the Boneless will seek to hurt me by wresting you from me and using you ill?"

"Nay, I—I was wroth and embarrassed, and I—I did not think. . . ."

"'Tis good, then, that I did, isn't it?" he observed coolly, so, however unwillingly, she felt chastened, as he had intended. "Lady, you do not know the Northland—and I do. Besides that I would not have it said that I favor you overmuch, Sliesthorp is crowded with traders from all over the world—and many of them are rough, dangerous men; for *Víkingrs* are not the only warriors and pirates to sail the seas. Much as you loathe it, this rope around your neck is as much for your own protection as 'tis to prevent you from running away from me. It marks you as my property and lets other men know that they will have to do battle with me if they would claim you for their own. Now, if you would not be stared at, do you get inside the ox-cart."

His hands strong about her slender waist, Wulfgar lifted Rhowenna up and settled her as comfortably as was possible in the vehicle. Then he instructed the driver to get under way, and with a crack of the driver's whip and a sudden lurch as the previously placid oxen started in response, the ox-cart lumbered forward. The road between Hollingstedt and Slies-thorp was well traveled and maintained, and heavily defended, being girded to the south by the vast system of earthworks known collectively as the Danevirke and which was similar to Offa's Dyke, Rhowenna saw. Flower-filled meadows and reed-grown swamps abounded along the road; and Sliesthorp rose in the distance, protected to the north, west, and south by an extensive, semicircular rampart topped by a stout palisade and bounded on its outer edge by a deep moat. To the east, defense was provided by the shallow waters of the Haddeby Nor cove. The town was divided into three sections by road tunnels with gateways piercing the rampart, and it was through the western gate that the ox-cart carrying Wulfgar and Rhowenna entered, wheels clattering over the bridge across the moat, and then beneath the tall wooden watchtower. It was cool and semidark in the road's tunnel portion, which was six feet wide, wedge-shaped, and planked, the roadway beneath paved with stones. Then the vehicle was through the passage, back into the sunlight; and the town unfolded before the ox-cart.

Covering a full sixty acres and laid out in a surprisingly orderly fashion, most of the enclosed land on which Sliesthorp had been built was crowded with huts, workshops, store-houses, and barns and stables, although open spaces, by the three cemeteries and along the single stream that wended its way through the center of town, had been left for itinerant traders to pitch their tents and stalls. Narrow wooden streets and walkways meandered past timber and wattle-and-daub dwellings with thatched roofs, their gable-ends fronting the streets, with barns and stables and the occasional outhouse behind. Fences enclosed the small plots, on which there was often a well, too; and decaying animal sacrifices to the North-land's gods hung on poles before many of the structures. At the north end of town, instead of a wharf, a strong, curved wooden breakwater, nearly five hundred feet long, to whose massive bollards heavy vessels could be moored, stretched from the rampart into the sea; rowboats ferried men and cargo to and from the anchored ships. Smaller craft landed on the beach and were drawn up on the sand for loading, unloading, and repairs.

Rhowenna had never before seen anything like the town—or so many people in one place. Sliesthorp boasted a thousand inhabitants, Wulfgar told her, and their ranks were now swollen to twice that number by the hundreds of traders and travelers who came to the town and marketplace during the summer months. The streets and walkways hummed and bustled like a hive aswarm with bees, with sweating bodies pressed close in the summer heat, and with all kinds of activity. The air was pungent with smoke from cook fires and with spicy aromas that, however fragrant, could not disguise the vile stench of garbage and offal that strewed the gutters. The clamor was deafening; raucous talk and laughter, boisterous song from the alehouses, and the shouts of the merchants and artisans hawking their wares dinned ceaselessly in one's ears. *Víkingr*, Slavic, and Arab slave-traders, their chained captives in tow, vied for space alongside a multitude of traders of all nationalities, as well as potters and weavers, metalworkers and carvers of bone and horn. All along the streets and walkways, pelts and wool blankets spread upon the ground displayed goods from all over the world. Pots of salt from the port of Noirmoutier, in the Frankish kingdoms, sat beside jars of oil, bolts of cloth, wooden trays brimming with jewelry, and heavy basalt millstones from the Germanic kingdoms. From the kingdoms of both had come jugs of rich, costly wines; plain pottery for everyday use and expensive, delicate glassware for special occasions—or for the wealthy, who could afford it; and highly prized weapons and armor. Barrels of wheat, jars of honey, bolts of woolens, and tin from the British kingdoms were arrayed alongside baskets heaped high with amber and walrus ivory and fresh-caught fish; stacks of pots and dishes of soapstone; mounds of woolens, hides, and furs; and coils of ships' rigging from the Northland kingdoms. Wares imported from the Slavic kingdoms were among the rarest and most luxurious of all: baskets of fruits and nuts; pots of spices and jars not only of honey, but also of wax; bolts of exquisitely woven silk, piles of furs, and open wooden caskets spilling over with jewelry and silver. Local craftsmen showed their own goods: garments and leather boots and slippers; fine combs, needles, flutes, and gaming pieces of bone and horn; and glass beads that were strung on silver necklaces, along with amber and jet, crystals and carnelians. The clanging of hammers upon anvils reverberated as blacksmiths worked bronze and iron.

To these last were herded various of the women who had been abducted from the village and the fields of Usk. Iron slave collars were fastened about their throats, marking them as those chosen to continue the journey to the Northland. The remainder of the Usk women—like the cattle and pigs, the sheep and goats that were led to the marketplace to be bartered or sold to the highest bidder—were peddled to new masters; and Rhowenna knew, with a terrible sense of outrage and despair, that she would never see the faces of those women again. But whether they were the lucky ones, she did not know.

"Did you—did you have to sell them?" Her eyes shone with anger and tears as she gazed up at Wulfgar at her side.

"What would you have had me do, lady? Keep them all? I could not. They were not all suited to a life of slavery in the Northland. Those I sold were too old or frail or sickly; they would not have survived the first winter on the shores of the Skagerrak—for our winters are hard, lady. They are long and dark and bitterly cold. So 'twas a kindness in a way to those women and better for me to barter them away for goods and coins to share among the men aboard the *Dragon's Fire*, who might have cried foul at their portions of the profit otherwise. This is the way of the *Víkingrs*. For two hundred years, those of the Eastlands and the Southlands have been our enemies, and we have raided and battled them. But commerce and war are a man's business, lady, and so I do not expect you to understand them. Come.''

The tug upon the tether around Rhowenna's throat was gentle; still, the rope chafed her tender skin, burning her. She could only imagine how a heavy iron slave collar would feel, weighing against her collarbones, cutting into her flesh. To her relief, she and Morgen—who was guarded by Flóki the Raven—had been spared that indignity at least. Despite the fact that they were captives, the princess of Usk and her waiting woman were entitled to some privileges, it seemed— at least until it was learned whether Prince Cerdic or King Pendragon would pay the ransom that would be demanded for Rhowenna's safe return.

With Morgen and Flóki trailing behind, Wulfgar led Rhowenna to several of the stalls, where he bought a change of clothing for both her and Morgen, a pair of leather boots each, and lovely combs carved from reindeer antlers. Then he took the two women to a bathhouse, where, for the first time in days, Rhowenna was able to have a proper bath, in a real tub filled with steaming-hot fresh water instead of cold seawater. After she had entered through the low doorway, stepping down onto the sunken, hard-packed earth floor inside, and her eyes had adjusted to the relative darkness within after the brightness of the day, she saw by the flicker of the rushlights burning in clay bowls placed all around that the crude, wattle-and-daub hut contained just one room, which was full of steam that rose from an iron cauldron of boiling water set upon the fire blazing at the heart of the stone hearth in one corner. Nearby sat empty wooden buckets and a large, iron-hooped wooden tub, beside which were baskets filled with thick woolen cloths and bars of soap. Wulfgar spoke briefly to the stooped old man and frail old woman who were the proprietors of the bathhouse, then handed them a few coins. With the wooden pails, the old man began slowly to fill the tub, while the old woman bent over the baskets, removing some of the folded cloths and a single bar of soap, which she laid upon a low stool by the tub. Turning back to Rhowenna, Wulfgar said:

"You and Morgen will bathe here and clothe yourselves in your new garments. Nay, do not trouble to thank me for this, lady, for 'tis not the kindness you believe it to be, but the law of the Northland that a master must provide for his slaves. And right now, I *am* your master, lady, no matter that you are loath to call me such." He untied the tether around Rhowenna's neck, then, drawing the scramasax at his waist, cut the rope that bound her hands behind her back, while Flóki the Raven did the same for Morgen. "Lady"—Wulfgar's voice, although pleasant as he continued, also held a note of warning—"do not be so foolish as to think that because we have loosed your bonds, the two of you can escape. As you can see, this hut has no windows, and Flóki and I will be waiting just outside the only door."

This last at least relieved Rhowenna's mind of the fear that he and Flóki intended to stay and to watch her and Morgen at their toilette—or even to join them; for the *Víkingrs* appeared to have little regard or desire for privacy, no matter the activity. She had thought of Wulfgar stripping himself, and then her, and then pulling her with him into the tub that was surely big enough for two to share, and she had felt a strange, unsettling shiver run through her, as though she were growing feverish, coming down with an ague. Now the feeling dissipated, leaving behind only a sense of welcome expectation and pleasure as she gazed at the tub and thought of being really clean for the first time in days.

Wulfgar, Flóki, and the old man, who had finished filling the tub, left the bathhouse; but the old woman stayed, just cracking the door a little to bring in additional buckets of water that the old man drew from the well outside and left on the stoop. Not knowing which, if any, of the other *Víkingrs* might make use of the hut and so feeling that wisdom dictated prudence, Rhowenna turned to Morgen and spoke to her in the language of Usk.

"Our dark coloring is not common among these Northmen, Morgen, so 'tis likely that this old woman will remember us; and I do not know what tales she may tell about us later, or to whom. For that reason, you will bathe first, and I will assist you, as though I were, in truth, your waiting woman and you, the princess of Usk."

"If that is your wish, my lady. However, 'tis my own feeling that now is the ideal time to attempt our escape—for we may not get another chance so good!" Morgen's voice held a note of impatience and excitement. "Old women are sometimes stronger than they look; but between us, we can surely overpower this one who has been left to guard us. We can hit her over the head—with one of those hearth stones— tie her up with the ropes the Northmen were so foolish as to leave behind, and lose ourselves in the crowds outside. If we are fortunate, we will find a trader from Britain or perhaps even Walas to help us!"

"Nay, we would not even get past the door, before which Wulfgar Bloodaxe and Flóki the Raven stand even now, if Wulfgar spoke truly to me—and I see no reason to doubt that he did. I do not mean to pass up any opportunity to escape, Morgen. But at the moment, 'tis futile to try. Get in the tub."

When her own turn in the wooden tub finally came, Rhowenna sank gratefully into the water, which was still wonderfully warm, kept so by the old woman's dropping hot hearth stones into it now and then, and removing those that had grown cold. This practice produced additional steam that Rhowenna found exhilarating. She longed to linger in the tub, to soak herself for hours. But she knew that at any moment, Wulfgar and Flóki could reappear; so, taking up the bar of soap, she began to lave herself vigorously and to wash her hair. When she had finished rinsing herself—with pails of the well water, which was so unexpectedly cold that she gasped from the shock of it—she stepped out onto one of the woolen cloths and toweled herself off with another, her body tingling, invigorated by the steam and the hot water followed by the cold. After that, she dressed in the plain, workaday gown of undyed wool that Wulfgar had bought for her. Then she and Morgen combed and braided each other's hair.

"Perhaps there is another way we could gain our freedom, my lady," Morgen remarked slowly as she worked at the tangles in Rhowenna's tresses. "Flóki the Raven is . . . interested in me. He looks at me . . . well . . . in the way that Wulfgar Bloodaxe looks at you, my lady. 'Tis a look I know well—and understand. If I were . . . nice to Flóki, perhaps I could persuade him to let us go, to help us to escape."

"And perhaps he would only take what he desired—and then put a slave's iron collar around your neck, Morgen! Nay, I cannot permit you to sacrifice yourself in such a manner. We must bide awhile yet. My father will surely ransom us if Prince Cerdic will not; and in the meantime, we can best serve Usk by learning all we can about these Northmen, so we can better defend ourselves against them in the future."

"Of course, you are right, my lady. 'Tis only that I have always been like a wild thing, who must live free or die, and this captivity weighs heavily upon me."

"In that, you are not alone, Morgen. Perhaps I chafe less strongly against it only because my own freedom has always been limited by my duty to Usk. I have often wondered what my life would be like if I were not a princess. I have sometimes wished I could just run away and be nobody," Rhowenna confessed, thinking of Gwydion and how she had yearned to go away with him somewhere, anywhere—if only he had asked her. *If only* . . . Those were the two saddest words in the world, she thought. Even so, she discovered to her surprise that the ache in her heart at the memory of Gwydion had now lessened, faded to a dull hurt, like an old wound long healed, with only a scar and an occasional twinge left to remind one of it.

"How strange to hear you say that, my lady." Morgen's face bore a rueful smile. "For I frequently have longed to be a princess—and now, in an odd way, what we both wished for has come to pass. Well, the priests do say that God works in mysterious ways."

Or is it as Wulfgar told me: that the old gods still exist and are ever capricious? Rhowenna wondered—but did not speak the words aloud.

There was no time for further conversation, for just then, the door of the bathhouse swung open to reveal Wulfgar and Flóki, who had obviously grown tired of waiting and decided that the two women had had ample time to complete their toilette. Rhowenna was glad then that she had not dallied in the tub, but was dressed and ready to depart—although some of her ebullience at once more being clean faded when Wulfgar again tied the rope around her throat and bound her hands behind her back.

On the way back to the ox-cart, Wulfgar bought a basket of fruits and nuts from a Slavic trader; and once the vehicle was under way, he and Flóki, with their dinner knives, peeled apples, sloes, and plums, and cracked open hazelnuts and walnuts, feeding Rhowenna and Morgen chunks of the fruits and pieces of the nutmeat. Wulfgar's strong, slender fingers felt moist and sticky and disturbingly intimate against Rhowenna's lips as he pressed the fruits and nuts upon her, now and then slowly tracing the outline of her mouth, tugging gently at her lower lip, and wiping away the juices of the succulent sloes and plums, which trickled down her chin.

"Don't," she implored, unable to bite back the whispered word that issued from her lips at the loverlike caresses of his fingers.

"Don't what, lady?" he inquired softly, feigning innocence of her meaning, although she knew, from the desire in
his eyes and the strange half-smile that curved his mouth, that
he knew only too well the unsettling effect he was having
upon her and took satisfaction in it. "Are you not hungry—
as I am hungry?" Now it was she who pretended innocence
of his own meaning, the double entendre he had intended
with his words. Her eyes fell before his; a blush rose to her
cheeks. "With your hands bound, how can you eat if I do
not feed you, lady?"

"You . . . you could untie me," she suggested.

"Nay, I prefer this method—or, even better yet,
this. . . ." Wulfgar's voice trailed away as, taking a small
slice of plum between his teeth, he suddenly bent his head,
taking Rhowenna unaware, and pressed his mouth to her own.

With his tongue, he slowly pushed the plum slice between
her lips, so it lay sweet and seeming to melt upon her tongue
as his own tongue followed it inside, twisting lingeringly
inside her mouth, touching, tasting, setting her atremble with
the wild, unexpected thrill that suddenly shot through her,
making her feel dizzy and breathless and faint. Startled,
frightened by the flame that seemed to ignite at the core of
her being to leap and to spread through her entire body,
flickering and burning, she tried to yank away from him. But
his hands cupped her face now; his fingers were ensnared in
the tresses at her temples, imprisoning her, and she could not
free herself from his grasp. For an endless moment, his tongue
swirled the plum slice over her own tongue, teasing, tantalizing, spreading mellifluous juices before, at long last, he released her, his eyes smoldering with passion and knowing—
mocking her. Fury and shame and some other dark thing
loosed from deep inside her roiled within Rhowenna; she felt
a wild urge to spit the plum slice into his face. But reading
her mind, Wulfgar laid his hand against her mouth, drawing

his forefinger slowly, erotically, along her lower lip and saying:

"I would not, lady, if I were you." He paused, allowing this warning to penetrate. Then, his voice low, husky, he demanded, "Swallow it."

So soft in her mouth had the plum slice grown beneath his taunting tongue that it hardly needed to be chewed. Still, it was with difficulty that Rhowenna choked the piece of fruit down her throat, feeling as though, somehow, it were a part of Wulfgar that she took deep inside her, a thought that, unbidden, conjured other, even more intimate images in her mind, acts she had unwittingly witnessed the *Víkingrs* forcing upon the other women during the battle on the shores of Usk and, later, aboard the *Dragon's Fire*. Until the marauders had swooped down upon her homeland, she had known little more than the rudiments of how a man bedded a woman. Now, no matter how hard she had tried to close her eyes and ears against enlightenment, she was no longer so innocent as a maiden should have been.

"You said . . . you said you would not force yourself upon me!" Her tone was accusing.

"'Twas only a kiss, lady—little enough payment for the garments and the bath and the basket of fruits and nuts, I am thinking."

"And what will be the price of your clothing and housing and feeding me until Prince Cerdic or my father pays the ransom you will demand for me, I am wondering?" she shot back defiantly, a scornful mimicry of his manner of speaking, her eyes blazing with the violet fire of amethysts in the sunlight, although he thought that there was fear, too, in their depths.

"Lady, I said I would not rape you; that much is true. But I did *not* say that I would not try to bring you willingly to my bed. I have wanted you from the first moment I laid eyes on you, and I will have you if I can.'' The declaration was blunt, matter-of-fact.

''You speak of lust—''

''And you would rather hear words of love? Those, also, I can speak, and will if you will listen.'' He paused for a moment, as though gathering his thoughts. Then he continued, his voice soft and melodious, as, with his words, he sang to her a bard's song.

''Lady, I have never seen a woman more beautiful than you. Your skin is whiter than the snowy breasts of the wild swans that float upon the meres of summer in the Northland. Your eyes are the violet of the heather that blooms upon the hillsides of my homeland, your cheeks the rose of the morning sun that rises on the eastern horizon and sets the Skagerrak aflame, your lips as crimson as the sail of a longship, kissed by the wind—as I would kiss you, softly, like the breeze that stirs the reeds of the Northland's heaths, and then more fiercely, like a storm at sea. Gently would I nuzzle your shell-like ears, your perfect breasts, as the roe deer feed among the lichens and moss of the forests that rise, ever green, against the northern sky; and so would I stroke your trembling thighs until they opened to me, spread wide like the wings of a falcon in flight, soaring upon the clouds, as I would teach you to soar. I would bury my face in your raven hair and against your milk-white throat to breathe the heady fragrance of your woman's scent—and myself in you until you wept my name for joy and cried out your sweet surrender. Aye, all this would I do, and more, for love of you, lady.''

''You—you must not say such things to me,'' Rhowenna breathed, although, despite herself, she had thought his words more eloquent even than Owain the bard's songs, which had sometimes been so beautiful that they had brought tears to her eyes. ''Your words are lies you spin as a spider does its web—to deceive and to ensnare. I have seen for myself how a Northman uses a woman—violently, brutally, so she cries out not in surrender, but in agony at the pain inflicted upon her!''

''It does not have to be like that, lady—nor have I ever used any woman in such a cruel fashion. This, I swear by the gods, so you will know I speak the truth.''

Rhowenna did not answer; she did not know what to say. No man had ever spoken to her as Wulfgar had. He was not like the other Northmen; she had recognized that from the beginning. Now she told herself again that he was her enemy, her captor, and that she hated him. But in her heart, she knew that it was not so simple as that. He confused her, filled her with strange, conflicting emotions she had never felt before. Almost, she wished he had beaten and raped her ruthlessly, for then could she have hardened her heart against him, knowing with certainty that he was deserving of no less than her abhorrence and contempt. But instead, he had offered her his protection and assistance; he had kept her safe from the other *Víkingrs*, and for that had claimed nothing more than a few kisses as his price. Was that such a bad bargain? Deep down inside, Rhowenna knew that it was not.

Heavily laden with the goods the *Víkingrs* had traded for in Sliesthorp, the ox-cart trundled on toward the port of Hollingstedt, wheels clattering over the road, the great system of earthworks that was the Danevirke rising to the south, like Jormungand, the giant Midgard serpent that the Northmen believed girded the world. On the western horizon, the mammoth ball of fire that was the summer sun sank slowly toward the sea, its rays turning Wulfgar's hair to gilded flame and making Rhowenna's fair skin glow with the luminescence of a pearl. Side by side, the two of them sat in silence, and their thoughts were long thoughts.

From the sandy shores in the distance, the calls of the seabirds rose, achingly sweet and forlorn, a cry to the heart.

Chapter Nine

Olaf's Markland

From Hollingstedt, the three longships sailed on up the coast of Jutland, past small islands and long beaches rippled with sand dunes, until they gained its northernmost reaches, a region known as the Skaw. From there, the vessels struck out across the Skagerrak, toward its northwestern shores; and presently, the end of their long journey was in sight. Like the rest of the women, Rhowenna stood upon the deck of the *Dragon's Fire*, silenced and daunted by the vast, craggy, heavily forested mountains that hove up in shades of dark green, blue, and purple in the distance ahead, their snow-capped peaks piercing the clouds, cutting a jagged oblique into the robin's-egg blue of the sky, where hundreds of sea-birds soared and cried hauntingly along the coast. The mountains of Walas had been but hills compared to these huge, towering alps, whose steep, rocky sides fell away sharply into deep, narrow valleys through which white-watered rivers ran, and shallower, wider expanses of marsh and heath, where the morning mist still clung to the low-lying hollows of the land and swans and ducks called, floating upon still, reed-grown meres. The sea was so clear and so pristine and dazzling a blue that the glare of the sunlight reflecting off the waves hurt Rhowenna's eyes, and she held one hand to her brow to shade them.

"Lady, you see the Northland at its most beautiful," Wulfgar remarked from where he stood at the tiller, guiding the *Dragon's Fire* toward the fjord-riddled coast, "for its summers are as glorious as its winters are bleak. The sun shines long hours during this season; even at the midnight hour, it can still be seen in the sky in those regions of the Northland that lie at the edge of the Frozen Sea that flows into the Grey Sea, which is dark and rough and so cold that great chunks of ice float upon its waves. There do we Northmen hunt whales and sea cows—the walrus—and seals whence come the rigging for the sails of our longships, and the tusks of ivory we trade in the marketplaces. But here"—with one hand, he indicated the sweep of wild shore ahead—"here is where we live. Here is home."

"Home for you, Wulfgar Bloodaxe—but not for me," Rhowenna reminded him quietly, beset with longing of a sudden for the familiar, gentler green mountains of Walas. Her heart ached at the thought that perhaps she would never see them again, or the shores of the Severn Sea. "Here have I been brought against my will—a stranger, a captive, a slave. Never will your Northland be home to me."

"Never is a long time, lady, and who but the gods know what our future holds in store? Save perhaps for the spaewife Yelkei, a yellow slave from the Eastlands, who reared me and who sees in the fires and mists and her castings of the rune stones what cannot be seen by other mortals, who possess not her power of prophecy. 'Twas she who sent me in search of you, lady. 'Twas she who said you would be mine. And now you are—as the gods ordained. And if 'tis also their whim that you call the Northland home, you will, lady; for the gods do with us as they will, and we are but shells upon the sands of life's strands, cast hither and yon by the great sea of fate.''

"Perhaps," Rhowenna conceded slowly. "But even if 'tis my destiny that I be compelled to spend the rest of my life here in your Northland, 'twill still not be home to me. And that, neither your gods nor you can change, Wulfgar Blood-axe, I promise you. Walas is my home, and come what may, I shall never forget that!" Her voice was low, fierce, and her hands clenched at her sides, so her knuckles shone white and her nails dug into her palms.

"Do you not think, then, to call Mercia such when you are wed to Prince Cerdic?" Wulfgar asked, a note of curiosity in his tone.

"My thoughts about Mercia and my betrothed are none of your concern, and so I shall not make you privy to them," she rejoined stiffly.

"You just did—for if you found joy in the match your father arranged for you, you would be glad to tell me that, to use the knowledge like a scourge against me, to hurt me, knowing how I desire you. Instead, you are silent; so you are no more eager, then, to lie in Prince Cerdic's bed than in my own, are you? Still, you will submit to him—although, like a fox the hound, you do seek to elude me, lady, and doubtless pray every night to your Christian God that I do not grow weary of the chase."

"Cerdic of Mercia is a prince and soon to be my husband—not a heathen marauder who savagely plundered my father's kingdom, committing mayhem and murder before kidnapping me to hold me hostage for ransom!"

"Lady, if I thought that such would bring about your surrender, gladly would I marry you and make you a queen of the Northland, I swear it! Only tell me that you will be mine, and when I sit upon the high seat in Olaf the Sea Bull's great mead hall, you shall sit at my side as my bride—and not at my feet as my slave."

"You are mad!" Rhowenna cried softly, stricken by the sudden, unwelcome, unnerving thought that perhaps Wulfgar would force her to undergo some pagan wedding ceremony and then proclaim her his wife, his for the taking if she dared to refuse him.

"Mad with wanting you, lady? Aye, I'll not deny it. To look at you is to feel a thunderbolt from Thor's hammer, Mjöllnir, coursing through my blood and my loins. Lying beside you these past nights and willing myself not to touch you, to take you, has been an unbearable torture to my heart and soul. Yet have I compelled myself to endure it—for your sake—and claimed no more than a few kisses from your lush red mouth that, soft and trembling, invites the hard feel of a man's certain possession. As that fox-hunting hound strains at its leash, lady, so do I chafe impatiently at my own restraint where you are concerned, longing to be rid of it. Do you think that Cerdic of Mercia will prove any different, that he will want less of you than I? You do not love him—how can you when you do not even know him? And if your father were willing to marry you to one sea wolf, why not to another? What does it matter if 'tis I and not Prince Cerdic to whom you plight your troth?"

To her despair, Rhowenna had no good answer to that.

"It matters," she insisted, the words sounding lame even to her own ears.

"In time, 'twill cease to," came the sure, cavalier response.

"You are arrogant, Wulfgar Bloodaxe."

"And you are proud, lady, and strong-willed. But my own will is stronger, as you will come to learn, as the fox learns of the will of the hound when the chase is done and she is run to ground by him. Yield to me, lady! You will not regret it, I swear it!"

"Nay, I cannot! I will not!" Rhowenna's face was anguished as she spoke the words, and her mouth quivered, her white throat worked, so Wulfgar knew she was more tempted by his offer than she would have him believe.

Without a doubt, her future must look very bleak to her at the moment, with her being so very far from home and not knowing whether, in truth, her betrothed or her father would pay the ransom demanded for her safe return. The idea of being his, Wulfgar's, bride instead of his slave must therefore hold a certain undeniable appeal, which he had counted on. That Rhowenna had rejected him annoyed but did not truly trouble him. He had not expected her acceptance, but only hoped to give her food for thought, to weaken her resolve. Satisfied that he had accomplished this, Wulfgar spoke no more, but turned his attention to the sounder in the bow, watching for the signal that would indicate that they were nearing the shoals, that the sea had grown shallow enough that the sail must be lowered, the rudder raised, and the oars put to use. When the time came, he gave the orders easily, with an authority and assurance he had not so much felt as pretended in the beginning, after he had fought Knut Strongarm for captaincy of the vessel.

In the end, when the *Dragon's Fire* was at last moored to the wharf that stretched into the sea, Wulfgar took possession of Olaf the Sea Bull's markland just as easily, somewhat astonished by how simple it proved. It was as Yelkei had told Wulfgar: Olaf's wife and sons were dead; the husbands of his daughters had the spines of jellyfish, and as they had not protested his assuming command of the *Dragon's Fire*, they did not now voice objection to his seizing Olaf's markland, but slunk away home to their wives. So there was no great battle as Wulfgar had half feared. In fact, no man resisted him as, after the traditional wassailing in the Sacred Grove on Olaf's markland to give thanks to the gods for a successful voyage and raid, Wulfgar strode through the gates of Olaf's palisade and into the great mead hall of the *hof*. The *thegns* and freedmen left behind to guard the longhouse in Olaf's absence were stunned and disarranged by the news of their master's death. Instinctively, they looked for guidance and did not question Wulfgar's commands, which the warriors who had been aboard the longship were seen to obey without hesitation. Only Olaf's concubine, Ingeborg, protested, shrieking and tearing like a crazy woman at her long, greying blond hair—although not from any real grief at Olaf's demise, Wulfgar soon discerned, but from fear of what was to become of her now that her paramour was dead.

Disgusted, Wulfgar slapped her across the face to bring her to her senses, then directed her to pack her clothes and jewels, and to be gone from the *hof* within the hour—he cared not to where. Olaf's concubine was not the woman Wulfgar wanted as mistress of his longhouse. Ingeborg was sly and grasping; he felt sure she had cheated Olaf outrageously over the years, hoarding much of what the Sea Bull had given her to manage the *hof* and to spend in the marketplaces. Wulfgar was equally certain that once she had departed, Ingeborg would waste no time in hurrying to Ragnar's longhouse to inform him of her master's death and Wulfgar's claiming of Olaf's markland. Still, there was no way, Wulfgar knew, that he could prevent that news from spreading like wildfire, so it seemed a wasted effort to try. The most he could realistically hope for was that neither Ragnar nor Ivar had yet returned from raiding the Southlands, thereby giving him time to secure his position as the markland's *jarl* and to fortify the palisade against his father and half brothers in case they should decide to march forth and attack him. At the very least, they were bound to come to demand that he relinquish the prize he had snatched from them—the princess of Usk—and if he did not deliver her up to them, they would surely declare war against him. Worse, perhaps they would even call for an assembly of the *Thing* and insist that he be branded an outlaw. Then he would be an outcast in the Northland, driven from his markland, deserted by his men, unprotected by the laws, having no rights whatsoever, no hope of succor from even the lowliest slave, upon pain of death for any and all who aided and abetted him. Wulfgar would not let that happen.

He gave instructions for ox-carts to be driven to the beach so the goods aboard the *Dragon's Fire* could be unloaded, as well as the decaying bodies in the shallow cargo hold. Then, with great reluctance, he ordered the mighty longship itself dragged onto the shores of the Skagerrak, for interment in the burial mound of Olaf the Sea Bull. Wulfgar could not dishonor his dead lord by doing any less. Still, he deeply regretted the loss of the vessel, his first command, and resolved to set the men to work building another longship as soon as possible. In the meanwhile, there was much to be done to put the markland in order. Many of the fields lay fallow and needed to be planted, come next spring; byres and fences were tumbling down, and the *hof* itself was a veritable pigsty. It was no wonder, he thought as he abruptly viewed the longhouse through Rhowenna's assessing eyes, that as she gazed about the dismal great mead hall, she looked so disheartened, her mouth and shoulders drooping.

"Lady, I would you had received a better welcome," he told her gently. "As you can see, my lord, Olaf the Sea Bull, had little care for aught beyond his cups and comfort. But now that I am *jarl* here, I will soon set matters aright."

Before Rhowenna could respond, Ingeborg reappeared from the lord's private sleeping chamber beyond the great mead hall, bearing a large jewel chest and still shrilling about the treatment she had received at Wulfgar's callous hands. In her wake trailed several slaves she had pressed into service, dragging her heavily laden coffers between them. She cast at Wulfgar a glance of utter loathing before tossing her head and flouncing out of the *hof*. From beyond its low doorway, with wry amusement, he heard her commandeering two of the ox-carts to carry her and her possessions away; he made no attempt to countermand her orders, thinking himself lucky to be well rid of her and with so little trouble.

"Come, lady." Wulfgar held out one hand to Rhowenna, leading her reluctantly drawn figure into the gloomy sleeping chamber Ingeborg had vacated. "Since I have claimed you as my slave, and mine alone, this is where you will sleep— with me," he announced casually, "for the women in the slave pens may be used freely by the *thegns*, and so I will not have you there. That being the case, if you would be comfortable this night, you would do well to clean my sleeping chamber first, before attending to my great mead hall. Also, my men and I will be hungry tonight and will expect to be well fed, so you had best see to the kitchen, as well. You may have as many of the other slaves as you need to help you with your tasks; I will ensure that they follow your directions."

"I am—I am to be as mistress here, then?" Rhowenna asked tentatively, still not quite certain of the role he meant her to play.

"Aye, that is my desire. I have just thrown Olaf's shrewish concubine out on her ear, and there is no other woman here with your knowledge of how to manage a lord's household, lady. In this way will you earn your keep while you are under my protection."

"And is it your intention that I—that I earn it also in your bed, my lord?" Now that he was a *jarl* of the Northland, she could address him thus, as his rank alone demanded, without feeling she demeaned herself by speaking the title.

"If that is *your* desire, lady."

"'Tis not—and well you know it!"

"Aye, for so you have told me often enough. Still, 'tis a woman's prerogative to change her mind, and that, you will do in time, I am thinking." He reached out and, with his hand, cupped her chin, tilting her face up to his and running his thumb slowly across her lower lip. "I have learned that much comes to a man who waits, as a wise wolf bides patiently among the reeds at the edge of the mere, waiting for the lone swan to draw near before pouncing on it."

His analogy was all too clear. Her eyes flashing sparks, her cheekbones high with color, Rhowenna jerked her head away from him, causing him to laugh softly.

"I am not so unwary as your careless swan, my lord!"

"Not now, perhaps," Wulfgar conceded. "But 'twill take time to send messages to Mercia and Walas, to Prince Cerdic and to your father, time for their replies to reach us here in the Northland, time for you to be safely returned to them if the ransom demanded for you is paid—in short, time enough for much to happen, much to change between us, lady. Time, you see, is on *my* side, and 'tis a powerful ally, as you will come to learn. Meanwhile, I will wait and watch, like the wolf who stalks the swan."

"And I will wait and watch, also, my lord," Rhowenna rejoined, falsely sweet, "for the time when I may take flight, homeward bound."

At that, Wulfgar's mocking smile turned so abruptly to a dark scowl that she could not restrain the mirth that bubbled from her throat at her having got a bit of her own back against him. It was, Wulfgar realized suddenly, the first time he had ever heard her laugh; and her face, as lovely and distant as the swan to which he had likened her, was transformed with radiance and warmth, growing even more beautiful, he reflected, like the frosty, breathtaking beauty of the tundra when touched by the midnight sun. He inhaled sharply at the sight of her, her head thrown back a little, the slender white column of her swan's throat bared, her eyes half closed, her moist mouth parted. So would she look when being made love to by a man, he thought, and he felt his loins tighten with desire for her, and a sudden, wild urge to throw her down where she stood and to claim her as his, only his, forever his.

Something of this must have shown upon his face, Wulfgar recognized; for after a long moment, Rhowenna's laughter slowly died away, and she stared up at him breathlessly, as still as a startled doe poised for flight, the tiny pulse at the hollow of her throat fluttering like the wings of a moth beating helplessly against a flame.

"Lady . . . Rhowenna . . ." he murmured, his voice low and thick, speaking her name for the first time, so she would know that now that he was a *jarl*, he considered himself her equal.

His eyes darkened with passion as he drew her into his arms, his fingers entangling the tresses at her temples, turning her face up to his, his mouth finding hers, his tongue cleaving her lips, thrusting deep into the dark, moist cavity of her, seeking . . . finding. The taste of her was sweeter than costly Rhenish wine, he thought, and he savored it, only dimly aware of her small fists hammering against his broad chest as she struggled to free herself from his strong embrace—futilely. For Wulfgar did not release her, but went on kissing her hungrily until at long last, with a long, soughing moan of helplessness and defeat, Rhowenna melted against him, her hands slipping up to twine about his neck. Her fingers burrowed in his long mane of tawny hair, twisting and tightening convulsively as his tongue wreathed hers, searching out the innermost secrets of her mouth until her lips softened beneath his, yielded tremulously, a scarlet rosebud unfurling to surrender the nectar at its heart. She gasped for breath. Feverishly, his mouth burned across her cheek to her temple then, pressed kisses upon the silky strands of her hair, her shell-like ear. The scent of her was intoxicating; she smelled of soap and sunshine and spindrift. Gently, Wulfgar bit her earlobe and felt his blood leap and surge as she inhaled raggedly and shuddered hard against him, her full breasts soft and swelling against his chest, exciting him beyond belief. He bent her back, his lips sweeping down her throat to those breasts with which Rhowenna taunted and tempted him so unconsciously, he was sure, unaware of how alluring they felt to him, their nipples taut and straining against the light woolen fabric of her gown, hard twin little peaks he longed to nibble with his teeth, to suck with his mouth, and to lave with his tongue until she moaned and writhed beneath him with a desire to match his own. He buried his face between her breasts, his hands sliding down to her shoulders, tugging impatiently at the sleeves of the gown he yearned to tear away from her savagely, stripping her naked.

"Lord?" a voice called tentatively from beyond the hide-curtained doorway of the sleeping chamber. "Lord?"

"Not now, damn it!" Wulfgar snarled, his breath coming harsh and fast, his arms tightening about Rhowenna, feeling her stiffen and, regaining her senses, begin once more to struggle against him as the mood was inevitably lost, the spell broken. Knowing that what they had shared could not be recaptured at the moment, he reluctantly released her, his eyes raking her intently, ravenously, for a long moment before, with a muttered curse, he strode to the doorway and murderously yanked back the curtain. "What in Hel is it?"

"Ah! My timing is indeed as bad as I feared." Flóki the Raven took half a step backward, a rueful smile playing about the corners of his lips, although his eyes were wary, as though he believed he would be soundly cuffed or kicked for the interruption. "I am sorry, lord, but as you gave no orders not to disturb you, I thought that you would wish to know right away that Ingeborg instructed the drivers of the ox-carts to convey her and her belongings to Ragnar's markland."

"Aye . . . I expected as much," Wulfgar said slowly, some of his anger draining away; for in truth, had he wished to remain undisturbed, he ought to have given orders to that effect. He was not yet accustomed either to the responsibilities or to the privileges of his new rank as *jarl*; that he could demand that he be left alone was an unfamiliar notion—one to be savored at his leisure. But Flóki had been right to interrupt him with the news of Ingeborg's destination, which would surely have an impact on them all.

"Do you wish me to send riders after her to bring her back, lord?" Flóki asked.

"Nay, for I'll not have her as mistress of my *hof*, and she'll not be happy with less than that, but stirring pots of trouble in the kitchen and sowing seeds of dissension in the fields. Why Olaf ever tolerated her, I'm sure I do not know; no doubt, she was why he spent so much of his time in his cups! Nay, Flóki." He shook his head. "If not from Ingeborg, Ragnar will learn soon enough from some other that I am *jarl* here now. Such news travels fast, as will the news of our raid's success, also; so there is no point in chasing after her. Let her go—but post men in the watchtowers to give warning if Ragnar or his sons should approach."

"It shall be done, lord," Flóki declared, then pivoted on his booted heel.

Allowing the curtain to fall back into place then, Wulfgar turned back to Rhowenna, acutely aware of how violently she trembled as he neared her. From the corners of his eyes, he had watched how she had quickly turned from the doorway, so Flóki would not see her disarray; and how, with shaking hands, she had fumbled to draw up her sleeves and to smooth back into place the strands of her hair that had been pulled loose from her long braid; and how she had then crossed her arms over her breasts, hugging herself tightly and swaying a little on her feet, as though she would faint. Now, as she stood with her back to him, her head bowed, Wulfgar almost took pity on her. She was yet innocent, a maiden, and frightened by his passion for her. But then he thought of her lying in the arms of Ragnar Lodbrók or Ivar the Boneless—or both—taught cruelly the lessons he would teach her with such caring and tenderness; and he strengthened his resolve to win her however he could.

"Lady . . . Rhowenna . . ." He spoke quietly, noting sadly how she tensed as he laid his hands upon her shoulders, caressing her lightly, pulling aside her braid to brush his lips against her nape. "My desire for you is such that I press you too hard, perhaps. I am a man, with a man's wants and needs, and I have not had a woman since the festival of Eostre, this past spring—and never a woman like you. Still, I will wait until you are ready and willing to receive me, as I have said I would do. That being so, I will leave you now, so you may perform the chores I have set for you—and if you would not bestir me to jealousy and rage, do you keep your eyes cast down while about your work, like the modest maiden I know you to be, and tempt no man upon my markland to forget that you are my slave and woman. For know you this, lady: I will slay the man who dares to touch you, who would seek to earn your favor by helping you to escape from me—and he will not die pleasantly, I promise you, but a death you will not care to have upon your Christian soul. Do you understand?"

"Aye." The word was soft, broken, her earlier defiance and laughter stilled now, as though she feared to arouse him again.

And Rhowenna had such apprehensions, for quite simply, she did not know if she was strong enough to resist another such onslaught upon her senses. No man, not even Gwydion, had ever dared to make so bold with her, to kiss her so fiercely, so ardently, forcing her lips to part, to yield to his plundering tongue, taking her breath—and her reason, scattering her senses to the four winds. She could not seem to think when Wulfgar kissed her, but only to feel exquisite sensations that he had wakened within her, a fire in her blood, spreading and burning, charring her bones to ashes and leaving her weak, dizzy, pliant, as fluid as quicksilver, like wet clay in his embrace, his to shape and to mold as he willed. She was powerless against him, dependent upon him for her food, her clothes, her very life; she should have hated him for that. She did not know what was wrong with her that she did not. She did not understand these strange, disturbing emotions and sensations he evoked inside her. She thought she must be a wanton or mad to feel as she did in the arms of her enemy, her captor, the man who had stolen her from Usk and made of her a slave. Had Flóki the Raven not interrupted them when he had, Rhowenna had no doubt that Wulfgar would in moments have been forcing her down to slake his lust on her upon the pelts that covered the pallet on the hard-packed earth floor.

At the thought, she inhaled raggedly, one hand going to her tremulous mouth, knuckles pressing hard to still the quivering of her lips, to hold back sobs of confusion and despair. Presently, as she became aware of the silence in the sleeping chamber, she realized dully that Wulfgar had indeed left her, slipped away as quietly as a stealthy predator on the prowl; and recovering some of her composure, she turned finally to the tasks he had assigned her.

Only the burning whale-oil lamps that hung from the smoke-blackened, freestanding poles that supported the thatched roof chased away the shadows with which the sleeping chamber was long and dark. Little light came through the two small, high-set windows that were covered with pigs' bladders instead of being set with glass. The room itself— little more than a lean-to attached to the great mead hall, really—was sparsely furnished. Piled high with a multitude of pillows and fur blankets, the huge, thick, eiderdown-stuffed wool pallet that lay upon the floor was its only luxury. Other than this, the sleeping chamber contained only a few coffers, low stools and cushions, and a big wooden bathtub ringed with iron hoops. Striplike tapestries hung upon the walls; fur rugs were scattered upon the floor, and in one corner was a small stone hearth. That was all. When she thought of her own sleeping chamber in Usk, with its large bed, wooden dressing table, polished bronze mirror, bronze bathtub, iron brazier, and stone floor, she knew with certainty that she had come to a hard, barbaric place, to a way of life much more difficult than she had known before Wulfgar had swept her up in his arms and carried her on board the *Dragon's Fire*.

The great mead hall was as dark with gloom and smoke as the sleeping chamber, and so was equally depressing, lacking even such basic furniture as the trestle tables and benches that had filled her father's own great hall, although a large loom stood in one corner. On the dais at the sleeping-chamber end, between two massive, intricately carved pillars, there sat a high seat; but even it was just a more elaborate version of the low stools to be seen elsewhere. At the opposite end was the kitchen, no more than a small area separated by a wooden screen from the rest of the great mead hall and boasting few conveniences besides a shallow wooden tub for washing pots and dishes, which were stored in chests that sat alongside barrels and jars of provisions. Just beyond the kitchen, in the great mead hall itself, was a domed baking-oven of stone. Save for that, meals themselves, it seemed, must be cooked over the central hearth. Facing the kitchen was a modest storeroom, largely empty when it ought to have been filled with supplies.

Everything was layered with soot and dust, and festooned with cobwebs, as though it had not been cleaned in many a long year; and Rhowenna knew she had her work cut out for her. Hesitantly, remembering what had passed between them only moments ago in the sleeping chamber, she approached Wulfgar, who stood to one side, giving commands to his men. When he had finished, she asked him to translate her instructions to the slaves allotted to assist her; and presently, several women laden with cloths and pails of hot, sudsy water were busy scrubbing the walls and the freestanding poles, while others took down tapestries, carrying them and the cushions and rugs outside to beat them vigorously until they were free of their burden of dust. Still other women labored in the kitchen and at the hearth and oven, preparing fruits and vegetables, roasting a sheep Wulfgar had ordered slaughtered, and baking fresh bread for supper. Male slaves emptied overflowing slop buckets and, armed with scythes and rakes, were dispatched to the heaths and marshes to cut rushes to lay upon the floors, there being none of the grassy plants dried and in storage, for this custom was not prevalent in the Northland. The *thegns* and freedmen Wulfgar had put to work, as well, cleaning weapons and armor, and repairing the palisade's fortifications. Only Morgen, the "princess" of Usk, was spared from the hard chores, which no doubt suited her just fine, Rhowenna thought with a trace of wry amusement as she glanced at Morgen sitting idly on the edge of the dais, a piece of tapestry that required mending half sliding from her lap, a cup of wine and a bowl of fruits at her side.

Despite their terrible ordeal, Morgen was obviously enjoying the role she played to the hilt, her lovely face cool and haughty—so Rhowenna, stricken with a twinge of guilt, wondered if she herself had often looked so at her father's royal manor, distant, disdainful; and she thought of Wulfgar's calling her proud, and she knew in her heart that it was so. Generations of royal blood ran in her veins, and all her life she had been made aware of that heritage and taught to honor it. Now she was a captive, a slave, and she saw the world through different eyes—not as the secure, happy world she had known, but as one fraught with peril and hardship and suffering. No matter what happened, she knew she would never again be the same woman she had been before the Northmen had descended upon Usk. Much of her innocence of youth was now lost to her, she realized, and she would never find it again. The thought saddened her; with difficulty, she forced herself to put it from her mind, remembering suddenly the words of advice her mother had often spoken to her:

Yesterday is an old sheet of parchment whose words can never be rewritten or its mistakes blotted clean; but tomorrow is a new page, and wise are those who take up quills afresh instead of wasting precious time by rereading old scrolls long yellowed with age.

She would heed her mother's sage counsel, Rhowenna told herself fiercely. Come what may, she would not look back, but only ahead. Determinedly, she pressed on with her work.

It was not, of course, to be supposed that the longhouse could be set to rights within a day. But by the time the sun had dipped below the western horizon, leaving behind a grey twilight that would not fade to darkness for many hours still, she had made a good start. The *hof* at least was clean, and there was a hot, appetizing supper waiting for Wulfgar and his men. They wolfed the meal down with gusto, drinking and shouting and laughing boisterously as they toasted one another to celebrate their successful voyage and raid, and told the tale of their battle with the Usk men, which Håkon, the *skáld*, wove into a spirited song. Morgen had the good grace to blush when he sang her praises as the "princess" of Usk.

Rhowenna was both attracted and repelled by the *Víkingrs'* unbridled behavior. Truly, she thought, they were savages, sitting cross-legged on their cushions on the floor, using their strong hands to tear off huge chunks of the meat roasting on the spit over the hearth, pouring onto their heads quantities of wine and ale from overflowing horn cups, and openly kissing and fondling the slave women, sometimes pulling them down upon the floor of the great mead hall to slake their lust upon them, while the rest of the men roared encouragement and approval. To Rhowenna, seated on the dais at Wulfgar's feet, such raucous, ribald revelry was shocking and mortifying. Her father's housecarls had never demonstrated such lack of restraint. Still, she was forced to admit that the *Víkingrs* also possessed a vitality, a zest for life that she had seldom before witnessed and that held its own strange, wild, earthy appeal; these were men who lived hard and died hard, unafraid of what tomorrow might bring. There were few warriors greater.

When supper was done, Wulfgar rose slowly and took up one of the broadswords for which he had bartered in Sliesthorp; and one by one, quieter now, the *thegns* came forward to kneel before him and to place their right hands upon the blade's gold hilt, swearing solemn fealty to him, their lord, their *jarl*. His heart swelled with pride at how high he had risen from the depths into which his father and half brothers had cast him. His only regret was that Yelkei was not there to see the oath-swearing that her prophesying had wrought. Then Håkon sang a mighty *thegn*'s song, followed by a soft, melodious love ballad, the strains of his lovely, carved harp echoing on the wind that swept gently through the open door of the great mead hall, setting the whale-oil lamps and rushlights aflicker; and of a sudden, it seemed that there was magic in the night that was not really night at all, but a gloaming, aglow at its edges with the far-distant flame of the midnight sun. Abruptly, Wulfgar caught Rhowenna up in his arms and strode toward his sleeping chamber, stumbling slightly along the way, so she knew then, with a sudden lurch of her heart, that he was as drunk as the other men, although he held his liquor well.

Drawing back the hide curtain, he carried her inside and laid her upon the pallet, his eyes holding hers steadily as he stripped off his leather tunic and sealskin boots and tossed them aside. Then, after a moment, he bent over her, pressing her down, his gilded mane of hair falling about his bare, broad shoulders, glowing like a nimbus in the shadowy half-light cast by the whale-oil lamps, making him seem like one of his ancient pagan gods. Rhowenna's breath caught in her throat at the way the light gleamed upon his bronze flesh, shimmering and dancing with each sinewy ripple of the powerful muscles that corded his arms and layered his chest and belly. In her breast, her heart pounded with apprehension mingled with a strange, leaping anticipation that caused her blood to quicken, her body to tremble.

"Lady, tonight . . . tonight was a night of which—all my life—I have dreamed," Wulfgar said, his words soft and slurring, his eyes shining with wonder and triumph. "How I would that you knew what it has meant to me! But how can I make you understand—you, a princess? I was . . . nobody, Rhowenna, nothing, a bastard my father would not acknowledge, and belonging nowhere. My mother, a Saxon woman taken captive by my father, died when I was just a lad; Yelkei reared me after that, she herself a yellow slave from the grassy steppes of the Eastlands. She and my mother were the only two people who ever loved me. To the rest of the Northland, I was naught but a lowly *bóndi*, undeserving of life's rewards or, at death, of a place in Valhöll, Odinn's great mead Hall of the Slain, in Asgard. Can you imagine what that was like for me, Rhowenna? I hardly dared to hope that the gods would grant my dream of becoming a warrior, much less a *jarl*. But now they have, and I would share it with you, who might have been my queen and chose instead to be my slave. But in truth, 'tis I who am enslaved. I could take you—I *want* to take you! But I will not unless you wish it, for I have given you my word. But I *would* kiss you, Rhowenna, and lie beside you and hold you through the night if you bid me do no more than that."

Stretching out one hand to caress her cheek, he slowly lowered his mouth to hers and kissed her lightly, once, twice, before he claimed her lips more firmly, nudging them apart with his tongue that teased and twined with her own. Startled, touched despite herself by his words and gentleness, Rhowenna did not at first resist. She had feared that in his drunkenness, Wulfgar intended at last to rape her callously; she had not expected tenderness and respect for her wishes, much less his confession of his ignoble birth and humble back-

ground, of his innermost hopes and dreams. It had not occurred to her before to wonder *why* he was different from the
other *Víkingrs*; it had been enough that he was. Now she
glimpsed the lonely boy inside the man and saw him as more
than just her captor, a man with emotions far deeper and
more complex than she would ever have suspected, and with
demons that haunted him. She had not known he was illegitimate; she could only guess what his life had been like until
now—hard, wretched, solitary, with only his impossible
dreams to comfort him, dreams that had this night come true.
He was right; how could she possibly understand what that
meant to him? In her life, all things had come easily to her,
save for Gwydion, who had not come to her at all, who had
never spoken to her as Wulfgar did, impassioned words of
love and desire, words as beautiful as the strains of music
that drifted from beyond the curtained doorway, plucked by
Håkon, the *skáld*, upon the strings of his wild harp, a song
for lovers and dreamers.

Wulfgar's kisses tasted of mead, a taste so familiar upon
Rhowenna's tongue that almost, she could imagine she were
home again in Usk, lying in her own bed—save that no man
had ever shared it with her, except Wulfgar in her dreams.
Wulfgar held her now in reality, his kisses bestirring her
traitorous young body, kindling within her the hot, licking
flame she had felt before in his embrace, as though it had
been smoldering inside her all along, waiting for him to stoke
it anew. Fueled by his insistent lips and tongue and hands,
the fire burgeoned, seeping through her veins, like a strange,
languorous fever overtaking her, dizzying her, clouding her
senses, setting her body ablaze. She must shake it off, she
told herself dully; she must make him stop. He had promised
he would do no more than hold her, kiss her—and she should
not have permitted him even those liberties. No matter that
Wulfgar had aroused her compassion, her empathy, he was
still her enemy; why did she keep forgetting that?

Bewildered, frightened now by the feelings he evoked within her, Rhowenna attempted to fight them and, at last, to fight him, too. But her strength was nothing compared to his, her fleeting struggle that of a swan against a wolf, her defeat swift as his hands easily caught her wrists and, with surprising gentleness, pinned them to the pillows beneath her head.

"There is no need for this, sweeting," he whispered huskily. "Did I not say that I would not take you against your will? I want only to taste the sweet nectar of your lips, to hold your body close to mine, and to feel you tremble against me as a woman does when she is wakened to passion by a man. Don't be afraid. I won't force you; I won't hurt you. By the gods, I swear it!"

His mouth claimed hers once more, his tongue slowly tracing the outline of her lips before again plunging deep between them to taunt and to wreathe her own tongue, as though he entwined it with silken ribands that he would tie in a love knot to hold it captive—as she was held captive until, releasing her wrists, his hands swept down to tangle in her long black hair. Impatiently, he pulled the thong from the end of her braid, loosing and spreading her tresses so they rippled like an ebony sea about her, shimmering in the diffuse light. His fingers sailed upon its waves; like a gust of wind, he lifted one thick strand, drawing it across her face and her throat before wrapping it about his own throat, binding them together.

"Rhowenna . . ." he muttered thickly as he buried his face in her hair, inhaling deeply the sweet, heady fragrance that clung to her locks, born of the heather with which she had scented the water in which she had bathed earlier, just before supper. "Rhowenna . . . *kjæreste* . . ."

Like Wulfgar, she had drunk too much mead, she thought, else surely she would not feel like this—burning with a treacherous fire and dazed by his kisses and caresses. Or mayhap she was really asleep—and dreaming, a midsummer night's dream of a midnight sun that shone in a forgotten, faraway land of a more ancient, atavistic world, a land where time stood still and darkness never came, only a strange and magical twilight touched by flame. Tendrils of smoke wafting from the whale-oil lamps garlanded the sleeping chamber, giving it a primitive, mystical air, as though it had become an unreal place, a place that existed only in the realm of the old gods, or in her dream. Wulfgar's breath was a wind primeval against her flesh—sultry, savage with quickening as he rained hot kisses upon her face and hair. His fingers wove through the sweat-dampened tresses at her temples, disheveling, ensnaring, compelling her head back to bare the long, smooth white arch of her throat. Purring low in his own throat, like some predatory animal, he scalded her there with his lips before he found the tiny pulse fluttering at the base of the slender column, and his tongue stabbed her with its heat, setting her aquiver with the sudden, wild tremor that coursed through her. All the while, his hands moved with skill and assurance upon her body, embracing, exploring, and exciting her, so she felt as though she no longer had any strength or will to resist his increasingly fierce, demanding kisses and bold, sensuous caresses.

Of their own volition her hands slid up his naked, hard-muscled chest, sheened and slick with sweat, to fasten about his neck, drawing him down to her; for, despite herself, she longed for more of him. She felt as though, somewhere deep inside her, a dam was bursting, unleashing a flood of want and need that sluiced through her to sweep her up as ruthlessly as a madding sea, bearing her swiftly, helplessly, toward some distant, unknown, uncharted shore—and Wulfgar was the northern star that guided her there, bright and golden in the gloaming. Her skin felt so incredibly sensitive that his every touch scorched her, like sparks cast from the strange and beautiful flickering lights that he had told her of while aboard the *Dragon's Fire*, that she would see shining in the night sky of the Northland, and that were the flashing swords of the Valkyries, the helmed maidens who, on their magnificent white horses, came to fetch home the Einheriar, the brave warriors killed in battle, to Valhöll, Odinn's great mead Hall of the Slain, in Asgard.

"The Valkyries are as fair as you are dark, lady," Wulfgar had said to her, "and every *Víkingr* prays to lie in their arms at his death. But willingly would I wander the Shore of Corpses to the barred gates of Hel, lady, to lie in *your* arms instead."

And so now, he lay, his powerful body weighing her down as he clasped her to him, his mouth and hands everywhere upon her, his hard, massive thighs holding her prisoner, brushing intimately against her own thighs, making her acutely aware of his virility and desire. She had never been so close to a man before. A low whimper escaped from her throat at the feel of him, at the caress of his strong hands upon her shoulders, pushing the sleeves of her gown down her arms to expose her light woolen shift beneath, her breasts that strained against the thin-woven fabric, rising and falling quickly, shallowly, with her every ragged breath, their dusky-rose nipples taut, alluring.

"Don't, Wulfgar. Please, don't," Rhowenna pleaded softly.

"Shhhhh, sweeting. You cannot sleep in your gown."

Slowly, he eased it from her, leaving her clad in her soft, loose shift, which clung to her body enticingly, revealing not only the white slope of one shoulder, but also the generous swell of her ripe, round breasts, the soft curve of her hips, and the long, lean line of her graceful legs. A door was opened in the great mead hall beyond and a gust of wind swept beneath the hide-curtained doorway of the sleeping chamber, ruffling the long, raven skeins of her hair and billowing the white folds of her shift about her, so that to Wulfgar she looked very like a lorelei, the beautiful, enchanting sirens of the seas' far strands and who, with their bewitching songs, would tempt a *Víkingr* to his death, luring his longship into shattering upon the rocks. The whale-oil lamps flickered in the draft, alternately illuminating her face and then casting it into shadow. Her sloe-violet eyes were closed; her thick, sooty lashes spread like delicate wings against her cheeks; her moist mouth was parted. Wulfgar's eyes and his lips drank her in as his palms cupped her breasts possessively through the fabric of her shift, his thumbs gliding in a slow, circular motion across her nipples, sending waves of pleasure radiating through her body. The neckline of her shift was wide, so it was easy for him, after a moment, to slip it off one shoulder, pulling it down low to expose her breast. His mouth trailed fervent kisses down her throat to the deep valley between her breasts, then closed hungrily over the dark-pink nipple he had bared. Greedily, he suckled her, his tongue swirling, tantalizing, causing Rhowenna to inhale sharply and to shiver with delight and then with a wild, exigent desire as an unbearable, burning ache erupted at the very core of her being, so she longed instinctively to be filled by him. Sensing her need, Wulfgar slid his hand lower, tugging at the hem of her shift, dragging it upward.

"Nay!" she cried, suddenly afraid and beginning desperately to struggle once more against him, twisting and writhing to free herself from his embrace. "Nay, don't! Please don't, Wulfgar!"

For a long moment, Rhowenna thought he would not heed her entreaties, and her heart pounded with both fear and the passion he had aroused in her. But finally, sighing and swearing softly, Wulfgar rolled off her, flinging himself down next to her on the pallet, his breath coming in hard rasps. Trembling, she fumbled with her shift to cover herself, abruptly stricken and ashamed by what she had almost allowed to happen between them. She did not understand how she could have let him kiss and fondle her so; truly, he was a devil who had tempted her to wickedness, and she was a wanton to have responded to him as she had. At the thought, tears began to trickle without warning from her eyes, glistening like silvery dew upon her cheekbones in the shadowy light before dripping slowly, like rivulets, into the hair at her temples.

"Hush, sweeting. Hush," Wulfgar said kindly, half turning now to draw her into the circle of his arms, cradling her head gently against his shoulder and stroking her hair soothingly. "You've no cause to weep. Much as it tried my heart and soul, I kept my word. You are a maiden still."

He meant to comfort her with his words. But to his dismay, Rhowenna only sobbed all the harder, and Wulfgar did not know why—nor, strangely enough, did she.

At long last, she slept—and dreamed a haunting dream of a great, burning sun that shone in a sky blacker than black, and of a mammoth, crimson-sailed longship that carried her far beyond the charted seas, to the place where it was written that dragons were, and the old gods reigned, and Wulfgar stood upon a distant shore, his gilded head thrown back, his hand outstretched to her, strong and sure and waiting.

Chapter Ten

The Chatelaine

When Rhowenna awoke in the morning, Wulfgar was gone, leaving behind on his side of the pallet only the deep indentation of his powerful body to tell her that he had slept beside her. If not for that, she might have convinced herself that what had passed between them last night had been only a dream such as she had so many times before, or that she had only imagined it in a mead-soaked stupor. But although she longed to believe otherwise, she knew that his kissing and caressing her had been more vivid than anything her imagination could have wrought. She could not deny the truth of that; still, the light of day brought no understanding of her own behavior in the shadowy gloaming of last night. She had never in her life felt so confused as she did now, so incapable of sorting out her emotions. She yearned for guidance, but there was no one to whom she could turn, no Gwydion now to weave a tale that would satisfy. There was only Wulfgar—who wanted her and who bided his time, knowing her to be vulnerable. The thought unnerved her. How long could she continue to resist him when in his embrace her own body traitorously betrayed her? She did not know, and she prayed that Prince Cerdic or her father would ransom her quickly.

As Rhowenna rose from the pallet, there appeared in the doorway two of the slave women who had assisted her with the cleaning yesterday. Both were Saxon captives, so she was able to speak to them, and she learned that for this reason, Wulfgar had assigned them to serve as her waiting women. They carried several garments she was to have as her own, as well as a small ivory casket of jewelry, all of which had come from the bartering at Sliesthorp. When she had finished sponging off with hot water from the soapstone bowl the waiting women had also brought, they helped her to dress, showing her how to fasten at her shoulders, with two beautifully wrought oval bronze brooches, the sleeveless scarlet tunic that went over her finely pleated white gown, in the fashion of the Northland. No girdle of fine mesh or laced leather, such as was worn in the Southland, was among the clothes. Instead, a chain of colored beads was suspended between the brooches; and from this hung the implements of a chatelaine—a needle-case, a pair of small scissors, and the key to the storeroom, as well as her own small dinner knife, which Wulfgar had returned to her. Then the waiting women bedecked Rhowenna with necklaces, armlets, and bracelets of gold and silver, which, it was explained to her, a lady of the Northland wore as evidence of her husband's or her paramour's riches. Next, the women, each taking a side, combed her long black hair back from her face and plaited it in two thick braids into which they wove a profusion of ribands. When they were finished, they handed Rhowenna a polished-bronze mirror, which had also come from Sliesthorp, Wulfgar having apparently given considerable thought to a woman's wants and needs.

Seeing her reflection, Rhowenna felt that for the first time since being taken captive, she was garbed as befitted her rank, although she never would have worn such finery at home, except for special occasions. Yet this was the everyday dress of ladies of the Northland, she was informed by the waiting women. Suddenly, she felt a longing for the plain, workaday gown of undyed wool that she had worn yesterday; for this clothing and these adornments marked her as Wulfgar's concubine. It was as though she had, in truth, lost her maidenhead to him last night, and now was no more than his slave and whore. She had a wild urge to snatch off everything he had bestowed upon her, and she was only deterred by discovering, in answer to her inquiry, that the coarse slave's garments he had bought for her in Sliesthorp had been taken away by him earlier, the waiting women knew not where. She must wear what she had on.

Two spots of color staining her cheekbones, Rhowenna drew back the hide curtain of the sleeping chamber to survey the great mead hall. Wulfgar was there, talking earnestly to Flóki the Raven and a few of the other *thegns*; and although the rest of the warriors had not yet stirred from their sleeping quarters all along the *langpallar*, the slaves were up and about their morning chores. Upon his arrival, Wulfgar had made it clear that there would be no slackness or slovenliness tolerated under his authority, and this warning had been taken to heart, it seemed. Rhowenna observed with approval that the fire in the central hearth had been stoked; and as she smelled the fragrance of the thick porridge bubbling in a cauldron on the blaze, she became aware that she was very hungry. Still, like the slaves, she must attend to her duties before breaking her fast.

As Wulfgar was absorbed in conversation, she hoped to escape his notice; she did not know that he had spied her the moment she had appeared in the doorway of the sleeping chamber, that he had, in fact, been watching and waiting impatiently for her to appear. Now, as she started toward the kitchen, he caught her wrist, drawing her into his arms and kissing her deeply before she could protest or struggle, prompting low laughter and a few good-natured jests from Flóki and the other men, who had come to know and to like her.

"Good morning, sweeting," Wulfgar drawled lazily after a long moment, with a slow, knowing grin. She yearned to scratch his eyes out as they raked her appreciatively, delighting in her beauty and her body so finely arrayed. The fury that sparked in her own eyes that he should act as though he had taken her last night and had found the experience pleasurable indeed seemed to add to his enjoyment at her expense. Still, it would not be wise to provoke him before the rest, she knew. He might feel the need to demonstrate his power over her with more explicit actions here and now. "I trust that you . . . slept well?" he asked.

Unable to trust herself to speak, she merely nodded, humiliated by the blush she could feel deepening on her cheeks as, unbidden, the memory of him pressing her down upon the pallet stole into her mind. Would he do as much to her tonight? she wondered, mortified as she realized she felt tantalized as much as fearful at the thought. Aye, he would do as he pleased—tonight and every night until she at last submitted to him, yielded herself willingly to him, desiring him as much as he desired her. He was a monster, a fiend to torture her so, she told herself, far worse than all the other *Víkingrs* put together—when she had hoped and half believed he was better. But how could she escape from him, and even if she did somehow manage to flee, where could she go, knowing so little, as she did, of this Northland? Yesterday, when she and the rest of the women had been brought from the *Dragon's Fire* to the longhouse, she had seen the fenced meadows where the horses ran free in the summer, horses that could be ridden to chase her down; and the kennels in which the hunting dogs were kept, dogs that could be set to track a lone woman as easily as they tracked game. Even if she were able to steal a small boat, who knew what might befall her on the long journey between the Northland and Walas? Much as she wished otherwise, common sense told her that realistically, until she was ransomed, there was surely little hope of her getting away from Wulfgar.

When he released her reluctantly, Rhowenna moved quickly lest he take her back to the sleeping chamber to finish what he had only started last night. The insolent, unexpected smack he gave her bottom as she walked on toward the kitchen jarred her to the bone, adding injury to insult. How dare he treat her in so ill-bred a manner? she fumed to herself, although she knew with certainty that it was to make his possession of her plain, so no other man would dare to touch her or even to think of helping her to run away from him. And if she were honest with herself, Rhowenna knew she must admit that perhaps this itself was for her protection, as well; for who was to say whether another man, after assisting her to escape, would not turn on her and force himself upon her once they were well beyond Wulfgar's reach? Surely it was as she kept reassuring herself: that her anger and embarrassment and the advances she suffered at Wulfgar's hands were preferable to what she might endure at those of another man.

In the kitchen, Rhowenna saw that the slaves had already milked the cows, for buckets white with foam sat to one side, along with crocks of honey and butter, and loaves of the bread baked yesterday, as well as eggs gathered earlier from the chicken coop. But she knew from experience in her father's royal manor that bread and eggs and porridge were not enough to feed a great hall full of hungry men, and so she ordered what remained of the roasted sheep from last night set out, as well as bowls of fruits and nuts. There was no cheese, and she made a mental note to find out whether this was due simply to the previous mismanagement of the household and markland or whether this was a staple unknown in the North-land. In addition to the milk, she directed that mead, ale, and beer be served. All the while, Rhowenna thought to herself how cramped and inefficient the kitchen was, how inconve-nient the great mead hall was, both lacking trestle tables and benches, so the slave women must sit upon the low stools or the floor to prepare the meal and be constantly stooping to wait upon the *thegns*, who, having been rousted from their pallets, were now taking their places on the cushions around the central hearth. Given the vast forests she had seen, the dearth of furniture could not be due to an equal dearth of wood, so there must be some other reason why there was none. She would ask Wulfgar about it; surely, some of the male slaves or the freedmen could construct something so simple as trestle tables and benches if she were to explain the rudiments of what she wanted. There were other things she would change, too, Rhowenna decided resolutely. After all, if Wulfgar was right, she might be here for a while; and just because the Northmen lived like savages, there was no cause why *she* should. She was civilized, a lady, a princess; she must not let herself forget that. She must not let her spirit be crushed, her dignity stripped from her, as had obviously been the fate of many of the poor slave women who toiled in the kitchen this morn.

Only Morgen, as she had yesterday, escaped the work, sitting languidly on a cushion on the dais between the two huge pillars at the sleeping-chamber end of the great mead hall. She had spent last night locked in the storeroom, whose door had been guarded by Flóki. She, too, had been given two slave women to wait upon her, and clothes and jewelry, and now, she was even more lavishly attired than Rhowenna. Morgen's pleated gown was the color of amber; her indigo overtunic was bordered by wide bands of elaborately embroi-dered riband and fastened with gold brooches at her shoulders. Countless necklaces of gold and amber draped her neck, and armlets and bracelets of gold and silver gleamed at her arms and wrists; even rings, which were rare and thus costly, adorned her slender fingers. Her black hair was intricately braided, woven with ribands, and pinned atop her head, giving her an undeniably regal air. Even Rhowenna, knowing the truth, could believe Morgen a princess.

When the morning meal was finished and the last of the pots and dishes were cleared away, Rhowenna discussed with Wulfgar what she had in mind in the way of furnishings for the great mead hall and the kitchen. To her surprise, he said she might do as she pleased to make the longhouse more comfortable; and presently, freedmen armed with axes were dispatched to the woods to choose and to cut down trees suitable for Rhowenna's purposes. She herself, she learned, was to be permitted to roam the markland freely, so long as she was accompanied by some of the *thegns*—for her own protection rather than to prevent her from escaping, Wulfgar informed her with a bland smile, so she knew he was on guard against her instinctive urge to flee and would thwart any such attempt. After ensuring that the household chores were under way, she and a few of the other slave women, laden with baskets, ventured down to the seashore, where they searched for seaweed, with which Rhowenna planned to make laverbread. If Wulfgar would allow one of the pigs in the pigsty to be butchered, she could fry the laverbread in the rendered pork fat and make hog's-head cheese, a jellied meat, at the same time, a method her practical mother had always favored.

As it had ever since her abduction, Rhowenna's heart ached when she thought of her mother and father; she wondered how they fared without her in Usk, so distant from the Northland. Although she had been gone from her home only days, to her, it seemed like forever, as though she had lived her years there in another life far away and long ago—or in a dream. It was as though only the Northland existed for her now.

Earlier, she had taken off her slippers; and now she thought that even the sand here felt different from that of the beaches of Usk, rougher, grainier, and that the water felt colder, despite the warmth of the summer sun. As she filled her basket with seaweed, it suddenly occurred to Rhowenna that she had been doing something quite similar when the Northmen had attacked Usk; and for a moment, she glanced around uneasily, half fearing that here, too, she would face an assault. While aboard the *Dragon's Fire*, Wulfgar had told her that Northland feuds were infamous, with Northmen battling one another as frequently as they did their enemies of the East-lands and the Southlands, and that the *Víkingrs* often hired themselves out as mercenaries, also, to the Greeks and to the Slavic kingdoms especially. But to her relief, she saw no one hovering near except the other slave women and the *thegns* who guarded them.

When the baskets were full, Rhowenna and the rest walked back to the longhouse. Upon the wooden racks used for drying fish and fruits and vegetables, she hung the seaweed to dry in the sun. She would make the laverbread and the hog's-head cheese tomorrow; upon hearing her plan, Wulfgar had agreed to slaughter one of the pigs. Having ridden out earlier on Olaf the Sea Bull's huge black horse, which he had also confiscated for himself, Wulfgar had since returned to the *hof* from inspecting the fields and was now busy in the palisade, overseeing the repairs he had put into progress the day before. As she draped the strands of seaweed over the drying racks, Rhowenna could feel his intense eyes upon her, devouring her. Still, although his watching her unsettled her, she did not hurry at her task, for its completion meant a return to the shadowy interior of the longhouse. Thinking of her father's great hall during the long, dark winter months, she could only imagine the dreariness of the *hof* during the Northland's "murky time," as Wulfgar called it. But surely she would be long gone by then, she thought; surely Prince Cerdic or her father would have paid her ransom by then, and Wulfgar would have returned her if not to Usk, at least to Mercia.

That her current life here in the Northland was in some respects a glimpse of the life she would spend in Mercia as a stranger in a foreign land, with unfamiliar customs and raiment and foods, was a notion on which Rhowenna did not care to dwell. There could be no comparison between being a slave and being a princess—even if Wulfgar *had* allotted her the duties of his chatelaine—and Mercia was a civilized kingdom whose Saxon inhabitants, once barbaric heathens, had long ago converted to Christianity, unlike these savage Northmen. Further, Prince Cerdic would be her husband, caring and considerate, surely, as his gift to her of the gold necklace set with amethysts had demonstrated. That even so, he, too, would want of her what Wulfgar desired was a thought she determinedly shoved from her mind. It would be different with Prince Cerdic, Rhowenna told herself. His taking of her would be properly sanctified by the Church; he himself would be kind and gentle, understanding her maidenly fear and respecting her as his wife—not seeing her as merely a vessel to receive his lust, as Wulfgar did, murmuring his bard-song lies to beguile her into surrendering to him. Nor would Prince Cerdic press upon her such kisses and caresses as Wulfgar did to arouse within her that strange, leaping flame, that fierce, wild yearning that only a wanton would feel. In Prince Cerdic's arms, she would be safe. Only deceit and danger, dishonor and disillusionment lay in Wulfgar's embrace.

Picking up her empty basket and turning to go into the longhouse, Rhowenna's attention was caught by the return of some of the freedmen who had gone out earlier to the forest. They drove an ox-drawn sledge to which numerous logs were roped; here was the wood with which to begin building the furniture she wanted. Despite herself, she felt a tiny thrill of anticipation at the sight. She would soon have the *hof* at least *looking* as though it were inhabited by civilized men instead of barbarians, even if it were not. Carrying her basket against her hip, she went to speak again to Eirik, the chief wood-carver, still not certain he grasped what she had in mind. After a few minutes of struggling conversation in which Rhowenna addressed him in the Saxon tongue and Eirik responded in the language of the Northland, Wulfgar materialized at her side to translate. More than once during their dialogue, Rhowenna heard the Northland word *seng* but was not certain of its meaning; it was not, she thought, a term she had heard previously—and was not table *bord* in the Northland tongue, and bench, *benk*? Confused, she wondered if even Wulfgar had understood what she meant by furniture.

"Aye," he said in answer to her question, his voice dry, "I may be a 'heathen' and a 'savage,' as you have called me, lady. But I am not so ignorant that I have mistaken your meaning. Even if Olaf the Sea Bull possessed none, I have many times over the years seen tables and benches and other furniture at the *hof* of Ragnar Lodbrók. But most are used only on special occasions, such as feast days, we Northmen not being so soft and needful of luxuries as the warriors of the Eastlands and the Southlands—which is why we will someday rule them all, lady, as we already rule the seas.

"Even now, we have footholds in the Slavic, the Germanic, and the Frankish kingdoms, as well as in Frisia, Caledonia, and Erin. 'Tis only a matter of time before we conquer Britain and Walas, too. This summer, Ragnar sailed up the river Seine to sack Paris again, for plunder with which to support an army. If he gets it, he and his sons will hire mercenaries and, like a horde of flies upon honey, will descend on the kingdoms of Britain; for 'tis Ragnar's burning ambition in life to be overking of all of Britain, subject no longer to the Jutish king across the Skagerrak, to whom he must pay tribute and homage in the Northland. So you see, lady, 'tis not just a ransom worth your weight in gold that you will represent to Ragnar, but also perhaps a stronghold from which he may launch his campaign to subjugate the kingdoms of Britain and to place the Saxons firmly beneath his booted heel, Prince Cerdic of Mercia among them!''

"I—I don't understand.'' Rhowenna was puzzled and somehow frightened by Wulfgar's words. "What—what do you mean, my lord?''

"Only this: Despite your father's betrothing you to Prince Cerdic, Usk and Mercia will never be aught save uneasy allies at best; for between the Celts and the Saxons, there has ever been enmity. It may be, then, that in exchange for your honor and—Ragnar will take pains to convince him—your life, your father will find it wiser in the end to strike a bargain with Ragnar; for allies are often born of expedience and friends made of those with common foes. Ragnar has three legitimate sons, none of whom would scruple at setting aside their wives and marrying you if it served their ambition and purpose. Then would your Usk become Ragnar's stepstone into Britain—although once the old wolf and his cubs had devoured the sheep, they would no doubt turn on the shepherd who let them into the fold, I am thinking.''

"A fact my father will be wise enough to grasp," Rhowenna declared, not without pride. "Besides, my father fears the Christian priests and so would never barter me to a heathen!''

"Perhaps, lady. But I tell you that there are Northmen who are not so fearful of your priests or of your God and who would swear oath to worship Him if such would win for them what Ragnar hopes to attain.''

To Rhowenna, this was a terrible blasphemy. Yet from what she herself had seen of the *Víkingrs*, she could not doubt that Wulfgar spoke the truth. She shuddered at the thought; for as, unbidden, Father Cadwyr's fanatical image stole into her mind, she knew that the priest would view the conversion of a heathen to Christianity as God's most highly esteemed work and would counsel Pendragon accordingly should the opportunity arise, urging him to join forces with the Northmen against the Saxons—and allaying his suspicions that the Northmen would, after consuming Britain, also swallow the whole of Walas.

"Now you know why, above all else, Ragnar Lodbrók and his sons will come for you, lady, why I sought to have Morgen take your place as the princess of Usk." Wulfgar's voice was grim. "A father whose daughter has been dishonored and is heavy with child, besides, is more often than not a man determined to see her wed to her seducer and so a man, also, with whom a bargain may be more easily struck. Believe me, lady: If Ragnar should somehow learn your true identity and succeed in wresting you from me, if your father should balk at paying what I suspect will prove Ragnar's ransom demand, Ragnar will force you himself or turn you over to his son Ivar the Boneless for sport; and if afterward they cannot get you as a bride, and a stronghold in Usk as your dowry, you will wind up their slave and their whore. Doubt that not, lady. I know them, down to their bones. Father and sons are all hungry for power and ruthless in their pursuit of it—and you are but a woman and a maiden, whose feelings will mean nothing, less than nothing, to them."

"But if all you say is true, how can I permit Morgen to fall into their clutches?"

"She is no virgin," Wulfgar stated bluntly, shrugging. "Her fate at their hands will be no worse than what it would have been in my slave pens, as she must have guessed. So there is, in truth, little risk to her. As long as she commits no crime, neither Ragnar nor Ivar will kill her. As I told you in Sliesthorp, there are laws here in the Northland that govern how a slave must be treated. Besides, 'twas Morgen's own choice to trade places with you, and she made it freely. By doing so, she proved herself both bold and clever; and I will do what I can to protect her as I protect you, lady. And perhaps the messengers I have dispatched this morning to Prince Cerdic and to your father will return to the Northland before Ragnar Lodbrók and Ivar the Boneless sail their longships homeward. But if the gods decree otherwise, I will not sacrifice you to spare Morgen, lady. There is too much at stake for that. It would avail her naught and bring you a certain and grievous ruin—to say nothing of the formidable weapon it would place in Ragnar's grasping hands.''

For a long moment, there was silence between them, each pondering the shared knowledge of what Wulfgar would allow Morgen to endure if it would save Rhowenna from a like fate. Tears stung Rhowenna's eyes at the realization, for with it came the understanding that Wulfgar, too, could be hard and remorseless when he chose. Had she not seen evidence of that once before, when he had beheaded Knut Strongarm? Even so, she could not fault Wulfgar's reasoning; it was all too obvious that he had thought things through very clearly. At last, her voice throbbing with emotion, she spoke.

"You—you are right, of course. I—I must think of Usk. Without me, Ragnar Lodbrók cannot compel my father to accede to his demands, and so Usk and its people will be safe. That is enough; that is all that is important."

"Have you no thought for yourself, Rhowenna?" Wulfgar inquired gently, his voice holding a curious note as he gazed at her searchingly. "For your own needs? In your place, another woman would think only of herself."

"I am a princess, and I know my duty."

"You are also a woman—with feelings—are you not?"

"Aye. But I have learned over the years that sometimes 'tis necessary for a princess to deny her own emotions for the sake of her obligations to kingdom and crown."

"Is that what you did when your father betrothed you to Prince Cerdic? Is that why you agreed to the match? For do not tell me that you wished to wed him when I know that you did not!"

"Nay, I did not want to marry him, 'tis true—but only because I—because I . . . loved another, my kinsman Gwydion." Rhowenna's face softened with sadness and regret as she spoke Gwydion's name, and her eyes glowed with a faraway light that filled Wulfgar with anger, jealousy, and a terrible fear, of a sudden, that he could never win her heart, that she had given it away to another and so had nothing left for him. He had never once thought that she might be in love, that some man other than he had embraced her, had tasted her sweet mouth, drinking long and deep of its nectar, and had caressed her milk-white throat and breasts.

"Lady, your words are a blade in my heart," he said, his voice low, rough with emotion. "Why do you seek to wound me with this revelation of your love for another when you know how much I love and desire you, that I would have made you my queen instead of my slave, and would still? Have you so little care, then, for my feelings? Or are you as fickle and faithless as any other woman? By the gods, I had not thought so. But why else would you lie in my arms and kiss me as you did last night if your heart belongs to your kinsman?"

"How can I reply when I do not myself know the answer?" she cried softly, turning her face away from him in shame that he would speak of last night and how she had responded to him. One hand fluttered to her slender throat, as though to still the sudden, wild beating of the pulse that lay at its delicate hollow. "No man has ever had of me what you have taken from me, my lord; and although I would hate you for it with all my heart, I find I cannot. I do not understand these strange feelings you have stirred within me. 'Tis as though my mind and my will melt away when you touch me—" A small, ragged sob issuing from her throat, Rhowenna broke off abruptly, stricken by her confession, her eyes cast down to avoid his, her mouth so vulnerable and tremulous that Wulfgar longed to possess it with his own as a thrill of triumph shot through him at her anguished admission. After a long moment, she continued. "Through you, a sinful pagan, does the devil, who is unholy and iniquitous, tempt me to wantonness and wickedness, I fear, to test my faith as a Christian maiden; and I pray earnestly for my swift deliverance and, if that be not granted me, for strength to hold fast against you as long as need be." When she paused, drawing a long, uneven breath that revealed how difficult she feared that the struggle against him—and against her own self—would be, he was filled with elation. Then, her voice poignant with sorrow, she went on. "As for my heart, if once it belonged to my kinsman Gwydion, it does no longer; for he would not have it in his keeping—"

"What?" Wulfgar exclaimed harshly, shocked that any man could not want her as his and angered by the hurt and rejection she had so obviously and painfully suffered. "What fool was he? Was he blind that he could not see your rare beauty? Deaf, that he could not hear your siren's song of enchantment? Mute, that he could not speak to you the words of love and desire for you that I would shout unto the very halls of Asgard, the barred gates of Hel, if the gods and Hela, who is Death, would deign to hear my cry?"

"Nay." Rhowenna shook her head slowly, her countenance wistful, her gaze distant, as before. "He was only a man who did not dare to dream."

"I am not such a man as that, lady. For I *do* dare to dream. I dream of holding you in my arms and of feeling you tremble with passion beneath me, your white thighs spread wide to receive me as I fill you to overflowing with a nectar far sweeter and headier than wine, as I would show you if you would but yield to me. I dream of waking every morning for the rest of my life to see you lying beside me, the waves of your raven hair rippling across the pillows, a black sea in which I would gladly drown forever. I dream of watching your soft body ripen and swell with a babe of my making, here"—he laid his hand upon her belly, a tender caress that made her shudder, despite herself, with a sudden, strange longing, a deep, instinctive, maternal ache she had never before felt. "I dream not only of life within you, but also of life *with* you, of you sitting beside me in my great mead hall, your face aglow with the light of the fire and of the whale-oil lamps of many a long, dark winter's eve. I dream of growing old with you. I dream that when I die in battle, 'twill be you instead of a golden Valkyrie who comes for me, and that we will live together until the very end of time, on some enchanted isle that is neither my Asgard nor your Heaven, but a place for souls who love so deeply that they can never be parted. All this, I dare to dream for love of you, Rhowenna. What more would you have me say?"

"Say that you will take me home to Usk, my lord," she implored quietly, although the reply was not what her heart prompted her to speak, and the hand she laid upon his arm trembled not with fear, but with the passionate yearning his eloquent words had aroused within her. No man had ever spoken to her so, plucked the strings of her heart so surely that they echoed with a melody so sweet she ached to sing a harmony in answer. "Tell me that, Wulfgar, if you love me as you claim."

"Gladly would I take you there, although I should sicken and die of unrequited love and desire for you at our parting; so much, I know in my heart. But I have no way at present to return you to Usk, Rhowenna. The *Dragon's Fire* was Olaf the Sea Bull's longship, not mine; even now, it lies in the hollow of a heath on this markland, waiting to become part of Olaf's burial mound when the priest of Odinn at the *templum* in the Sacred Grove has finished his preparations to speak the funeral prayers to the gods. And I dare not take you on board a cargo vessel, where your beauty and desirability might bestir its captain and crew to turn upon me and to slay me, so they can take you prisoner and rape you at their leisure before selling you at a slave market—or, if they should somehow learn your identity, hold you hostage themselves for your ransom. Either way, you would represent a profit to such men, lady, many of whom are *Víkingrs* or other sea wolves, as well as traders. Do you understand?''

"Aye." Rhowenna nodded, swallowing her disappointment, inwardly torn by the knowledge that it was not so acute as it ought to have been, that some tiny, traitorous part of her was glad she must remain in the Northland, with Wulfgar.

Turning from him, carrying her empty basket, she went at last into the longhouse, into the gloomy great mead hall, where the fire burned in the central hearth—and now, of a sudden, she felt a pang at the unbidden thought that perhaps she would not be there to see it of a long, dark winter's eve in the Northland.

Chapter Eleven

Swift Flies
the Summer

The summer was short in the Northland, and seemed to fly by so swiftly that Rhowenna, whenever she thought of it, could not believe how long she had been gone from Usk. Yet, strangely, despite being Wulfgar's captive and slave, she could not honestly have declared herself discontent. Because he had given her the duties of his chatelaine, her days soon settled into a pattern that was not dissimilar to that of her life in Usk. Time no longer hung heavily on her hands, as it had aboard the *Dragon's Fire*, but was taken up by her multitude of tasks as mistress of the *hof*. It was almost as though she were, in fact, Wulfgar's wife, Rhowenna sometimes reflected, such was the respect and deference with which she was treated by all, the way in which her soft-voiced commands to the *thegns*, the freedmen, and the slaves were obeyed. Still, she would have been surprised to learn that this was due as much to her own noble nature as it was to Wulfgar's august authority. She did not realize how her outer beauty and grace, her inner caring and compassion touched the hearts of even the hardest of the men, who, no more than Wulfgar, had never before known her like.

To the *thegns*, Rhowenna was a living symbol of their lord's boldness and virility; that he should hold such a coveted prize was proof indeed of his might and worth as a *jarl*, and so of their own as his warriors. Thus did they also come to revere her, as Wulfgar did. As the days passed, she learned that they were not quite the savages she had at first thought them, that although still boisterous, they usually comported themselves more decorously, the ribald revelry they had engaged in during the voyage and on the night of their homecoming being celebrative rather than everyday behavior. To the freedmen, Rhowenna quickly became a mistress who valued their skill as artisans and laborers, fishermen and farmers, and who was never too busy to praise their talents and to take pride in their work. She soon knew all their names and their jobs, from Gudrod, the temperamental potter, to Arngrim, the taciturn blacksmith, from Magnus, the tranquil fisher, to Thorvald, the thoughtful shepherd. They were, she discovered, not so very different, after all, from the people of Usk, the craftsmen and *ceorls* she had known and cared for all her life. To the slaves, Rhowenna seemed from the beginning a savior who did whatever she could to better their lowly lot, for she could not help but pity them. There were no slaves in Walas; and even though there were laws to govern the treatment of those in the Northland, the slaves were often miserable. All worked long, hard hours; the women bore the additional burden of being prey for any lustful *jarl* or *thegn* who desired them, and this practice, Rhowenna could not stop. But at least she could make certain the slaves were not denied proper food or clothing, and she had a kind word for everyone.

To the longhouse, Rhowenna brought not only order and cleanliness, but also a sense of dignity and grace that it had previously lacked and that the *Víkingrs*, with their—to her, startling and unexpected—love of beauty and art and poetry, approved and appreciated. Knowing she was accustomed to finer things, sensing how important her surroundings were to her, and wishing to please her, Wulfgar had the craftsmen fashion exquisitely painted wooden panels, which were pegged to the timber walls, as was the custom in many a wealthy household; and to these were fastened big, elaborately formed bronze hooks on which to store, when dismantled after meals, the trestle tables and long benches the woodcarvers built. On the dais sat a thronelike chair that served as Wulfgar's high seat. An abundance of whale-oil lamps and rushlights brought light into the shadows, and sweet-smelling rushes strewed the hard-packed earth floor. There were trestle tables for the kitchen, as well, and shelves now to hold pots and dishes, with barrels and chests neatly lined up underneath on the floor. To all this, Wulfgar made two further—and swiftly completed—contributions: The hide curtain in the doorway of the sleeping chamber was replaced by a stout, ornately carved oak door with iron fittings and a sturdy lock; and in the sleeping chamber itself stood a massive bed—the *seng*. That word had puzzled Rhowenna the day of Wulfgar's discussion with Eirik, the chief woodcarver, but she now knew its meaning as she learned daily more and more of the language of the Northland.

When the door and the bed were installed, Rhowenna's heart turned over in her breast; for she knew they meant that although Wulfgar perhaps would keep his word and would not force her to submit to him, he was determined to win her surrender, nevertheless. He continued his loverlike assaults upon her body and senses, and she did not know how long she could go on holding out against him. She was virtually his wife in all but his bed; and even there, she lay in his embrace at night, trembling with the feelings he had wakened within her and went on nurturing, filling her with an undundurable ache she knew instinctively that only he could ease. Fiercely, trying to convince herself of it, she told herself that she wished he would not kiss her, would not caress her. Once, she even asked him not to touch her again; but he only laughed softly and said that that had not been part of the bargain, that he had promised only not to rape her.

Still, although it was potent with meaning, the bed, made of oak, was undeniably beautiful. Eirik and his cadre of woodcarvers must have labored many days and long into the nights to finish it, Rhowenna thought when she first saw it, and she was touched despite herself by the work and obvious care that had gone into it. The two tall, highly detailed posts of the headboard each resembled the dragon-headed stempost of a longship; the headboard itself had intricately carved upon it a great, stalking wolf at the edge of a reed-grown mere, upon whose quietly rippling waters a graceful swan floated— beautiful, serene, unaware. The footboard and its shorter posts were a luxuriance of forested mountains sweeping to the sea. Ells of walrus hide stretched between the sideboards supported the eiderdown-stuffed wool pallet.

"Do you like it?" From behind her, Wulfgar's hands slid slowly back and forth along her shoulders and arms; his breath was warm against her nape, making her shiver. "'Tis built so it can be dismantled for traveling. The *konungrs* and rich *jarlar* often have more than one such bed in their *hofs*; sometimes, they are even interred with them, as in his longship, Olaf the Sea Bull was with his own possessions and food and drink for his afterlife as one of the Einheriar, in Valhöll."

"The bed is lovely," Rhowenna admitted honestly, for it was not the bed itself, but only the thought of sharing it with him that disturbed her—although why it should be any different from the deck of the longship or the pallet alone, she did not know.

"I would make love to you in it, *elsket*." His lips brushed her hair, her ear, the side of her neck, sending another shudder of excitement through her. "Why do you not yield to me? You know that you want me as much I want you. You cannot deny that."

"Nay, I cannot," she rejoined softly, after a long moment; for in her heart, she knew that he had spoken truly. Despite everything, she did desire him, her enemy, her captor. She did not know why, but it was so. "But I *will* deny you, Wulfgar. You are a heathen, and I am a Christian, betrothed to Prince Cerdic, whom I cannot wed and to whose own bed I cannot go as a sullied bride, lest he cast me off and I be compelled to return home to Usk, disgraced, a disappointment to my father and mother, a sinner in the eyes of the Christ and the Church."

Wulfgar sighed heavily at her reply. Still, he would have pressed her, would have argued the issue further, would have carried her to the bed and laid her down upon its soft pallet to try with his mouth and tongue and hands to persuade her to give in to him. But there came a knock upon the door and then the sound of Flóki the Raven's voice, saying:

"Lord, I am sorry to disturb you, but 'tis important. One of the messengers you dispatched to the Southlands has finally returned—from Mercia, lord—and he has Prince Cerdic's answer to your ransom demand for the princess!"

Hearing this news, Rhowenna felt her heart give a sudden lurch and then begin to hammer violently in her breast, and Wulfgar's hands tightened so painfully on her shoulders that she flinched. For an eternity, it seemed, neither she nor he moved or spoke. Then, at last, he released her, turning to open the door.

"Come," he demanded quietly, holding out his hand to her, his face impassive, his eyes hooded so she could not read his thoughts, although there was a certain grimness about the corners of his mouth, a tenseness to his body that let her know how unwelcome he found the missive from Mercia.

Perhaps even if Prince Cerdic had agreed to pay her ransom, Wulfgar would not return her, Rhowenna thought, startled by the abrupt realization that this prospect neither frightened nor dismayed her as wholly as it ought, but gave her instead a peculiar pleasure. Surely, she had been beset by some madness to feel so. Despite the freedoms he had permitted her, she was still his prisoner, his slave; she should be glad to escape from him, not experiencing such a queer pang at the idea of never seeing him again.

Aye, I am mad, or ill, she told herself, *or else Wulfgar has entranced me with some Northland magic. Perhaps that old slave woman who reared him, Yelkei, has cast a spell upon me to tempt me from my loyalty and my duty to Usk into wickedness and wantonness in Wulfgar's arms—for did he not say that she was a spaewife, that she possessed the power of prophesy born of fires and mists and the rune stones? Surely, such a one is a witch.* . . . But then Rhowenna remembered her own prophetic dream and how, for it, she had feared to be accused by Father Cadwyr as the devil's handmaiden; and she knew that she was being unfair to the old slave woman. It was Wulfgar himself who attracted her, despite herself. *Have I somehow fallen in love with him?* she wondered. *Nay, that cannot be. Of course it cannot.* . . .

Determinedly dismissing the notion, she followed Wulfgar from the sleeping chamber, anxiously settling herself in her position at his feet as he sat down on the high seat upon the dais between the two large pillars at the end of the great mead hall. Unless he was swearing oath, it was not the custom in the Northland for a man to kneel before his lord. Instead, with his right fist, the messenger, Naddod, struck his chest over his heart in a brief salute to Wulfgar before handing him a scroll of parchment sealed with beeswax, into which was stamped what Rhowenna recognized as Prince Cerdic's seal. Breaking the seal, Wulfgar slowly unrolled the scroll, frowning as he stared down at it.

"''Tis not written in the *dönsk tunga*,'' he announced finally, referring to the language of the Northland, "but some tongue I know not."

"Latin, lord"—Naddod elucidated—"which, begging your pardon, lord, Prince Cerdic charged me to say that he doubted that you would understand, as 'tis the language of the learned, and despite your calling yourself a *jarl* of the Northland, you are, in truth, naught save an unlettered pagan barbarian and a *Víkingr*."

"Well, by the gods, that is a case of the troll's calling the dwarf ugly"—Wulfgar's snort of laughter rang out amid that of the *thegns* at this insult—"coming from a Saxon sea wolf whose own ancestors were both savages and pirates, and a bold statement, besides, for a man whose betrothed I hold utterly at my mercy! Either this Cerdic of Mercia is a prince I'd like to cross blades with, or else he's a fool; and if the latter is so, why, then, he's not deserving even of my scorn! Say on, Naddod. Did Prince Cerdic tell you what is written herein this scroll?"

"Aye, lord, and he commanded me to commit it to memory and to repeat it to you thus: 'To Wulfgar Bloodaxe, *jarl* of the Northland, I greet you. In reply to your letter regarding my betrothed, Rhowenna, princess of Usk, I must inform you that as her dowry has never been delivered to me, I consider that both our betrothal and the treaty with Usk have been broken, and so I feel no obligation to pay from my own coffers the gold demanded as my lady's ransom. You must do with her as you will. Hereto, I have affixed my seal this fourteenth day of August in the Year of Our Lord 865.' Signed 'Cerdic, prince of Mercia.' "

"By the God of the Runes and Valhöll!" Wulfgar roared, slamming his fist down on the arm of his chair, then springing to his feet and throwing the scroll to the floor. "The man's a contemptible, callous coward with more care for his purse than for what is right and honorable toward his lady, who is powerless against this wicked wrong done her! Whatever the reason for it, 'tis not her fault that her dowry has yet to be delivered to him. By Thor's hammer, my battle-ax is too good for the likes of him; why, I'd sooner use a horsewhip to teach that Saxon dog a lesson!'' Still, his eyes glittered not murderously, but with an eager, triumphant light when he gazed down at Rhowenna, and she knew he was thinking, as she was, that she was not yet to leave him, and that she could no longer use her betrothal as an excuse for refusing to lie with him.

Frightened more by this than by his anger, which she knew was not directed at her, she cringed at Wulfgar's feet, stricken that Prince Cerdic, not knowing whether she was treated well or ill, should so cruelly relegate her to her fate in the North- land. This was not what she had thought to hear from the man to whom her father had betrothed her, the man who had sent her the gold necklace set with amethysts, which she had believed such a caring, considerate gift, a mark of his esteem for her. That he should now so easily and heartlessly abandon her for lack of her dowry filled her with despair. Something must have happened, she thought with a sudden sense of foreboding. Although Prince Cerdic's missive had hinted at no discord between them, her father would never, without just cause, have reneged on his agreement with Prince Cerdic. Was Mercia now once more Usk's foe, then? Rhowenna shivered at the idea, for in her heart, she knew that Usk was not strong enough to fight off a concerted attack from Mercia and Glamorgan or Gwent, especially after the brutal raid by the Northmen, during which Wulfgar had taken her captive. She worried for her parents, and for Gwydion, and thought how ironic it was that she might actually at this moment be safer in the Northland, under Wulfgar's protection, than in her own homeland.

How prophetic was that observation, Rhowenna was to think over a fortnight later, when the *thegns* in the watchtow- ers sounded their horns in warning, and one of the men descended his ladder to report grimly to Wulfgar that a band of armed men approached the palisade, at their vanguard, mounted upon a snowy white horse, Ivar the Boneless, son and heir of the great Ragnar Lodbrók, a *konungr* of the Northland.

Chapter Twelve

The Reckoning

Rhowenna had dreamed a horrible dream the night before. She had dreamed of wandering on the shores of Usk, and of crimson-winged sea dragons, breathing fire and death, their riders dismounting to plunge into the frothy brine, shouting mighty battle cries, weapons raised high to lay waste to Usk, at the vanguard of the warriors a gold-headed demon. Tears streaming down her cheeks, she had run and run through the melee, frantically turning over one by one the corpses that lay facedown, strewn upon that bloody earth. To her horror, every man had borne the face of her father, every woman, that of her mother. She had screamed and screamed at the sight; but as is often the way of a nightmare, no sound had issued from her throat until she had wakened herself with her shrieks and sobs, and Wulfgar, too, her heart pounding, her body drenched with a cold sweat.

"Shhhhh, *elsket*," he had murmured soothingly, gathering her into his arms, stroking and kissing her gently as he had cradled her against his chest. "'Twas only a dream, only a bad dream, that's all. I'm right here beside you, and I won't let anything happen to you, I swear it. You're safe, sweeting; you're safe here with me. So, hush, now. Hush."

But hours had passed before Rhowenna had finally fallen back to sleep. Now, as she heard the horns sounding their warning, she thought of her dream last night and of the horns echoing up and down the coast of Usk before the Northmen in their longships had swooped upon her homeland; and she was gripped by a fearful premonition. So strong was this feeling of foreboding that she did not move when Wulfgar turned and spoke to her, but stood where she was, caught up in the chaotic images of violence that, unbidden, erupted in her mind, memories of the actual battle at Usk, when she had been taken prisoner, and unreal scenes from her dreams. Her countenance was pale; her violet eyes were wide and dazed and scared, uncomprehending as, abruptly grabbing her, Wulfgar pulled loose several strands of hair from her braid and then, bending to scoop up a handful of dirt, rubbed her face and gown with it.

"There, that's better; you are less likely to attract Ivar's attention, I am thinking. Now, go back inside the *hof*, to the kitchen, and stay there until I send for you, Rhowenna," he ordered harshly, afraid for her and savage in his fear. Then, angered by her lack of response, he snarled, "Do as I say, wench!" giving her a rough little shove toward the longhouse.

Rhowenna did as Wulfgar had commanded then, her heart racing, her hands trembling as she gathered up her skirts and hastened into the *hof*, to the kitchen. She had been in the process of making laverbread when the horns had begun their clamor; and now, despite her agitation, she forced herself to continue her work. But even so occupied, she could not quell the dread that filled her at the news that Ivar the Boneless was coming.

By now, Rhowenna knew the sequence of events that had

followed the tale told by the *skáld* Sigurd Silkbeard in Ragnar Lodbrók's great mead hall: how it was that Wulfgar had sailed to Usk to take her captive before Ivar the Boneless could seize her as his own prize and why Ivar would feel he had a right to claim her from Wulfgar. But in the beginning, some days after their arrival in the Northland, word had reached them at Wulfgar's markland that neither Ragnar nor his sons had yet returned from their respective raids upon the Southlands; and so, as the summer had flown by, it had been easy for Rhowenna to push the threat of their homecoming to the back of her mind. Some part of her, she now realized, had even half thought—half hoped—that Ragnar and his sons would be killed in battle while away a-*víking*, as Olaf the Sea Bull had been killed. But now, the threat they posed to her, and to Morgen, could no longer be dismissed. Ivar the Boneless was alive; he was here.

Through a chink in the longhouse's timber wall, Rhowenna watched as the gates of the palisade swung open to admit the band of riders who galloped inside; and as she spied the man mounted upon the pure-white steed at their fore—Ivar the Boneless, surely—her breath caught in her throat and her heart seemed to stop beating for an excruciating eternity before starting up again with a frightening jerk. It was *he*, the gold-headed demon of her horrifying dream last night, a sinister portent not to be ignored by one whose dream of Wulfgar and the Northmen's raid upon Usk had come true. Her sense of impending doom grew; she shivered uncontrollably. Without even realizing she did so, she grasped the gold Celtic crucifix about her neck and began to pray, her lips moving soundlessly, the laverbread forgotten.

In the bailey, Ivar drew his prancing horse up short, lifting one hand to bring the rest of his *thegns* to a halt behind him. For a long moment, he did not dismount, but sat there staring down at Wulfgar, in his eyes that strange, leaping light Wulfgar had seen that winter's day of the roe-deer hunt, on his face that peculiar half-smile that somehow bespoke both challenge and admiration, and that caused the fine hairs on Wulfgar's nape to lift. Yet, for the first time in his life, he found to his surprise and fierce gladness that he was able to look at Ivar without a sense of lowliness and jealousy, of dread and humiliation; and he somehow knew he would never again feel those emotions in Ivar's presence. Hatred still roiled within him at the memory of Ivar's ill-treatment of him over the years, his refusal to recognize him as a brother; but now Wulfgar's feeling was that not only of a man toward his enemy, but toward his equal. As though Ivar sensed this, he at last spoke.

"Well, well, Wulfgar," he drawled, in the habitually insolent tone Wulfgar recalled only too well, "it would seem that the gods and the Norns have granted you their favor; for your fortunes are much improved since last I saw you. The lowly *bóndi* has risen not only to the rank of *Víkingr*, but also to that of *jarl*. Who would have thought that your saving of my sword hand would reap such rewards? But, then, the gods have ever been fanciful, have they not? And what they bestow today, they may as easily take away tomorrow."

"'Twas your life I saved, Ivar," Wulfgar rejoined tersely, blandly ignoring Ivar's veiled threat and deliberately addressing his half brother by his given name instead of his title, relishing the way in which Ivar's brows rose in reaction to that, his eyes hardening a little, and his half-smile tightening at the corners.

"Aye, but my life would have been nothing without my sword hand, which, as you can see"—with an elegant motion born of his body's uncanny limberness, Ivar raised his hand and flexed his wrist to demonstrate that it had lost none of its strength or suppleness—"is quite mended and still serves me as well as ever."

"As does my battle-ax serve me. What do you want, Ivar?"

"A cup of *nabid* would do for a start—or is the bold

wolf, in truth, yet such a scraggly animal beneath his newly acquired fine fur that he would deny me the hospitality of his *hof*?'' The words stung, as intended; for they were an insulting reminder of the fact that Northmen prided themselves on their hospitality, which they would not refuse any but an outlaw, not even a foe.

"If an animal is scraggly, 'tis due to the fleas who bite him. Once rid of them, why, then his true coat is revealed,'' Wulfgar observed smoothly, his smile sardonic, his blue eyes glinting with a guile and malice to match Ivar's own.

"Your wits have grown sharp.''

"Aye, now that they are no longer dulled by those who fear to have their own barbs returned in kind.''

"What are a few barbs between adversaries?'' Ivar shrugged nonchalantly, a fluid motion that seemed the merest ripple of his shoulders, sinewy with muscle. "A trifling annoyance, perhaps, but no more than that—hardly enough to inspire fear in one who wields a gilt-bronzed shield against them. But my tongue thirsts from all this talk. I have always been a man of action myself. Do you offer *nabid* or nay?''

"Aye, if you would have it. Do you and your men dismount and come inside. You will not judge my great mead hall so grand as Ragnar's, perhaps; but it serves me well enough, because 'tis mine. For that alone, the taste of the *nabid* served therein is sweet upon my tongue, although you may find it a trifle sour, Ivar, I am thinking.''

"Well, we shall soon see, shall we not?'' With a curt command to his *thegns*, Ivar swung down from his saddle to follow Wulfgar into the longhouse.

Inhaling sharply, unable to conceal his surprise, Ivar momentarily drew up short as he beheld the interior of the great mead hall, the ornate twin pillars flanking the dais at the far end, upon which sat Wulfgar's high seat, the elaborately carved chair that had replaced what had previously been little more than a low stool. Slowly, his eyes narrowed, Ivar gazed at the beautifully painted wooden panels pegged to the walls—even the wooden screen that set apart the kitchen had been so decorated; the striplike tapestries, cleaned and so expertly mended by Rhowenna and Morgen that the repairs were hard to see; the long, intricate bronze hooks for storing the tables and benches; the furniture itself, uncommon in the Northland and, so, highly prized; the fresh rushes mingled with sweet-scented heather that strewed the hard-packed earth floor; and the abundance of whale-oil lamps and rushlights that illuminated even the shadowy corners.

Still, Ivar said nothing as Wulfgar gave orders for the tables and benches to be set up and for food and drink to be brought, then settled himself upon the high seat, motioning for Ivar to join him at the high table, along with Flóki the Raven, as well as Ivar's own second-in-command and some of the other, higher-ranked warriors. Neither Rhowenna nor Morgen was anywhere in sight, Wulfgar noted with relief. Rhowenna was in the kitchen, he knew; Morgen, he correctly assumed, had been locked in the storeroom by Flóki for safekeeping. It was the slave women who waited upon the men, bringing forth pitchers of *nabid* and *bjórr*, and from the hearth and the oven, platters of flaky fish baked on iron-barred griddles and served with vegetables, berries, and nuts; bowls of steaming beef stew made with potatoes, onions, and carrots, and seasoned with salt, garlic, and cumin; and fruits and slabs of cheese and thick, crusty, hard bread, along with the pork-fried laverbread and jars of honey and butter. It was as fine a midday meal as any ever served at Ragnar's *hof*, and Wulfgar's heart swelled with pride as he gazed at his laden high table, glad that he should not be shamed by having but scanty fare to offer Ivar.

As the men ate, the talk at the high table was of inconsequential matters; and such was Ivar's behavior that had Wulfgar not known him so long and so well, he would surely have been deceived into thinking that Ivar had come to the longhouse this day as a friend instead of a foe. But Wulfgar was on his guard and so not gulled into making this mistake; and at last, as the meal drew to a close, Ivar began to tell the tale of the great raid made five years previously by Björn Ironside and Hasting.

With a fleet of sixty-two vessels, the two *jarls* had ventured as far into the Southlands as north Africa, sacking towns all along the way and filling their longships with gold, silver, and exotic prisoners known as *fir gorm*, blue men, and *blá-menn*, black men. Eventually, during the course of their journey, they had penetrated the Middle Sea, where Hasting had led upon Italy a raid that had since become legend in the Northland. Spying a great, white-walled city he had believed to be no less than Rome itself, but judging that its defenses were impenetrable, Hasting had sent a message to its inhabitants, falsely proclaiming himself a dying chieftain far from home and in need of a Christian burial. Taking pity upon him, the city had opened its gates to admit the now "dead" Hasting and his procession of *Víkingr* mourners. Once at the graveside, Hasting had, during the funeral ceremony, risen from his coffin to plunge his broadsword into the officiating bishop, after which he and his men had rioted in the streets, committing mayhem and murder. In the process, Hasting had somehow learned that the city was not Rome, after all, but Luna. Incensed by his error, he had ordered the city burned to the ground and all the townsmen slaughtered. The women he had spared, taking them captive to sell them later, as slaves, to the Moors.

"So it was that Hasting profited from his mistaken raid," Ivar ended the story to a roar of laughter from the listening *thegns*. Only Wulfgar did not share in the mirth, for he knew in his bones what Ivar was leading up to with the tale; and finally, as the laughter in the great mead hall died away, Ivar continued, his voice low now, as insidious as a serpent. "Now, then, Wulfgar, it seems that, like the bold Hasting, you, also, would profit from a mistaken raid. But the prize you plundered, Ragnar would have claimed as his own; and so I have come to bring you word from him, your king, that he would have you deliver it unto him. So, where is she? Where is the princess of Usk, whom my father sent me to Walas to fetch?'' Ivar paused for a moment. Then he said softly, ''Twould not be wise to deny that you have her, Wulfgar, for I know that you do.''

"Aye, she is here,'' Wulfgar answered reluctantly at last, glancing at the storeroom, where Flóki had locked up Morgen when the horns had blown their warning.

"And unharmed . . . untouched? I ask because I heard that you had taken one of the Usk women as your concubine, Wulfgar. Yet you did not see fit to show her to us, to have her sit beside you at the midday meal. . . . So, naturally, one must wonder: Can it be because you have dared to claim not only a markland, but also a princess as your own?'' Ivar's brows rose faintly in inquiry, but his saturnine smile did not quite reach his narrowed eyes, which were as hard and icy as an arctic winter.

"That would be not a barb, but a blade to crack a gilt-bronzed shield, then, would it, Ivar?'' Wulfgar needled, deliberately mocking, so Ivar should not guess how his stab in the dark had struck home. "But, nay, 'tis the princess's waiting woman who is my concubine. You've not seen her because she is willful and disobedient, and so I punished her earlier by relegating her to the kitchen, where she does the work of a scullion this day. However, I will send for her if you wish.''

"And for the princess, as well,'' Ivar reminded him dryly.

"All right,'' Wulfgar agreed slowly, his face impassive as he forced himself to remain outwardly calm, although, inwardly, he was a mass of turmoil; for he knew that this was a crucial moment. If Ivar, clever Ivar, should suspect that

Rhowenna, not Morgen, was the princess of Usk . . . "Flóki, do you fetch my concubine and the princess."

"Aye, lord."

Rhowenna was elbow deep in soapy water, washing pots and dishes in the kitchen when Flóki came for her, although she was scarcely aware of her actions, even so. She labored perfunctorily, from habit, accustomed to busying her hands at a woman's tasks. Her mind was a room away, in the great mead hall, with Wulfgar, wondering anxiously what was happening between him and Ivar the Boneless. Although all seemed amicable enough, her sense of dread had not lessened, but deepened. Now, after she dried her hands, she slowly followed Flóki from the kitchen. Her palms were wet again, she realized dimly, sweating profusely; nervously, she wiped them on the cloth she still carried, unconsciously wringing it between her hands. Her face was ashen; her eyes were huge as they met Wulfgar's own; her body trembled as, not knowing what to do, she bowed her head and sank respectfully to a curtsy before the high table.

"Well, I see that the strap I laid to your backside has much improved your manners, wench," Wulfgar growled as he gazed down at her, so, gratefully, she understood from his lie that he knew how frightened she was and was giving her a plausible reason to appear so. "Perhaps you have now learned that although I have chosen you as my concubine, and accorded you the privileges of such, I can just as easily send you to the slave pens."

"Aye, my lord," Rhowenna replied quietly, as though duly chastened, glimpsing, from beneath the fringe of her lashes, the man she knew was Ivar the Boneless.

As, surreptitiously, she watched him, Ivar abruptly stood and walked toward her. Towering over her, he stretched out one hand and, cruelly grabbing the back of her hair, roughly jerked her head back so he could see her face. Involuntarily, she gasped, stricken, for his resemblance to Wulfgar was unmistakable. They were brothers, she thought—and Wulfgar had never told her. Suddenly panicked, she wondered wildly if everything he *had* told her had been a hideous lie to deceive her into surrendering to him. But then Rhowenna saw the murderous rage that flared in Wulfgar's eyes at how Ivar touched her, and she recalled his bitterness at being a bastard his father would not even deign to acknowledge; and she knew to her relief that whatever lay between Wulfgar Bloodaxe and Ivar the Boneless, it was not love.

"Well, I suppose the wench is comely enough after a fashion—although 'tis hard to tell, since you have had her toiling like a drudge all morning and she is none too tidy at the moment." Ivar's cold blue eyes raked her indifferently, making her shudder as unbidden in her mind rose an image of this man kissing and caressing her brutally, as Wulfgar had warned her Ivor would do. After a tense moment, spying Flóki emerging with Morgen from the storeroom, Ivar released Rhowenna, turning his attention to Morgen, who was so finely dressed, with not only the gold circlet of Usk, engraved and nielloed, about her head, but also silk ribands intertwined in her intricately braided hair, that she did, indeed, look every inch a princess. "That is the princess of Usk?"

"Aye." Wulfgar nodded, his eyes warning Rhowenna to stay where she was, silent and unassuming, drawing no further attention to herself. "As you can see, she has not been harmed or touched, but has been well cared for and treated with every courtesy and consideration due her rank. But if you have come on Ragnar's authority, Ivar, to wrest her from me for the ransom she will bring as your hostage, your ride here was for naught. In response to my own demand for payment for her safe release, I have received a message from Cerdic, prince of Mercia and her betrothed. It seems that as the princess's dowry was never delivered to him, he considers both the betrothal and the treaty with Usk broken and feels no obligation to come to his lady's rescue. Nor have I heard from her father, Pendragon, king of Usk.''

''Nor will you,'' Ivar declared shortly, with a supercilious smirk as he strode to stand before Morgen. Reaching out, his fingers digging viciously into her cheeks, he compelled her face up to his, his eyes dancing with spiteful amusement at how her own shot sparks at him, how she attempted—futilely—to wrench free of him. ''When I arrived in Usk, 'twas to discover that you had been there before me, Wulfgar, and had taken half of what Ragnar had ordered me to obtain. In a way, you actually made it easy for me. Usk was neither expecting nor prepared for a second attack to follow so swiftly on the heels of the first—and I had three times as many longships and men under my command. The palisade fell on the third day. Pendragon is dead. I slew him.''

Stunned, heartbroken, Rhowenna could not repress the low wail of agony and denial that issued from her lips. But even in her sudden state of shock and sorrow, she instinctively recognized not only her own danger, but also that battle threatened as Ivar glanced at her sharply, shrewdly, and Wulfgar stealthily laid his hand upon the scramasax sheathed at his belted waist. Like an animal, Morgen, too, sensed the abrupt deadliness of the moment, and she began again to struggle furiously against Ivar, reclaiming his attention and crying out to Rhowenna in the tongue of Walas, ''What is it? What is it, my lady? What has happened?'' so it seemed only natural that Rhowenna, her supposed waiting woman, should answer. Inhaling raggedly, fighting to hold her tears at bay, she spoke with anguish to Morgen in their own language, translating what Ivar had said, knowing that Morgen's knowledge of the Northland tongue was not yet so great as hers and praying that Ivar would grasp this fact and would attribute to it her own grief and Morgen's initial lack of response at the news of Pendragon's death.

Hearing what had come to pass, Morgen started to scream with wrath and pain and to strike out at Ivar blindly, clawing at his face, leaving bloody gouges upon his cheek before he backhanded her savagely with his fist, violently knocking her to the floor, where she lay, sprawled and dazed and weeping. Flóki's indrawn breath was a hiss of ire as his hand swept to the hilt of his own scramasax; and Rhowenna did not know if Wulfgar's sharply uttered "Nay!" was a command to stop Flóki from drawing the weapon or herself from running to Morgen's side. She, at least, paid it no heed; and as she bent over Morgen, the two of them clung to each other, Morgen sobbing wildly.

"I'll kill him! I'll kill that bloody bastard! Oh, my lady, my lady! We'll never get home now! We'll never see Usk again!"

"Shhhhh, don't say that! Don't say that! We will! Somehow, we *will* get home, I swear it! Mayhap this heathen Northman has but lied for some cruel purpose of his own. Perhaps my father . . . my father is not truly dead. . . ." But in her heart, Rhowenna did not believe this; for in her horrifying dream last night, had he not been a corpse—and her mother, also? Her mother . . . A harsh sob of terror and torment caught in Rhowenna's throat at the thought, choking her. What had happened to her mother?

"Oh, my lady, I am sorry, so very sorry." Morgen's voice, while still raw with fury and loathing, tremulous with affliction, was nevertheless quieter now. "I am selfish, thinking only of myself—and not of you and the grievous blow you have suffered at this Northman's ruthless hands."

"I must know . . . I must know what became of my mother," Rhowenna murmured dully to herself, hardly aware of Morgen's words. "My lord . . . my lord"—for fear of what he would see in her eyes, she did not dare to look at Ivar as she addressed him in the Northland language—"the princess . . . the princess would know her mother's fate."

"Tell her that Igraine, queen of Usk, is dead, too. Tell her that as proof of all I have said, I offer this." From the pocket of his leather tunic, Ivar withdrew a gold necklace set with amethysts, which Rhowenna recognized at once as Prince Cerdic's gift to her, plundered by Ivar from her jewelry chest in her sleeping chamber in her father's royal manor.

It was all true, then, as she had feared. Still, it was all she could do to keep from keening like a banshee again; she bit her lower lip so hard to remain silent that she drew blood, tasted it, coppery and bittersweet, in her mouth, upon her tongue. Now she knew why her dowry had never been delivered to Prince Cerdic, why he had refused to pay her ransom, why he did not care what happened to her. She was no longer of any use to him. Her father's palisade had fallen before the onslaught of Ivar the Boneless and his *Víkingrs*; her parents had been killed; their royal manor ravaged, perhaps even burned to the ground; Usk's people slaughtered, perhaps to the last man. For Rhowenna did not delude herself that Ivar's attack had been no more than a raid that, however brutal, had at least been brief. Nay, he had engaged in a long, hard battle. Perhaps even Gwydion now lay dead.

"The—the Queen?" Morgen asked hesitantly, her dark-blue eyes stricken as she saw the pain upon Rhowenna's face. "She—she is dead? The Northmen murdered her, also, my lady?"

"Aye . . ." Rhowenna whispered brokenly, drawing another long, uneven breath as she fought to keep from giving way to the sorrow and hysteria that threatened to overcome her.

A blinding rage and hatred such as she had never before felt welled within her breast. She could commit murder at this moment, she thought numbly; she could drive a dagger deep into Ivar's black heart, and never feel remorse for the deed, but take joy in his death.

"Damn you to Hel, you filthy whoreson!" Morgen spat in

the tongue of Walas; and although Ivar did not comprehend the words, he got the gist.

He laughed, an ugly sound, as he gingerly touched his wounded cheek, then deliberately wiped his fingers across Morgen's upturned face, marking her with his blood, in the way a hunter did himself with the blood of his kill. Then, without warning, seizing hold of her hair hurtfully, he kissed her, grinding his mouth down on hers hard and long before, at last, he released her, his eyes raking her lewdly, lingering on her heaving breasts—although only his own men laughed, and the sound had a nervous ring; for in that moment, something vital and terrible leaped between Ivar and Morgen, and the air was fraught with a tension so strong as to be almost tangible.

"If you know that you can expect no ransom for the princess of Usk, why have you come here, Ivar?" Wulfgar slowly stood, longing fervently to comfort Rhowenna, his heart aching for her—and he not liking at all what had passed between Ivar and Morgen. From that, he knew that the danger to them all was not yet over, that Ivar and his warriors could turn upon them at any moment, a violent battle erupt in the great mead hall. "From your boasts, 'twould seem that you have the princess's dowry in your possession. So, what more do you want?"

"The princess herself, of course, as you must surely have guessed by now—or are you blind, as well as bolder than is wont for a bastard *bóndi*?" Ivar turned from the two women back to Wulfgar. "It may be that Cerdic of Mercia can be persuaded of the error of his ways, or that whoever manages to rise to power from the ruin of Usk will want her to secure his claim to that kingdom's throne. Regardless, one of her rank is always valuable for coin or barter, and so Ragnar means to have her. He has ordered you to surrender her and me to bring her to him. He is your king; he will not look lightly upon your failure or my own to comply with his demand. So, do you give her up or nay, Wulfgar?''

"Even a king may not just take what is not his, but fairly won by his *jarl*, unless he wishes to start a feud—or a war.''

" 'Fairly won' is debatable, since you would not have known about the princess of Usk and her dowry had not a foolish yellow bird of Ragnar's dared to chirp in a cage not her own. Still, Ragnar's raid upon Paris this summer was quite profitable. He is even now hiring an army of mercenaries. I feel certain that he, as I, would welcome a battle to test their mettle before they march upon the kingdoms of Britain.''

"Indeed? What a pity, then, that *you*, at least, would not be there to see it, Ivar." Wulfgar glanced pointedly around the great mead hall, where his own warriors outnumbered those of Ivar by two to one.

"I thought that perhaps that might prove your answer," Ivar rejoined coolly, seemingly unruffled by the veiled threat to his life, although his eyes shone like blue flame and his body was suddenly as taut as a bowstring. "And since I am not so hotheaded as you, Wulfgar, I came prepared to offer you a bargain instead of the point of a blade. Bring the yellow slave from the Eastlands inside!" he called to his *thegns*, causing Wulfgar's nerves abruptly to tighten like thong. "Bring the spaewife, that spawn of Nidhögg, bloodsucking dragon of Náströnd!"

Yelkei! Wulfgar had not seen her earlier, in the bailey; his fear for Rhowenna had been paramount in his mind, and Yelkei was a small woman and had ridden double, mounted behind one of Ivar's men, besides. But she *was* here, he saw now as she was momentarily silhouetted in the frame of the open door, the sunlight bright behind her. Then her stooped figure began slowly to shuffle toward him in such a way that he realized of a sudden, enraged, that she had been badly beaten, whipped viciously but skillfully as punishment, surely, for telling him the *skáld* Sigurd Silkbeard's tale; and he thought that with his bare hands, he would throttle Ivar in that moment.

"Do you draw steel on me now, 'twill be without provocation, Wulfgar, after I have proposed to you a fair trade; and no man will trust you after that, and the *Thing* will have just cause to brand you a traitor to your king and an outlaw," Ivar warned softly, his smile mocking, disdainful. "And that, I should find a pity, indeed; for you should not be a foe worth having if your honor were lost, and then I must kill you as I would a mongrel dog instead of in battle, as I long to do and will when the time comes. Now, you've that yellow witch to tell you when that will be—for all the good it may do you—and I'll take the princess of Usk and go in peace until we meet again, when perhaps I'll slay you." Reaching down, he hauled Morgen roughly to her feet, laughing shortly as she struggled in vain against him. "A feisty wench I shall enjoy taming. Had the men of Usk had half the mettle of their princess, I should not have slaughtered them like sheep. Come!" he shouted to his warriors. "Let us ride!"—and he was gone in a flurry of dust churned up by the horses' hooves as, after striding from the great mead hall, he and his *thegns* thundered from the palisade.

"*Elsket*, I am sorry." Wulfgar's voice was gentle as, slowly loosing the hand he had clamped down hard upon Flóki's wrist to prevent him from yanking his broadsword from its sheath and running with it after Ivar, he pulled Rhowenna to her feet and into his arms, holding her trembling body tightly but tenderly against him. "I am sorry for your loss, sorry for all the pain that has been caused you. By the gods, I would undo it if I could, I swear!"

"You have risen high, Wulfgar, since last I saw you—but not so high that you are become a god yourself, to change what is written in the stars," Yelkei croaked in her raven's voice, her black eyes shrewd as she stared hard at Rhowenna, then glittering with malicious amusement as she glanced out through the open door, where Ivar had vanished. "Although you have learned something of the gods' devious ways, I am thinking, to trick Loki's wolf, with fine-woven silk ribands— as Týr did with the chain called Gleipnir. But now, you had best beware, lest your own hand, too, be bitten off at the wrist! Haaa! How I should love to see Ivar's face when he learns what a fool you have played him for!"

"Be silent, old woman!" Wulfgar hissed, angered, despite his gladness at seeing her and his love for her; for his love for Rhowenna was greater still. "Naught here save myself and my lady know of what you speak; nor will I risk having it babbled about in Ragnar's *hof*, because you could not hold your venomous serpent's tongue! 'Twas *you* and your prattle of power and prophesy that brought about all that has come to pass! Truly, you are lucky Ivar did not cut your tongue from your head, but only lashed you for carrying to my ears the tale told by the *skáld* Sigurd Silkbeard that summer's night in Ragnar's great mead hall!"

"'Twas not due to luck, but because of Ivar's fear of my witchery that I may still speak the truth to you, Wulfgar, thankless though you may find it. My tongue, I would not part with—and for all his bravado, Ivar did fear its curse upon him. But the beating I gladly endured for your sake, who are the child of my heart; 'twas a small price to pay, indeed, for all you have gained—and will yet achieve, Wulfgar. But, come. We may talk of all this later. Right now, your lady is ill with grief, and Flóki the Raven burns with a fire that may rage out of control if not dampened. Do you take your lady to your sleeping chamber, while I prepare a potion for her that will ease the burden of her anguish for a little while, so she may rest. Then speak you to Flóki. The woman he would have will come to no harm yet for a time at Ivar's hands; Ragnar's great longship lies at anchor in the harbor, and he will not prove so hot as Ivar to breach the maidenhead of one whose virginity he thinks may still hold value.''

''I hope that you are right, Yelkei.'' Wulfgar's face was grave with worry as he gazed down at Rhowenna, who wept quietly against his chest. ''For she who took my lady's place was ridden hard at the battle of Usk—and mayhap even before, if I am any judge of a maiden—and so Ragnar and Ivar will learn if they seek to climb into her saddle. But you are right; I must see to my lady. Come, *kjæreste*. Let me put you to bed.'' Sweeping Rhowenna up in his arms, he carried her unprotesting figure into the sleeping chamber and laid her gently on the bed, the touch of his hand a loving caress as he brushed her hair back from her face and the tears from her cheeks. ''Oh, sweeting, what I would give to have it all to do again!'' he whispered fiercely, anguished by the shock and agony that filled her wide violet eyes. ''I would not so much as breathe your name to Olaf the Sea Bull!''

''And what would that change, Wulfgar, save that I, not Morgen, would now be in the cruel hands of Ragnar Lodbrók and Ivar the Boneless? Usk would still lie in ruins; my parents . . . my parents would still be . . . dead—Ivar would still have killed them—'' Sobbing softly again, Rhowenna closed her eyes, feeling as though a ponderous weight were bearing down on her, crushing her, as she thought of her father and mother, images she could not put from her mind: her father, laughing in his great hall, wine cup in hand; her mother sitting before the large loom, her beautiful face illuminated by the fire and the candlelight. ''Oh, Wulfgar, it hurts,'' she said, reaching instinctively for his hand, for comfort. ''It hurts so bad.''

''I know, *elsket*, I know. So I felt when, as a lad, I lost my mother, Goscelin. Here.'' Gathering Rhowenna in his arms, Wulfgar lifted her a little, so she was cradled against him. ''Here is Yelkei with the sleeping potion. Do you drink it down now, and try to rest.''

Obediently, Rhowenna did as he commanded, too dazed by the day's events, too grief-stricken to object. She did not care if the yellow slave, Yelkei, poisoned her; she even half hoped that it was so, although she could think of no reason why the old woman would want to do such a thing, save that Yelkei was a witch, and therefore wicked, in league with the devil. For how else could she have known that Rhowenna, not Morgen, was the princess of Usk? But when she looked up at the old woman's wrinkled moon face, into her perceptive black eyes, Rhowenna saw nothing but kindness and pity, and she felt suddenly ashamed of her suspicion.

"You need not fear, lady. 'Tis only a mixture of herbs and spices," Yelkei told her, as though reading her mind. "For all that Wulfgar blames me for what was the gods' decree, I wish you no harm. You will sleep now—and dream no dreams."

And at last, it was as Yelkei had predicted: Rhowenna did sleep—and she did not dream.

Book Three

Swan Road
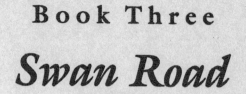

Chapter Thirteen

Surrender the Night

The Shores of the Skagerrak, the Northland, A.D. 865

Now that Ivar the Boneless had ridden away with the woman he thought was the princess of Usk, Wulfgar knew he and his markland would be safe for a time from Ragnar Lodbrók and the army of mercenaries he had been amassing since his return from the Southlands. Wulfgar would have liked nothing better than to slay Ivar and the band of *thegns* who had accompanied him, and might have done so with few losses to his own warriors. But that would have brought Ragnar down upon him; and even while aboard the *Dragon's Fire*, Wulfgar had known he and his men were no match for Ragnar's larger forces. If Ragnar marched upon him, Wulfgar would be defeated and probably killed in the battle. Even so, only the thought of what Rhowenna would suffer should that prove his fate had compelled him to stay his hand against his half

233

brother; for he would rather have wandered the Shore of Corpses to the barred gates of Hel than to have swallowed his pride and stood silently by, while Ivar had manhandled both Rhowenna and Morgen. Yet to have acted, as reckless Flóki would have done, would have been foolhardy, Wulfgar knew. Still, he felt guilty and ashamed that he had done nothing, that Rhowenna had learned in so cruel a manner of her parents' deaths, and that he had allowed Morgen to be carried away from Flóki, who so plainly loved and desired her.

"Curse you, Wulfgar! If you balked at slaying Ivar because he is your half brother, why did you not let me do the deed?" Flóki asked angrily later. "Gladly would I have slit his throat or driven my blade through his heart—and well you know it!"

"Aye, as would I also have done, for there is no love lost between Ivar and me—"

"Then, why—"

"You know why, Flóki!" Wulfgar snarled, scowling darkly. "And if you don't, you're a fool! Ivar is not just my half brother, but the son and heir of my father, the great Ragnar Lodbrók, a *konungr* of the Northland. Even my half brother Halfdan, who is so ambitious and hungry for power that he would gladly slay Ivar and Ubbi both to claim Ragnar's throne, does not dare to lift a hand against Ivar for fear of our father's reprisals. Are you so eager to lie in the arms of a Valkyrie that you would have Ragnar come here with his army of *thegns* and mercenaries to slaughter us all like sheep, as Ivar did the men of Usk?"

"Nay, of course not. But neither would I see the princess of Usk held at Ragnar's and Ivar's mercy!" Like a caged beast, Flóki paced the floor, restless and agitated.

"Nor would I; but there was no other choice, and so I did what I must. A *jarl* cannot think only of himself, Flóki, but must think of those who are bound to him, as well. Still,

Yelkei has spoken truly, I believe; the princess is in no danger at the moment. Unlike Ivar, Ragnar will not be so desirous of harming one who may yet be of use to him.''

"Aye, well, I hope that you are right, lord." Flóki's reply, while grudging, was calmer at least. "For I did not like Ivar's behavior toward the princess, as though she were a common slave he might have as he pleased, and no royal maiden at all!"

"We will get her back," Wulfgar insisted stoutly. "In the meanwhile, we must concentrate on completing the new longship, so 'twill be ready if Ragnar decides to declare war on us, or to see us all branded as outlaws by the *Thing* so that we are compelled to flee from the Northland."

Together in silence, each dwelling on his own thoughts, the two men walked down to the strand, where, resting on its log rollers, the new longship that Wulfgar had ordered built was slowly taking shape. Soon, it would be completed; and as he gazed at it, his heart burst with pride stronger than any he had ever before felt. Not only was the vessel his own, but also of his own design. Eirik and his cadre of woodcarvers had outdone themselves to bring it to fruition, Wulfgar thought, as he looked up at the towering stempost and sternpost that seemed to pierce the sky. The dragon's-head stempost was long; the mouth was open, breathing wooden flames; the dragon's outstretched neck was gracefully curved and unusually notched down its length with scales that stood upright; its throat was deeply and beautifully chiseled with countless runes and other magic symbols and scenes of battle and of tales of the gods. The bow of the longship formed the beast's belly; and along the vessel's sides, Eirik and the rest had engraved a set of sweeping wings, so it appeared as though the mighty creature had folded them against her body. Also notched with upright scales, the dragon's-tail sternpost rose behind, culminating in a triangular point. Never had there been a longship so magnificent; even Ragnar's own great vessel would pale to insignificance alongside it, Wulfgar told himself. In honor of Rhowenna, he had decided to call it the *Siren's Song*.

A basket in hand, she and several of the other slave women had come down to the beach from the longhouse, to catch fish and to gather seaweed in preparation for the *mørketiden*, the long, dark winter that would soon be upon them. Already, the days had grown cool and shorter; the leaves had begun to turn on the deciduous trees of the dark forests; and snow had fallen in upper reaches of the mountains. Presently, winter would spread its white mantle over the heaths, the meres, and even the strands. Before then, cattle, sheep, pigs, and chickens must be butchered; game from the woods must be hunted and killed; and fish must be speared or netted, all to be preserved by being dried and smoked, salted, or pickled, and sealed in barrels or jars so there would be food enough to last through the long months of winter and none on the markland would go hungry. Vegetables, fruits, and grains, too, must be prepared and hoarded.

Now, as Wulfgar watched Rhowenna at her work, he thought that even had he not loved and desired her, he would have been a fool not to have kept her with him; for truly, he could not have accomplished half so much or managed the markland half so well without her guidance. The knowledge and training she had received as the princess of Usk had proved invaluable to him, and he had not hesitated to make use of it. As, with his stern but fair authority, he had won the hearts of his people, so she had won them with her goodness and gentleness and grace; and if she were at times proud, stubborn, and defiant, well, were not those faults his own, also? Aye, he had chosen well, he thought. He and she were like what the *Víkingrs* called hacksilver, two halves of the same coin. If only Rhowenna would come to see that, would agree to be his wife, and would yield to him in bed, gladly would he go down to the barred gates of Hel at his death, having known on earth the blessings of Odinn's Valhöll.

Sensing Wulfgar's eyes upon her, Rhowenna glanced up from where she waded in the seawater off the shore, her long skirts drawn up and tucked into a belt she had borrowed from his coffer and fastened about her hips. She shivered as she looked at him, but it was not from the cold water that lapped about her bare legs, and not with the fear of him that she had felt in the beginning, but with an ache that deep down inside, she knew was both love and longing for him. If she were honest with herself, she could no longer deny that. Despite everything, Wulfgar had found his way into her heart, and she could not now imagine her life without him. Over and over, she had told herself that she was vulnerable because of her deep grief at the deaths of her parents, that she had become like a coracle adrift upon madding seas—blown off course, lost, and alone—and he was like a haven in the storm. But in her heart of hearts, Rhowenna knew that it was more than that. Still, she withheld herself from him, anguished and afraid. Wulfgar was her enemy, her captor. How could she have forgotten that? How could she have fallen in love with him?

He was nothing at all like Gwydion, nothing at all like any man she had ever before known, able to swing a warrior's battle-ax at one moment and to sing a bard's song the next. Despite herself, the juxtaposition intrigued her, as the man himself fascinated her. Surreptitiously, through the ebony strands of hair that had come loose from her braid, she studied him, her eyes drinking him in. Tall, fair, and handsome, he stood with his head thrown back, his long mane of hair gleaming golden in the sun and rippling like wheat in the wind, as the hard muscles in his strong, supple body rippled with his every movement, speaking to something within her that yearned wistfully to answer, a slow, swooning sensation that

made her feel as though she were melting inside, trickling
down into one of the quiet pools of the Northland forests. His
blue eyes shone with pride and excitement at the longship of
which he would soon be master. The vessel was nearly finished. The hard work was done; the rest was simply a race
against time now, until winter fell.

Winter. Rhowenna could hardly believe that so much time
had passed since Wulfgar had abducted her from her home.
Once, she had prayed desperately to go back to Usk, and he
had had no longship in which to take her. Now that he would
soon have a vessel, she had no home to return to. Ivar the
Boneless had destroyed it. The first messenger Wulfgar had
sent to Usk had not come back; perhaps he had been killed
in the melee when Ivar had descended upon the small kingdom. After Ivar had taken Morgen away, Wulfgar had dispatched another messenger to Usk, in an attempt to discover
if anyone or anything had survived the battle with Ivar. But
there had not yet been enough time for the messenger to get
there and back; and Rhowenna held out little hope that when
he did return, his report would contradict Ivar's story. All she
had cared for, all that had mattered to her was gone; she had
no one and nothing save Wulfgar.

Abruptly startled from her reverie by the sound of shouts,
she spied Naddod racing down the shore, his sealskin boots
sending foam and sand flying. Something had happened, she
realized, glancing around fearfully, thinking that perhaps
Ragnar Lodbrók and Ivar the Boneless had decided to march
on Wulfgar's markland, after all. Leaving her half-full basket
on the strand, she, too, began to run toward Wulfgar, instinctively relying on him to protect her. But then she understood
at last what Naddod was yelling and that, to her relief, they
were not under attack.

"Whale!" Naddod cried again. "There's a whale, lord,
stranded on the beach!"

At that, to Rhowenna's astonishment, all the men—*thegns*,

freedmen, and slaves alike—working on the longship threw down their tools and, shouting and laughing, began to rush down the shore to where a whale lay on the sand. Awed, even frightened by the sight and size of the gargantuan creature, Rhowenna halted a little distance away. She had never seen a whale so close; it was as big as a longship, bigger, dwarfing her and everyone else around it. In its natural milieu, the sea, it could be a dangerous animal, she knew. Yet at the moment, it was helpless, belly down on the beach, making no attempt to return to the sea, despite the white-foamed combers that swept in upon the sand. Had the whale's sides not heaved now and then, she would have thought that it was dead.

"How did it get here?" she asked Wulfgar, puzzled and pitying the great beast, for it would surely die if it did not get back to the sea.

"Sometimes, we just find them like this," he explained, shaking his head at the mystery of it. "It's as though they deliberately cast themselves upon the strands. No one knows why."

"Can't you—can't you do something for it? Tow it back out to sea?"

"Nay, and even if we could, 'twould only return. I've seen it happen before with some of the smaller whales. 'Tis destined to die here—and perhaps it came here for that reason. Only the gods know. But its sad fate is our glad fortune, lady. 'Twill mean hide for rigging, and meat and blubber and oil for the lamps this winter. 'Twill mean that no man must die on a whale hunt this season, leaving behind a widow and fatherless children. But do you go back to the *hof*, Rhowenna; for although 'twill be a kindness for the men to kill the whale, to end its suffering, its slaughter will not be a pretty sight, and you will not care to see it, I am thinking."

"Nay, you are right. I will not, my lord."

Still, for some strange, unknown reason, Rhowenna found it difficult to turn away from the magnificent, doomed crea-

ture. Its image haunted her all day, as did the thought of its
dying, alone, beyond its vast home of the sea. In some way,
she felt a kinship to the beast washed up upon the strand, as
the tides of destiny had brought her also to the Northland;
and she knew that she did not want the whale's lonely fate to
become her own. Her parents were dead, and even if somehow Usk had survived, whoever now sat upon its throne
would view her only as a political pawn. Her own father had
used her as such; how, then, could she expect another man,
who bore no father's love for her, to do any less? The thought
of being bartered away yet again to someone like Prince
Cerdic of Mercia was more than Rhowenna could endure.
She felt torn inside; she longed for the pain to end. Surely,
she owed Usk no more than what she had already given;
surely, she now deserved something for herself, a chance for
something more than just a life of mere survival or, worse,
an uncertain death.

Still, when Wulfgar entered their sleeping chamber that
night, Rhowenna shuddered at what she thought to do; and
she wished fervently, of a sudden, that he had, after all,
forced himself upon her in the beginning, so she would not
now be compelled to bear the responsibility for her surrender
to him. In some ways, it would have been easier that way,
she felt; for if afterward he had loved her truly and deeply,
she could have forgiven him for constraining her to admit
what was in her heart for him. But she was a woman grown,
and he had given her both the privilege and the burden of
deciding for herself the path in life she would take. She should
be glad of that; it was a mark of his respect for her, although
a small, scared part of her wished perversely that he had
instead chosen for her, had taken upon his own strong shoulders the accountability and risk that must now be hers alone.
Aye, risk, Rhowenna thought again anxiously; for to love
someone, to trust someone, was to open yourself to hurt and
to rejection. What if all Wulfgar had told her of his love had

been lies? How deeply that would wound her. And what if he rejected her, as Gwydion had? At least she had not lain with Gwydion; she had had that thought to comfort her when he had turned away from her. If she gave in to Wulfgar, she would not even have that balm, however meager, for her pain.

Yet, when she gazed at him, Rhowenna saw only love and desire for her in his blue eyes, no guardedness that would have warned her that he withheld a part of himself from her out of malice or deceit, no shadows that would have hinted at an inner self confused or conflicted where she was concerned. His eyes were honest, frank, assured, surveying her in that way he had that made her blush and tremble with the emotions welling inside her; for no man had ever looked at her as Wulfgar did, as though he knew her intimately, down to her very bones. At the thought, the slow-burning fire his glance ignited inside her spread like a fever through her body, making her shiver as though delirious, with mingled fear and excitement. Her mouth went dry, and the pulse at the hollow of her throat throbbed. Without warning, the night wind that whipped through the forests and across the heaths and meres beyond the palisade lulled, as though before a sudden storm; and the sleeping chamber itself seemed strangely to fade away into the smoke that filled it, leaving Rhowenna's senses focused acutely on Wulfgar. Her breath caught in her throat, and she cast down her eyes so he would not guess that this night would be different from all the rest she had spent in his arms, in his bed.

To give her a modicum of privacy, he seldom used the bathtub in their sleeping chamber. But he had been to the bathhouse, she knew. For earlier when she had seen him, he had been covered with blood from the slaying and butchering of the doomed whale; and now, despite the chilliness of the night, he was naked to the waist and dripping water. His bronze flesh glistened in the fire and the lamplight, so that the hard muscles beneath seemed to shimmer and to ripple, exciting her, making her long to touch him, to feel him touching her. Overcome by a wave of violent emotion, she half turned from him, clutching the material of her loose, thin-woven white shift tightly to her, but whether to ward him off or to contain herself, she did not know, could not have said.

"Rhowenna?" Slowly, Wulfgar came to stand behind her, his hands upon her arms, sliding up her shoulders to draw her long, unbound hair aside so that he might glimpse her face. His breath was warm against her cheek, her ear, making her shiver as he spoke again. "*Elsket?* You are very quiet tonight. Something troubles you?"

"Nay . . . aye . . . I don't know. The whale has preyed on my mind. I still do not understand why it would cast itself upon the strand, knowing that it would die."

"Why do you not yield to me, knowing that there is no other man for you—nor will there ever be?" When she was silent, he laughed softly, gently tugging the fabric of her shift from her tight hold, until her shoulders were bare, and his lips and hands caressed them. "Perhaps the whale is but as stubborn and foolish as you, lady."

"I . . . I do not want to end up alone, Wulfgar," she confessed softly, her voice catching on a ragged breath that caused his hands to tighten so suddenly and painfully upon her shoulders that she winced. "I do not want to die alone, at the hands of my enemies."

"You are not going to die, *kjæreste*, and I am not your enemy." His voice was low, husky in her ear before he slowly turned her around to face him, his fingers weaving through the strands of hair at her temples, tilting her head back so he could see her face. Beneath his hooded lids, his eyes gleamed dark with passion. "Surely, you know that by now. For have I not told you in more ways than I can count how much I love and desire you?"

"Aye, Wulfgar, you have. Still, I am afraid."

"Of what? Of me? Why, sweeting? Tell me!"

"I . . . I do not want to be hurt again."

"There is always pain for a maiden the first time she lies with a man. But 'tis only a small one that soon passes—and the only hurt I would ever cause you, Rhowenna. By the gods, I swear it! I am not like him to whom you gave your heart before. Do you give it into my keeping, you will learn that. Yield to me, now, and I will show you. In your heart, you know that it must come to that in the end, that you have no one now save me, and that I will not let you go, not ever!"

"Aye . . ." she breathed, an anguished consent.

His mouth claimed hers fiercely then, as he joyously sensed that at long last, she would be his; and without warning, the passion that had crouched like a predator within him, and within her, too, suddenly sprang upon them both to devour them. Wulfgar growled low in his throat as his lips swooped to capture hers again and again, as though he could not get enough of her. His mouth was hard and demanding against hers; his tongue was soft and insistent. His teeth grazed the tender flesh of her lower lip, and Rhowenna tasted her blood upon it as a thrill of pleasure and pain such as she had never before experienced shot through her, arousing and exciting her, filling her with savage yearning. She had not guessed, had not known that it could be like this, wild and violent, an emotion, a want so purely primeval that it was feral, animalistic. Boldly, Wulfgar's tongue ravaged her mouth, dizzying her and making her so weak that she knew she would have fallen had he not held her so tightly.

He was so tall and so powerfully built that he felt like iron against Rhowenna, making her feel as small and fragile as a child, and so pliant that all her bones seemed to have dissolved inside her as, of its own eager accord, her body melded itself to his. Beneath her palms, she could feel his bare arms, his muscles tightening and quivering as he clasped her to him;

and she recognized the strength that was his, and wondered if, with such power, he would hurt her inadvertently. She shuddered a little with apprehension at the thought; and Wulfgar, intuiting her sudden maidenly fear, tightened his embrace about her, his mouth sweeping hotly down her bared throat to her breasts, as though to give her no time to think, but only to feel. His hand was at the simple riband that tied her shift at the neck, his fingers deftly unknotting the bow, pulling it free, so the shift itself slipped from her shoulders and would have fallen to the floor had she not, with a soft, sharp cry, caught it at the valley of her breasts, holding it there as though she would never let it go, her now half-naked body quivering with all he had wakened within her. At that, tearing his scalding mouth from her shoulder, Wulfgar drew a little away, his eyes boring into hers, his indrawn breath a hard rasp.

"Do you want me to stop?" he asked, his voice harsh with arousal and emotion.

For what seemed an eternity, Rhowenna was silent, her face torn with indecision and fear and desire; and a muscle flexed tensely in his set jaw as he awaited her answer; his hands clenched her arms so tightly that she knew she would have bruises there tomorrow. Then at last, drawing a long, uneven breath, she whispered, "Nay," and swallowing hard, closing her eyes, and turning her head away, her hands shaking, she slowly loosened her grasp on her shift. After a long moment, Wulfgar released her arms, and as he did so, she felt her shift slide from her body, float like a gossamer cloud to the floor, leaving her standing utterly naked before him. She heard him inhale sharply, then felt his hand beneath her chin, turning her face back to his.

"Look at me, Rhowenna!" he commanded softly. "You are beautiful, more beautiful even than I ever imagined; and I want you as no man has ever wanted a woman, *elsket*. . . ."

His hands tangled roughly in her hair; his mouth seized

hers again, his tongue plunging deep, taking her breath as, without warning, he swept her up in his arms and carried her to the bed. There, he laid her down, still kissing her until, reluctantly, he loosed her to cast away his boots and breeches. Feeling his eyes upon her, embarrassed and shamed by her nakedness before him in the fire and the lamplight, Rhowenna half rose, reaching down to draw about her his huge wolfskin, which lay upon the bed, only to feel his hand close about her wrists, preventing her from covering herself.

"Nay, *kjæreste*," he said softly but firmly as he bent over her, pressing her down again, pinioning her hands on either side of her head. "I will not let you hide yourself from me, as though our lovemaking were a thing of which we must be ashamed, to be done beneath blankets and in darkness. I will see you—all of you—and I will watch your face when I come into you, so I will know what you are thinking and feeling when I make you mine. These things, I will not permit you to conceal from me, any more than I now permit you to conceal your body from me. I will have all of you, Rhowenna—not just your body, but also your heart, your mind, and your soul; for 'tis for those things that I love you. Without them, what happens between a man and a woman is but a moment's lust, a fleeting pleasure, as easily found with some other, and thus meaningless, without value. Do you understand? Nay, how could you? For you are a virgin yet. But I will take you; I will teach you, and then you will know I speak the truth. . . ."

Wulfgar's mouth closed over hers once more, his tongue parting her lips, invading her, pillaging the sweet secrets of her mouth, leaving her weak and dazed and breathless, filled with fear at the magnitude of what she was letting him do, and yet, as well, with a perverse, perfidious, perilous excitement that was like nothing she had ever before felt. Like a wild wind, it caught her up and swept her away, and helpless against it, Rhowenna gave herself up to it and let it carry her where it willed. Time turned, and kept on turning; it might have been minutes, or hours. She did not know as she lay in his arms and let him do as he wished with her. She knew nothing but the sensations that engulfed her as he touched and tasted her endlessly, as though time had stopped and he had all the time in the world to kiss her and to go on kissing her, his tongue darting forth to follow the lush curves of her mouth, teasing, tantalizing, opening her lips to entwine her own tongue.

"Sweet," he muttered huskily against her lips. "Sweeter than wine is the taste of you. Gods, how I want you! *Heks!* Witch! You have bewitched me, I swear—"

His mouth abruptly silenced any reply she might have made before burning across her cheek to her temple, the fragrant strands of her hair, scent sweet and inciting in his nostrils. Like the long, feathery branches of a dark, ancient pine in a mystic forest, blown by an unseen wind, her tresses tangled about her and Wulfgar, irrevocably binding them together as his lips tasted the length of her white throat, his tongue licked the salty sweat from its hollow and that trickled down between her breasts. Gently, his teeth bit the soft spot where her nape joined her shoulder, sending an erotic thrill of pain and pleasure shooting through her before the bite turned into a kiss that scorched its way to her breasts, swollen and aching with passion, straining eagerly against his mouth and tongue and hands as, her head thrashing from side to side, she arched and writhed against him, instinctively craving more.

Wulfgar's breath caught in his throat at the sight of her. Her skin was so very white that he exulted in it, feeling a deep satisfaction that it should be claimed, covered, and possessed by his own bronze flesh, that this pale Celtic princess should be his, only his, forever his. His blue eyes glittered as they devoured her, palms closing covetously over her full, upthrusting breasts, pressing them high as his mouth lowered to suck again and again of their nectar, first one and then the other, teeth grazing their hearts, tongue stinging like a bee, flicking her nipples into hard, roseate buds bursting to unfurl.

Her arms wrapped about his neck; her fingers burrowed through his long mane of golden hair, urgently drawing him down to her. As though she were the earth, Rhowenna drank him in, soaking him up as thirstily as though he were necessary to sustain her existence, as though he were draining her very soul from her body and then pouring it back in, the wine of life. He intoxicated her. His body was as hard as horn, in sharp contrast to the fine blond hair on his chest that was like silk beneath her palms and against the sensitive tips of her breasts; his muscles were sinewy, serpentine, rippling beneath her fervid lips, her caressing hands; his flesh was slick with sweat, glistening in the diffuse light that illuminated the shadowy chamber. He tasted of salt, elemental, atavistic, like the wind and the sea, crumbling her maidenly defenses as surely as the breakers that swept in upon the strands of the Northland crumbled the land, molding and shaping it as they willed, as Wulfgar did her. She was breathless in his wake, kissing and touching him everywhere she could reach, discovering, exploring, and charting him as he charted her, mapping every line, every curve of her body, kissing and stroking her shoulders, her breasts, her belly, the inside of her thighs, her spine from her buttocks to her nape, his tongue making her shiver both with desire and delight.

Like a white-watered stream through the mountains, like the tendrils of smoke that wreathed the sleeping chamber, he twisted and twined himself about her, lips and tongue and hands unstill, working their devilish spell upon her until she was like fire and ice, burning and melting beneath him, a mass of quivering sensation raised to a feverish pitch. Her womanhood throbbed with a searing ache, an unbearable hollowness she longed to have filled by him; and at last, Wulfgar spread her thighs wide, touching her where no man ever had, a quick, light stroke that was torment in the face of her agonizing need, making her whimper like a wounded animal, a low moan that she only dimly realized came from her own throat. Then, slowly, deliberately, in an encroachment so intimate that Rhowenna wanted to die, he plunged his fingers full length into her well of cinnabar softness, into the dark, secret heart of the mellifluous, engorged petals of her that trembled and opened to him of their own eager, exigent volition. Her breath caught on a ragged sob as he then withdrew his fingers just as torturously, spreading quicksilver heat, before sliding them into her again and yet again. His tongue was in her mouth, mimicking the sweetly agonizing movements of his hand, the flicking of his thumb against the pulsing key to her desire, honing her passion for him to a keen, dagger edge that stabbed her like a blade, making her strain desperately against him, driven by blind, primitive need, frantic for release and fulfillment.

"Please, Wulfgar . . ." Rhowenna entreated softly, her violet eyes flying open to see him poised above her, bronze and naked in the shadowy half-light, his own blue eyes dark with desire, glimmering with triumph, his bold shaft hard and heavy with desire.

She shivered at the sight, suddenly afraid of what was yet to come, understanding that what had gone before was but a tantalizing prelude designed to ready her to receive him. There was between them an eternal moment as highly charged as a storm, the air fraught with promise and portent. The fire and the lamplight flickered and danced, casting eerie, elongated shadows on the walls; the smoke swirled high, sinuous and somehow mystical, making her feel like a vestal offering and Wulfgar seem like one of his ancient pagan gods from a place older than the earth, older than time itself. It was as though in all the heavens, only they two existed, wanting, needing, destined for this joining.

"Rhowenna," he groaned. "Rhowenna . . ."

And then, at last, he took her, the hard, questing sword of his manhood driving swift and deep and true into the sheath of her, burying itself to its hilt, splitting her asunder in a breathtaking moment of penetrating, white-hot pain that was all-vanquishing, all-consuming. She gasped, then cried out, a low wail of surrender that he smothered savagely with his lips, filling her mouth with his tongue as he filled her with himself, throbbing within her, lying still atop her to accustom her to the feel of him inside her, stretching and molding her to accept him. Until now, she had never truly known what to expect, had never truly comprehended this absolute invasion, this quintessential possession that made of a maiden, a woman; and of a man, a conqueror. How could there be pleasure from this subjugation? Rhowenna did not know, and tears trickled from the corners of her eyes at the thought that perhaps there was none to be had, that Wulfgar had lied to her, after all.

"Shhhhh, sweeting," he murmured as she whimpered against his lips. Gently, he kissed the tears from her cheeks, his hands stroking her hair soothingly. "Hush. I know that it hurt. But the pain will pass in a moment, and then you will know only pleasure, I promise you. Trust me. I love you. I love you with all my heart."

Slowly, steadily, he began to move inside her; and it was then as though her body no longer belonged to her at all, but had become a part of Wulfgar. His hands were beneath her hips, lifting them to meet his own as he thrust into her powerfully, again and again, faster and faster, dark flesh melting urgently into pale as he quickened against her, his head buried against her shoulder, his harsh, uneven breath hot against her skin. From the woolen pallet wafted the scent of their mating, sharp and sweet, as, to her surprise and wonder, the pain Rhowenna had felt at first gradually gave way to pleasure that grew stronger and stronger within her, until she felt as though she would burst from it and did not know how she could

possibly withstand it. Surely, she would die, and yet, perversely, she felt as though she would die, as well, if she did
not find some release from the nameless thing that had seized
her, that she did not yet understand but instinctively sought.
Feverishly, she clutched Wulfgar, enwrapped him, enfolded
him, taking him deep inside her, the world spinning away
into nothingness as she moaned and strained desperately
against him, rushing headlong with him down a dark, wending passage that led from deepest seas to highest mountains,
where a sun-touched midnight sky above seethed and roiled,
and then, without warning, erupted violently into such splendorous fire that it was almost hurtful to behold, dazzling flame
setting them both ablaze, taking their breath, exalting them,
sealing them forever as it burned them to ashes until, finally,
with a last, ragged gasp, Wulfgar shuddered long and hard
against her, spilling himself inside her before they lay still,
hearts pounding as one.

In the quiet afterglow of their lovemaking, he held her
close against him, cradling her head against his shoulder; and
Rhowenna was filled with joy and wonder as she lay silently
in his embrace, marveling that he should have made her feel
as she had. In her wildest dreams, she had never imagined
that what happened between a man and a woman could be as
it had been for her and Wulfgar—beautiful and special in
every way. She had never in her life felt so close to someone,
to a man, felt so secure and protected, so fulfilled and beloved
as she did now. Idly, her hand trailed down his broad chest,
traced tiny patterns in the fine blond hair there until he caught
her wrist and, turning her palm up, kissed it tenderly, lingeringly. His blue eyes were loving and drowsy with passion,
his smile so tender that her heart turned over in her breast.

"I love you, Wulfgar Bloodaxe," she said softly.

"I know, *kjæreste*, I know, else you would not have sur-
rendered yourself to me; and my heart is overflowing with all
that it holds for you and for what you have given me in return.

I love *you*, Rhowenna of Usk," he murmured fiercely before his lips came down on hers again, desire for her once more sweeping through him like a strong, in-rushing tide.

His body moved to cover hers again, pressing her down; and eagerly did she open herself for him, not knowing then where his mouth ended and hers began. Outside, the wind sang its unbridled, melodious song to forest and heath and sea; and within, the fire and the whale-oil lamps burned low as she and he became again as one, no space between, urgent mouths and tongues and hands engaged until he swelled and surged into her, bringer of exquisite torment—and its joyous, sweet release. His exultant cry was as piercing as the call of the seabirds that haunted the sea-swept strands; dulcet, it mingled with her own when, at long last, she felt the hard, supple length of him shudder against her, and she trembled fierce with passion as, like a wild swan, white wings spread wide, she soared over seas and distant shores unto the very heavens, then came to rest ever so gently in his strong and loving arms.

Chapter Fourteen

Frey's Blessing and Loki's Mischief

Although she did not then know it, the short, swift days that followed that first night of lovemaking were the sweetest Rhowenna was to know for a long while. Yet even had she known what was so soon to come, she could not have savored those sweet days any more than she did. Never before in her life, not even with Gwydion, had she felt such happiness, known such sharing and intimacy with another human being as she knew with Wulfgar; nor had she ever experienced such passion. Time and time again, he swept her up to lay her down upon the soft woolen pallet of the beautifully carved bed in the sleeping chamber, there to work his devilish magic upon her, until she knew every plane, every angle of his body as well as she knew her own. There was nothing he did not know, did not teach her. As autumn hastened toward winter, she spent long, languorous, greying afternoons with him erotically tormenting and tantalizing her until she begged him to take her; and there were intense, feverish nights, as well, nights when, long after she had fallen into slumber, he came late to their bed to take her urgently, fiercely, without any preliminaries.

Wulfgar insisted that they be wed, although, to Rhowenna, the pagan ritual they would undergo had little meaning, and she knew that in the eyes of the Christ and the Church, and under the laws of Usk, she would not be truly and legally married. Still, because Wulfgar wished it, she gave in to his demand, and preparations for the ceremony went forth. It was to take place in the *templum* in the Sacred Grove on Wulfgar's markland. The feasting would last for nine days, and sacrifices would be made to the god Frey, who was the god of fertility and sexuality. To her horror, Rhowenna learned that the customary sacrifices for such an important occasion as the marriage of a *konungr* or *jarl* were nine young male slaves.

"Nay!" she cried, distraught, to Wulfgar when told this terrible news. "'Tis a heathen practice, a sacrilege!—and I will not wed with you if it means our marriage must be consecrated by the blood of men!"

"'Tis the way of the Northland, to which you now belong, lady!"

It was their first serious quarrel and upset them both dreadfully. In the end, they compromised, with the sacrifices still being planned, but in the form of cattle, sheep, and pigs, which had to be killed and butchered anyway for the fast-approaching winter.

At last, the day of their wedding arrived. Long before dawn, Rhowenna was wakened by her waiting women and Yelkei, and taken to the bathhouse, which was similar to the one she had first used in Sliesthorp and an important part of life in the Northland; for the Northland people were very clean, washing every morning. Despite her new and warm fur cloak made from the hide of one of the great white bears found far to the north, in the tundra, she shivered in the chilly darkness, and her new sealskin boots crunched on the frost-rimed ground in the stillness. It was Yelkei, looking even more witchlike than usual, who swung open the bathhouse door on its creaking iron hinges, her bony, clawlike hand seeming almost disembodied, spectral, as she wordlessly beckoned Rhowenna to enter. Slowly, beset, of a sudden, by a tiny frisson of fright, Rhowenna stepped inside. Because it was close on winter and cold, the steam that filled the bathhouse was like white clouds of mist; and although Yelkei and the waiting women had brought whale-oil lamps, Rhowenna could scarcely see inside the shadowy, dimly lighted interior. Like ghosts, the women moved to disrobe her; then, naked, she climbed into the bathtub. Sitting in the warm water, with the steam rising all around her, was like being sealed in a gossamer cocoon, she thought, quiet and eerie, as though a blanket had smothered the earth. The only sound was the ripple and dripping of the bath water as the women washed her hair and body so she would be purified for her wedding rite; and into her mind, unbidden, came the thought that the bathing ritual was not so very different from what her ancestors, the Picti and the Tribes, must once have practiced. Rhowenna had never felt so close to the old ways as she did now at this moment; and she wondered uneasily if the Christ would be very angry with her for taking part in the pagan ceremony that would shortly make her Wulfgar's wife.

Once the bath had ended, the women wrapped her naked body in her cloak, then led her back to the *hof*, to the sleeping chamber, which was empty, Wulfgar having been taken away for his own preparatory rites. In the center of the room, she stood, while the women oiled and perfumed and powdered her body, then dressed her in a beautiful, pleated gown of expensive blue silk from the Eastlands, over which went an exquisite tunic of purple silk banded at both bodice and hem by heavily bejeweled and embroidered widths of gold riband, and fastened with ornate gold brooches above each breast. Her long black hair the women left unbound, but plaited strands of it with fine, narrow ribbons of gold into tiny braids. Upon her head they placed a gold circlet, engraved and niel-loed, that Wulfgar had had made for her. Her neck was hung with a multitude of necklaces of gold and amber; armlets and bracelets of gold and silver adorned her arms and wrists; she wore rare rings upon her fingers.

When her toilette was completed, the women escorted Rho-wenna from the longhouse to the celebrative, consecrated ox-cart that was to carry her to the *templum* in the Sacred Grove. No common vehicle, the ox-cart was embellished with de-tailed carvings of runes, other magic symbols, and scenes of battle and from the tales of the gods. It was festooned with pine and spruce boughs, branches of berries from the sacred ash trees, acorns from the equally prized oak trees, and sprigs of mistletoe. Wulfgar's great wolfskin covered the top and hung down the sides. Naked to the waist, despite the cold, the nine young male slaves who, if not for Rhowenna's protests, would otherwise have been drowned in a secret pool after serving her, surrounded the ox-cart, silent, heads bowed, not daring to look upon her face; for as the bride of their *jarl*, she was this day the embodiment of the goddesses Freyja, sister to Frey; the unchaste Gefjon, to whom virgins prayed; and Nerthus, the Earth Mother. Only the priest, who stood at the heads of the yoked oxen, was permitted to glance at her with impunity as he led the vehicle to the Sacred Grove. Reverently, he handed her onto the seat of the ox-cart. Then, with a small lurch, the oxen lumbered forward at his com-mand, the cart wheels rumbling, and the procession began its solemn progression across the now-fallow fields and the wild heaths of Wulfgar's markland.

The sun had just begun to peek over the horizon, turning the dark sky a silver that gleamed with a cold, frosted flame, like a blade, and the earth into a crystal, fairy place when the pale light shone upon the sparkling rime that encrusted the trees and the land. Rhowenna's breath caught in her throat at the sight. Wulfgar had told her once, on board the *Dragon's Fire*, that the Northland was at its most beautiful in summer, but she thought she had never seen it look more splendorous than it did now, white and glittering, the dark, soughing forests sweeping up the craggy sides of the great, towering mountains whose snowy pinnacles seemed to pierce the very heavens. Truly, it was a place fit for the old gods, she thought—primordial, almost unearthly in its magnificence, this place of atavistic mountains and ancient forests, of burning sun and twilight darkness.

Then, at last, the Sacred Grove lay before them, so chosen because of the massive old evergreen tree that rose at its heart, its trunk so huge that even a *Víkingr* could not span it with his arms, its branches so long and feathery that they were like an immense canopy sheltering the Sacred Grove. Beneath the tree stood the *templum*, a simple structure consisting of little more than four elaborately carved pillars topped by a thatched roof; only *templums* at the Sacred Groves of *hofs* such as Ragnar's had walls. There, Wulfgar was waiting for her. Like the male slaves, he, too, was naked to the waist; but if he felt the cold, he gave no sign of it, for it was the lot of a warrior to endure, as he demonstrated by baring his torso to the frigid air. A gold circlet that matched her own was around his head; at his throat, he wore a gold torque formed by two dragon heads that met at his collarbones; armlets that were gold serpents coiled around his arms. As she descended from the ox-cart to walk slowly toward him, Rhowenna thought he had never looked more princely, more godlike.

Silently, they stood before the priest as he intoned the requisite prayers to Frey and the blessings upon them, then made the animal sacrifice and other offerings to the tall wooden statue of the god—with its customary exaggerated phallus—which had been erected beneath the *templum*. A little of the blood that had poured from the sheep's cut throat, the priest caught in a silver-chased cup, which he then filled

with wine; and this, Wulfgar and Rhowenna shared to sym-
bolize their joining, drinking deep. After that, each fastened
around the other's left wrist a wide gold wedding bracelet
especially engraved with the wolf and the swan that Wulfgar
had chosen as his seal. Then he kissed her, and the ceremony
was ended. She was his wife.

She had not thought to feel truly married after the pagan
rite; yet, strangely enough, she did. In rituals such as this had
her own ancestors wed, and their blood flowed strongly in
her veins, no matter the gold Celtic crucifix she wore around
her neck, beneath her gown. The Christ's priests would call
her a sinner, her marriage a blasphemy. Yet when she looked
into Wulfgar's eyes and saw his deep, abiding love for her
shining there, she could not in her heart believe that the Christ
would withhold his blessing of their union. Only on the ninth
and last day of feasting, when the second messenger Wulfgar
had dispatched to Usk finally returned, did Rhowenna doubt
this, did she seem to hear Father Cadwyr's invidious voice
whispering in her ear that God's curse was upon her. For the
scroll the messenger handed to Wulfgar was written not in
Latin, but in the language of Walas; and when Rhowenna
read it, the words struck her as hard as a devastating blow:

Usk survived, with Gwydion as its king, and he would pay
whatever ransom was demanded for her safe return.

Chapter Fifteen

Flight into Darkness

Rhowenna would never, so long as she lived, forget the anguish on Wulfgar's face in that moment when she read aloud Gwydion's letter. She was stricken by the missive's contents, but even more so by what she saw in Wulfgar's eyes. He was her husband; he loved her, and she loved him. Yet she knew that in that first instant, her heart had involuntarily leaped into her eyes, with hope that she might go home, to Gwydion; and she knew, also, that Wulfgar had seen it.

"Do you want to leave me, *elsket*?" he asked her later, in their sleeping chamber, after they had made love and she lay snuggled in his embrace. "Here in the Northland, a woman is permitted to divorce her husband if she wishes. Do you want to do that, to return to Usk?"

"Nay, oh, nay, Wulfgar," she said quietly but fiercely, wounded herself by the pain she had caused him. "'Twas only a moment's homesickness—that's all—a longing, really, for the time when I was young and innocent, and my parents—

my parents were still alive. Sometimes even now, I—I just can't believe that they're—that they're really dead."

"I know, *kjæreste.*" His voice was kind. "I know that 'tis hard. I know that your life and your world have been changed forever because of me, because I took you from Usk."

"Aye, but I would not go back, not if it meant never knowing you, never loving you, Wulfgar. . . ."

They made love again then, with a passion as unbridled as a storm, her hair a tangle of heather, ensnaring him, drawing him down to her. Her breasts were mounds of soft earth, molded by his palms. His breath was warm and inciting upon their rosy buds. His tongue was as moist as the spindrift that spewed from the sea to waft on the wings of the wind across the strands and heaths of the Northland, as salty as the taste of him upon her own tongue when she pressed her lips to his flesh. There was no part of her that he did not know, nor any part of him that was untouched by her. Clinging tightly to each other, they came together as, hard and swift, Wulfgar claimed her and, soft and deep, Rhowenna took him into her, sailing with him down a wild, tempestuous wind to a place that was neither Heaven nor Asgard, but a mystical isle of misted mountains and sylvan glades through which rushed and tumbled the quicksilver river of life before it swept finally, quietly, into a boundless, tranquil sea.

The gods are capricious.
And what they bestow today, they may as easily take away tomorrow, Ivar the Boneless had said, as Wulfgar was to remember for many a long day after he dispatched Gwydion's message to Ragnar Lodbrók, in the hope that obtaining the ransom for the woman he thought was Rhowenna, Ragnar would send Morgen back to Usk, never knowing how he had been deceived. Morgen would be glad to return to her

homeland; she would explain to Gwydion all that had happened, and if brazen Flóki truly wanted her, he could go after her. It would, Wulfgar thought, tie all the loose ends up quite nicely and settle everything to everyone's satisfaction.

And perhaps it would have, if not for the gods and Ivar the Boneless, who saw fit to thrust a malicious hand into the affair, and for the recklessness of Flóki the Raven.

It was Flóki whom Wulfgar entrusted with the delivery of the scroll; and truth to tell, when he first entered Ragnar's great mead hall, Flóki had no notion of doing anything rash, having heard Wulfgar's plan and agreed that it was for the best. But after Ragnar and his sons were apprised of the letter's contents, Ivar—who had been awaiting his chance—announced wickedly that while they could be certain the princess of Usk was unharmed, they could *not* be sure she was a virgin, and that perhaps they should verify that fact before sending her back to Usk, lest its new king think they had cheated him. A huge clamor of ribald laughter and lewd remarks erupted in the great mead hall at that; for with winter coming on, there was little for the *thegns* to do save to sit, play board games, and drink, and the *nabid* and the *bjórr* had flowed freely all day. Ragnar had swilled more than his share, and like his son Ivar, he was not loath to rape an unwilling wench. The only thing that had saved Morgen thus far was that he believed her to be the princess of Usk and her virginity of some use to him. Now that her ransom was to be paid, however, there was no reason not to take her; for now by the time she could inform Gwydion, king of Usk, of her fate, it would be too late. Ragnar would have her blood money in his grasping hands.

So thinking, he jerked Morgen up from where she sat at his feet and, throwing her roughly over his shoulder, carried her into his sleeping chamber, shouting back to his sons that they could have her when he was finished with her. It was all Flóki could do then to keep from running after Ragnar and cutting him down; but that would have been to sign his own death warrant, as well, and he was not quite so rash as that. Instead, in all the cacophony, he slipped from the great mead hall and sneaked around the side of the *hof* to the exterior door of Ragnar's sleeping chamber. It was fortunate, Flóki thought, that Ragnar had not decided to rape Morgen in front of all his warriors, and so had taken her to his sleeping chamber; no doubt, he had feared he had drunk so much that his shaft might fail him, provoking his men to laughter and jesting at his own expense. Stealthily, Flóki pressed his ear to the door and tried the handle to be certain it was not locked. It was not. After a few minutes, when he heard screams and what was clearly a struggle inside, he quietly eased open the door and stepped into the sleeping chamber. Ragnar had Morgen down on the bed and was tearing at her clothes, so intent on sating his lust that he did not hear the intruder. Again, Flóki thought about drawing his broadsword. But slaying a king was a serious crime indeed; and finally, he contented himself with creeping up on Ragnar and, with a heavy soapstone wine cup that lay on the floor, bashing him over the head, knocking him unconscious. With a groan, Ragnar rolled slowly off Morgen, falling with a thud to the floor, his head bleeding profusely from the wound Flóki had inflicted. Morgen's eyes were filled with fury and fright. But then she recognized Flóki.

"Shhhhh," he hissed, holding a warning finger to his lips. "Come on. I'm taking you out of here—now." Grabbing up one of the pelts from the bed, he continued, "I needs must bundle you up in this, lady, so no one will see you and try to prevent us from leaving."

"What about the King?" Morgen asked, looking with disgust at Ragnar's senseless form.

"If we're lucky, he'll be unconscious for hours, with no one the wiser; for no man—except perhaps Ivar the Boneless—will be brave enough to interrupt what all think is going on in here. By the time Ragnar finally does wake up, we'll be long gone."

Flóki wrapped Morgen up in the fur, then carried her outside, where he slung her over the front of his saddle, hoping that the sentries in Ragnar's watchtowers would not remember whether he had had the pelt thrown across his horse when he had ridden in. It was becoming dark now, so perhaps the guards would not be able to see him very well, or would be so busy quaffing wine or ale to warm themselves on this chilly evening that they would not bother looking too closely at him. To his relief, his luck held. Spying him coming, the gatekeepers merely opened the gates to allow him to pass, waving him on through and paying no attention when he galloped by. He could hardly believe he and Morgen had made good their escape, and so easily. Once they were out of sight of Ragnar's palisade, Flóki drew his steed to a halt and unrolled Morgen from the pelt so she could finish the remainder of the ride mounted pillion behind him.

"There will be a moon, lady," he observed as he gazed at the swiftly darkening sky. "We will be able to make it to Wulfgar's markland this night."

"And then? What then, Flóki?" Morgen's face was anxious.

He shook his head, his own dark, handsome visage creased with worry now that he considered the enormity of what he had done in attacking his king and stealing away the princess of Usk.

"I don't know, lady. I don't know."

Then, setting his heels to his horse's sides, he urged the animal on across the frost-encrusted heaths, racing the darkness and the moon rising slowly on the horizon.

* * *

There was nothing to do but to make a run for it, Wulfgar thought, his heart heavy as he listened to the story told by Flóki and Morgen. The crime Flóki had committed of assaulting his king was so terrible that Ragnar would not be satisfied with less than Flóki's death by the Blood Eagle, a hideous ritual. Wulfgar could not allow that to happen to Flóki, who had been his staunch supporter from the time of the duel with Knut Strongarm aboard the *Dragon's Fire*. Further, even if Flóki alone were to flee and Morgen return to Ragnar, since Flóki was Wulfgar's second-in-command, entrusted to deliver the message from Usk, Ragnar was sure to claim that Wulfgar was behind Flóki's actions, to use the attack as an excuse to march on Wulfgar's markland, to have him branded an outlaw by the *Thing*. The risk of remaining in the Northland was now too great even to consider; they must all flee and hope that Ragnar and his sons did not pursue them.

Wulfgar's longship, the *Siren's Song*, was finished, although she still sat on her log rollers upon the strand, unconsecrated, not yet named ceremoniously, unsoaked by the sea, her maiden voyage not yet made. He had planned to sail the vessel following his wedding rite, perhaps on a seal hunt in the Grey and Frozen seas, to test her. But there was no time for that now. They must put to sea and hope that the longship proved herself worthy of a *Víkingr*.

"But it means giving up everything you have gained, Wulfgar!" Rhowenna exclaimed, anguished, when he announced the decision he had made.

"*Elsket*, 'tis a great loss to me, aye. But it does not matter, if only we are together. What will become of you if Ragnar marches on my markland or persuades the *Thing* to proclaim me an outlaw? Nay, I cannot risk that. I *will* not. Go now. Gather those possessions you need most. We shall not sleep this night, but must make haste to escape before Ragnar wakes or is discovered before the dawn."

Seeing Wulfgar's determination, Rhowenna knew that it was useless to argue with him, and silently, she went to do as he had bade her, her heart overflowing with love and pain. That he should give up for her all he had gained was to her the greatest of both joys and sorrows; she could not help but think of Gwydion in comparison, whose own sacrifice in running away with her would have been small and yet who had not been willing to make it, rejecting and abandoning her to Prince Cerdic. Only Wulfgar had proved himself constant, and Rhowenna had never loved him more than she did in that moment.

By the light of the pale, sickly moon that had risen in the night sky, augmented by whale-oil lamps that flickered in the moaning wind, the longship was loaded and provisioned, then shoved over its log rollers into a sea that shone silvery dark and cold, roiling and white with foam. The vessel rocked on the waves, tugging so hard at the mooring ropes the *thegns* had tethered to temporary posts driven into the sand that it seemed it would tear free and take with it the only chance at escape. Rhowenna's heart pounded as she saw how violently the longship heaved on the rough water, for she knew that this was a bad time to be out on the sea, that even the *Víkingrs* did not care to take such a chance unless compelled to.

Wulfgar was shouting orders, the words ripped away by the wind, his face grim. Flóki was doing the work of ten men, in an attempt to make up for all the trouble he had caused. He knew that it was bad luck, an offense against the gods to set sail in a vessel that had not yet been consecrated or named in the sacred ritual; that for that reason, many of the warriors would consider the longship accursed; and, considering that if they embarked upon this voyage, they might be leaving their homeland forever, they would refuse to sail upon the *Siren's Song*, perhaps even rendering the vessel shorthanded. Then Wulfgar would be forced to press his male slaves into service. But in the end, there were enough *thegns* to man the oars, although the shifts would have to be staggered.

Shivering, Rhowenna stood with her white bearskin cloak pulled close about her to ward off the chill. She could hardly believe that the events of this night were taking place, were real; everything seemed to have happened so fast. She was almost as sick and frightened as she had been when the Northmen had descended upon Usk; for although she had never thought to call it so, the Northland had become her home. Glancing back toward the heath, she could see in the distance the palisade that surrounded the *hof* upon which she and Wulfgar had worked so hard, where they had built so much, planning a life together. Tears started in her eyes. Somehow, it was like losing Usk all over again; and when Wulfgar gathered her up in his arms to carry her to the longship, she buried her face against his chest so he would not see how she wept for her own loss and his. She must be strong, she told herself, as strong as he, who loved her so.

The sea frothed and swirled about them; the vessel pitched so, that it was several moments before he was able to hand her aboard. But finally, she and Morgen were settled in the stern, as they had been once before, on their journey to the Northland. As much for comfort and safety as for warmth, they huddled together between the coffers and sea chests on the deck. Flóki joined the two women, while Wulfgar took the tiller. Then, at last, the mooring ropes were cast off, and to the soft, low beat of the drummer's instrument, the oarsmen began quietly to row, the longship to move slowly out of the harbor, all aboard aware that if anyone spied them sneaking away like thieves in the night, an investigation would ensue and an alarm would doubtless be raised. But no one ventured forth in the darkness, lamp in hand, to witness the passage of the *Siren's Song* and to wonder why the vessel of the *jarl* Wulfgar Bloodaxe had put out upon such a rough sea, on such a cold, windy night.

Wulfgar did not know where they would go, although he had a vague notion of settling in the Frankish kingdoms, in Normandy, where many *Víkingrs* had already carved out marklands for themselves. So he set a northerly course, intending to follow the coast of the Northland up and across to the Shetlands and Orkneys, and thence down the shoreline of Britain, rather than along those of Jutland and Frisia, until he reached the Frankish kingdoms. He thought that this route might help to throw Ragnar off the scent should he pursue them. It also meant that if, instead, Ragnar, too, sailed down the coast of Britain, Wulfgar could turn the *Siren's Song* east, across the savage North Sea if he was compelled to, and end up, if the gods so willed, in harbors more familiar to him, harbors more accustomed to the sight of longships moored at their wharves, for the purpose of trading rather than raiding. Crossing the North Sea was not a course Wulfgar liked to consider taking; for it was a rough sea, frequently cloaked with mist and beset by storms, especially at this time of year, and no *Víkingr* willingly ventured across it. But it would be better than winding up as prisoners of Ragnar Lodbrók after the crime Flóki had committed against him.

Shuddering at the thought that Ragnar might somehow learn of Rhowenna's true identity, Wulfgar decided that if worse came to worst and the *Siren's Song* was taken captive and boarded, he would slay Rhowenna himself rather than let her fall prey to Ragnar and his sons. For if ever they discovered that she, the true princess of Usk, had willingly married Wulfgar, they would see it as a sign that she had considered him royal enough of lineage, blue enough of blood to claim her hand, a legitimate heir to Ragnar's kingdom and throne; and her fate would be even more cruel than slavery and whoredom. They would torture her and put her to death, Wulfgar thought, for daring to wed an upstart who had dared to aim so high. His child, too, if she even now carried a babe of his making, they would not suffer to live, but would expose it to the elements or put it to the sword, as was the custom for unwanted children in the Northland. As he glanced at Rhowenna's face, small and ashen in the moonlight, Wulfgar shivered again with fear for her; and he prayed to the gods that he would not be forced to kill her, that they would escape Ragnar's long, vengeful arm to build a new home together somewhere, some way.

But to Wulfgar's despair, the gods chose not to hear his prayers; for a few days later off the coast of Caledonia, when the grey dawn came, he spied in the distance a widespread sail as crimson as his own, and he recognized Ragnar's mighty longship, which was lying in wait. Such was Ragnar's rage at the assault upon him that he had gambled all on correctly guessing which course Wulfgar would choose to set and had himself daringly crossed the North Sea at a much wider point rather than to follow the safer shoreline route as Wulfgar had. Ragnar was now hard on the heels of the *Siren's Song*, bearing down rapidly from the northeast; and now Wulfgar wondered uneasily if his vessel was, in fact, accursed because he had not consecrated her to the gods and named her in accordance with the proper ritual.

The wind was with him, at least; but that was of little help, for it was also with Ragnar, whose own longship was as swift as the *Siren's Song*. It would be a race, then, between the two vessels and their captains, a test of skill, seamanship, and cunning; and Wulfgar had not Ragnar's years of experience at the tiller of a longship to draw upon. It was time for Flóki to spell Wulfgar at the tiller, but Wulfgar knew he could not relinquish the tiller now, when Ragnar was in sight. So he stayed where he was, his fatigue dispelled all at once by the sudden surge of adrenaline that pumped through his body, setting his pulse to pounding.

"'Tis he. 'Tis Ragnar. I would know his Dragon Ship anywhere," Flóki stated grimly as he stared at the red sail in the distance. "He has come after us, as the hunter pursues the hare, and is bent on driving us into some snare, I am thinking.''

"Aye, so I fear." Wulfgar's voice was grave and had a hard, serrated edge at the thought of how Ragnar had outfoxed him. ''That is why I will keep the tiller for now, Flóki, until I am too weary to stand. Till then, do you rest and conserve your strength; for although Ragnar may have won this round, the battle is not over, and I do not mean to make it any easier for him. 'Tis a long race we shall run, and with a fight at the end of it, I am thinking. So 'twould not be wise for us both to be exhausted then.''

''Nay, you are right, lord. Ah, Wulfgar!'' Flóki cried with remorse. ''I rue that I have with my rash action brought us to this terrible pass! But I could not just ride away and leave my lady to Ragnar's mercy. She, who is a virgin and the princess of Usk!''

Almost, Wulfgar was tempted to tell him that Morgen was neither, but in the end remained silent about how the two women had switched identities. If Ragnar should catch them, it might be that Flóki would blurt out the truth under torture or in a vain attempt to save Morgen against the attentions of Ragnar and his sons. Not even the fulfilling of Flóki's love and desire for Morgen was worth putting Rhowenna at such risk, Wulfgar told himself fiercely as he gazed at her pale, sleeping form curled up on his wolfskin in the stern, her own white bearskin cloak, for which he had traded a fine scramasax, wrapped around her. He thanked the gods that for the moment, she still slumbered, blissfully unaware yet of Ragnar's bearing down upon them. Would that she need never know, need never confront the threat the dawn had brought to them all, Wulfgar thought. She was weary to the bone, had endured too many grievous blows for one woman to suffer. Yet, with courage and conviction, she had borne them all, telling him, once, that God never gave anyone a burden too heavy to bear. This, however, Wulfgar did not believe.

The Christ might be merciful, as Rhowenna claimed; but the gods were not, as he had good cause to know—and perhaps the Christ was angry with her for marrying him, a pagan. It could be that all of her Heaven and his Asgard had turned against them.

Yet, despite the adversity they faced, Wulfgar still could not repress the thrill of excitement and exhilaration that shot through him as the *Siren's Song* lifted and surged beneath his feet, driving forward across the waves, the wind filling her sail so that it billowed and whipped against the grey dawn sky. She was his vessel, just as Rhowenna was his wife. Come what may, nothing on earth could change that, he told himself fervently. The thought filled his heart to bursting. He would do whatever was necessary to protect them both, he vowed savagely, even if it meant dying in the attempt and spending his whole afterlife not in the Valhöll, but on the Shore of Corpses, forever at the mercy of Nidhögg, the blood-sucking monster of Hel.

Chapter Sixteen

The Fish Hooked

For long days and nights, the *Siren's Song* played a cat-and-mouse game with Ragnar's own mighty longship, neither gaining nor losing leagues, but always running, with Wulfgar and Flóki both forced to call upon every ounce of shrewdness and strength they possessed to maintain the distance between the two vessels. Down the coasts of Caledonia and Britain, the *Siren's Song* fled, zigging and zagging in an effort to throw off her relentless pursuers, to no avail. Ragnar's knowledge and experience of the sea were much greater than that of Wulfgar. Like a sly fox, Ragnar seemed to anticipate Wulfgar's and Flóki's every move.

"We cannot shake him, lord." Flóki's face was taut with tiredness and worry. "He is going to keep on until he has run us to ground."

"I had hoped that Ragnar would grow weary of the chase. But in my heart, I know that you are right, Flóki," Wulfgar agreed. "Still, somehow, we must rid ourselves of him. If we put in to some harbor, he will be on us, like a bear fishing in a mountain stream, clawing us from the water to bite off our heads! Yet if we continue to sail on, he will chase us until we are too exhausted to go any farther, or out of fresh water and supplies. We simply *must* find some means of outwitting him!''

That night, while Flóki stood at the tiller, Wulfgar discussed their options with Rhowenna and Yelkei, he holding Rhowenna's hand tightly in his as they soberly contemplated their dismal prospects, each wondering if they would have a future at all. Her violet eyes were huge and dark in her white face, and her skin gleamed like a pearl in the moonlight and the light cast by the flames of the firepot, which she sat near for warmth. Yelkei's own eyes glittered blacker than black and, narrowed, were nearly lost in her wrinkled moon face as she squatted on the deck, listening to Wulfgar's words. When he had finished, she reached, without speaking, beneath the folds of her fur cloak to draw forth a small, deerskin pouch that he knew contained her rune stones. An icy grue chased up his spine at the sight; for the contents of that pouch had enabled her earlier to pierce the veil of time and peer into the future, and he did not know if she had but spoken of what she had seen or if he himself had brought her prophecies to pass because he had believed and acted upon them. For who, in truth, had the power to look into the minds and hearts of the gods? If such a gift were indeed Yelkei's own, truly she was a spaewife to be feared; and for a moment, Wulfgar nearly snatched the pouch from her yellow, talonlike fingers, so great was his trepidation that the curse of the gods would fall upon him for Yelkei's presumption. But as though sensing his sudden, wild desire, Rhowenna's hand tightened around his own; and seeing in her eyes something akin to what lay in Yelkei's, he stayed his hand, shuddering again and muttering under his breath.

"Silence!" Yelkei hissed, shooting him a censuring

glance. "If you are afraid, lie down on your wolfskin and go to sleep. If you are not, then do you keep quiet while I cast the rune stones, so I may hear what the gods would speak."

This was pagan and witchery, Rhowenna thought with a shiver, a blasphemy against the Christ and the Church, for which she would surely be punished. Yet she could not seem to leave the place on the deck where she sat, any more than Wulfgar could. Some unknown force held her there, as though she could hear in her mind the chanting of the blue-woad-tattooed Picti and the Tribes who had been her ancestors as Yelkei added fuel to the firepot, so its flames blazed high. As she passed her bony hand over them, sprinkling them with a fine powder she had taken from her pocket, they leaped with such intensity, spitting sparks and turning the colors of a rainbow, that Rhowenna and Wulfgar both started and shrank back a little, although they did not move from where they watched Yelkei's sorcery. She was chanting now, words in some strange language they had never before heard, clipped and chiming. Such was the spaewife's power to entrance that Rhowenna was only dimly aware that at the very back of the stern, Morgen was on her knees, crossing herself and praying, and that at the tiller, Flóki stood, making the ancient pagan sign against evil.

Now the stones bearing the nine runes that were the gift of Odinn were in Yelkei's hand, and she was shaking them so they rattled eerily, like the bones of the skeletons that hung in the Sacred Groves of the Northland long after the corpses had decayed, dancing and knocking in the wind, their eyes black abysses, like Yelkei's own. From the palm of her hand, the stones tumbled onto the deck and lay there, some faceup, others facedown. Rhowenna did not know what they meant; but Yelkei's quickly indrawn breath was sharp, and her eyes glittered. A short cackle of laughter erupted from her mouth, and then a cawing cry that was like that of a raven.

Nine times, Yelkei tossed the rune stones onto the deck,

and to Rhowenna's awe, nine times the stones fell as they had that first time, the same runes showing, the same runes concealed. Then, at last, Yelkei gathered them up and put them away in her pouch.

"Tell Flóki to steer the *Siren's Song* into the heart of the North Sea, Wulfgar," she croaked slyly, "there to hook a big fish worth the sea goddess Ran's hoard of gold from all the drowned *Víkingrs* who have paid her to journey from her domain to Valhöll."

"Art mad, Yelkei!" Wulfgar spat softly, angry and afraid. "Art a witch, in truth, who leads us all to our deaths, I am thinking! Even the boldest of *Víkingrs* would rather wander the Shore of Corpses to the barred gates of Hel than to cross the North Sea at its heart, where 'tis most treacherous. We will surely go down to lie in Ran's watery arms, wrapped in the strands of her seaweed hair!"

"Do you say that you yourself have not considered sailing the *Siren's Song* there to elude Ragnar, Wulfgar?" Yelkei's eyes seemed to pierce his very soul. When he did not respond, she snorted again with laughter. "Aye, you have; for within you, you know that even the great Ragnar Lodbrók will think twice about following us there, where the mist and maelstroms lurk like monsters to send a longship fathoms deep beneath the sea. Yet even that, I tell you, would be an easier death for your lady wife, for whom you fear so greatly, than what she would endure at the hands of Ragnar and his sons."

In his heart, Wulfgar knew that this, also, was so. Still, he hesitated, recalling a time, in his youthful manhood, when he had displeased his half brothers Ubbi and Halfdan for some now-forgotten reason. Seizing him, they had hurtled him headlong into an open barrel of *bjórr*, holding him under until he had thought that his lungs would burst from lack of air, that he would surely drown in the cask of wine. Again and again, they had jerked him up, only to plunge him back down once more until, at last, they had tired of the sport and released him. Gasping, coughing, and choking, sodden and dripping with *bjórr*, he had stood then, petrified, as Ivar, on his face a cruel, wolfish smile, in his hand a lighted torch, had stalked him, threatening to set him ablaze, all of them knowing that Wulfgar would catch fire like the whale-oil-soaked wick of a lamp. Now, as he remembered how his lungs had felt that day, Wulfgar did not know if he could bring himself to condemn Rhowenna to such a fate, to such a terrible death. But sensing this, she laid her hand imploringly upon his arm.

"Wulfgar, please, 'tis a chance, at least—mayhap the only chance for us. And I would rather die in your arms in the sea than to lie in the arms of Ragnar Lodbrók and Ivar the Boneless, I swear it!"

Tightly, Wulfgar embraced her at that, as though he would never let her go, kissing her feverishly and then burying his face in her hair, sighing so long and heavily that she felt the raw sob in his throat, which he choked down with difficulty.

"Flóki," he whispered hoarsely at last, "take us into the heart of the North Sea."

For a moment, inhaling sharply, Flóki seemed poised to refuse and argue against the order. But then, rising, Morgen moved quietly to stand beside him, slipping her arms about his waist and laying her head upon his shoulder.

"Please, Flóki," she murmured; and finally, nodding his head, his face grim, he headed the longship toward the open sea.

The dawn came, pale and leaden, and the wind had both winter's icy scent and a madding storm on its breath. Frost layered the mast, the crutches, and the deck, and clung to the sail, so that it shimmered like a fetch in the bleak light. Surely an ill omen, Wulfgar thought as, silently, somberly, he took the tiller from an equally solemn Flóki. Clouds the color of unpolished silver scudded from the west across the sullen sky, and mist clung to the dark, restless, shifting waves that swirled about the hull of the vessel.

"This is madness!" Flóki broke at last the stillness heavy between them. "There is a storm blowing up somewhere in the distance. I can feel it in my bones."

"Aye, so can I."

"But still, you do not intend to turn back toward the coast?"

"Nay, if the storm comes, we will ride it out here. Nay, do not try to dissuade me, Flóki. My mind is made up—and truth to tell, you've naught but yourself to blame for it," Wulfgar reminded him, not wanting to quarrel, "although I do not hold it against you. In your place, I should have done the same, such is my deep love for my lady. Now, do you get some rest. 'Tis going to be a long day and an even longer night, I am thinking; for I do not believe that the storm will overtake us before dusk, if it catches us at all. If the gods be willing, we can outrun it, mayhap. At least, 'twill hit Ragnar's longship first." Wulfgar gazed at the western horizon, where the crimson sail that was their nemesis was barely visible. "Unless he chooses now to turn back, to give up the chase, and to put in to a harbor on the coast."

"He will not." Flóki laughed shortly, harshly. "Like the gods, he is against us!"

It was soon seen that this was the case. Ragnar's longship pressed on, the rising force of the storm wind in the distance such that he began actually to gain upon the *Siren's Song*, which was far enough ahead for the moment to catch only the dying gusts, not powerful enough to propel the vessel as quickly as Ragnar's own was being driven forward. As the day wore on, the sky growing steadily darker and Ragnar's longship steadily gaining, Wulfgar knew to his despair that Flóki had spoken truly, that the gods were against them, that they were not going to be able to outrun the storm, as he had hoped. Along toward dusk, he gave orders for the hide coverings that protected the vessel when it was moored to a wharf to be brought forth and stretched across the bow and the stern, to provide a modicum of shelter, and for everything that could be, save for the men's sea chests, to be crammed into the shallow cargo space beneath the deck, in preparation for what he feared was about to descend upon the *Siren's Song*.

The temperature had fallen drastically in the last several minutes; and now the mist, which had never dissipated, wafted up from the sea, in ever-thickening sheets that twined like a shroud about the longship, so only the wind's piercing its veil permitted Wulfgar to see what lay ahead—and behind. Black thunderheads massed and roiled in the seething sky. Like a portent, the first hard drops of rain struck the deck, a warning of what was soon to come. He should strike the sail, Wulfgar knew. Yet his gut instinct told him that somewhere behind him, Ragnar's own sail was still boldly spread, bearing swiftly down on him; and so he set his teeth against the order that would have rendered the *Siren's Song* virtually helpless.

"Rhowenna! Get back beneath the hide!" From fear, Wulfgar spoke more harshly than he had intended, startled by her suddenly coming to stand behind him, her long black hair whipped loose from its braid, tangling wildly about her, her face uplifed to the spurts of rain.

"Nay, I will not!" Rebelliously, she shook her head, grasping his arm to hold herself upright as the deck rolled and pitched ever more fiercely beneath their feet. "Whatever happens, I want to be here by your side when it comes!"

"That is foolish! A storm is about to hit us, and you are in danger of being swept overboard! By Odinn!" Wulfgar roared when, still, she did not move, her chin set stubbornly, but her eyes so beseeching that it was all he could do to stand firm against her. "Do as I say, wench, else I'll tie you up myself and throw you in the hold! By the gods, I swear it!"

He knew from the sudden tears that started in her eyes how he had hurt her; and grabbing her, he kissed her hard and savagely before abruptly shoving her down beneath the hide. "Now, stay there, and do not come out again!" His bronze visage was such in the sudden flash of lightning that exploded in the heavens that, biting her lower lip so hard that she drew blood, Rhowenna could only nod her obedience mutely, not trusting herself to speak, for fear that he would actually strike her.

Still, she could not resist peeking out from where she huddled with Morgen and Yelkei beneath the hide across the stern, cringing at the violent crack of thunder that followed the lightning and seemed to split the very firmament asunder. All at once then, the rain came, so ferociously that it ripped apart the sheets of mist in moments to reveal, as though by some dreadful witchery, the black sky, the even blacker sea, and the longship that loomed up suddenly, it seemed, from nowhere. Not only the storm, but also Ragnar Lodbrók was upon them. But even more wild and terrifying than this evil sight was the vision of Wulfgar himself, making Rhowenna's breath catch with fear in her throat. Having turned the tiller over to Flóki, Wulfgar stood like an avenging god at the center of the deck, his golden hair streaming from his face in the wind and rain, his sable cloak flapping like a raven's wings about him. His legs were spread wide, as were his uplifted arms. In his right hand, he held his battle-ax, shouting above the roar of the storm, "Hear me! Hear me, O great Odinn, god of warriors, and give me your blessing! Odinn! Odinn!" and to her horror, as Rhowenna watched him, another bolt of lightning erupted in the heavens, seeming to strike his upraised weapon. For an eternity, the blade glittered silvery in the coruscating light. Then, without warning, it appeared to explode in a dazzling burst of unholy blue fire that streaked like a shooting star up the mast, now bare of its sail furled and lowered, causing all who saw the ball of eerily glowing flame to fall to their knees, petrified that Wulfgar himself had called down upon them the wrath of the mighty god Odinn. And in that shocking, horrifying, glorious moment, when it seemed that perhaps Wulfgar himself had become a god, Ragnar's heavy, sodden crimson sail, which his men had been desperately attempting to lower, tore violently loose from its bottom spar, the flapping corner striking him hard in the chest and knocking him overboard into the turgid, churning sea.

Through the pelting rain, all could see him bobbing helplessly amid the waves. Yelling frantically, his *thegns* began throwing barrels and oars into the water, in the hope that he could remain afloat long enough to be rescued.

"Row!" Wulfgar demanded harshly of his own men; and like the primordial thunder of Thor's hammer, Mjöllnir, pounding across the firmament, the drummer's instrument began to sound a barbarous beat, and massive muscles straining with effort, the warriors bent their backs to their oars, forcing the *Siren's Song* through the storm, toward Ragnar's longship. "Row, you bloody bastards! Row as you've never rowed in your life!"

And they did, the vessel groaning and creaking as it struggled to stay afloat, to press on, tossing and heaving upon the rough swells of the sea, the waves sluicing across the deck, the rain battering it unmercifully. Wulfgar had gone mad, utterly mad, Rhowenna thought as she clung to the side of the stern to keep from being washed away as the water flooded in, only to rush out again as the longship leaped from the sea, then plunged back in again. They were going to sink, she knew, to drown in those cold, dark, terrible waves that roiled with a fury to match the storm's and Wulfgar's own as his voice lashed his *thegns*, a cruel and hideous whip that goaded them on. Like a wildman, he had flung off his cloak and stripped off his tunic; now, naked to the waist, he stood, his battle-ax sheathed at his back, his hands on Flóki's own to hold the tiller as they drove onward through the blinding rain until it seemed that Wulfgar intended them to collide with Ragnar's vessel, to smash headlong into it, sending both longships straight to Hel. But then, in an awesome feat of strength and daring, Wulfgar and Flóki hauled on the tiller, and the *Siren's Song* spun about on her keel to roll and to pitch alongside Ragnar's vessel.

Now, as were several of the other men, Wulfgar was running, staggering across the deck to snatch up a heavy coil of the walrus hide usually used for rigging; but these ropes had, attached to their ends, grappling hooks designed to haul in kills from sea hunts and to secure enemy vessels for boarding. These hooks, Wulfgar and the warriors were now flinging violently into the sea, where Ragnar rose and plummeted on the waves, clinging for life to a plank ripped up from the deck of his longship and tossed into the sea in an effort to save him.

"Hook him!" Wulfgar shouted fiercely, as though the men fought to capture a whale and not a king of the Northland. "By the gods, a casket of hacksilver for those who hook that son of a whore! Hook him! Odinn! Odinn!"

Ragnar and his own men went crazy then, seeing what Wulfgar intended; and Rhowenna, her eyes riveted to the vicious, fantastic scene, knew then that this could not be happening, that this could not be real, but must be a dream, a horrible nightmare from which she could not seem to awaken. Again and again, as great tridents of lightning stabbed the sky black with the evil night that had fallen, so the sharp hooks gleamed viciously with each cast as they flew through the wind and rain into the swollen, frenzied sea. The thunder bellowed and boomed, as though the gods themselves warred in the heavens, as though the Ragnarök, the twilight of the gods, were at hand. The longships surged and fell, timbers straining and moaning so fiercely that it seemed as though the vessels would break apart in the storm. The wind howled like

Garm, the hound of Hel; the rain shattered down, a hail of stinging barbs. Wulfgar and his fiendish warriors had metamorphosed somehow into the gruesome monsters of the Shore of Corpses, Rhowenna thought dully, shocked, stricken as, incredibly, a hook struck its mark, and then another, so deep that Ragnar could not stifle the long, hoarse cry of agony that was torn from his throat and lost in the wind. Still a third hook drove like a blade into his flesh; and then, as though Ragnar were indeed a whale or a walrus, Wulfgar and the rest pulled his bleeding body onto the deck of the *Siren's Song* just as the two longships at last, and perhaps inevitably, collided with a deafening crash that jarred Rhowenna to the very bone. Timber shrieked, scraping, splintering until one proud dragon could fight no more and sank swiftly into the gaping maw of the dark and perilous sea, a rich bounty to be claimed by Ran.

Chapter Seventeen

Aella's Snake Pit

Although not mortally, the *Siren's Song* was indeed badly wounded, Wulfgar saw by the dawn that broke, bleak but at least clear, upon the horizon after the long, terrible night. They had ridden out the storm beneath the hides stretched across the longship, rudder and oars drawn in finally, leaving the vessel to the mercy of the wind and sea. In his hope to outrun the storm, Wulfgar had waited too long to order the sail furled and lowered, so there had been no time to take down the mast and to stow it upon the trestles that rose from the deck. During the storm, it had been struck by lightning, the top third charred and, breaking away, sent hurling into the sea, crippling the longship. The strakes on the side that had struck Ragnar's own mighty vessel were deeply gouged, although the rivets had somehow held fast. Those on Ragnar's longship had not, loosening from the repeated blows against the *Siren's Song*; the strakes had buckled and given way, and the vessel had sunk. Wulfgar could, however, no longer be certain the caulking of tarred animal hide between the strakes of the *Siren's Song* would hold. He needed to put in to port somewhere to effect repairs; and he thought how ironic it was that the nearest harbor should be the mouth of the river Humber, in that kingdom of Britain, Northumbria, ruled by Aella, who had put a rich price on the head of Ragnar Lodbrók.

Yet as Wulfgar gazed at his father lying trussed hand and foot upon the deck, he found to his deep anger and frustration that despite himself, regret stirred in his soul for this man who had given him life, and that there was pity in his heart for this great king of the Northland, this worthy foe, once so high, who had been brought so low. Gladly in his fear and rage of last night in the storm, Wulfgar would have sunk his grappling hook into Ragnar's head or heart, slaying him. But this morning, with those turbulent emotions drained from him, with Rhowenna lying safe beside him, Wulfgar somehow could no longer summon his hate; and he thought that, after all, he did not care to have upon his conscience his own father's death.

His face impassive, he rose to move toward Ragnar's prone figure, hunkering down beside him and staring at him silently. Sensing Wulfgar's eyes on him, Ragnar blearily opened his own. Last night, he had thought to drown in the treacherous sea into which his own sail had knocked him. Then, when he had felt the savage hooks pierce his body, tearing his flesh, he had been certain at least one had stabbed some vital organ and that he would die. When he had been roughly hauled onto the deck of the *Siren's Song* and bound hand and foot, he had believed he would surely bleed to death. But he was an incredibly strong giant of a man; and now that none of these things had come to pass and he was still alive, he knew that the gods had in mind some other fate for him, and he chafed against what he feared would be the ignominy of it. He wished violently that he had not retched up the foul seawater he had swallowed, that it had poisoned him or swallowed the breath in his lungs, that the bleeding of his wounds had not been staunched as well as possible under the circumstances by Wulfgar's woman. Had he proved able to free himself from his restraints, Ragnar would have thrown himself overboard or cut his own throat.

"Why did you not kill me—or at least let me die?" he asked sourly, coughing a little, his face as grey as the morning light. "Then would I already be in Valhöll."

"I do not know—save that when I was born, you allowed me to live instead of leaving me for the wolves to devour or the foul weather to finish on a Northland heath," Wulfgar confessed honestly.

"Aye, well, better I had done so than to listen to Goscelin's insistence that you were my son and no one else's, and giving in to her tears by permitting you to take suck from her breast."

"Do you then look at me and doubt still that you are my sire? People say that I bear a strong and marked resemblance to Ivar—and although I've no love for him and no liking for his looks, either, I am forced to admit that seeing him is like looking at my reflection in the polished-bronze mirror of my lady wife."

"Were you his twin, I'd not give a damn!" Ragnar insisted scornfully; then he spat contemptuously on the deck at Wulfgar's feet. "Nor claim you as the seed of my loins, you bloody bastard *bóndi*! I curse the day you were born, and the day you slew Loki's wolf so Ivar might live; for 'twas that act that freed you to climb so high that you became a great threat to my sons, to my kingdom and throne. I should have smothered you at birth; I should have killed you the day of the hunt rather than let Björn Ironside and Hasting goad me into allowing you to take oath at the festival of Eostre; and when you stole the princess of Usk and Olaf the Sea Bull's markland, I should have marched on you and destroyed you, or had you named an outlaw by the *Thing*!"

"Then why did you not?"

"Because that yellow witch from the Eastlands put a curse on me, that's why. She swore by the gods that if ever my hand struck you down, however indirectly, I should die a coward's death, unsung, unremembered, and that none of my sons would live to rule after me. It would be as though I never existed; and by the God of the Runes and Valhöll, I'm the greatest *Víkingr* ever to sail the seas, and I'll be remembered as such! A thousand years from now, long after you're less than worms' excrement and forgotten, rotting on the Shore of Corpses in Hel, the *skálds* will still sing my praises in the Northland. But mark me: When I'm dead and swilling mead and whoring with the Valkyries in Valhöll, I will have my revenge, for Ivar will rid himself of you soon enough."

"Are you sure?" Her black eyes glimmering avidly, Yelkei squatted beside Ragnar, her head cocked to one side, like that of a raven when it has found something to interest it.

"You've no cause to curse Ivar, you evil old witch!" Ragnar hissed, his eyes narrowing. "Nor would that stay his hand against this bloody bastard *bóndi*, anyway, I am thinking; for there is aught in Ivar's soul that belongs not to a *Víkingr*, but to Loki and Nidhögg and Hela."

"Aye." Yelkei nodded thoughtfully. "It may be that you are right, for Ivar has always been like a maggot, crawling into the labyrinth of a man's heart and soul to feast on his dreams. But malice and guile are poor weapons compared to the greatest of them all, Ragnar Lodbrók: ambition and determination; and while Ivar has his share of both, make no mistake, the flame that burns within him is as cold as the tundra in winter compared to what burns within Halfdan, white-hot, like the blazing midnight sun of summer."

"Aren't you forgetting Ubbi?" Ragnar inquired mockingly.

"Nay." Yelkei chortled contemptuously. "For in truth, he

is no more than a crude lump of peat that Ivar and Halfdan will consume between them.''

''Be that as it may, your foundling here shall not live to see it!''

''Are you sure?'' Yelkei prodded again wickedly, her eyes alive with malice.

''Aye, for he is weak; even now, his soul balks at slaying me.''

''What you think of as a weakness is his greatest strength; for from it spring all his strengths: his love, his honor, his loyalty, his courage, and his conviction. Wulfgar''—Yelkei turned to him—''do you give Ragnar Lodbrók into my keeping, to do with him as I see fit; for in truth, 'tis not meet that you kill your father, and I've an old score to settle with him, besides, the reason for my curse upon his soul.''

''And what is that?'' Wulfgar asked, curious, for never in his life had Yelkei made mention of this, although he felt, of a sudden, that the answer would make much clear to him.

''Many years ago, when I was scarce older than your lady wife, I myself was a princess, a princess of the people who ruled the grassy steppes of the Eastlands as far as the eye could see. But then Ragnar came, with his *Víkingr* hordes, and made of me a slave. I was the bride of a prince, and carrying his child; and I wept and begged Ragnar to ransom me. But after the many long months it took for his message to reach my people, who were nomads, and for the coffer of gold and silver and jewels my husband sent in return for me to be delivered to the Northland, Ragnar broke his promise and would not release me. By then, Goscelin had borne you, her son and Ragnar's; and after three days, her milk had dried up, while my own milk, for my own son, born a month before you were, still flowed. Ragnar thought to put you to suck at my teat so Goscelin would cry no more, but I had not milk enough to feed two. And so, one day, when my son screamed loudly with hunger, Ragnar picked him up by the heels and, swinging him hard, bashed his tiny head against the wall of the *hof*—my son, who would have been a king of the Eastlands.'' Tears trickled slowly down Yelkei's face at the memory. ''As I sat there, with you and my dead son in my lap, I saw that his blood had marked your face in the way of a hunter, a warrior; and I knew then that my son had chosen you to fulfill his own destiny, to become a king, Wulfgar Bloodaxe. All I have done has been to accomplish that end. Now, do you give me Ragnar Lodbrók, to do with as I will, in the name of my son.''

''You may have him, Yelkei,'' Wulfgar said softly, deeply moved by the unbearable sacrifice she had suffered for him, ''and if the gods are willing, I will be a king of the Northland, I swear it!''

The storm had blown the *Siren's Song* many leagues off course. Wulfgar's sun board, a bearing dial marked with compass points and held to the rising or setting sun, and his sun shadow board, which determined latitude by the shadow cast by the sun at midday, were frequently useless to him in the mist that blanketed the North Sea. He resorted, therefore, to finding his way by means of his sunstone, a strange, crystalline rock that was yellow in color but that when held at right angles to the light from the sun, turned instantly a dark blue. This enabled him eventually to seek out the proper latitude that would take them to the kingdoms of Britain, to Northumbria; and some days later, on a shortened sail, the *Siren's Song* limped into the mouth of the river Humber. By now, winter had arrived in earnest; and to Wulfgar's relief—although he did not fear the Saxons, of whom he reckoned his own *thegns* were worth at least fifty men apiece—the harbor was inactive, with only some crude sailing vessels and rowboats in evidence, nothing that his own longship, injured though it was, could not easily outrun, if need be.

The villages and farms that dotted the coast were likewise quiet, for the Saxons were holed up like hibernating bears for the winter, smoke wafting from what Rbowenna informed him were called chimneys, of which there were none in the Northland. His eyes narrowed thoughtfully as he studied them. Having previously perceived the advantages to this method of ridding a house of smoke, Wulfgar asked her why she had not demanded that such a hearth be installed in the longhouse, when she had not hesitated to hound him for furniture.

"Because, my love, a chimney is not so easily built as a bed—and, if improperly constructed, will explode when a fire is lighted within it," she explained, then blushed with shame and embarrassment as she saw how his eyes danced wickedly at her inadvertent analogy.

"Like a man, you mean," he teased, pulling her into his arms and kissing her mouth.

"There is nothing wrong with your construction," she said before she thought, flushing even more scarlet as the impulsive words left her lips.

"Hmmm. I am very glad you think so, *elsket.*"

Satisfied that there was no immediate threat to them, Wulfgar ordered the anchor dropped in the port and the mooring lines tied to the wharf. He was somewhat amused by the sight of the few villagers and farmers, who were out and about, running away with fright when they spied the *Siren's Song*. Still, he did not discount the possibility of an armed band's returning, and posted guards around the longship, sending a handful of other *thegns* to inquire about procuring the materials they needed to repair the vessel and to discover whether there were lodgings available nearby. Presently, the warriors came back to report that supplies necessary to mend the longship were readily at hand and that there was an abandoned farm not far from the shore, the apparent victim of a *Víkingr* attack, which could be made habitable with a little hard work.

As Wulfgar had expected, it was Yelkei's wish to sell Ragnar to the Northumbrian king, Aella, whose seat was in the city of York, north of the river Humber. But having no good reason to trust that Aella was an honorable man—he had, after all, seized his kingdom and throne by overthrowing its previous king, Osberht, with whom he was still feuding—Wulfgar had decided to wait until the *Siren's Song* was once more seaworthy before dispatching an emissary to York, with the news that Ragnar Lodbrók had been taken prisoner. Meanwhile, inspecting the farm that had clearly once been prosperous but was now abandoned, Wulfgar saw that if the stone cottage, stables, and byres were cleaned and repaired—they had been set afire, and most of the thatched roofs were gone—the farm could indeed be made livable and would serve them well as winter quarters, fronting a small, sheltered cove and so having a beach onto which the longship could be dragged to ride out the winter. He moved the *Siren's Song* there at once to work at restoring her to her previous condition; and thus began what Rhowenna was to think of ever after as the quiet time. They bothered no one; no one bothered them. It was as though time stood still and, after the winter snow fell, silent and deep, they had somehow been cut off from the rest of the world.

The stone cottage was adequately appointed, with a hall, a kitchen, and two small sleeping chambers, one of which she and Wulfgar claimed for themselves. The other was taken, with a defiant glance in Wulfgar's direction, by Flóki and Morgen, who plainly expected resistance to the arrangement. But much to Flóki's obvious surprise and confusion, although Wulfgar raised one eyebrow coolly at this presumption, he said nothing at all, thereby giving tacit approval to whatever might take place behind the closed door at night. Rhowenna was safe in his arms, Wulfgar thought; that was all that mattered. And Flóki and Morgen, who had risked so much, deserved whatever happiness they might find together now. Yelkei slept on a pallet in the hall, where she kept both one eye and a scramasax on Ragnar, who now wore an iron slave collar that had been fortuitously discovered in the empty slave pens, and with which Yelkei had chained him to an iron ring set into one of the hall walls, so he could not escape. Ragnar appeared to accept his captivity calmly, even affably; but not one of them made the mistake of forgetting that he was a cruel, dangerous man who would slay them all if afforded half the chance. Rhowenna continued to tend the tears in his flesh made by the grappling hooks, while Wulfgar stood wordlessly by, battle-ax in hand, lest Ragnar seek to grab hold of her and do her some injury. The warriors bedded down in the stables, while the byres were given over to housing the livestock that had escaped during the *Víkingr* assault and that the men now rounded up—a cow, a goat, a litter of pigs, and some chickens. Food was scanty; but between what Wulfgar bartered for in the villages and the winter berries, nuts, and roots that Rhowenna, Morgen, and Yelkei managed to forage from the land, hunger was held to a dull, gnawing ache in the belly, which was at least tolerable.

Life had never been harder, more uncertain. But at night, when Rhowenna lay in Wulfgar's embrace, she could forget everything but him; and when she thought of all he had gained and then given up for her, her heart overflowed with all the love it held for him. She knew that so long as she lived, there would never again be any man for her save Wulfgar. When she found out she was to have his child, she was filled with joy that not even the worry for her that shadowed Wulfgar's eyes could dim.

"'Twill be all right, my lord, my love, I promise you," she reassured him softly after she had told him the news and they lay in bed, basking in the sweet afterglow of their lovemaking. "I am strong, and you are stronger yet. Together, we will manage somehow."

"Oh, Rhowenna, *kjæreste*!" he whispered fiercely, his hands tightening on her slender hips, his face buried against the softness of her naked belly, where their babe grew within her. His lips kissed her feverishly there. "I do not know what I ever did that the gods should have blessed me with you! I love you! Gods, how I love you. . . ."

Once more together then, they lay, breast to breast, thigh to thigh, no space between or in their hearts for any other; nor would there ever be. His hands were beneath her hips, lifting her to meet his own until the rapturous flame that burned between them was more brilliant than the Northern Lights that scintillated gloriously in the night sky of the Northland, more beautiful than the boundless sea that swept in upon the bold and wild strands.

It could not last. In her heart, Rhowenna knew that the winter was but an interlude in their lives, a moment out of time. Spring would come, and did, the snow that had enwrapped them like a white silk-spun cocoon melting away, the world once more intruding. The repairs to the *Siren's Song* were finished; and finally, when the new green shoots budded across the land, Wulfgar could no longer delay sending a messenger to York, to Aella, king of Northumbria. They could not keep Ragnar a prisoner, chained up forever; they dared not simply abandon him—not only because of Wulfgar's promise to Yelkei, but also because if Ragnar were somehow to get free, he would hunt them to the ends of the earth. So it was that one morning, the *thegns* dragged the longship into the sea, and then, with Wulfgar at the tiller, the vessel sailed slowly up the river Humber until it reached the river Ouse. There, they dropped anchor; and dressed in his best and mounted upon a fine steed Wulfgar had gained in trade at a nearby village, Flóki the Raven galloped away toward York. In a leather pouch at his waist was the missive Rhowenna had written in the Saxon tongue to Aella and sealed with wax into which she had pressed Wulfgar's seal.

A few days later, Flóki returned, with an escort, horses, and an ox-cart as elaborately carved as any Rhowenna had ever seen; and when she read the letter he carried from Aella, granting Wulfgar and the rest of them safe passage through Northumbria, they set off at once, leaving behind a handful of warriors to defend the *Siren's Song* in case of an attack. The short journey reminded Rhowenna of her voyage upon the *Dragon's Fire*, for Northumbria was one of the most powerful kingdoms of Britain, and as a result, there were towns and marketplaces and farms aplenty, as rich as any she had seen along the coasts of the Frankish and Germanic kingdoms and Frisia. But most wondrous of all was the city of York itself, a site of importance and authority since the time of the Romans, who had based the Sixth Legion there. It was, Rhowenna thought, even more splendid than Sliesthorp, enclosed by a vast wall, with towers that had stood from the days of the Romans, and, lining the narrow streets, a multitude of impressive buildings of timber and stone such as she had never before seen. Grandest of all was that which housed Aella's court, the huge great hall to which she and the others were escorted and that was the seat of his power. There, they could only gape at the high, raftered ceiling; at the richly embroidered tapestries and displays of weapons and shields that adorned walls lined with iron scones into which torches were set, and windows fashioned of rare glass, which admitted the sunlight; at the ornate dais at the far end, where Aella sat upon a high-backed chair so intricately carved and detailed that it was daunting, gilded with gold and cushioned with red silk, a high seat, a throne indeed fit for a king.

Aella himself, Rhowenna knew, was not of royal blood, but a commoner who had dared to usurp the throne, and held it not securely, but precariously; for its deposed king, Osberht, had amassed a great army and was now bent on reclaiming his lost kingdom. Aella was handsome enough, she supposed, his hair, mustache, and beard short-cropped in the current Saxon fashion; but his eyes hungry for power and disdainful mouth told her he could be cold and cruel. On his proud head, he wore a gold crown set with jewels; his hard-muscled warrior's body was accoutred in the costliest of furs and silks from the Eastlands; so important to him must elegance be that Rhowenna felt that even had they worn their finest raiment, she and Wulfgar must appear as barbarians before him. But then she reminded herself that not only was she of royal blood, the princess of Usk, but that while men such as Aella might rule great lands, it was men like Wulfgar who ruled the even greater seas. She lifted her head proudly, and although Wulfgar did not deign to kneel, but stood defiantly, head unbowed, she swept Aella a graceful, practiced curtsy that caused his eyebrows to lift in surprise and his courtiers to whisper speculatively among themselves before Wulfgar angrily yanked her to her feet and deliberately, in the Saxon tongue, so Aella would understand, warned her, "You are my wife and, as such, will kneel to no man save me!" Then, staring coolly, challengingly, at Aella, not waiting for him to speak, Wulfgar announced, "I am the Dane Wulfgar Bloodaxe, *jarl* of the Northland, here to speak for the yellow woman Yelkei, a princess of the Eastlands who holds captive the great King Ragnar Lodbrók of the Northland, whom she would sell to you for the price you have put upon his head."

"So your message would have me believe." Aella's tone was haughty, and the half-smile that twisted his lips was derisive and did not quite reach his narrowed eyes that glinted as hard as stone in the sunlight that streamed in through the windows. "But a king has many enemies, and so, if he is wise, must be ever on his guard against treachery and deceit.

How do I know that your prisoner''—his eyes flicked over Ragnar's chained figure—''is indeed who you say he is, that this is not some trickery of your own, Viking, to relieve me of my gold?''

''I give you my word that 'tis not. However, if you doubt me, my lady wife, who is not of the Northland, but of the land of Walas, and so a Christian, will swear upon the holy crucifix of your priests that 'tis indeed Ragnar Lodbrók who stands prisoner before you.''

''My lady, is it true what this pagan says, that you are a Christian,'' Aella asked then of Rhowenna, ''and prepared to swear upon the cross of the Christ and the Church that he who stands in chains before me is, in fact, Ragnar Lodbrók, knowing how you will imperil your immortal soul should you give false testament before God and these witnesses?'' His hand indicated the courtiers in the great hall.

''Aye, my lord,'' she answered.

''How came you then to be wed to this heathen?''

''My lord, I myself was taken captive last summer during a Viking raid upon my homeland of Usk; and what maiden, Christian or nay, would not choose to become a bride rather than a slave and a whore of her captor?''

''Yet in the eyes of the Church and the Law, you are both.''

''In the eyes of the Northland, she is neither.'' Wulfgar spoke softly but in a voice so savage that it sent a shiver up the spines of all who heard it, on his face a murderous expression. ''And you shall not call her such again, lest you would feel the bite of my blade at your neck.''

An audible, collective gasp rose from the courtiers at that; and Aella, gripping the arms of his chair so tightly that his knuckles shone white, half rose, as though he would strike Wulfgar down. But then, much to Rhowenna's surprise, after a long, tense moment, Aella chose to be amused and slowly settled back onto his seat, giving a low laugh, his eyes gleaming.

"For all that you are a pagan, you are a bold warrior, Wulfgar Bloodaxe; and I have pledged you safe conduct, besides. Being a Christian, I'll not risk my soul by breaking my bond, for I've no wish to burn in Hel forever—as your . . . lady wife will burn, I promise you, if she swears to a lie upon the crucifix." Then, turning to the elderly priest who stood at his side, Aella said, "Father Wynfrith, do you the honors, and let us see if the maid is indeed a Christian and speaks the truth."

The priest stepped forward, motioning Rhowenna to kneel before him. For a moment, remembering what Wulfgar had told her, she hesitated. Then, insisting firmly, "I kneel to no man, but to the Christ, my lord and husband, as is the way of my people," she sank to the floor, bowing her head and clasping her hands before her, responding quietly but surely to the questions put to her by Father Wynfrith, and then to his prayers. Finally, her hand laid upon the plain wooden cross he held out to her, she swore that their prisoner was indeed Ragnar Lodbrók, then kissed the crucifix and crossed herself as the priest gave her his blessing.

"I am satisfied, my lord," Father Wynfrith declared, turning to Aella, "that the lady is both Christian and honest, and that the man who wears the iron slave collar is, in fact, Ragnar Lodbrók, the accursed Viking who has plagued these shores of Britain for more years than I like to remember, and who will be justly served by a death sentence for his crimes, my lord."

"Aye, so he will." Aella nodded. Then, addressing Ragnar, he continued, "Ragnar Lodbrók, you are a king of the Northland and a mighty warrior. But verily do I say unto you that now, you shall die at the hands of a man who is an even greater king and warrior than you; and on the lips of bards far and wide, for all time, will be the tale of how I slew you and sent your soul straight to everlasting Hel!"

"I am no Christian, Aella of Northumbria, but the greatest *Víkingr* in all the Northland." Ragnar spoke for the first time, seeming unperturbed by the other's boast. "So much as you may wish it, when I die, I'll not go down to wander the Shore of Corpses to the barred gates of Hel, but be borne by a golden Valkyrie to Valhöll, Odinn's great mead Hall of the Slain, in Asgard, where I shall drink and whore and spit in the eye of your Christian God, who is weak and so whom I do not fear."

"By God!" Aella roared at that, leaping to his feet, his eyes blazing. "You shall learn His strength and to fear Him before you die, Ragnar Lodbrók, I promise you! You shall learn as they learned in the Garden of Eden, from the mouth of the serpent who was all-evil! Seize him!" he cried abruptly to his guards. "Bring him!" Then, his robes flapping, Aella strode, enraged, from the great hall, leaving the rest to follow.

To an enclosed courtyard filled with gardens abloom with spring flowers, he led them, to the place at its heart where, beneath an apple tree, lay what Rhowenna realized was a huge, deep, circular cistern that must have been built during the time of the Romans, so ancient and crumbled was the low stone wall that surrounded it. The well had long since gone dry. But as she neared the edge and looked down into the shadowy abyss, she saw that the recent spring rains had left a muddy puddle of water in the bottom, from which rose the pungent, sweet-sour stench of apples long rotted and fermented. But what filled her with utter horror was the fact that the core of the cistern was so infested with snakes that it seemed alive, coiling and crawling and creeping. Even Ragnar's face turned pale, and his eyes bulged at the sight. Only Yelkei's yellow face was still, emotionless; her eyes were as fathomless as the writhing black depths of the well.

"Do you fear the Christian God now, Ragnar Lodbrók?" Aella asked in the taut, terrible silence that had fallen as all recognized what he intended. "Or must you needs feel the fangs of His wicked servants pierce your flesh before you are enlightened as to His strength?"

"Even then, I shall not fear Him," came the brave reply.

"Lower him down!" Aella ordered tersely.

"Wait!" Yelkei cried of a sudden, a raven's shriek; and although the guards did not understand the foreign word she had uttered, they instinctively drew back a little from Ragnar's figure. "I would speak with him first." When Wulfgar had translated what she had said and Aella had nodded his permission, Yelkei slowly approached Ragnar. "'Tis your fate to meet your death here this day, in this land you once thought to conquer for your own," she croaked. "But before you die, there is something I want you to know." Then she bent very close to him and whispered in his ear; and at that, from Ragnar's throat erupted a long, terrible shout that seemed to echo forever as, without warning, Yelkei struck him hard between the shoulder blades, shoving him into the snake pit.

The chain that dangled from his iron slave collar clanking and whipping against the stone wall of the cistern, he fell, landing heavily, with a hideous squishing sound, in the midst of the mucky water, the decaying apples, and the slithering serpents. Instantly, at least two of the snakes struck, their fangs sinking deep; and as, groaning now with pain, his head bleeding profusely, Ragnar slowly staggered to his feet, Rhowenna observed, ill and horrified, that a serpent had fastened itself to his cheek. With a vicious curse and a violent jerk, Ragnar tore the creature loose and flung it away, then began to swing the chain and to kick with his booted feet at the rest, so they hissed and curled up, their heads raised high, bobbing and weaving before striking.

"Ah, gods!" Wulfgar muttered sickly at Rhowenna's side. "Whatever else he is, Ragnar is Odinn's warrior and deserves to die as one—in battle!" And with that, he brought forth the gleaming broadsword he had taken away from his father when Ragnar had been hooked and hauled aboard the *Siren's Song*, and now, with a mighty heave, threw it down into the well, at Ragnar's feet. "Because you are my father—whether either of us wishes it so or nay," Wulfgar called down, "that much, I owe you!"

"And I owe you more, no doubt; but 'tis a debt I'll not pay—nor would I have, you miserable, ill-gotten bastard!" Ragnar yelled as he bent to snatch up the weapon and began to slash furiously at the snakes that assailed him. "I do curse the day I ever laid eyes and a hand on that bloody Saxon bitch, Goscelin, your mother! I'd curse you, too, Wulfgar, with my last, dying breath, if I didn't know in my heart that 'twould be a waste of time and air, that that yellow witch of the Eastlands would lift it somehow and turn it back upon my own. So I'll say naught, save that sooner or later, a man who dares to aim higher than gods shall surely suffer a great fall."

"That, you would know better than I," Wulfgar declared, with a mocking smile, so only Rhowenna and Yelkei guessed at the pain that twisted inside him, thrashing like the serpents in the cistern, that his father should hate him to the bitter end. "Die well, Ragnar Lodbrók."

"As I lived, Wulfgar Bloodaxe."

The broadsword flashed silvery in the sunlight as it rose and fell ever more slowly, the shimmering runes along its length little by little blotted out by the venom and blood that dripped from the blade. Ragnar's face and limbs grew discolored and puffed and swollen with poison; at last, he sank to his knees, retching, then crumpled over, his body racked by violent convulsions that caused him to flail wildly about the well, slinging the vomit, the muddy water, the rotten apples, and the slimy, hacked pieces of the dead snakes so hard in every direction that the spectators shrank back in alarm. Then, finally, he was stilled by the onslaught of paralysis. After a short while, his breathing stopped; and he lay faceup, his blue eyes staring blindly into the sun, nearly lost amid the turgid folds of his grotesque, bloated corpse.

Wulfgar's own eyes stared skyward, as well, where in his mind, he watched the winged, snow-white charger that galloped forth from the clouds, on its back a gilt-haired, silver-mailed Valkyrie, singing gloriously, come to carry his slain father home.

Chapter Eighteen

The Blood Eagle

They were standing again in Aella's great hall. Of how they had come to be there, Rhowenna had only a dim recollection. She had felt so dizzy and ill at the vile manner of Ragnar's death that she had thought she would faint; and only the look upon Wulfgar's face, the understanding that he needed her desperately in that moment, had kept her on her feet, clinging to him as he had clung to her, so it had seemed they had held each other upright. Aella sat once more upon his throne, laughing, a gold-chased wine goblet filled to overflowing in his hand, raised high to toast his victory over the great Ragnar Lodbrók, once a king of the Northland and now a corpse in a snake pit. Slightly startled, Rhowenna realized dully that she, too, was holding a cup of wine, as was Wulfgar; but neither of them drank to Aella's triumph, only to Ragnar's death, as was the way of the *Víkingrs*. Then Wulfgar said:

"I'll trouble you now for the price on Ragnar's head, due the princess Yelkei, if you please, King Aella. Then we'll go, and haunt your shores no more, for our way lies south, and we've a long journey ahead of us.''

"But you cannot leave now," Aella insisted, smiling, his tongue darting forth to lick his wine-soaked lips, in a manner that reminded Rhowenna unpleasantly of the serpents in the snake pit. "The hour is late, and the roads across the moors are rife with brigands in these uncertain times. I cannot keep my word and guarantee you safe passage if you would set out when 'tis nigh on dusk. Nay, Wulfgar Bloodaxe, you and your companions must stay and have supper with me and spend the night beneath my roof. Far better that than some villager's shabby lodgings, some peasant's dungy byre along the wayside, you must agree. In the morning will be time enough to settle our account and for you to continue on your way.''

This was all said politely enough. Still, Rhowenna recognized, as Wulfgar did, that Aella, for whatever his true reason, did not mean to let them depart just yet and that if they pressed the issue, they were as likely to wind up his prisoners as his guests.

"Very well." Wulfgar spoke at last. "We shall partake of your hospitality, then, and make an early start tomorrow; for I should not like to leave my Dragon Ship too long at anchor in your harbor, King Aella, lest my army of *thegns* grow restless and forget that we came here for trading instead of raiding.'' This threat was as courteously veiled as Aella's own had been.

Yet, despite this warning, they were not to depart from York, after all; for in the morning, Aella showed his true colors by having Wulfgar and Flóki thrown into a dank, barred cell and Rhowenna, Morgen, and Yelkei locked up in a tower. When assaulted by Aella's guards, Wulfgar and Flóki fought wildly, savagely, like maddened Berserks, killing several of their attackers and wounding many more. But in the end, by the sheer weight of numbers, Aella's men overwhelmed them, and they were taken captive and stripped naked to the waist; then iron slave collars were fastened about their necks, each with a long chain at the throat that ended in manacles that were clamped shut around their wrists. The women were treated more gently, their hands bound, with ropes, behind their backs. Then all were herded before Aella in his great hall, who laughed mockingly at Wulfgar's struggles against both his captors and his bonds, his expression murderous as he glared at Aella.

"What is the meaning of this, you treacherous whoreson?" Wulfgar demanded, his breathing harsh and labored from his futile attempt to free himself. "Is this how you would keep your word to us that we might come and go in peace?"

"If you had read my missive more carefully, you would have grasped that it was worded in such a way that my guarantee to you of safe passage was good for yesterday only," Aella sneered, stroking his beard absently. "Today, I may slay you if I please, and my conscience will be clear. However, fortunately for you, that is not my pleasure. I am greatly in need of a scapegoat, you see, and you will serve most admirably for my purpose. My God!" Aella burst out suddenly, rising from his throne and pacing the dais before them. "I could not credit it when I received your message, telling me that you bore Ragnar Lodbrók captive in your train! I feared that it must be some sly trickery indeed devised by Ragnar and his sons to conquer all of my kingdom of Northumbria. But then I realized that however you came by him, you honestly did not know—"

"Know what?" Wulfgar's voice was sharp, his eyes so intense, so searching that Rhowenna could almost see the wheels turning in his mind as he swiftly considered and rejected one possible explanation after another until, at last, his body abruptly tensed as though he expected to receive a mortal blow.

"Why, that late this past autumn, a great army of Vikings

landed in East Anglia, led by the sons of Ragnar Lodbrók,'' Aella elucidated, each word falling lethally into the sudden silence. ''They are even now marching toward York; and while I thought it prudent to execute Ragnar, lest he somehow escape to ride at their vanguard, I now needs must find someone else to blame for the evil deed, someone whom I may use to my advantage to barter with Ragnar's sons, if necessary.''

''So that is what we are to be, is it? Coins at your bargaining table?'' Wulfgar's eyes blazed with fury and fear for Rhowenna at the thought that surely now, they would all be undone. ''Damn you to Hel, you filthy bastard! Listen to me! I've known Ragnar's sons all my life. They haven't come here to barter, you fool, but to conquer all of Britain; and to do it, they'll kill you and every other Saxon king who stands in their way.''

''Well, we shall soon see, will we not?'' Aella smiled smugly, confident of his own ability to prevail. Then, motioning to his guards, he demanded, ''Take them away!''

With that began the long months that in her mind, Rhowenna was to think of ever after as the dark days. In the tower where she, Morgen, and Yelkei were kept locked away day and night, time crawled by in endless hours they spent alone, shut off from the rest of the world, devoid of any news, even some small message or word that might have given them hope, have let them know how Wulfgar and Flóki fared or even if the two men were still alive. But there was nothing. Neither the guards posted outside the tower door nor the waiting women who brought meals and bath water daily spoke to the three women; nor was there any chance for them to escape. Rhowenna and Morgen played long games of chess and draughts and fox-and-geese; Yelkei cast her rune stones and muttered to herself. All the while, Rhowenna's child grew within her, her soft, round belly slowly burgeoning; at night, she longed for Wulfgar and wondered desperately about his fate, exhausting herself, making herself ill as she wept into her pillow to muffle her sobs at the thought that perhaps her babe would never know its father.

Then, finally one morning when summer was nearly upon them, Rhowenna stood at the tower window, and her heart leaped to her throat; for she saw what she had feared ever since Aella had imprisoned them, what she had hitherto seen only in her dreams: On the road to York, there marched the greatest army she had ever beheld, at its fore, Ivar the Boneless, mounted on a showy white steed.

Seeing this vast horde approach and realizing at last the truth of Wulfgar's words to him, Aella fled from the city to join forces with his archrival, Osberht, both kings agreeing that under the circumstances, they would be wise to set aside their differences until they had rid themselves of the *Víkingr* threat, after which they might resolve their own quarrel. Thus decided, they returned to York to reclaim the city that Ivar the Boneless had taken from them without so much as unsheathing his broadsword. Breaching the poorly maintained Roman walls of the city, Aella and Osberht bravely led their forces into battle against the Northmen; but, in the end, could not hold their ground, and broke and scattered before the ranks of the Berserks, the *Víkingrs*, and the mercenaries Ragnar had assembled before his death, to conquer all of Britain. In the fierce fighting, Osberht and eight earldormen were slain. Aella was taken captive; and it was then that Ivar learned that Wulfgar and Flóki were caged in Aella's dungeon, and that Rhowenna, Morgen, and Yelkei were confined in Aella's tower.

When the three women were led from the tower, Rhowenna felt certain that they went to their deaths. Yet it was not for herself that she grieved, but for her unborn child, alive and kicking so hard in her womb, as though sensing her distress.

She pressed her hands to her belly, rubbing gently there, in a vain attempt to quiet the babe. It was a son, she thought, a strong, healthy son, like his father; and she wept to think that the child would not live to draw breath, to see the light of day. Then her tears of sorrow became tears of joy as she spied Wulfgar standing in the great hall to which they had been brought, and before the *thegns* could stop her, Rhowenna ran to him, crying out with all her heart held for him. As tight as she could, she embraced him, sliding beneath his manacled wrists so she might feel his arms about her; and cupping his face in her hands, she kissed him feverishly, as he kissed her, muttering her name hoarsely as his lips brushed the tears from her cheeks. Then, at last, together, they turned to confront Ivar the Boneless, who sat, now a king, on Aella's throne, while Aella himself stood nervously to one side, between Ubbi and Halfdan.

"While it gives me no end of pleasure to see you alive and well, Wulfgar," Ivar drawled dryly, "I must confess that the feeling is somewhat mitigated at seeing you in chains. But then, King Aella here has told me a strange tale of how you came to his court, with my father, the great Ragnar Lodbrók, as a prisoner in your train, an iron slave collar around his neck. Now, while I find that difficult to believe, I must admit I have heard other such rumors up and down the coast of Britain all spring; so perhaps 'tis fitting, after all, that you are shackled like a slave. Aella claims that you brought Ragnar here to York to sell him for the price on his head, and that when you learned Aella did not mean to kill him, but to hold him for ransom instead, you found the Berserks' Way and shoved my father into a snake pit. Is that true, Wulfgar?"

"Nay, 'tis not," Wulfgar answered, calmly enough. "Oh, I did bring Ragnar here to sell him all right, Ivar, and he died in Aella's snake pit—that part's true enough—which you may see for yourself if our father's corpse is still lying there.

But 'twas not I who decided to slay him or who ordered him cast in to feed the serpents, either.''

"Well, we shall find out shortly whether or not you speak the truth, will we not?'' Rising, Ivar glanced sharply at Aella, continuing in the Saxon tongue. "I have been too busy making war upon you and Osberht to explore much of this city or of this longhouse, either, else I should have known before now of Wulfgar's presence here and looked sooner into this matter of my father's supposed death. But now, I would see this infamous snake pit for myself. Bring him," he commanded his brothers; and as these had been Aella's own words to his guards regarding Ragnar, Rhowenna felt sure that Aella thought himself imminently to receive a like death at the hands of Ragnar's sons.

The gardens in the courtyard were a riotous profusion of blooming flowers, whose thickly sweet perfume hung heavy in the air, almost but not quite masking the scent of decaying apples, which Rhowenna believed she would never forget as long as she lived. Her stomach churned, and despite the heat of the warm day, her hand was as cold as ice in Wulfgar's own. After Ragnar's death, Aella had ordered the snake pit covered with a heavy wooden lid, which, at Ivar's command, several of the *thegns* now heaved from its resting place to reveal the cistern itself. As they did so, a foul, nauseating stench wafted up from the dank, dark bottom of the well, and Rhowenna swayed a little on her feet; Wulfgar, his eyes filled with concern for her, held her close to steady her.

"I did not believe it. I did not *want* to believe it; but 'tis Ragnar, in truth," Ivar said at last as he stared down into the snake pit at the skeleton that lay there. Its long mane of hair was dark with mud; bits of flesh still clung to its bones. Around its neck still was Ragnar's distinctive gold torque; on its arms were his armlets and bracelets of gold and silver. Its bony fingers still clutched the hilt of his broadsword. "Aella, no *Víkingr* worth his salt would have slain my father in this bizarre fashion; 'twould have taken the mind of a Saxon for it, I am thinking. So I know that 'twas you who gave the order that he die here. Now all that remains to be sorted out to my satisfaction is the identity of the one who pushed him in.''

'''Twas that yellow witch yonder who did that!'' Aella declared hastily. ''She did bend near to him to whisper something in his ear—I know not what—so he roared like a madman; and then she hit him hard on the back, knocking him in.''

''What did you say to Ragnar, Yelkei?'' Ivar asked, as calmly as though they discussed the weather and not the killing of his father.

''That is for me to know. Still, perhaps someday I'll tell you—or mayhap nay.''

''You've an accursed tongue that has always been as forked as a serpent's, speaking in lies and riddles and prophecies. Perhaps today I'll cut it from your head—or mayhap nay. Was it written in the stars that Ragnar die here, by your hand, I wonder; or was it your own predictions and machinations that brought about his fate, Yelkei?'' The question was rhetorical, for Ivar answered it himself. ''You will say that only the gods know the answer to that, and no doubt, that is true. That being the case, let us move on, then, to what is more obvious. Now, since he was collared and chained like a slave when he went into the snake pit, I know that my father had not his weapon in his hand then; so who did throw it down to him, that he might die like the great *Víkingr* he was—in battle against his foes?''

''I did,'' Wulfgar responded quietly, although, in his bones, he felt certain Ivar had already known the answer.

''Of course you did—although not even for that did Ragnar speak to what was in your heart, Wulfgar, I am thinking, but left his debt unpaid.'' On Ivar's face was a peculiar expression of understanding, almost of pity, Rhowenna thought, puzzled that Ivar should feel such for Wulfgar. After a long, silent moment, Ivar spoke again, addressing one of his *thegns*. "I do stand in debt, in my father's stead, that he died not a coward's death. Fetch an armorer or a blacksmith to strike off that slave collar from around Wulfgar's neck."

"And Flóki's, also," Wulfgar insisted, eyeing Ivar steadily.

"Ah, aye, there is still the matter of Flóki the Raven, is there not?" Ivar's voice was lightly mocking. "A man who dared to assault his king and to steal from him a rich prize. 'Tis hard to imagine . . . isn't it? All this"—his sweeping hand encompassed all those, including himself, who stood in the courtyard, and the snake pit, where Ragnar lay—"for love of the princess of Usk." He stared hard at Morgen in Flóki's arms, thereby missing the malicious light that danced in Yelkei's eyes at that, and the sudden fear that leaped to Wulfgar's own; for surely, no truer words had ever been spoken than those unwittingly uttered by Ivar the Boneless just now. "What shall I do with you—all of you—for that, I wonder? I needs must think long and hard on that."

Presently, the armorer was brought; and after half an hour of tedious chiseling, both Wulfgar and Flóki were freed of their iron slave collars and chains, and stood, slowly chafing their necks and wrists, where the heavy metal had, in the beginning, rubbed raw, bleeding wounds, now scabbed over. In all the time it took to cut through the iron, Ivar, silent, seemingly lost in reverie, kept everyone standing in the sun. He himself seemed not the least perturbed by the delay, as though he had all the time in the world and so was not in any great hurry to get on with the business at hand—although no one present thought that when the armorer's task was completed, Ivar would not claim retribution for his father's killing. Still, only when the last manacle had been forced open and tossed to the ground, did Ivar finally speak again.

"Now, it seems to me that Ragnar's death may be laid at many a door, including his own; for if many long years ago he had not lusted for a black-haired, yellow princess of the Eastlands, he might not have come to this pass. Who can say but the gods whether a man's fate is inevitable, or if he only makes it so by his actions? But this, I know: Regardless of what led up to it, 'twas you who ordered his death and who determined the manner of it, Aella; and for that, you must pay the penalty exacted for the slaying of a king of the Northland." Then, glancing toward Ubbi and Halfdan, Ivar said, "Strip him, and tie him facedown over the snake pit, that he may glimpse Náströnd long ere he steps foot upon its corpse- and monster-ridden shore, there to wander for nine days and nights to the barred gates of Hel."

Ignorant of what Ivar intended, sensing only the excruciating pain and the horror that would come of it, Aella struggled like a man possessed against Ubbi and Halfdan—to no avail. In the end, Aella was forcibly stripped naked and compelled facedown over the snake pit, spread-eagled across its gaping maw, his hands and feet bound to short posts driven into the ground along the sides of the crumbled wall that surrounded the cistern. When it was done, Ivar, drawing his glittering broadsword from the scabbard at his back, slowly approached the well, stepping up onto its low stone wall and then, like an acrobat, with uncanny agility and grace, swinging one leg across to the other side, so he stood with Aella directly beneath him. Then, after raising the blade high, Ivar deliberately brought it down so the point slashed into Aella's flesh, cutting a fine crescent-moon from Aella's shoulder to his lower back, first one side and then the other, torturously, so Aella was unable to restrain the agonized cry that emanated from his throat. With a mocking smile, Ivar tossed the bloodied weapon to Wulfgar, as though daring him to use it. But after catching it instinctively with one hand, Wulfgar, his face grim, only lowered the broadsword to his side; and with a low laugh, Ivar turned his attention back to Aella. With his bare hands then, Ivar slowly peeled back Aella's skin to expose his backbone and ribs. Ivar broke the ribs away one by one from the backbone before grasping Aella's lungs and pulling them from his body so they lay spread like an eagle's bloody wings upon his mutilated back.

Aella was dead. Of course he was dead. He *must* be dead, Rhowenna told herself dumbly—shocked, horrified. No one could have survived that terrible, inhuman ritual. Yet it seemed that she could still hear his hoarse screams of torment ringing in her mind as Ubbi and Halfdan, slicing through the ropes that bound the fallen king to the short posts along the stone wall, pushed his corpse into the snake pit, where it fell with a sickening thud on top of Ragnar's skeleton. Lifting his outstretched hands to the heavens, so the blood ran down his arms, Ivar threw back his head and shouted, a wild, mighty cry. "Odinn! Odinn!" So much in that moment did he resemble Wulfgar standing on the deck of the *Siren's Song* that night of the storm upon the North Sea that it was, to Rhowenna, like seeing her husband's other half, a dark, terrible side of him that she did not know, did not want to know; and overcome by horror, she slipped finally, mercifully, to the ground, in a dead faint.

Casting down Ivar's broadsword, Wulfgar knelt swiftly beside her, gathering her into his arms and cradling her against his chest, his face stricken as he glanced up to see Ivar standing now on the edge of the snake pit, his eyes burning with a feverish triumph and bloodlust that warned Wulfgar that his half brother's revenge was not yet finished.

"Seize them!" Ivar commanded; and the next thing Wulfgar knew, he was being hauled up roughly from the ground by a group of Ivar's men. "Hold them!"

As he had Aella's guards, like a Berserk, Wulfgar fought Ivar's *thegns*. But as Aella's own had been, Wulfgar's struggle was in vain. Presently, he and Flóki both stood furiously, fearfully, breathing hard, forcibly restrained by the many strong hands that constricted them, preventing them from breaking free. Like Aella, they were ignorant of what was to come, knowing only the dread it inspired within them as, his mouth curving in a terrible, mocking caricature of a smile, Ivar jumped down from the stone wall; then, like some predatory beast, he began slowly to stalk toward Morgen. Her eyes widened with terror, then narrowed with hate and understanding; her nostrils flared, like those of some wild animal scenting danger. Her fingers curled into punishing talons, she lifted one hand to claw at Ivar's cruelly handsome visage. But he caught her wrist in a brutal grip, then, with his fist, he backhanded her across the face before, tearing at her clothes, he forced Morgen to the earth and ground his mouth down on her, hard.

Then, one by one, while Wulfgar and Flóki, tears trickling from his eyes, stood and watched helplessly, Ivar, Ubbi, and Halfdan raped her.

Chapter Nineteen

The Great Army

When Rhowenna awoke, it was to the slow, rhythmic movement of an ox-cart, in which she lay upon a pallet, and to Yelkei's wrinkled moon face bending over her, black eyes anxious, as though the yellow woman had feared that Rhowenna would never regain consciousness. But upon seeing Rhowenna's eyes flutter slowly open, Yelkei nodded to herself, giving a small cackle of satisfaction. Then, turning away, she reached into one of her many deerskin pouches and, with crushed herbs and roots, and wine from a leather flask, she prepared in a wooden bowl some dark potion, which she pressed to Rhowenna's lips.

"Drink, lady," Yelkei commanded softly. "Now that you are awake at last, 'twill help to revive you and to give you strength. You have suffered a bad shock—the ritual of the Blood Eagle was too much for you, I fear—and I would not have you lose the child, when 'twas because of it that you were spared by Ivar the Boneless and his brothers, I believe."

"What . . . what are you talking about, Yelkei?" Rhowenna was startled to hear how weak her voice sounded.
"What has happened? Where is Wulfgar? Where are we—
and where are we going?" The questions came softly but
swiftly, as though she feared the answers.

"Shhhhh. You must not tire yourself, lady. Drink, and I
will answer as best I can." Obediently at last, while Yelkei
held the bowl, Rhowenna drank until it was empty. Then
Yelkei spoke again, responding to what was uppermost in
Rhowenna's mind. "Do not be afraid. Wulfgar is alive and
well; he rides ahead of us, with Ivar and his brothers, as does
Flóki the Raven, at Ivar's command. For although another
man would have slain them outright, there is something dark
and cold in Ivar's soul that stayed his hand against them, that
compelled him instead to raise the stakes, to draw out the
game a little while longer yet. Some might call it evil, and
that is a part of it, I am thinking; but I myself would name it
fear. Aye, for all that he holds him prisoner, deep down
inside, Ivar is afraid of Wulfgar. I know not why, save that
they are like hacksilver, two halves of the same coin." Yelkei
unknowingly voiced aloud Rhowenna's own thought when
she had seen Ivar poised over the snake pit, shouting to
Odinn, bloody arms upraised unto the heavens; and now,
remembering, she shivered, despite the warmth of the spring
sun that stretched toward summer.

"Having conquered all of Northumbria and been paid to
go in peace by what ealdormen who still remain, Ivar now
departs," Yelkei continued, "leaving behind a puppet to rule
in his name—Egbert, an earl of Northumbria who was exiled
from Britain and sought refuge in the Northland, as Ragnar's
thegn. 'Tis southwest we travel, to march now on the kingdom
of Mercia. For, like his father, Ragnar, before him, Ivar
means to conquer all of Britain, to rule as Bretwalda over all
the Saxons and Angles and Jutes who are its peoples."

At the thought of being taken into Mercia, home of Prince

Cerdic, Rhowenna shuddered again violently, filled of a sudden with a terrible foreboding. For the thousandth time, she cursed herself for a fool for not reading Aella's letter to Wulfgar more carefully, more closely; for if she had, they would never have stayed in his royal manor to be imprisoned by him; they would not now be at the mercy of Ivar the Boneless and his brothers.

"Yelkei, what happened after I fainted?" Rhowenna asked slowly after a moment, sensing somehow that there was still something more, something Yelkei had held back, had not told her. But when Yelkei did not reply, her lids hooding her fathomless black eyes, her glance flicking away, Rhowenna became aware of Morgen huddled in a corner of the ox-cart, trembling and rocking herself, her arms wrapped tightly about her knees; and instinctively, Rhowenna knew then what had occurred. "Oh, God," she breathed, tears starting in her eyes. "Oh, God . . . Morgen. Morgen . . ." Then, somehow, Morgen was in her arms, and Rhowenna was holding her tight, stroking her hair and crooning to her as the two women rocked each other, Morgen weeping hard but quietly against Rhowenna's comforting breast. "I'm sorry. I am so sorry, Morgen," Rhowenna whispered.

"I only wanted . . . to go home," Morgen said, sobbing softly. "I didn't want to stay in the Northland! I didn't want to fall in love with Flóki the Raven! But he made me love him, and now—and now—Oh, Rhowenna! Ivar and his brothers . . . they forced Flóki—they forced him to watch, while they—while they took me—God, how Flóki must hate me now! Every time he looks at me now, he'll remember. He'll remember what they did to me, and he'll think of me as their whore, and he'll never love me again—Oh, Rhowenna! That's what hurts! I could live with the other. 'Tis losing Flóki that hurts so much that I just wish I were dead!"

"Hush! Hush! Don't say that! 'Tisn't true—and I don't believe that of Flóki, either! A man who loves you as much as Flóki does isn't going to turn away from you because of this terrible thing that has happened to you, through no fault of your own. He is more likely to murder Ivar, Ubbi, and Halfdan in their beds!''

"And be killed himself for his trouble—for they'll be expecting that, won't they? They'll be on their guards against him, always sleeping with one eye open," Morgen insisted, quieter now as she brushed away her tears, as though angry and ashamed at having given way to them.

"Wulfgar will be watching, too, Morgen. Trust me. He won't let Flóki do anything rash, I promise you—and somehow, some way, we'll get through this, all of us, together. By the Christ and Wulfgar's gods, I swear it!"

It was apparent from the massive size of the Northland army and the range of its resources that Ragnar Lodbrók had planned his campaign well, and perhaps would have survived to lead it to victory over all of Britain had he not flown into such a wild rage at Wulfgar and Flóki, and gone chasing after them, sending his sons on to Britain, with his great army. Still, Ivar himself was an equally capable leader, as was proved by his taking of Northumbria. Now as, toward sundown, they halted their march for the night, Rhowenna observed from the ox-cart that in addition to horses and other supplies, Ivar had also confiscated a number of pavilions from the Saxon kings and ealdormen. Being so well-sheltered as a result, he allotted to Wulfgar and Flóki each a small hide tent such as were used by the Lapps of the northern tundra, which his army had brought from the Northland. Once these were erected, Wulfgar and Flóki came to the ox-cart, having been prevented from doing so before then.

Wulfgar's eyes were haunted by shadows that filled Rhowenna with pain when she saw him, and as he lifted her from the vehicle, embracing her tight, she clung to him ardently, returning his hot, feverish kisses in equal measure. But Morgen huddled in the ox-cart, hiding her face in shame, not looking at Flóki until he compelled her chin up and kissed her full on the mouth—deeply, fiercely. After that, crying out, she flung her arms about his neck, clutching him desperately, holding on for dear life as he swung her down from the vehicle, then carried her wordlessly to their tent, letting the flap fall shut behind them.

"She thought that he would not want her," Rhowenna remarked quietly as she and Wulfgar stood, watching the two lovers disappear. "She thought that he would hate her, that he would never love her again, but would think of her only as the whore of his enemies."

"He hates what was done to her, aye," Wulfgar acknowledged soberly. "But Morgen herself, Flóki only loves all the more. How could he not? Because they took their revenge on him as they did, with his woman, while they forced him to watch, my half brothers spared his life. So Morgen's sacrifice was not in vain, Rhowenna; had she not been there, they would have killed him. They may yet. They may kill us all in the end." Wulfgar's voice was raw and desperate. "Still, I cannot, at the moment, see any way out of this for us, *elsket*. It amuses Ivar, in his mockery, to treat us as his honored guests—providing horses for me and Flóki, the ox-cart for you and Morgen and Yelkei, Lapland tents for us. As you can see, Ivar has even returned my battle-ax and Flóki's broadsword. But we are prisoners just the same, all of us; for Ivar knows that neither I nor Flóki will make any foolhardy attempt to fight our way free of this ravening horde and ride off, endangering the lives of you and Morgen and Yelkei in the process or leaving you behind to the mercy of my half brothers. Yet, as he did of old, Ivar taunted me all day, hoping to provoke me into some reckless act." Wulfgar laughed shortly, harshly. "He even informed me that he sent some of his men to seize my Dragon Ship, and that it does even now lie off the coast of East Anglia, with his own, waiting for me.''

"Then if we could escape—"

"Nay, we cannot, sweeting." Wulfgar shook his head. "At least, not right now—and even if somehow we could, 'twill be time soon for your lying-in"—he laid his hand gently upon her full, round belly, where their child grew within her—''and you'll not be able to travel. Nay, we must wait and play for a while this strange and deadly game that Ivar directs. But our chance will come, I promise you. 'Tis only a matter of time, I am thinking. So, enough of this. Come. Yelkei will have supper hot on the fire by now, waiting for us; and after we are done eating, I would lie with you and make love to you, *kjæreste*, while I still can. For soon now, although such is my desire for you that I loathe even the thought of doing so, I know I must stop, lest I risk doing some injury to you or the babe.''

Darkness fell as they ate by the fire; and afterward, in the way that lovers do, Rhowenna and Wulfgar made another kind of fire between them, and of the crude Lapland tent that was their shelter, a magic place, a cocoon spun of the moon, the stars, and the night wind that soughed across the sweeping moors of Northumbria, bringing with it the scent of the distant sea. He held her on her side, wrapping himself about her so they fitted together like the few rare spoons she had seen at the supper table in Aella's great hall, and entering her so gently that his passage into her was like the long, deep sigh of pleasure that escaped from her lips. His mouth upon her nape, his hands upon her breasts, her burgeoning belly, he thrust into her, slowly but strongly until he could feel how she opened to him, her thighs parting even farther, her nether lips ripe and swollen, bursting with her sweet berry juices, mellifluous as he moved inside her. One of her arms rested above her head, her hand tangling and tightening in his long mane of golden hair as she cried out, soft and low with rapture, and then turned her face so her mouth found his, yielding, opening to receive his tongue as she received him, trembling hard and sweet with passion as, at last, he spilled himself inside her.

In the quiet afterglow, they lay together as they had when making love, Wulfgar stroking Rhowenna's belly tenderly, tracing tiny patterns there and thinking how much he loved her, that if ever he should not have her, the very light would go out of his life forever and he would surely die—and be glad of it. But even such a love as his was not enough to hold at bay the sounds of the ribald revelry of the *Víkingrs* preying upon their captive Saxon women, which echoed through the night to intrude upon him and Rhowenna; and as he lay beside her, Wulfgar could sense the long thoughts on which she dwelled in her mind, and feel the tremor of her heart in her soft white breast. For that, he cursed and damned Ivar to Hel, that she should lie in her husband's arms and fear being forced to lie in Ivar's.

"Wulfgar," she whispered at last, "if ever Ivar—"

"He won't. Don't even think about it. I would slay him first."

"Flóki could not." Her voice was low, tremulous.

"I am not Flóki."

"You are a man—one man—just as he is, not a god. I must know, Wulfgar. Somehow, I need to hear you say it . . . that you would still love me if—"

"Oh, *elsket*, how can you even wonder?" he asked, his heart aching that she would doubt him, if even only a little. "I would still love you! I will always love you! You are the other half of my heart, my mind, my soul! Don't you know that?"

"Aye . . . for you are mine, my love. Make love to me again, so I can pretend we are back in our *hof* on your markland, in the bed you had made for me and where you

first showed me what it was to love a man—to love you—
then and always. In my dreams, I am there now, with you
beside me. Take me home . . . home to the Northland, Wulfgar—if only for a little while. . . ."

"Home, *kjæreste*? Once, you said that you would never
call it that."

"I did not know then what I wanted, what I needed."

"And what is that?"

"You, Wulfgar . . . only and forever you."

Like the night mist twining itself about the hills and hollows
of the land, he enfolded her then, his mouth softly fierce upon
her lips, her breasts, her belly as he led her up a wending
mountain path of the Northland, past fairy rings and elfin
trees to a place where Thor's hammer, Mjöllnir, split the
heavens asunder, and Rhowenna knew she soared higher than
the gods in Asgard before floating gently back to earth, to
drift like a swan upon a wild Northland mere.

The great army marched on, warring and killing, maiming
and burning, ravaging and raping their way down Northumbria and into Mercia, terrifying all in their path. Burgred, the
king of Mercia, who had wed the sister of Aethelred, the
king of Wessex, sent a message to his brother by marriage,
entreating the help of the West Saxons against the *Víkingrs*.
Between Aethelred and his brother, Alfred, the West Saxons
marshaled their own army and, departing Wessex, marched
to join Burgred's own forces, meeting outside of Nottingham.
Meanwhile in Northumbria, the Saxons had revolted against
Ivar's puppet ruler, Egbert; compelled into exile again, he
had this time sought refuge with Burgred, in Mercia. The
Northumbrians had chosen another Saxon, Ricsige, as their
king; and for the time being, the *Víkingrs* had lost control of
the kingdom. So, initially, they declined to engage Burgred's

army and accepted payment to go in peace from Mercia, back
to York, to reclaim Northumbria.

But then, hearing that Burgred sheltered the traitorous Egbert, Ivar grew so enraged that he swept down on Burgred's
troops, decisively routing them, so Burgred was then himself
forced into exile, in Rome. After his victory, Ivar appointed
one of Burgred's earls, Ceolwulf, as the tributary king of
Mercia, provided that Ceolwulf hold himself and his kingdom
ready and willing to serve Ivar, Ubbi, Halfdan, and any other
Víkingr kings or *jarlar* who dared to follow them into Britain.
This binding pledge upon Ceolwulf, Ivar secured with both
oaths and hostages, learning from the mistake he had made
with Egbert. Carrying away his hostages to ensure Ceolwulf's
loyalty, Ivar then marched on that portion of Mercia that was
the holding of Prince Cerdic—for Cerdic alone of all the
Mercian royalty had refused to pay his share of what, in later
years, was to come to be known as danegeld.

When she discovered, to her horror, where they were
headed, Rhowenna was terrified; for it seemed to her that
everything since her first dream of Wulfgar—the attack upon
her father, the attack upon Usk, everything—had been leading up to this point in her life. No matter how she tried, she
could not shake off her deep sense of foreboding, her fear
of exposure. There were men at Cerdic's court who would
recognize her, who could identify her, the envoys he had sent
to teach her the Saxon tongue and customs. Still, there was
no reason to think that she would ever even see the inside of
Cerdic's royal manor, his great hall, that she would be anywhere other than in the ox-cart or in the Lapland tent when
the battle, if it came, took place. Always, if there was a
conflict, Wulfgar made sure that she was well back from the
front lines, where he and Flóki—ever alert lest they get a
scramasax in the back from one or another of the three brothers—were compelled to fight alongside Ivar, Ubbi, and Halfdan.

It was toward the end of summer, and she was very near her time now, besides. Yelkei thought that the child would come within the next few weeks, so Rhowenna was especially careful to stay close to her, not only because the *Víkingrs*, believing Yelkei a witch and a true spaewife, were afraid of her, but also because she was to serve as Rhowenna's midwife.

Suppressing her worries, Rhowenna tried to remain calm as the great army continued its march southwestward, toward Cerdic's principality, which lay at the edge of the border between Britain and Walas, separated by Offa's Dyke from Usk—so near and yet so far from her homeland, to which she no longer desired to return. But then the gods, ironically in the form of a Christian priest, once more thrust a capricious and terrible hand into her affairs.

To Ivar's message demanding that he pay for peace or show himself at the head of his army, Cerdic sent a short, rude reply, then massed his forces along the walls of his stronghold, where he waited for Ivar's own troops to appear. The ensuing battle was long and bloody, lasting for three days and nights, during which time Ubbi was slain in a daring charge from the stronghold's gates by Cerdic himself, much to Ivar's rage. For when Ubbi fell, his standard-bearer was also cut down; and seeing the banner of Ubbi Lodbróksson trampled upon the bloody ground, half of Ivar's army, believing that it was he who was dead, fled the field. But in the end, Ivar caught and rallied them; omnipresent on his snow-white steed, he marshaled his forces to attack with renewed vigor, overwhelming Cerdic's troops at long last, overrunning the stronghold, and taking Cerdic himself prisoner.

Now, in the great hall of his royal manor, Cerdic knelt upon the rush-strewn stone floor, his hands bound tightly, with rope, behind his back, his head laid on a wooden block, and, resting lightly, tauntingly, at his bared nape, Ivar's broadsword, poised to perform the execution that was retribution for Ubbi's death. Present to witness the delivery of Cerdic's death blow were Halfdan and Wulfgar, along with Flóki and some of Ivar's and Cerdic's *thegns*. A dark-robed Christian priest, clutching a wooden cross on an amber-beaded gold chain and muttering prayers for the prince's soul, stood at Cerdic's side, and before him knelt his sister, the princess Mathilde—tall, golden-haired, blue-eyed, and lovely, weeping and pleading with Ivar to spare her brother's life, to no avail.

"Only think: If you had not been such a pinch-purse, Cerdic," Ivar drawled dryly, "you would not now feel my blade at your neck. But then, you have made a habit of refusing to discharge your debts, have you not? Even the princess of Usk you would not ransom from Wulfgar Bloodaxe there, although she was beautiful and your betrothed— and a pleasure to bed, as well I and my brothers know, Cerdic. We all had her, you see. So, alas, she's only a whore now, and belongs to Flóki the Raven there. But I thought that since you took such an interest in her once, you might wish to bid her farewell; so I've ordered her brought here."

As he heard this frightening piece of news, Wulfgar started, his heart leaping to his throat, his hand reaching for his battle-ax. But then he remembered that Cerdic had never seen Rhowenna, so would not know her from Morgen, and that the envoys from Cerdic's court, who had met her and so who would know her, were not likely to be present at the moment in the great hall—being counselors, teachers, rather than earls, and thus of relatively small importance. Taking a deep breath, he forced himself to relax.

Presently, escorted by two of Ivar's men, Morgen appeared—wide-eyed and pale-faced, terrified as she glanced around the great hall, instinctively searching for Flóki's handsome bronze face. Upon finding it, she gathered her courage to walk slowly forward as, with a languid wave of his hand, Ivar beckoned her toward him.

"Well, Cerdic, there she stands before you, the woman who would have been your bride had you not proved yourself so faithless and cheap a lover," Ivar jeered, sliding his blade beneath Cerdic's chin to compel his head up, so he might gaze upon Morgen. "Is she not as comely and charming as I remarked—if a trifle used now?"

"My lord"—the priest spoke before Cerdic could answer, addressing him—"I do not know what manner of strange and cruel game this Viking barbarian seeks to play with you, but I beg you: Do not listen to him. 'Tis some trickery to deceive you for some purpose I know not, some mockery to make a fool of you, to rob you of your princely dignity before you meet your Maker, in Heaven—"

"Why, what nonsense, what babble is this?" Ivar asked, startled, his eyes narrowing sharply of a sudden as he brought the point of his weapon to bear at the priest's chest. "What say you, priest? What mean you? Spit it out, man, at once, or I'll cut your heart out where you stand, I swear!"

"But—but . . . surely, you know, King Ivar," the priest insisted nervously. "This woman is not the princess of Usk! She is only a serving maid, named Morgen."

"So that is what Yelkei said to Ragnar before he died!" Ivar's eyes gleamed with sudden understanding—and then he began to howl with laughter. He was still laughing when, with a swift and supple flick of his uncannily boned wrist, he brought the point of his blade to rest at Wulfgar's throat, pressing lightly until a bead of blood appeared there and Wulfgar was forced at last to loose his hold on his battle-ax he had snatched from its scabbard at his back, to let the weapon slide with a clatter to the floor. After a long, taut moment, Ivar's laughter slowly died away. Then, his eyes hard and angry, he said softly, "Halfdan, do you go and fetch Wulfgar's lady wife, and bring her here to me now."

Chapter Twenty

The Princess of Usk

For a year of her life, she had feared and dreaded this moment; yet now that it was upon her, Rhowenna found that she was strangely unafraid. She walked slowly by Halfdan's side, and much to her surprise, he did not try to hurry her, made no attempt to drag her ruthlessly along in his wake, as she had expected he would. More than once, he even took her hand in his and slipped his arm about her waist to help her over a rough patch of earth, so she did not fall.

"Why do you show me such kindness, my lord?" she asked him.

"I do not even myself know the answer to that, lady, save that I have always thought you more regal than the other— and Ivar a fool, that he did not see it," Halfdan confessed. "You are the true princess of Usk, and Wulfgar's wife, and have made fools of us all; and for all that, I suppose I should wish to slay you. But the truth is, I do not. For although neither my father nor brothers would ever own him, I have always known that Wulfgar was Ragnar's son and my brother, as well, the same as Ivar and Ubbi; and in the end, blood is blood, and, bastard or nay, a brother's a brother, I have always thought. Wulfgar has outfoxed us all, but I bear him no grudge for it. In truth, in my heart, I think he may be the greatest *Víkingr* of us all; and I think Ivar knows it, too, and that's why he fears him.''

"Does he?"

"Oh, aye, lady, he does," Halfdan asserted. "For at the core of his soul, Ivar's rotten, as cold and dead as a wolf frozen on the tundra—and what's more, he knows it. He's like an Eastlander—dark and cunning and malicious; he'd as easily stick a blade in your back or pour poison down your throat as to meet you face-to-face in battle—and that's not the way of a *Víkingr*. But a man cannot change his nature, and Ivar's too proud of his to waste his evil deviousness against less than a master opponent. In all his life, he's found no worthier foe than Wulfgar; and I think he believes that so long as Wulfgar lives, he will, too—inside. But once Wulfgar's dead and buried, why, then, who in the world will there be to give Ivar a game worth playing? So 'tis like a snake with its tail in its mouth—a venomous circle. Ivar wants Wulfgar dead, and yet he doesn't—and that's why he fears him.''

"And you do not?"

"Nay, lady, I fear no man, only the gods—and my own accursed ambition," Halfdan said, and smiled. "Like Ragnar, 'twill be the death of me in the end, I am thinking.''

They spoke no more, for they had come at last to Cerdic's royal manor; and now, each was alone with long thoughts, wondering what would happen inside. His hand beneath her elbow to steady her, Halfdan escorted Rhowenna into the great hall. Then, with an unexpected but chivalrous nod to Wulfgar to let him know that she was unharmed, Halfdan left her standing in the center of the floor. Rhowenna's heart turned over in her breast as her eyes found Wulfgar's, and she saw that his hands were tied securely, with rope, behind his back, and that the point of Ivar's broadsword lay at Wulfgar's throat and had drawn a drop of blood there.

"Lady," Ivar addressed her, "I commanded Halfdan to bring you here, because I have just now heard a fantastic tale, in which yon wench"—he indicated Morgen—"was said to be naught save a serving maid, which can only leave you as the princess of Usk."

"Where is the *skáld* who has sung you this strange and incredible song, lord?" Rhowenna asked, slightly startled to hear how calm and collected she sounded, as though, now that her true identity was revealed, she was become again the proud princess she had once been. Tossing her head, she stared haughtily at Ivar. "Was he wounded in the battle, and is he now delirious with fever, or is he merely drunk on *bjórr* or *nabid*, this *skáld*?"

"Neither, lady, and no *skáld* of the Northland, either, but a priest of Christendom, and so an honest teller of tales, I am thinking. There stands he, and since you are a Christian lady, do you go and swear upon his crucifix that he has lied to me, and I'll trouble you no more."

"That, she cannot do, lord." The priest spoke, drawing Rhowenna's attention for the first time; and as he slowly lowered his hood from his face, she gasped with shock, as though she had been struck a mortal blow.

"Father Cadwyr!"

"Aye, my lady, 'tis indeed I—once your confessor and of whose ear and blessing you must stand again in need from the look of you!" The burning black eyes she remembered with horror raked her deliberately, eyeing her swollen belly pointedly.

"Then 'tis true!" Flóki the Raven burst out suddenly, accusingly. "She *is* the princess of Usk! Gods, you bastard!" he spat heatedly to Wulfgar. "You knew! You *knew* that

Morgen was not the princess, and still, you stood there and watched and kept silent, while your half brothers raped her, you whoreson!''

"In my place, Flóki, would you not have done the same? Were you not willing to strike down Ragnar, your king, for your own love?" Wulfgar queried quietly, so Flóki's eyes fell, and he hung his head with shame. "I am the only man Rhowenna has ever known; she carries my child, Flóki! And Morgen was no virgin, as you must have guessed when first you took her."

"Aye, but I thought . . . I thought 'twas you who—"

"Nay, 'twas not."

"Flóki, 'twould seem from your words that you knew naught of this deception, but were Wulfgar's unwitting dupe," Ivar observed. "Therefore, I give you leave to depart, taking with you the maid Morgen, if you wish. But do you go in peace, and swear never again to raise your blade against me or mine, so I may consider the score between us settled."

"That sounds fair enough to me, lord," Flóki confessed, after a long moment, "and so I shall do, if Wulfgar Bloodaxe, my *jarl*, will give me leave to do so."

"I will," Wulfgar said.

"By the gods, then," Flóki pledged his oath, "I do so swear never to take up arms against you or yours again, Ivar the Boneless, so long as I may live."

"Then I've no more interest in you, and you are free to go," Ivar declared. Flóki took Morgen's hand, and with a last, anguished glance back at Wulfgar and Rhowenna, who were truly alone now in all the world, save for Yelkei, the spaewife, he led her from the great hall. "Now, then, Wulfgar," Ivar continued softly, reaching out—the point of his broadsword still at Wulfgar's throat—to seize Rhowenna and to draw her slowly toward him, "as you've won your way from a mere *bóndi* to a mighty *jarl* of the Northland, played us all for fools, and dared to claim a princess as your wife, who may guess how much higher still you will seek to climb? I would serve myself well, I am thinking, if I simply struck off your head and had done with it, as I intend to do with Cerdic. But then our game would be ended, and as I've none so interesting a foe as you, I am loath to see that happen, I'll admit. So here is what I'm going to do instead: I'm going to let you live, in exchange for which I'll kill your child when 'tis born, and then put one of my own into your wife's belly!"

Wulfgar went crazy then. Rhowenna could feel the murderous rage that rolled up inside him, so that despite his bonds, he lunged forward wildly, like some savage predator, snarling and tearing free of the men who restrained him, as though, with his teeth alone, he would rip out Ivar's jugular vein. Even Ivar took a hasty step back from those blazing blue eyes that burned to his very soul, and jabbed the point of his weapon warningly against Wulfgar's throat, cutting open a small wound that trickled blood.

"Careful, Wulfgar—or you die th. moment, with your wife still alive and at my tender mercy. Or mayhap I'll simply slay her and your babe both, right here and now."

This last threat, especially, was enough to make Wulfgar go absolutely still, his breath coming in hard rasps, his eyes like blue flame. Slowly, tangling his hand roughly in her hair to hold her still, while Wulfgar watched powerlessly, Ivar bent and kissed Rhowenna full on the mouth, his tongue forcing her lips to part. She did not struggle, she did not move, she did not breathe, knowing that while a woman might not call her body her own if a man were bent on taking it by force, her heart, her mind, and her soul were hers alone for the giving. And those things, Ivar the Boneless would not have of her; those things, he would not even touch within her, so wholly were they Wulfgar's—and his alone. When, finally, Ivar released her, puzzled and angered by her lack of fight, he said:

"By the gods, 'tis not royal blood, but tepid water that

runs in your veins, lady! Morgen the maid had a good deal more spirit and backbone than you, I swear!''

"That is because you do not understand quiet courage, Viking, or inner strength." Prince Cerdic spoke again at that. He had remained silent before, the better to raise the odds of his not drawing Ivar's attention further to himself, thereby spinning out the thread of his precarious existence a little longer than it might otherwise have been. "My lady," he continued to Rhowenna, "once, I would have bid you welcome here; now, I can only bid you farewell, and for that, I am sorry. Had I laid eyes on your beauty ere you were kidnapped from Usk, I would have paid all your ransom demanded, and more. Instead, I did you a great wrong, which has brought you to this pass, and I regret it more deeply than I can say. I've no right to ask—but since I go this day to meet my Maker, in Heaven, and would stand before Him with a clear conscience, I do crave pardon and beg you to forgive me for my transgression against you."

As she gazed at Cerdic kneeling before the block, Rhowenna thought that but for his own avarice and a trick of fate, he, not Wulfgar, would be her husband; and while Cerdic was handsome enough in the same dark fashion Aella of Northumbria had been, with his short-cropped hair and beard, still, she had grown accustomed to a long tawny mane of hair on a man and a smooth-shaven face against her skin.

"I forgive you, my lord," she said to Cerdic, "for your loss was my gain, and so I am the richer for it."

"Then there is one thing more I would beg of you, and that is this: one kiss from your sweet scarlet lips, fair lady, for your less-than-gallant betrothed, a fleeting taste of what might have been had I not suffered my purse and my ambition to rule me."

"Because you are to die, I will grant what you ask, but only the kiss of peace, my lord, and no more. For the rest belongs to him who is my gallant husband, to whom I have gladly and willingly pledged my faithfulness and my heart.''

'' 'Tis enough, then; 'twill serve, my lady.'' And then, as Rhowenna solemnly bent near to him, cupping his face to kiss first one cheek and then the other, Cerdic whispered quietly but urgently in her ear, ''There is one thing, at least, that I can offer you, my lady, and for my soul's sake, so I will before I die. Beware the priest! He is a traitor to your people, a Judas whose treacherous soul I bought with thirty pieces of silver from my purse. 'Twas through him that I learned how best to lay the trap I used to strike at your father, Pendragon, in the hope of winning Usk for my own, thence to march upon the whole of Walas and proclaim myself its king. And when the attempt upon Pendragon's life failed, 'twas Cadwyr who counseled your father to betroth you to me, that I might gain by marriage what I could not seize by force; and in this way did I seek to use my poor, innocent, goodhearted sister, also. Now I am punished, fallen prey to men even more ambitious than I, such is the nature of man, a savage and predatory beast. Still, I think I might have loved you in the end.''

As she stepped back from Cerdic, Rhowenna did not dare to glance at Father Cadwyr, for fear of what he would see upon her face, in her eyes, such was the anger that churned within her at the revelation of his betrayal of Usk, of her father, of her. Trembling, she went to stand at Wulfgar's side, burying her face against his chest as, at last, Ivar lifted his broadsword high and then brought it down with a single, swift, hard stroke to cut off Cerdic's head.

Mathilde's screams filled the air as blood from her brother's body spurted on the floor, spreading across the stones to seep into her gown. Mumbling pious platitudes, Father Cadwyr moved to comfort her, while Ivar began issuing orders to secure the royal manor and the prisoners. Struggling fiercely, Wulfgar was taken away to the dungeon, while Rhowenna and Mathilde were confined to a tower, with Yelkei being sent to attend them. Mathilde, a gentle woman, lay on the bed there, weeping hysterically until Yelkei gave her a potion that put her to sleep. Then the spaewife said to Rhowenna:

"Lady, 'tis rumored that there is an army of Usk warriors marching toward Cerdic's markland. It seems that lacking you as his bride, he instead betrothed his sister to Gwydion, the king of Usk, and had already signed the necessary scrolls and delivered to Gwydion her dowry when Ivar swooped to make war on this stronghold. The princess Mathilde was to depart for Usk within the fortnight. But instead of sending his sister, Cerdic was compelled to dispatch a message to Usk, demanding men and arms to support him in his battle against Ivar, as was agreed by the treaty Cerdic and Gwydion made between them. The missive reached Usk too late to be of any assistance to Cerdic; but 'tis claimed that Gwydion means to have his bride ere returning home, that for her sake, he'll not leave her to the mercy of the *Víkingrs*; and if that is the case, then I have thought of a way in which to save you and your child from Ivar the Boneless. So, do you listen sharp now, and hear my plan. . . ."

The deadly potion was bittersweet, and as she drank it down, Rhowenna could not help but wonder with a deep shudder if it would, in fact, kill her and her babe. All day long and well into the night, she had lain in the tower, moaning and screaming, pretending to be in labor, terrified that she would actually bring it on with her exertions—although Yelkei had told her that the draught would delay the onslaught of childbirth. Now, as she felt the potion begin to take effect, Rhowenna closed her eyes sleepily, drifting steadily downward, toward a deep and dark unconsciousness, her last waking thoughts of the anguish she must cause Wulfgar and whether she would ever see him again in this life.

* * *

"I am sorry, Wulfgar," Yelkei whispered, and in her empathy, seeing the torment upon his handsome bronze face as he bent over Rhowenna's still and silent figure, the spaewife had no need to feign the tears that streamed down her cheeks. "I did everything I knew to do, but still, I could not save her. I have seen it before: The hips of your lady wife were too small, and the child was too large to travel through the narrow passage that leads into this world. She and the babe are in Asgard now."

"Rhowenna of Usk was not a pagan, but a Christian, old woman—and would even now be in Heaven had you let me inside this tower to perform the necessary rites!" Father Cadwyr glared at Yelkei malevolently. "Instead, she died unshriven!"

"She did not want you at her side, priest! She died calling not only on the Christian God, but also on the gods of the Northland and other ancient gods, whose names I had never heard before and so did not know. For she said that at last, in her hour of darkness, she had come to understand that the one God was the many, and that the many were the One, but that you, priest, served none save the Devil and were a traitor to Usk and to your king!"

"Shut your mouth, you evil old witch!" Father Cadwyr cried, and struck Yelkei violently across the face, sending her sprawling upon the floor, blood spurting from her bottom lip.

Yelkei's knife flashed in her hand then, but at that, Ivar spoke coldly:

"Priest, from what little I know of the Christian God, you are a disgrace to your robes. You've no respect for a man's tortured soul, or for the powers of a true spaewife, either! Halfdan, take this miserable servant of Christendom out into the courtyard, and hang him!"

"I will, and with pleasure," Halfdan growled, grabbing

hold of Father Cadwyr's terrified, protesting figure and forcibly dragging him away.

Following that, there was only silence in the tower, broken only by the sound of Wulfgar's tormented, racking sobs as he held Rhowenna's limp body in his arms, cradling her head against his chest, rocking her gently, and stroking her long, unbound hair as though it were something very precious and very fine. Even Ivar was still, unwillingly moved by this outpouring of love and grief; for although he had known many emotions in his life, these two alone had surely eluded him, and he envied Wulfgar them, despite the pain they had so obviously caused him. After a long while, Yelkei murmured:

"The last words of your lady wife were of you, Wulfgar. She said that she wished to be buried on the shores of Usk, from where you took her and where she would wait until the end of time for you to come for her again."

"'Twill be done, then. Gwydion of Usk arrives tomorrow morn, with the ransom he is to pay for the princess Mathilde's release. When they leave, they may take the body of your lady wife with them, Wulfgar, back to Usk," Ivar declared. He was so distinctly troubled by Wulfgar's silence, by what he glimpsed in Wulfgar's eyes, as though their vital flame had blown out, had been forever extinguished, that he failed utterly to notice the faint, sly smile of triumph that curved the corners of Yelkei's mouth.

"My lady, art mad, in truth!" Gwydion cried as he stared at Mathilde, aghast. "Ivar the Boneless did swear to me that you were yet chaste. But now I think that the pagan bastard must have lied to me and that his rape of you has unhinged your fragile woman's mind!"

"He did not touch me, my lord," Mathilde insisted, with

quiet fierceness. "For when it seemed that he would do so, Rhowenna of Usk rose bravely to stand between us. She looked him, unafraid, in the eye and said, 'Ivar, I had not thought so, but art a fool who does not learn from his mistakes?' And although I knew not what she meant, he pondered her words, then laughed and said that he was no fool, that he would get for me the purse he had not got for her. But we are wasting time, my lord, when every moment is precious! Rhowenna is alive, I tell you! But she shall surely die, in truth, if you do not pry up the lid on her coffin so that she may breathe! Please, my lord, I beg of you! Oh, please!''

Finally, as they had just crossed over Offa's Dyke into Walas and so were no longer in any immediate danger, Gwydion raised his hand to signal a halt to the men who accompanied him. Then, dismounting, he walked back to the ox-cart in which lay the wooden coffin that carried home to Usk the mortal remains of his beloved kinswoman, Rhowenna. For an eternity, it seemed to Mathilde, he just stood there, lost in reverie, his hand resting on the lid. On his face was such an expression of sorrow that she understood that to him, Rhowenna had been more than just a kinswoman, and her heart went out to him. Mathilde also knew that Gwydion believed her mad. But then, as though he could not bear to throw away the chance, the hope, however small, that she had spoken truly, he bade his men force open the lid on the coffin and then bent to gaze inside. So it came to pass that his was the first face Rhowenna saw when, wakened from her now-natural slumber by the noise of the hammers and the chisels, and the feeling upon her skin of the heat of the bright summer sun, and of the caress of the sea-kissed wind, she slowly opened her eyes.

"Gwydion!" she breathed, hardly daring to believe that she was still alive, that he stood before her in reality and not in a dream. Tears started in her eyes at the realization. "Oh,

Gwydion, at long last, after all this time, I have come back to Usk!''

And such was his joy at that, that it was some moments before he realized that the last word she had whispered had been ''Usk'' and not ''you.''

Chapter Twenty-one

The Reckoning

With autumn nipping at their heels, the great *Víkingr* army marched from Cerdic's principality back to Northumbria, to York, to reassert their authority there over the Saxons who had defied them. Afterward, the *Víkingr* forces descended again on East Anglia, where, at Thetford, they established a base to serve as their winter quarters when the season came. Then, at Hoxne, they engaged and defeated the troops of Edmund, the king of East Anglia who was later to become a saint and martyr, and executed him; so it began to appear as though there would not be a single king left in all of Christendom when Ivar had finished carving out his own and greatest kingdom of all.

Through all this, Wulfgar behaved so strangely that people began to speak of him as mad; and in battle, he fought so wildly and savagely that it seemed he had found the Berserks' Way—or else that he hoped to be slain. Even Ivar, in those days, kept out of Wulfgar's path, haunted more deeply than he cared to admit by Wulfgar's soulless eyes; for Ivar felt somehow as though he looked into a polished-bronze mirror and saw his own reflection in that blind and empty gaze. In the evenings, in the abandoned great halls of dead kings and earls, Halfdan sat and contemplated the two men silently, looking thoughtful and troubled. Yelkei, too, watched and waited and, for the first time that any of them could ever remember, held her tongue.

But then, one night, there came to Ivar's fire a bard, Owain by name, with a tame ferret wrapped around his arm and a wild Celtic harp slung over his shoulder. He was not a *skáld* of the Northland, but still, none offered him insult or injury; for a bard was a caste unto himself, respected by all, welcome anywhere to sing for his supper, and might as easily be found in some peasant's cottage as in the great hall of a king. After he had hungrily consumed his bowl of thick, savory mutton stew, a hunk of hard bread spread with honey and butter, and a cup of mead, Owain slipped from its soft leather drawstring case his harp, made of ash and beautifully carved. He tuned the strings, then plucked a few scattered notes and chords before beginning to play a soft ballad; and despite himself, as Wulfgar heard the foreign but achingly familiar words Rhowenna had used to sing, something sparked deep inside him and started to burn like a rare candle in the wind. After a moment, he somehow could not refrain from drawing near to the fire and the harper, Yelkei like a shadow at his side.

The ferret sat upon Owain's shoulder, its tiny eyes gleaming in the firelight, its nose and whiskers twitching; and Wulfgar thought how Rhowenna would love it, and there was a lump in his throat at the thought. The bard played for a very long time; for save in his own land of Walas, he had seldom, to his surprise, had a more appreciative audience than the *Víkingrs*, whose warrior souls stirred to music and poetry and art, knowing death so intimately and so being the more strongly drawn to all that enriched life. Then, at last, laying aside his harp, Owain took notice of Wulfgar's interest in the ferret. With a treat he took from his pocket, the harper tempted the small creature down his arm and then into Wulfgar's hands, saying:

"Her name is Cariad. 'Tis a word that in the language of Walas means—"

"*Elsket* . . . beloved." His head bowed, Wulfgar gently stroked the beast's soft fur, pretending to concentrate on the ferret, so the bard could not see his face.

"Aye." Owain nodded. Then he laid his hand on Wulfgar's shoulder and drew near to say, very low, so no one should overhear, "She is alive, your beloved, Wulfgar Bloodaxe. She bade me tell you so and that you have a fine son—Please, my lord, if you must break my wrist, have mercy, and choose not the hand that plucks my harp—"

"Lying bastard! How much did Ivar pay you?"

"Nothing, nothing. I do speak the truth, I swear it! Ask the yellow woman!"

Wulfgar inhaled sharply at that, turning to stare hard at Yelkei, his eyes leaping of a sudden with hope and a wild blue fire that was like the eerie blue spheres of light born of a highly charged storm.

"Yelkei . . . ?" His voice was low and pleading.

"'Tis true, Wulfgar," she confessed, half fearful and ashamed that she had kept this knowledge from him, although she had thought it in his best interests to do so. "I did not tell you before, because your lady wife said that if she survived, she would send Owain the Bard to me—for she would trust no other messenger or her words to a letter that might fall into Ivar's hands—and that if Owain the Bard did not come, there was no need for you ever to know what she did for love of you and your child—"

"What did she do? I don't understand. How can she be alive? Yelkei, I held her lifeless body in my arms, and kissed her breathless mouth—"

"Nay, 'twas but the deep, dark sleep from which one sometimes does not awaken. Your lady wife drank a potion I mixed, Wulfgar, so that abysmal slumber would come upon her. Far to the east beyond the Eastlands, there are tribes even older than my own, who know the secrets of such things, and one of their ilk did teach me, many years ago. But 'tis dangerous. Too much of this, too little of that, and one slips across the gloaming into Asgard, or Hel. So, 'twas best we did not tell you before now; for had you known, had you not believed your lady wife truly dead, Ivar might have guessed at our trickery—But now, Owain the Bard is here, and all is well—although he has been a long time coming. . . ."

"The time of your lady wife was long and difficult, my lord," the harper explained, as, taking up a soft hide cloth, he began to polish his harp. "'Twas not an easy birth. Then, afterward, the childbed fever set in, and we feared to lose her still. So I saw no point in telling you she lived, when it seemed she might yet die, grieving you all over again. Since her recovery, I have spent many weeks trying to find you, my lord. As well you know, all of Britain is in a state of war and upheaval, and when King Ivar travels, he moves hard and swift, so his enemies have little warning of his approach."

"There is still more, Wulfgar," Yelkei said, "for men do fear to cross a true spaewife, especially when she has paid them well for their silence; and so I've messages of my own to impart. Flóki the Raven serves you still as your second-in-command, and he has gathered the *thegns* who accompanied you here to Britain but were scattered by Ivar's men when they seized your Dragon Ship; and thanks to your famous prowess in battle, your own warriors have been joined by many others eager to pledge oath to you. Together with Flóki, they have reclaimed the *Siren's Song*, and he captains her now in your stead. She lies just off the coast of East Anglia, awaiting your return."

"I can't believe it! 'Tis just too much to take in all at once!

I am overwhelmed with emotion—'' Wulfgar broke off, trying to contain himself. Then, after a long moment, he continued. "Yelkei, you have been busy." His voice was wry with the first hint of humor she had seen from him since he had held Rhowenna's still and silent, drugged figure in his embrace, and Yelkei was immeasurably cheered. But then his face turned dark with sorrow again, and he cried softly, "Ah, gods! I should have been there for her, Yelkei! To think of Rhowenna giving birth to our child, without me, frightened and alone—''

"Frightened? Aye." Owain smiled kindly, clucking to the ferret in Wulfgar's hands and giving the creature another treat. "'Tis an awesome thing, the birth of a babe. But never you fear, my lord. Your lady wife was not alone, although 'twas you for whom she called out, and no other. She grieves that you have yet to see your son."

"My son . . ." Wulfgar's face was filled with wonder at the thought.

"A fine, strong lad, like his father—so says your lady wife."

"And does he have a name, this son of mine?" Wulfgar inquired.

"He does, my lord. Your lady wife calls him Leik the Bold."

"Leik the Bold. Rhowenna chose well."

"I am beginning to think so, my lord," the harper remarked enigmatically, folding away the cloth with which he had polished his harp and sliding the instrument itself into its case. "Come, Cariad." He patted his shoulder, and the beast leaped on it from Wulfgar's hands. "The hour grows late, and there are songs to be sung on the morrow." Slinging his harp over his shoulder, Owain stood. "My lord. Princess Yelkei. I will bid you a good night."

"Good night, Owain the Bard, and thank you, for everything," Wulfgar answered. Then he turned to Yelkei, saying, "You made plans with Rhowenna. Now, 'tis long past time that you made plans with me, as well. The horses Ivar has confiscated are valuable and, so, closely guarded; 'twould be hard to steal even one, much less two. So, we will do better with a small sailing boat to make good our escape to the *Siren's Song*, I am thinking—''

"East Anglia has its fair share of traders and fisher folk, and Thetford is no exception. There are rowboats and small sailing boats beached upon the banks of the little river from Thetford that leads to the Great Ouse and thence to the Wash and the North Sea. The theft of one vessel will surely not be noticed; many have been abandoned by the villagers who fled at the approach of Ivar's great army—''

"We'll need provisions, too, for the journey south, down the coast of East Anglia—''

"Those, I can get—''

"Then we will steal away just before dawn—Yelkei, you should have told me that Rhowenna was alive! I curse you that you did not!''

"You will have cause to thank me for it in the end, I am thinking. Remember that to you, my tongue has always spoken truly—and that there is purpose in all I do. Before, you did not know what it was to lose what mattered most to you in all the world. Now you do, and you will be the stronger for it, as the fire and the folding of the metal strengthen a blade. Now, let us speak no more. Ivar is watching us—Nay, do not glance in his direction! Ah, 'tis too late! Too late! Now he knows! He knows that something has happened tonight to change you.''

"Oh, Yelkei, how? How can he possibly know?''

"The light of your soul has come back into your eyes.''

Before the pale, cold light of day glowed at the edge of the horizon, Wulfgar and Yelkei sneaked from the great hall of the abandoned manor Ivar had appropriated for his own winter quarters. The mist that billowed in with the wind across the sweeping land hung thick and low in the hollows, and as he slipped through its veils in the darkness lighted only by the silvery, ringed moon and dimming stars that still shone in the sky, Wulfgar thought of Flóki out on the rough North Sea, blind in the mist, and was glad the *Siren's Song* lay instead safe at anchor at the mouth of the river Blackwater, off the southeastern shore of East Anglia. At this hour, the night was as quiet as the grave, save for the distant, wild, and forlorn cries of the wolves and birds, and just as eerie, giving Wulfgar and Yelkei the feeling that they had stepped from the earth that was real into one that was mystical and fey, a siren's place. Frost encrusted the ground, crunching beneath Wulfgar's booted feet as he slowed his pace to accommodate Yelkei, whose legs were not nearly so long as his and so who could not walk as fast as he. Every now and then, he glanced back over his shoulder, for all the good it did him. In the mist, he could not see if anyone was following them, although he thought he would have heard the crunch of boots upon the rime, if so. But perhaps he would not over the pounding of his heart, the harshness of his breath, making white clouds in the wintry air. From behind him now, Yelkei's own breath came in quick, hard little pants as she struggled to keep up; and Wulfgar realized then that he was now running along the reed-grown riverbank, through the mist, running like a lithe, mighty stag bounding and leaping in flight, as though his very life depended on it, his long hair streaming from his face in the wind. He knew he must stop and wait for Yelkei, but he could not seem to halt, or even to slow down. Something wild and primitive had seized hold of him, now possessed him, and he was both the hunter and the hunted, running from the darkness that swallowed all in his wake, and toward a distant, bright and shining light that was like the North Star, guiding him home.

At last, when he reached the place where the rowboats and sailing boats of the Thetford villagers were beached upon the riverbank, Wulfgar did stop, his heart racing, his lungs ready to burst from the chilly air he had drawn into them. Exhilaration surged through him. His face was flushed; his eyes gleamed with an excitement that was like that before a battle; and as he gazed toward the east where, he knew, far away, lay the dark and boundless North Sea, it came to him of a sudden, somehow, that his destiny awaited him there.

Gasping for breath, Yelkei trudged up beside him, small and stooped beneath the heaviness of the leather sackfuls of supplies she carried slung over her shoulders. So all-consuming had been the unknown, unbridled thing that had gripped him that Wulfgar had not even felt the weight of his own burdens. But Yelkei was not young, and now he felt shame that she had been forced to hurry because of him. Still, she said naught, as though she understood the madness that had come so unexpectedly upon him. Instead, dropping her bags to the ground, she began to move among the rowboats and sailing boats that lay like hulking beasts among the reeds that lined the riverbank.

"That one," she said after a moment, choosing a sturdy sailing boat.

Wulfgar nodded his agreement; and quickly, they loaded their provisions, then started to push the vessel into the water. But then Yelkei paused, her head cocked a trifle, listening intently, her eyes narrowed and alert.

"Someone comes—Nay, there is no cause for alarm," she reassured him as he reached for his battle-ax. "'Tis Owain the Bard."

Now Wulfgar could hear, as well, the harper's rich, melodious voice, singing in hushed tones, and see the light of the whale-oil lamp he carried in one hand, flickering like foxfire in the mist. His wild Celtic harp was still, secure in the leather drawstring case that hung at his shoulder, along with another sack that contained his belongings. From beneath the strands of his long, dark chestnut hair that whipped about his face in the wind, Cariad's glowing eyes peeked from where she, too, clung to his shoulder.

"Owain, what do you here?" Wulfgar asked quietly at the bard's approach.

"Since your lady wife returned to Usk, many nights has she sat beside the fire in the great hall, cradling her son at her breast, and telling him tales of the Northland, and of his mighty father, Wulfgar the Dane. Now, it comes to me that there is a song in my mind and in my heart which will not go away, and I must learn the words to the melody." So saying, he set the whale-oil lamp and his sack down on a thwart of the sailing boat, then laid his harp carefully in the bottom for safekeeping. After that, he, too, bent his back to the task of shoving the vessel into the water. "Come. We must hurry. King Ivar was already astir when I slipped away, and on his face as he glanced at your empty pallet, my lord, was a strange and haunting smile that I did not care to see."

Swiftly, between the three of them, they launched the sailing boat into the mist and water. Then Wulfgar took up one oar and Owain, the other, while Yelkei sat in the stern, her hand on the tiller. Much to Wulfgar's surprise, the bard's slender hands proved as sure upon the paddle as upon the strings of his harp; but then Wulfgar remembered that Usk, too, lay at the edge of the sea, and that Rhowenna had spoken of often riding the white-foamed waves, in a peculiar round boat she had called a coracle. No doubt, having been her father's harper, Owain, also, was no stranger to boats or to water. Rhythmically, the oars rose and fell in the imperceptibly thinning mist until, finally, the vessel was far enough from shore that the paddles could be drawn in and that Wulfgar could hoist the mast and the lugsail, and secure them. With a plaintive sough that echoed the distant cry of the night creatures, the freshening wind caught the white, four-sided sail so it billowed wide, sending the vessel skimming over the quietly rippling waves.

By now, dawn streaked across the horizon, the sun pale and grey in the sullen sky pierced the last wisps of lingering mist, so the glimmering river wended like a riband of long, dark silk before them. Wulfgar took the tiller from Yelkei then. Squatting in the bottom of the sailing boat, she opened the sacks of provisions they had brought, filling wooden bowls with chunks of cold meat, a handful of berries and nuts, and a thick slice of hard bread each, and, from a leather flask, pouring cups of mead. In silence, the three of them broke their fast, eating hungrily; for their exertions and the cold air had quickened their appetites. Even Cariad devoured the tidbits Owain fed her until the meager meal was done. Wulfgar felt ashamed that they had no better to offer the bard; but then he reminded himself that he and Yelkei had planned for only two, and that Owain had accompanied them of his own free will and so must accept what was given, without complaint.

The wind stayed with them; and the days of their journey passed peacefully as they wound their way west along the little river, then north up the Great Ouse to the Wash, finally turning east into the North Sea, rounding the mammoth bulge of East Anglia to follow its coast south. As the winter wore on, the weather grew steadily colder. But Yelkei had brought a firepot to warm them; and when the sea grew too rough for sailing, they put in to shore, where they foraged for supplies and, dragging the vessel onto the sands, turned it upside down over themselves for shelter if there were no other to be found. They took turns spelling one another at the tiller; and now and then, to pass away the time, Owain withdrew his chess-board from his bag, and he and Wulfgar played long, fierce games of strategy and battle. But more often, observing Wulf-gar suddenly grow silent and gaze off into the distance, lost in reverie, dwelling on his thoughts and memories of Rho-

wenna, the bard brought forth his harp and sang ballads of
Walas that echoed the haunting ache in Wulfgar's heart for
his lady wife.

At last came the day when they sailed past the mouth of
the river Stour; and Wulfgar's heart swelled within his breast,
for he knew that their journey to the *Siren's Song*, lying in
wait for them at the mouth of the river Blackwater, was nearly
at an end. But then, staring off into the distance, at the
far point of land that was the Naze, Yelkei said abruptly,
"Wulfgar, your eyes are younger and keener than mine, and
mine are blinded by the morning sun, besides. See you a
white sail there on the horizon, coming hard and fast upon
us?" and as he glanced to where she pointed, he spied another
vessel bearing swiftly toward them.

"'Tis only some fisherman, most like, who seeks to net an
early catch," Wulfgar said, but with a sinking heart, he
realized that it was none other than Ivar the Boneless, and a
frisson that had nothing to do with the frigid winter air chased
up his spine.

His hand trembled a little on the tiller, with the sudden
surge of adrenaline that coursed through him. Somehow, Ivar
must have learned the contents of the messages that had
passed between Yelkei and Flóki, Wulfgar thought, and upon
realizing he, Wulfgar, had fled and discovering he had gone
west by boat, along the little river, and not southeast by horse,
Ivar had known the route Wulfgar must follow. Taking the
shorter, overland route, Ivar had mounted up to ride southeast
from Thetford and, in Colchester or some other place, had
got a vessel to intercept Wulfgar at the Naze, to cut him off,
to drive him into the island-riddled harbor formed by the
inward curve of the small peninsula. The islands . . . At the
thought of them, grimly did Wulfgar understand then, down
to his very bones, what Ivar intended—the *holmganga*, the
island going, which was the name given to a formal duel
between two *Víkingr* warriors.

Like fathomless, twin abysses in her yellow countenance, Yelkei's black eyes swallowed the wan light of the faded winter sun, while Owain's own green ones glittered with the brilliance of raw green stones; and his indrawn breath was so sharp that Cariad chittered nervously and hid her pointed face against his neck as the oncoming sail quickened its pace, seeming to shoot forward like some strange and fantastic bird winging its way upon the wind. Steady, Wulfgar held the tiller, so their own sailing boat stuck to its speed and course, he seeing no other choice but to enter the harbor and to hope that they could hide among the islands. For although his vessel leaped valiantly across the waves, it was not so fast as Ivar's own, which, little by little, gained on them, so Wulfgar knew he could not turn and outrun it. Unbidden into his mind came the memory of his hooking Ragnar, his father, and hauling him like a seacow aboard the *Siren's Song*; and Wulfgar knew that Ivar would not hesitate to bring his sailing boat alongside them and, to prevent them from fleeing, use his own grappling hooks to secure their vessel.

Rapidly, Ivar closed the distance between them, until it seemed to Wulfgar that he could hear his half brother's mocking laughter on the wind, could glimpse the fluid-boned hand that guided the second tiller so skillfully—as it ever had held a tiller in their youth, when they had fished among the fjords along the coast of the Northland. Wulfgar could remember how Ivar had laughed at him then, too, at his own clumsy, inexpert handling of the tiller, in comparison to Ivar's own deftness. The memory was so vivid that although those days were twenty years gone and he could now hold his own against any who sailed the high seas, Wulfgar felt suddenly as awkward as he had then as a lad, the butt of Ivar's malicious jesting; and his hand tightened so hard on the tiller that he fumbled its course, and Ivar's sailing boat drew ominously even nearer.

Hide-and-seek they played then, among the small islands, flitting along the shorelines, Wulfgar's face bleak as he now saw that although he had dared to hope otherwise, Ivar was not alone, but was accompanied by Halfdan. Wulfgar knew that he could not fight them both, that together, they would kill him. Then, afterward perhaps, Ivar would discover that Rhowenna was still alive, had borne her husband a son, and then she and Leik would never be safe so long as Ivar lived. It was this thought that frightened Wulfgar most of all. For Yelkei and Owain the Bard, he had no fear; his half brothers would slay neither, afraid of the spaewife's power, revering the harper's talent. For his own self, Wulfgar feared only for Rhowenna's and Leik's sake. For them, he *must* prevail!

Such was the violence of this thought that his hand tightened once more on the tiller, inadvertently hauling the sailing boat off balance, so that it rocked on its keel, then heeled hard to one side, and he could hear it scrape upon the bottom of the shoals just off shore. Cursing himself vehemently for a fool, he hurriedly steadied the vessel, attempting to turn it back away from the breakers that rushed in upon the snowy island strand. But it was too late. The sailing boat was running up onto the sands; and whipping around a near point of the island, where he must have been lying in wait for them, Ivar was upon them. They would never get the vessel pushed back out into sea fast enough to escape, Wulfgar realized with a sinking heart. Hastily lowering the mast and sail, then leaping out into the icy, frothy combers, he, Owain, and Yelkei dragged the sailing boat inland instead, so it would not be dislodged and carried away on the waves. Once the vessel was secure, Wulfgar hurriedly threw off his cloak and stripped off his tunic, scarcely feeling the chilly wind against his bare skin as he mentally prepared for the fight he knew must come. Then, grabbing his shield from the bottom of the vessel and drawing his battle-ax from its scabbard at his back, Wulfgar stood, waiting for his half brothers to reach him, feeling somehow as though he had been waiting all his life for this moment, as though, at long last, his destiny lay at hand.

Now, Ivar and Halfdan were lowering their own mast and sail, jumping into the breakers to haul their own sailing boat up onto the beach drifted with snow and rimed at its edges. When it was done, they began slowly to walk toward Wulfgar. In that instant, it seemed that his world contracted sharply to that place where they stood upon the island shore, as though the gods or some other unknown force had deliberately woven it into a cocoon of grey silk spun from the leaden winter sky, sealing beyond it the cold breath of the wind, the frosty murmur of the sea, hushing the day, although it was only that his heightened senses shut the sounds out and became so keenly attuned to his half brothers that they all three seemed to breathe as one. Ivar's eyes shone with excitement, triumph, and even a hint of madness in that moment as he came finally to a halt a few feet away, his body as taut and graceful as a wolf poised for attack, and his smile was a wolfish smile, as though he scented victory at hand.

"A good race, Wulfgar. But now 'tis done, and we are come near to the end of our game, I am thinking. You have deceived me once too often for me to let you slip through my fingers yet again. What a pity for you, when you have so much to live for, after all, eh, Wulfgar?" Ivar paused for a moment. Then he continued softly. "For she is alive, your lady wife, is she not?" The question was stated in such a way that it did not demand an answer; so Wulfgar knew that Yelkei had been right that night in the abandoned great hall when he had first learned that Rhowenna lived: His eyes had given away the truth to Ivar. "May I ask how? Nay? Ah, I understand. You think that if you remain silent, Wulfgar, I'll believe that I'm wrong and that, truly, she is dead. But I will not, I assure you." When still he received no response, Ivar shrugged, laughing softly. "No matter. I was merely curious as to how you managed to deceive me. However, perhaps I can guess: 'Twas some dark Eastland potion of Yelkei's, no doubt, which brought on a sleep so deep that it resembled death . . . ?'' He turned to the spaewife, his eyes hard and angry. ''By Odinn! If you were not a true spaewife, I'd slay you where you stand, you meddlesome old witch! Still, you will be deservedly punished, I am thinking, when Wulfgar lies dead at my feet; for he has ever been the child of your heart, has he not?''

''I do not want to fight you, Ivar,'' Wulfgar insisted, his voice low but vibrant with emotion. ''I do not want to kill you. Despite everything, we are brothers—''

''You are no brother of mine, you bloody, upstart bastard, but a mockery the gods sent here to earth to plague me! *I* am Ragnar Lodbrók's greatest son! Yet every time I gaze upon you, 'tis like looking into a polished-bronze mirror and seeing a stranger staring out of my own eyes, a stranger who is somehow even greater than I. The Greeks have a name for what you are to me, Wulfgar: my nemesis. I cannot suffer you to live; I cannot suffer you to die. Still, one way or the other, once and for all, this day will end what is between us! And when you are dead, Wulfgar, I promise you: I will sail my mighty Dragon Ship to Usk; and there, I will take your lady wife for my own, my whore, and I will slay your son— for she *did* give you a son, did she not, your fair Rhowenna? Aye, a son like his father—ever to haunt me, like a ghost, lest I destroy you both!''

With that, Ivar stripped off his own cloak and tunic, took up his shield, and drew his broadsword from the sheath at his back; and as the pale, harsh winter light caught the blade, it gleamed silvery with menace, its runes writhing in a macabre dance along its deadly length, the zigging and zagging swirls of its pattern-welding shimmering like wraiths kneeling to drink from the blood channel at its heart. Wulfgar shuddered at the sight; and as he remembered the name of the terrible weapon—Soul-Stealer—a chill settled deep in his bones, as though a goose had just walked over his grave. But then he thought of Rhowenna and Leik; and a strength summoned from some deep, inner source welled inside him, and his hands tightened on his battle-ax and his shield; his eyes burned with blue flame.

"Halfdan, do you join Ivar in this madness?" he asked tersely. "Mean you to turn your own blade upon me, also, or to strike me in the back during the battle?"

"Nay, Wulfgar." Halfdan shook his head. "This is Ivar's game, not mine, I swear it!"

Ivar gave a low, scornful snarl at that, his eyes glinting with malice and derision, as though to taunt Halfdan into forswearing his soul; but Wulfgar merely nodded, satisfied that he need not fear to feel from behind the unexpected bite of Halfdan's scramasax or broadsword.

Although by his compelling it to take place upon an island, Ivar had given some semblance of formality to the forthcoming duel, it was not truly a *holmganga* in a formal sense, Wulfgar knew. There was no ring formed by four posts and a rope to limit the area of combat, beyond which if one of the opponents stepped, he was deemed to have run away from the fight; no white cloth spread upon the ground at the center of the ring, to show when blood had been spilled and so honor satisfied; no seconds to wield the shields of the swordsman, the axman. Instead, this was to be a bloody, no-holds-barred conflict, a duel to the death.

The sun was a flat, glimmering disk in the sullen sky, its edges as cold and sharp as the two blades that glittered in its sickly frosted light. Across its face, grey clouds scudded like billowing mist, as ominous as before a storm, although these were but the snow-thick clouds of winter, dark and dismal. The wind soughed plaintively across the harbor, so the thin layer of snow that blanketed the ground drifted up in streams and swirls, and the sea swelled and surged, white with foam as the combers rolled in to break upon the island strand. Spindrift spewed into the air, damp and tangy with salt. Above the sands, wings outstretched wide, the seabirds soared and called their achingly sweet, forlorn cries, piercing the silence otherwise broken only by the sigh of the wind, the rush of the sea. Nearby, Halfdan, Owain the Bard, and Yelkei stood as still and quiet as a hare whose quivering nose has caught the scent of a predator.

"Ah, 'tis a good day to die, is it not, Wulfgar?" Ivar asked mockingly. He threw his head back and low laughter emanated from his throat until the sound abruptly metamorphosed into a mighty battle cry as, without warning, he moved, his broadsword streaking forth like a flash of lightning, a lethal radiance in the dull-grey light.

But Wulfgar had fully expected some such sudden strike against him, and he was not taken unaware. The blow smashed down upon his swiftly upraised shield, jarring him to the bone, even as his own battle cry issued forth, his hand came up, his battle-ax glinting wickedly in the sun before dealing Ivar's own shield a fearsome whack that staggered both men and sent them reeling. Recovering, shouting to Odinn, they charged forward as, blades clashing, the terrible battle was joined with such ferocity that even Halfdan shuddered. The clang of metal upon metal echoed across the island and the sea, startling the seabirds, so they flapped and shrieked in the wind. Again and again, blade and battle-ax slashed and swung furiously at each other, scraping, clattering, hammering upon lime-wood shields until they cracked and splintered beneath the horrendous blows and were violently flung away as useless.

Equally tall, long of limb, and powerfully muscled, the two men were so evenly matched that neither could gain the advantage as the conflict raged on; Ivar's broadsword thrusting, hacking, and parrying; Wulfgar's battle-ax arcing, swinging, and falling, spinning deftly in his hands as he suddenly employed the long haft as a staff, driving the grip end into Ivar's stomach and beneath his jaw, sending him to stumbling and sprawling back onto the ground. Wulfgar lifted his blade high, then brought it down with all his might, intending to cleave Ivar's head in two. But with the flat of his broadsword, Ivar blocked the fatal blow, using his weapon to shove Wulfgar back so hard that he lost his own footing and fell. Swiftly regaining their balance, however, both men then lunged to their feet, standing motionless for a moment, their breathing so labored that the massive pectorals in their chests heaved and their gasping breaths blew white clouds of frost into the frigid air. Then the two men began to circle each other warily before once more shouting their battle cries and assaulting each other savagely.

Despite the cold, they were sweating profusely, so their bronze flesh glistened over their hard, rippling muscles— biceps that bulged and forearms taut and sinewy, corded thighs and calves that strained and quivered beneath leather breeches. Long, thin wounds now crisscrossed their naked torsos, weals that dripped blood, staining the snow as red as the crimson sail of a longship—so perhaps there was no need of the traditional white cloth on the ground, after all, Wulfgar thought dimly, experiencing a sudden, wild urge to throw back his head and to roar with laughter at the bitter irony of it. He did not want to slay Ivar, yet he knew that if he did not, Ivar would surely kill him. It was as Yelkei had said long ago: His and Ivar's destinies were inextricably intertwined; somehow, this was their fate, immutable, inevitable, written in the stars by the gods—as their duel appeared to those watching like a clash between titanic young pagan gods, each man proud, golden, handsome, not one to suffer defeat.

Time turned—and kept on turning. Wulfgar did not know how long they fought, although it seemed to him like hours, days. Every muscle in his body hurt. His limbs ached, had grown leaden from the unrelenting battle; he moved ever more slowly, staggering. But then, so did Ivar, seeming for the first time in his life to have grown clumsy, to have lost the fluidity, the grace of movement that had earned him his sobriquet, the Boneless. His hand came up and around in a particularly awkward, hacking slash of his broadsword; and Wulfgar, who had already begun an equally wild and ungainly swing of his battle-ax, could not halt its impetus as he realized to his horror what was about to occur. In that moment, time seemed to move in slow motion, to last an eternity as, powerless to stop it, he watched his weapon collide with Ivar's outstretched wrist, felt the sickening thud of the blade connecting with flesh, with bone, cutting clean through it.

Ivar himself felt nothing for an instant; the shock and agony of the devastating blow were so horrendous, so incredible that his brain initially rejected them, refused to absorb them, told him that they were unreal, even as his gut understood that they were not. Then, as he watched his broadsword go spinning and flashing through the air, he at last dimly grasped that his hand was still attached to its hilt, had been severed from his wrist; and he started to howl, unable to stifle the terrible screams that erupted from his throat as waves of excruciating pain stabbed like a thousand piercing barbs through him, and blood began to spew in sickening spurts from the stump that was his wrist. Crumpling to his knees, he intuitively, frenziedly, snatched up his nearby tunic and wrapped it tightly about his injury, while Wulfgar stood rooted to the ground, helpless to move, utterly stricken, not wanting to believe what he had done, praying to the gods that this was no more than a horrible nightmare. Nor did Halfdan, Owain, or Yelkei move, as though they, too, were petrified by what had happened, unable to accept, to believe that the great King Ivar the Boneless should be brought down in such a manner, when they, all of them, had secretly thought and feared that he was invincible, a demon, a god.

The leather of Ivar's tunic had grown dark and wet, and

still, the blood poured from his wrist, flowing into a scarlet puddle upon the snowy ground. Ivar was silent now, his madman's shrieks stilled, although his bearded visage was contorted with deep torment at the affliction he had suffered. But terrifyingly, as he gazed at his severed hand lying on the ground, his mouth was twisted in a ghastly caricature of a smile, and his eyes gleamed morbidly with a strange, unnerving satisfaction, almost triumph, Wulfgar thought as he stared at his half brother. Surely shock and pain must have unhinged Ivar's mind.

"By the gods, man! Do you not bind that wound tighter, you're going to die!" Wulfgar cried, somehow gathering his wits and finding his tongue at last, starting toward his half brother. "Halfdan! Build a fire, to sear the flesh shut, ere Ivar bleeds to death!"

"What is . . . the point?" Ivar gasped out softly, mockingly, his face ashen but his eyes blazing feverishly with a terrible flame. "'Twas my—'twas my . . . sword hand, you . . . bloody, accursed . . . bastard! I always—I always knew that you'd . . . have it somehow . . . in the end. 'Twas my fate, you see. Loki's wolf told me so . . . that day of the—of the deer hunt. When I looked into his eyes . . . I knew—I knew that he was your . . . brother spirit, and that you were . . . his, and that he had come because—because Ragnar and we had made of you a *bóndi*; we had . . . chained you, so to speak . . . just as, with Gleipnir, the gods chained Fenrir, so he bit off Týr's hand at the—at the wrist as punishment for the—for the gods' arrogance, for their deceit, for their fear of the—of the wolf Fenrir, who might . . . bring about their downfall. Thus Týr paid, Týr, the god of battles, who lost his . . . sword hand and so could . . . fight no more." Ivar paused, gathering his breath. Then he spat, "Damn you to Hel, Wulfgar! Why do you just stand there? Why do you not end my life now?"

"You know why: You are my brother. I cannot . . . I *will*

not turn kinslayer for you, Ivar. I will not!'' Wulfgar muttered fiercely.

"Damn you!" Ivar cried again. "You sold Ragnar to Aella!"

"Nay, 'twas Yelkei who did that, in revenge for Ragnar's murder of her son."

"You cannot leave me here like this! You cannot! I am maimed, and without my sword hand, I shall never be able to fight again. What is that but a life of endless torture for me? You are not so hard and cruel as to condemn me to that! I know that you are not, Wulfgar!"

"I will not listen to you, Ivar! You are out of your mind with shock and pain. Halfdan and the others are building the fire. We will seal the stump so the bleeding will stop. You can learn to wield your sword with your left hand."

"And with what will I hold my shield to defend myself, the reins of my horse as I ride into battle?" Ivar laughed shortly, bitterly. "You've never been a fool before, Wulfgar, so do not you be one now! Show me the same mercy you showed Ragnar when you handed his sword down into Aella's snake pit!"

"That was different! He was already a dead man!" Wulfgar declared stubbornly, turning away to begin walking toward Halfdan and the fire he, Owain, and Yelkei had built upon the beach and that now blazed high.

"And I am not? Wulfgar! Damn you, Wulfgar! You owe me! I set you free that day of the deer hunt! Now do you the same for me!"

In his heart, Wulfgar knew that all Ivar had said was truth, that it would be a mercy to kill him; yet, despite that, Wulfgar kept on walking. Then he heard Ivar utter very softly, in his voice an agonized note of entreaty:

"Please . . . brother."

Wulfgar halted in his tracks then, stiff and trembling with emotion, sudden tears stinging his eyes, a lump rising to his throat to choke him. With difficulty, he forced it down, say-ing, "This one stain of dishonor upon my soul, in exchange for your death . . . brother," and then he laughed as harshly and mockingly as Ivar had earlier, the laugh turning abruptly into a terrible, anguished cry. "Ah, gods! It sounds like a fair bargain to me!" Shouting to Odinn, the tears raining down his cheeks, Wulfgar whirled about and leaped forward, his battle-ax swinging high, glittering as bright and silvery in the sun as the mail of a golden-haired Valkyrie.

The song Blood-Drinker sang was a song of death; still, Ivar was smiling that strange caricature of a smile, and his eyes shone with a queer light of triumph as the blade bit deeply into his neck, taking his head.

Ceremoniously, they burned Ivar's body in the fire upon the beach. Afterward, although weapons were highly prized family heirlooms, handed down from father to son, Wulfgar raised Soul-Stealer high and, with all his might, flung the blade out into the sea. Like a beautiful white swan or a dragon breathing fire, it flew through the air, long neck outstretched, gleaming in the sun, until it dived straight downward to disap-pear forever beneath the frothy waves. Ivar the Boneless had been a king of the Northland, a great *Víkingr*; it was not right that his weapon be wielded by any other man.

"'Twas a glorious death at your hands he wanted, Wulf-gar," Halfdan said quietly as they stood together, staring out at the place where the blade had vanished, "what he sought all his life, I somehow do believe. 'Twas his fate and yours to come to this. You were everything he always wanted to be and could not: a true *Víkingr*, heart and soul, the stuff of which heroes and legends are fashioned; and he was the one thing you always wanted to be and never would have been: Ragnar's best-beloved son." Halfdan paused for a moment, dwelling on this irony. Then, at last, he turned to address the harper. "Owain the Bard, when you sing of this day, as you will, let the death of Ivar the Boneless remain a mystery. 'Tis not within most men to understand the fatal obsession in his flawed soul—and the burden Wulfgar now must carry on his own is enough.''

"So 'twill be, King Halfdan, if you will permit me to accompany you back to Britain," Owain said gravely. "For although I know in my heart now the remainder of Wulfgar's own verses, my song is not yet finished. 'Tis the tale of Ragnar Lodbrók and his sons, all four; and like your brother Ivar the Boneless, you, too, will prove a great *Víkingr*, I believe."

"Aye," Halfdan agreed, "for I'm a king of the Northland now, and I'll be king of Britain and mayhap even Erin, too, before I'm through. Still, 'tis Wulfgar who is destined to become the greatest one of us all, I am thinking. By the gods! I believe that before all is said and done, with his lady wife, fey Rhowenna the Fair, by his side, he will be king of all the Danes!"

Epilogue

Sweeter Than Siren's Snare

A Tall Red Sail

The Southern Coast of Usk, Walas, A.D. 867

Gwydion's heart ached with love and sorrow as he stared at the solitary figure who stood at the top of the stony, narrow, serpentine track that led to the beach below, overlooked by his palisade, which perched like a falcon's aerie above the strand. She came here every day, her son in her arms, to stand and to gaze out over the sea, searching, he knew, for a tall red sail spread wide against the blue spring sky and billowing in the wind as the sea dragon beneath heaved and plummeted on the frothy waves, drawing ever nearer.

That Rhowenna should love an enemy Viking! That she should have willingly become his whore, borne a child to him! Even now, after all these months, Gwydion could hardly believe it. Still, he would have taken her back, would have taken her as his wife, in a proper Christian marriage ceremony—for no matter what she said, she was not truly wed in the eyes of the Church and of the Law to that pagan barbarian she called her husband!—but she had obstinately refused even to consider his proposal. Now, sighing heavily, he thought that it was doubtless hopeless, useless, to implore her yet again to change her mind. Still, he felt he must try.

Slowly, he walked down to where, still staring out over the sea, Rhowenna stood on the high ground overlooking the beach below. Although she heard Gwydion's approach, she did not turn, but continued to study the far horizon, as though if she only looked at it hard enough, she could somehow magically make a crimson sail appear there. In her dreams, she had seen it; in her heart, she knew somehow that Wulfgar was still alive, that he would come for her and their child. But as though reading her mind and attempting to convince her otherwise, as he so often had since she had returned to Usk, Gwydion said:

"Wulfgar Bloodaxe is dead, Rhowenna! He *must* be dead, or else he has run off and deserted you, returned to the Northland and left you behind—and you've simply *got* to put him from your heart and mind, I tell you! 'Tis morbid and unhealthy of you to stand out here day after day like this, like a wraith haunting the shore. People are whispering about you, calling you mad—among other things not so pleasant—and if you're to be queen of Usk—"

"Gwydion, I am not!" Rhowenna declared impatiently, turning at last to face him. "Why can you not understand that? The princess Mathilde of Mercia is your betrothed, and if you had any decency or feeling for her, you would honor your agreement with Prince Cerdic to marry her. She loves you! She will make you a fine and devoted wife—"

"You would have—once—before that damned Viking carried you off and seduced and ruined you! How you can flaunt yourself here, with his bastard child in your arms—"

"Gwydion, please. We've been over this before, and I

don't want to hear it again. Wulfgar is my husband; our son is not a bastard. The royal blood of generations of kings of the Northland runs in his veins, and someday, he will be a great *jarl* there.''

''Nay, your marriage is not legitimate, Rhowenna; in your heart, you know that, for no Christian priest did speak his blessing upon you!''

''In my heart, since living in the Northland, among people who are, I think, something like what our own ancestors, the Picti and the Tribes, must have been, I have come to believe that all the gods are one God, Gwydion, and that to Him, each of us must find his own way. Mine lies out there.'' With a sweeping hand, Rhowenna gestured toward the sea. ''Wulfgar is *not* dead! I would feel it here, I tell you!'' She laid her hand upon her breast, where her heart beat strongly. ''He *will* come for me! He loves me! He—'' She broke off abruptly, her violet eyes shining, her heart swelling inside her, her scarlet mouth parting in a small gasp of surprise, of disbelief, of joy, of wonder.

For now, as though she had indeed somehow wished it there, there had appeared on the far horizon a single phantom rider as crimson as blood, mounted upon the spiny back of a monstrous sea dragon that rose and plunged upon the foamy waves, drawing ever nearer to the coast, as swift as the wind, as silent as the earth. Along the dragon's long, outstretched neck and upraised tail was a distinctive ridge of scales that Rhowenna knew belonged to the *Siren's Song* and none other.

''Wulfgar . . .'' she whispered, and then, ''Wulfgar!''— a cry from the heart as, clasping her son, Leik, tightly to her breast, she started forward eagerly toward the mighty sea dragon even now swooping toward shore, furling its wings, floating as gently as a swan now on the combers that rushed in upon the sands, watching, waiting.

''Rhowenna, nay! I love you!'' Gwydion insisted, his voice low and raw, as he seized her arm, staying her flight. ''Do not go to him. I love you! And you cannot love him! You cannot!''

''Oh, Gwydion . . . when my father betrothed me to Prince Cerdic and I thought I would die of love for you, you, who had so little to lose, would give up nothing out of love for me. Yet Wulfgar, who had gained so much, who had everything to lose, gave it all up for me. How could I not love him, then? He and I are like what we in the Northland call hacksilver, Gwydion, two halves of the same coin—one heart, one mind, one soul. Let me go to him. Please. If you do not, he *will* come for me. . . .'' Slowly, shuddering at the thought of a Viking warrior ever setting foot on the shores of Usk again, Gwydion at last released her, his face anguished as she said softly, ''Farewell, Gwydion.''

Rhowenna did not even hear him wish her, finally, sadly, Godspeed. She was already running urgently down the wending path that led to the beach below, wading headlong into the breakers that swirled white with froth about her, toward the strong and loving arms that waited, joyously outstretched, to pluck her and Leik from the sea.

Author's Note

Dear Reader:

I would like to take this opportunity to thank both my editor at Warner Books, Fredda Isaacson, for many reasons of which she is aware, and you, the reader, for buying and reading this book, *Swan Road*. I certainly hope that you enjoyed reading it as much as I did writing it. If you would like to write to me about Wulfgar and Rhowenna, or simply to receive a free copy of my semiannual newsletter about my books, you may address your letter to me in care of Warner Books, 1271 Avenue of the Americas, New York, New York 10020. Please enclose a business-sized, stamped, self-addressed envelope for reply—and on it, please be sure to print your name and address clearly. I read each and every one of your letters personally and am always delighted to hear from you!

Now, let me tell you a little bit about the historical and background material for *Swan Road*. As literature about King Arthur has become known as the Matter of Britain, and that about Charlemagne, the Matter of France, so I suppose that literature about the Vikings might be legitimately referred to as the Matter of Scandinavia—and there is a vast and wonderful body of works about the Vikings, dating back for centuries. Unfortunately, however, with the obvious exception of

Edison Marshall's classic, *The Viking*, most authors of modern romantic novels about the Vikings have tended to ignore the tales told of them by history's *skálds* and scholars. For *Swan Road*, I have drawn principally upon the stories of Ragnar Lodbrók and his sons, the Arthurian matter regarding Morgen Le Fey and Ogier the Dane, Scandinavian as well as Germanic mythology, and the Carolingian matter regarding Ogier the Dane.

Ragnar Lodbrók (Ragnar Hairy Breeches), the great chieftain, *jarl*, or king—depending on what material one reads—of the Northland, may or may not have actually existed. Because, like King Arthur, his image is overlaid with a heavy patina of mythical saga and heroic symbolization, today's scholars have argued both for and against his being a real historical personage. He is difficult to locate in both time and place, and various estimates make him at least 150 years old when he died in the snake pit of King Aella of Northumbria (who is known definitely to have existed).

However, I would like to point out that King Arthur, also, is difficult to locate in both time and place, and various estimates make him at least 100 years old when he was carried away to Avalon—having died in battle, no less. Yet since most modern scholars *do* give credence to a historical King Arthur, I see no good reason to discount the existence of Ragnar Lodbrók on bases that, over the years have gradually proved unconvincing with regard to King Arthur.

Generally speaking, Ragnar Lodbrók is credited with having had definitely three and possibly four sons: Ivar the Boneless (there are numerous spellings for his name; I have used the simplest), Ubbi (also given as Hubba, Ubba, and Ubbe), and Halfdan (also given as Halfdane and Healfdene). The fourth son is said to have been alternatively: 1) Björn Ironside, which involves equating Björn Ironside's father, Lothrocus, king of Dacia (Denmark) with Ragnar Lodbrók; 2) Sigefridus, which involves equating Sigefridus's brother Halfdan with Halfdan Ragnarsson or Lodbróksson (both forms are used), when they may not be one and the same; or 3) some other unnamed Viking. Because this fourth son is in dispute, I have felt free to appropriate him for my own use, giving him the name of Wulfgar Bloodaxe and making him a bastard, as is indeed perhaps one of the reasons why he remains such a shadowy, elusive figure.

Björn Ironside and Hasting (Hastein) actually did exist, and Hasting's mistaken sack of Luna, in the belief that it was Rome, is generally regarded as being factual—although it seems unlikely to me that he would have made such an error, being well acquainted, from numerous raids thereupon, with the European region. Flóki the Raven and Olaf the Sea Bull are my own inventions, as are Yelkei, the Eastland spaewife; the kingdom of Usk and all its inhabitants; and Prince Cerdic and Princess Mathilde of Mercia.

The invasion of Britain by the great army of Vikings and the events I have described happened essentially as I have given them—with the exception of any related to Prince Cerdic of Mercia. However, it must be noted that in reality, these events took place over a period of years, not months. For purposes of *Swan Road*, I have, of necessity, condensed the time in which they truly occurred. Kings Aella and Osberht of Northumbria, and King Edmund of East Anglia all did die apparently at the hands of Ivar the Boneless: Osberht in battle; Aella supposedly—in revenge for throwing Ragnar Lodbrók into the infamous snake pit—as a victim of the grisly Blood Eagle ritual I have described herein, although other sources state that he, like Osberht, died in battle; and Edmund by being brutally tortured, beaten, and shot with arrows before he was finally beheaded for refusing to renounce his Christian faith at Ivar the Boneless's demand. This massive Viking invasion eventually led to the establishment, in Britain, of the area known as the Danelaw.

Because the Vikings were, in truth, the masters of the seas, their influence was felt worldwide, in a way that I don't believe is actually realized by many people today. They raided far into what is now Russia, giving one of their many names, the *Rus,* to Russia. As the mercenary Varangian Guard, they served the rulers of Byzantium, modern Istanbul, Turkey. They raided south into Africa and west across the Atlantic Ocean, settling Iceland, Greenland, and discovering America. They also settled not only in Britain, but in portions of the Shetlands, the Orkneys, Scotland (Caledonia) and Ireland (Erin), as well as France, principally Normandy; the Low Countries (essentially Frisia), and Germany. Their ritual of naming and consecrating their longships with blood has come down to us in the rite today of smashing a bottle of champagne against the bow of a vessel to christen her before her maiden voyage.

The Viking religion, customs, society, and way of life are as accurate as I could make them, given that data about this time period in Scandinavia is relatively scarce and often speculative, much of it relying on the famous Sutton Hoo excavation, as well as a few other gravesites and archaeological digs, and rune stones erected to the dead. Because they were pagans, the Vikings had no respect whatsoever for Christian churches or priests, frequently sacking and burning the former, and killing the latter. Their crimes were considered especially heinous by all of Christendom, when, in reality, they were no better or worse than any other barbaric horde. In fact, where they could settle and live peacefully, they often did; and many times, because of their mercenary nature, they could be bought off with what later came to be called danegeld. In their own lands, Ultima Thule as a whole, they had strict laws and severe penalties for violations. I should also note here that longhouses such as those of Ragnar Lodbrók and Wulfgar Bloodaxe were known as *hofs* because their great mead halls, like their Sacred Groves, served as places of worship. Smaller farms, however, would not have borne this designation. The town of Sliesthorp was in later years called Hedeby.

I have also attempted to portray Ragnar Lodbrók and his sons as close to their true natures as my research led me to believe they were. Gang rapes of females captives were, apparently, not at all uncommon. Ragnar Lodbrók, for instance, is said to have raped a victim before more than thirty men gathered in his great mead hall, to the great sport of all present—except for the hapless woman, one presumes. It was indeed evidently his lifelong ambition to conquer Britain. His last words, supposedly spoken in Aella's snake pit, are said to have been, "How the piglets would be grunting if they knew the plight of the boar!" So perhaps this was his sons' incentive to invade Britain in his stead.

Ivar the Boneless was indeed, evidently, at the very least double-jointed and possibly a contortionist of considerable agility; he was also extremely cruel, being the one said to have perpetrated the Blood Eagle upon King Aella of Northumbria and to have brutally tortured King Edmund of East Anglia before beheading him. Following the murder of Edmund, Ivar the Boneless, en route from Thetford to Reading, did, in fact, mysteriously disappear from the pages of history, and no more was ever heard or known of him again—something I found particularly intriguing. It does seem strange that while various accounts of the deaths of Ubbi and Halfdan have come down to us, none at all is given for their greater brother, Ivar the Boneless.

Ubbi appears to have been, in reality, the "crude lump of peat" that I have described him as being; he was apparently killed in battle during the invasion of Britain by the great army, although other reports of his death are given.

It is said of Halfdan that he became a king of the Northland, Britain, and Ireland (Erin). He may or may not have been killed in battle at Strangford Lough, Ireland.

Of the fourth and last of Ragnar Lodbrók's sons, it is claimed many things, not the least of which is that he became king of all the Danes.

Rebecca Brandewyne